Mandy Magro lives in Cairns, Far North Queensland, with her husband, Billy, and her daughter, Chloe Rose. With pristine aqua-blue coastline in one direction and sweeping rural landscapes in the other, she describes her home as heaven on earth. A passionate woman and a romantic at heart, she loves writing about soul-deep love, the Australian rural way of life and all the wonderful characters that live there.

www.facebook.com/mandymagroauthor

www.mandymagro.com

MANDY MAGRO

Bluegrass Bend

First Published 2016
Second Australian Paperback Edition 2020
ISBN 9781489281050

BLUEGRASS BEND
© 2016 by Mandy Magro
Australian Copyright 2016
New Zealand Copyright 2016

Except for use in any review, the reproduction or utilisation of this work in whole or in part in any form by any electronic, mechanical or other means, now known or hereafter invented, including xerography, photocopying and recording, or in any information storage or retrieval system, is forbidden without the permission of the publisher.

This book is sold subject to the condition that it shall not, by way of trade or otherwise, be lent, resold, hired out or otherwise circulated without the prior consent of the publisher in any form of binding or cover other than that in which it is published and without a similar condition including this condition being imposed on the subsequent purchaser.

All rights reserved including the right of reproduction in whole or in part in any form.

This is a work of fiction. Names, characters, places, and incidents are either the product of the author's imagination or are used fictitiously, and any resemblance to actual persons, living or dead, business establishments, events, or locales is entirely coincidental.

Published by
Harlequin Mira
An imprint of Harlequin Enterprises (Australia) Pty Ltd.
Level 13, 201 Elizabeth St
SYDNEY NSW 2000
AUSTRALIA

® and TM are trademarks of Harlequin Enterprises Limited or its corporate affiliates. Trademarks indicated with ® are registered in Australia, New Zealand and in other countries.

Cataloguing-in-Publication details are available from the National Library of Australia www.librariesaustralia.nla.gov.au

Printed and bound in Australia by McPherson's Printing Group

In memory of my lifelong friend, Jacqui Benkler

What lies behind us and what lies in front of us is not as important as what lies within us, so whenever you get the chance, take your heart into Mother Nature, and allow it to breathe ...

PROLOGUE

Ivy Tucker manoeuvred through the drunken patrons of the popular Parramatta pub, making sure to smile at those who acknowledged her – it was all because of their cheers that she'd won the open mic night. The cool night air stung her eyes and cheeks as she stepped outside. She looped her scarf around her neck, part of her wanting to turn right around and head back into the warmth, but the crowd was becoming a little too boisterous. After a few uninvited arse grabs, two drinks spilt down her top and one particularly forceful bloke not wanting to take no for an answer, she knew it was time to head back to her aunts' friend's house. It had been a long day and she was dying to climb into the comfort of the warm, cosy bed in Pastor John's spare room.

Pulling her jacket tighter, she dragged her scarf up higher, the melodic thump of the music fading with each hurried footstep she took away from the pub. She wanted to get where she was going, and fast. Being accustomed to the relative safety of living in the small town of Bluegrass Bend, her aunts, May and Alice, had drummed into her the dangers of a young woman walking the city streets alone. She'd promised them she wouldn't be stupid enough to do such a thing, and now look what she was doing. She felt terrible going against their advice as well as feeling very naive for doing so, but it wasn't like she had much choice tonight.

Turning down a side street, she whistled a tune to try to keep her overactive mind from running off on a tangent. But the tune couldn't drown out the fact her footsteps echoed around her, nor that there was no traffic. She felt like she was in a ghost town. Goose bumps prickled her flesh. She stopped whistling. She walked faster. Damn all those stupid horror films she'd watched under duress with her friends as teenagers – half the time with one eye squeezed shut. Images of a flesh-eating Hannibal Lecter or a razor-fingered Freddy Krueger jumping out from one of the many shadows taunted her as she power walked like there was no tomorrow. She wished for a clear night sky, the glow of the moonlight unobscured by dense cloud. It hadn't been so daunting in the daylight with the hustle and bustle of everyday life but now all the shops were closed it was empty and lifeless and the darkness was making her imagination run wild – to the point where she thought she was being followed.

Halting mid-step, she sharpened her hearing as she spun around, her heart smashing against her chest like a boxer's fists. Her eyes darted from one side of the street to the other as she assessed her surroundings. Other than a stray dog rummaging through upturned garbage bins – which she dared not approach even though part of her wanted to take it home and love it like there was no tomorrow – there was nobody there. So, after a few more seconds of surveying her surroundings, and feeling confident she wasn't being followed, she laughed nervously at her overactive imagination, her breath escaping from her trembling lips in misty puffs, and shook her head.

Turning the last corner that led down to her car, the bright yellow glow of streetlights gradually faded away. The light of the one and only streetlight in the backstreet was barely enough for her to see a metre in front of her as it wearily flickered. She groaned. Trust her luck to park in the one street with a faulty light. Feeling extremely alone with the life of the pub now a fair distance behind her, and nothing but darkness in front of her, she picked up her pace to almost a jog – grateful that she'd worn her comfy boots, even as she cursed under her breath for parking so far away, all to avoid the high parking costs out the front of the pub. Now she wished she hadn't been so careful about her money. She would have paid a hundred bucks to already be within the safety of her car.

Only a little more to go …

The rushed clomp of her boots on the concrete echoed around the street, and the shadows seemed to loom out of every nook and cranny as though reaching for her. She wished she could close her eyes like she had as a child when something scared her, but with her clumsiness she'd probably run straight into a wall and knock herself out cold.

Finally reaching her car, she blipped it unlocked and a comforting sense of safety washed over her. She felt ridiculous for frightening herself so badly as she glanced at her watch glowing in the darkness. It was nearing one in the morning … where had the time gone? Her body was weary but she was still on a high, the night turning out to be better than she'd expected. Who'd have thought she'd win the open mic night? She couldn't wait to call her aunts in the morning to tell them the good news. Opening her boot, she carefully placed her guitar case in.

A crunch of shoes on gravel pulled her attention behind her. Spinning around, she squinted into the darkness, the strobe effect of the streetlight not aiding her as her eyes tried to adjust. But her ears were working perfectly and after hearing something moving near the industrial bin only metres from her she knew she wasn't imagining things anymore. Something just didn't feel right. She hoped the stray dog had followed her, but her instincts were telling her otherwise. The hair stood up on the back of her neck as fear froze her to the spot. She gripped the edge of the boot with sweaty hands.

'Hello?' she called out, her voice shaky. It was more of a question than a greeting.

Silence met her.

'Is anyone there?'

Still nothing.

'Please, if there is, show yourself.'

A tall silhouette stepped out of the shadows, one hand in his jeans pocket and the other tucked behind him. His strides were long and deliberate, and he remained unnervingly silent. The fractured light gave her a flicker of his features and she recognised him straight away. Dread filled her as he gave her a smile that made her stomach turn. She had to get into her car – now. Because this time, she knew he wasn't going to take no for an answer. Step by tiny step she began to ease around the side of the car so she could jump in the back door and lock it, but he dashed towards her and blocked her path, wedging her between himself and the corner of her open boot.

She screamed for someone to help her.

The man slammed his free hand over her mouth, bringing his face millimetres from her own. He reeked of alcohol but seemed to have regained some sense of balance after being thrown out of the pub a few hours ago. There was a hollowness in his eyes that freaked her out even more than his drunkenness, like he didn't possess a soul.

'You scream like that again and I'll have to hurt you good and proper. Got it?' His voice was spine-chillingly low.

Ivy nodded, heavy tears beginning to slide down her cheeks. She barely dared to breathe.

'Good girl.' He bent his head to sniff her neck and hair slowly. 'So, let's start afresh, hey?' He raised his malevolent eyes to meet hers. 'I know you knocked me back at the pub, and got your friend behind the bar to chuck me out, but I'm guessing you're just shy and you need a little bit of coaxing, like most of you sheilas do.' He took her hand, kissing the back of it.

Ivy felt a wave of nausea wash over her. She wanted to wrench her hand back but knew if she did, there'd be dire consequences.

Stopping at her elbow, he gave her wrist a firm yank, making her wince. 'So, because I'm such a nice guy, I'll give you another chance.' He smiled repulsively. 'Would you like to have some fun with me?'

Afraid to speak, Ivy shook her head, instinctively turning her face away. She was trembling all over and as much as she fought to gain control of her body, it only got worse.

The man gripped her jaw and forced her eyes back to his. He produced a knife from behind his back, pressing the tip into her cheek as his lips curled into a malicious grin. 'Does this change your mind at all? 'Cause it sure as hell would make me rethink a bad decision.'

Ivy's legs threatened to give way. 'Please, don't hurt me. I'll give you everything I have.'

The twenty-centimetre knife glimmered as he pulled it back, disgust contorting his features. 'I don't want your money, you stupid fucking woman. I want you – all of you.' He gripped her face tighter, leant in closer. The feel of his torso against her made her want to vomit. 'That pretty voice of yours got me so fired up that if I don't get a piece of you tonight I'm gonna go insane.' He brought the knife back up to her cheek and pressed the blade into her skin, laughing when she cried out in pain. 'You and me are going to have us some fun and you're going to do everything I fucking tell you to do – got it?'

Who the fuck did this man think he was? Adrenaline coursed through Ivy, making her want to fight for her dignity, and her life, as her sense of self-preservation finally outweighed her fear. 'No, I *don't* like it, and I won't be letting you touch an inch of me.'

'Yeah, we'll see about that then, won't we?' He pushed her backwards, shoving her into the boot.

Ivy turned her face from him, cheek resting against her guitar case.

Climbing roughly on top of her, he slammed his knees into her hips, pinning her down. She scratched, kicked, bit, punched, screamed – anything but lie there willingly – but fighting only spurred him on. He laughed sadistically as he finally got a secure hold on her, the knife now pressed against her throat.

'You're a feisty little one. I like that.' He pushed his pelvis against hers. 'Can you feel how much I want you?'

Ivy spat in his face.

Wrong move.

He wiped her saliva away with the back of his hand, eyes seething. 'You little bitch. You're gonna be real sorry you just did that.' He ripped open her jacket and then sliced at her shirt, the blade of the knife not only cutting through the material like butter, but also her flesh, all the way from the top of her pelvis to her rib cage. The pain was like fire entering her blood. She screamed in agony as the man laughed.

'Oops, well, that was a little bit of a misjudgement by me. Let's hope you don't bleed to death before I have my way with you.' He shifted his weight to get at his jeans, exposing the damaged flesh on her stomach and chest to the icy night air, the shock like an open flame against her wound.

'What the fuck do you think you're doing?' another man's voice said as heavy footsteps rushed towards them.

Her attacker's hand went to her neck as he covered her mouth with his other hand, the knife hitting Ivy's hip as he dropped it. His grip made it almost impossible for her to breathe. She gasped for air, unable to move with the man's whole weight on top of her. She could feel her legs going numb, and the throbbing across her stomach was excruciating. Blood dripped from her wound and she felt as though her life was draining from her. Was this how she was going to die? Was her body going to be found dumped in some dirty, dingy street? Her aunts would never get over the heartache.

'Don't come any closer, or I'll fucking kill her!' her assailant thundered.

The footsteps halted and a few heavy breaths followed. 'Just calm the fuck down, man, and think about what you're doing. You don't want to spend the rest of your life in prison because of some drunken mistake, do you?'

Ivy thought she could hear the man still taking cautious steps towards them, but she couldn't be sure. Everything around her spun as she began to lose consciousness.

'Listen here, *man*, if I were you, I'd do the smart thing and just fuck off, this has nothing to do with you. There's no need to be acting like some fucking hero … the little lady and I have come to an agreement.'

Ivy's saviour laughed mockingly. 'That's where you're wrong – this has everything to do with me. So, let her fucking go or I'm gonna break both your arms and legs before you've even had a chance to wave that knife in my face.'

Ivy tried to make out her rescuer by rolling her eyes as far sideways as they'd go, but with the angle she was at, as well as the lack of oxygen, it was impossible. He sounded so big and strong. How she wished he'd rip this monster off her.

'Please, help me,' she cried out instinctively, the words muffled by the hand across her mouth.

'Shut your fucking mouth, you whore.' Squeezing her throat even tighter, her attacker finally stole her ability to breathe. She clawed at his arm in a panic, wheezing as his weight forced out what air was left in her lungs. Somehow she scratched the hand across her mouth deeply enough to draw blood. Her abductor swore.

Hope filled her. She could smell the other man's aftershave now – it was heady and spicy. He was so close that she could almost reach out and touch him. He was about to save her. Or at least try to. Maybe she was going to live. Or maybe they were both about to die.

'You take another step and I'll –'

'You'll what? Bash me to death?' Her saviour sighed heavily. 'You're just another fucking coward who takes advantage of vulnerable women. So why don't you man the fuck up and take it out on me, hey? Let's see if you got any balls or if you're all talk and no action.'

Ivy felt her attacker's grip loosen as he turned to confront her saviour. 'You scrawny piece of shit. *Fuck off.*'

The newcomer took another step towards the boot. 'Looks like I'm going to *have* to teach you a lesson for attacking a woman.'

The man roared as he leapt off Ivy and out of the boot, pushing her head into the car's side. Ivy cried out as she felt her head smash against the edge of something solid, and then just as she heard a guttural sound – could it really be coming from her own lips? – her entire world went black.

CHAPTER 1

Healing Hills, Bluegrass Bend,
New South Wales

Screaming out as she woke, Ivy sat bolt upright, her heart in her throat. She tried to swallow but her mouth felt drier than the Simpson Desert. Sweat covered her. She kicked her tangled sheet off. Sobs escaped her as the adrenaline rush began to calm. Even after eight years, the nightmare was still the same, an exact replica of that horrific night. It made her feel as though she was right back there, being attacked by a sadist. She took a few moments to remind herself that it was just a dream; there was no-one standing beside her bed, waiting to slice her open with a knife or beat her to death with their bare hands. There was no threat of being raped. She was in the homestead, her safe haven, tucked up in bed with her aunts asleep just down the hall and her beloved eight-year-old Dalmatian, Bo, downstairs.

With the darkness of the night pressing in on her Ivy reached for her bedside lamp, quivering hands fumbling with the switch. She needed a well-lit room as much as she needed oxygen right now, and a drink of water wouldn't go astray either. Warm light flooded her bedroom, providing a sense of safety now that she could confirm there was nobody hiding in the shadows. It upset her that she couldn't seem to get past the horror of it all, no matter how much she wanted to. Grabbing her glass of water from the bedside table, she took a few big gulps, recalling her progress since it had all happened. It had certainly been a long hard road, and she'd come a long way, thanks to her aunts' support and her own work alongside their healing horses. But she was still trying to find her way back to her music.

With nausea swirling in her belly, she squeezed the soft feathery pillow she was already clutching as the tears that had soaked her lashes began rolling down her cheeks once more. She took a few deep, calming breaths. It had been ages since her last nightmare, and she wondered what had brought it back. Maybe it was all the stress she'd been under since finding out they might lose Healing Hills to the bank? Her heart squeezed even tighter with the thought. She groaned despairingly. She was over life being so hard. Over trying to heal the gaping hole in her heart the loss of her music had left. And completely over men after what her now ex-boyfriend, Malcolm Miller, had done to her two weeks ago. Finding him in bed with another man was beyond anything she could have ever imagined happening in her ongoing disastrous love life. It had shocked her to the very core. He was the kind of bloke every girl dreamed of – kind, good looking, strong, hardworking; she thought she was on a winning streak with him. Hell, she'd even imagined marrying him and having his children. How wrong she had been – yet again. She'd spent three days in her daggiest pyjamas holed up in her bedroom, torturing herself by watching her favourite rom-coms, and devouring tubs of Connoisseur cookies and cream ice cream – the entire time wondering what was wrong with her. What the hell was she doing so wrong to turn a straight man gay? Her aunts had eventually lost their patience and dragged her from the bedroom, screwing their noses up as they'd begged her to shower and eat something decent.

Rolling onto her side so she could snuggle further into her pillow Ivy grimaced as she recalled the gobsmacking encounter. It was as though she'd stepped straight into a scene in *Brokeback Mountain*. A shamefaced Malcolm had apologised profusely while desperately trying to gather the sheets to cover himself, and his extremely red-faced lover, and it was at this moment she'd hightailed it out of his bedroom. She hadn't seen or spoken to him since, and had no desire to – it had been quite obvious it was well and truly over between them. Apart from the shock and heartbreak of it all, it was Malcolm's secrecy that hurt her the most. Relationships were meant to be built on trust – she hated secrecy and believed if you didn't have trust, you didn't have anything. Once a man blew it, it was impossible for her to ever have faith in him again. Damn Malcolm for proving once more that men couldn't be trusted. They were all the bloody same. Why did it keep happening to her? What had she ever done to deserve it? And how much more heartbreak could a girl take before she gave up on having a relationship altogether? Maybe she should become a nun, devote herself to God so men were forever out of her life's equation. She chuckled at the thought. Yeah, right, as if that would ever happen when she was twenty-five and in her sexual prime. But damn love and all it stood for, because, in her expert opinion, it was overrated. Her mum had been right. All men did was cause heartache – Ivy's cheating father had proved that when he'd run off with a barmaid, never to be seen or heard from again. It had shattered her beautiful mum's heart and made her think death was easier than life. Ivy fought back the anguish that always had the power to crumble her into tiny pieces – even after sixteen years; she missed her kind-hearted, bohemian-spirited mum each and every day.

Completely shattered, she looked over at her bedside clock and grumbled under her breath. It was two in the morning and she needed sleep. Taking the last gulp of water from her glass she switched off her bedside lamp and threw the pillow she'd been clutching over her face. The anger the nightmare had evoked, along with the recollection of what Malcolm had done and the memory of playing music with her beautiful mother, inspired Ivy to make a firm promise that she would do everything in her power to overcome her fear of playing her guitar again. She'd already come so far, she thought, as her mind turned once more to that evening so long ago.

It was four years before she'd been able to sleep with the light off, her fear of the dark after being attacked beyond anything she'd ever felt as a child. On that fateful night, she'd learnt that bad men were real and that bad things didn't necessarily happen to someone else. Warren Young, the son of a bitch who'd attacked her, had stolen so much – her dignity, the innocent fearlessness she'd grown up with and the opportunity to make a go of her music. She shook her head, hating his name being in it. Warren had lost his own life that night and, as much as she loathed him, that saddened her, but it had been out of her hands. Over the years she'd come to accept there was nothing she could have done to make things any different, nor could her rescuer – he'd been defending his life, and hers, after she'd blacked out, or so she'd been told. Thank goodness he'd gotten her to the hospital as fast as he had, or she would be long gone from this life. Even though her recollections were hazy and she'd spent two days in an induced coma, she would never forget the fear of having a knife blade pressed up against her flesh, of seeing her life flash before her eyes, and of feeling her life seep out of the wound in her stomach. If only she'd had the chance to personally thank her rescuer, but he'd dropped her at the hospital and fled, for good reason. The police had later told her his name, but that had meant nothing. Being underage at the time of the crime and at the firm requests of her aunts to the police, she'd been kept out of the investigation after her statement. And why would the cops bother questioning her again when she couldn't give them any useful information or identify any mug shots? She'd never heard of Byron McWilliams, but she did find out which prison he'd gone to and had sent him a thank you letter. Byron never responded.

Among all the horrid recollections there was also a lot to be thankful for. And she knew, thanks to her training as a counsellor and her aunts' positive way of thinking, she had to keep a firm grip on the good things if she was ever going to get past this. Byron McWilliams had risked his life to save hers, and had already spent years in prison because of it, with a few more to go. She wondered what he'd do once he got out. After ignoring her letter she doubted he'd try to find her. And to be honest, she couldn't blame him. They all needed to get on with their lives. There was nothing to gain from reliving the past. She couldn't let that night steal her future any longer. It was time she climbed back into the saddle and somehow, some way, grabbed hold of the reins.

***

Racing down the stairs and through the sun-dappled kitchen, Ivy skidded to a stop to give her aunt Alice a kiss on the cheek, smiling at her bright pink polka-dotted pyjamas and matching fluffy slippers.

'Morning.' Alice graced her with one of her loving smiles as she tucked her long copper hair behind her ears. 'Did you have a good night's sleep love?'

Ivy shrugged. 'Not the best – but that's to be expected with everything going on.' She grabbed a grape from the fruit bowl on the bench and tossed it into her mouth.

'Yes, you do have a lot on your plate, my dear.' Alice reached out and cupped her face, her sandalwood perfume drifting. 'Just make sure you take time out to destress, okay?'

'I am, which is why I'm forcing myself to go for a jog this morning. It always makes me feel better.'

'That's good, love.' Alice watched her for a few more seconds before turning her attention back to the bowl she was stirring on the sink. 'Anything that can make you feel better is a good thing.'

Getting a whiff of something delicious, Ivy almost drooled. 'What's that glorious smell?'

'I'm baking some honey and oat bars.' Alice turned and opened the oven, peeking inside. 'And it looks like they're almost ready. Would you like one before you go for your jog?'

'No, thanks – it'll give me a stitch. But I'll be sure to have one when I get back.'

A groan drew their attention. Aunt May shuffled in, her pyjamas askew and her shoulder-length salt-and-pepper hair dishevelled. 'Morning all,' she said in passing as she made a beeline for the kettle. Ivy giggled. May always needed her morning cuppa before she could function properly.

'Morning Aunt May.' Ivy grabbed another couple of grapes. 'Right, I'm off, catch you in an hour or so.'

'Okay love,' May and Alice replied in unison.

With her well-worn Nikes pounding the winding dirt roads of Healing Hills and her earphones blasting one of her favourite country bands of all time, The Nitty Gritty Dirt Band, Ivy allowed her mind to go where it needed to. Jogging was a form of meditation to her, and she quite often solved things that were troubling her while out exercising.

Her mind decided it wanted to think about how she and Malcolm should have been celebrating her graduation as a counsellor after three long years of online study, but nope, life was throwing curve balls left, right and centre. She sighed. Although she'd only done what her aunts had encouraged her to by gaining a degree in her dream profession, she couldn't help but feel it was partly her fault they were in huge financial trouble. Her uni fees alone had cost close to eight thousand dollars a year. Little had she known her aunts had re-mortgaged the property to pay for them, among other things, including a hefty tax bill after forgetting to do their tax returns for the past couple of years. It was only after opening a letter from the bank by accident last week that she had finally discovered the truth. She'd then gone over the books with a fine-tooth comb, and discovered Healing Hills' running costs were heavily outweighing their income. She should have insisted May and Alice let her handle the bookwork years earlier, but out of respect for their wishes in leaving the business side of things to them, she hadn't. Hindsight could be an absolute bitch.

She and her aunts needed to do something, and soon. Times were undeniably tough – tough enough for their longstanding bank manager, Gerald Fromstein, to send May and Alice a gentle letter of warning saying that if they didn't catch up on the mortgage payments, he'd have no option but to allow the big wigs from the city branch to issue them a foreclosure letter. And there was no way Ivy was going to allow that to happen. Ever. This was her family home, as it had been for generations, and it was over her dead body that some toffee-nosed suit-wearer was going to waltz in here and take it from them like it meant nothing – because to her, and her aunts, and the people who came here for healing sessions with the horses, Healing Hills was everything.

But she had a solution – a good one. A mixture of excitement and apprehension washed over her. She was going to renovate the cottage her mother had left to her and sell it. Not an easy task, but certainly doable if Gerald agreed to loan the capital needed for the renovation. The money from the sale would most certainly get them out of their financial strife. And although it broke her heart to sell the home she'd spent the first nine years of her life in along with the many memories she had of her and her mum within its walls, Ivy honestly couldn't see any other way around it. She just hoped Alice and May would accept her offer of selling the cottage and pocket of land adjoining Healing Hills without too much fuss, because she wasn't going to take no for an answer.

Rolling her eyes at her seemingly on-going bad luck of late, she tried to keep her focus on the here and now – her motto of living in the moment something that had gotten her through the hardest of times. All around her the dawn fog shrouded the sweeping landscape in a thick white veil, the quietness a little eerie. The songs of the bellbirds would normally be filling the air around her, but this morning they were quiet and she couldn't blame the birds for their lack of effort – she could barely see a metre in front of her. She was a little crazy being out here on a morning like this – but desperate times called for desperate measures. She slowed her pace. After the heavy downpour last night the ground was muddy beneath her feet, and it was an achievement in itself to miss the water-filled potholes – some big enough to swallow a small dog whole. But, true to her usual form, she found one. She tried ungracefully to remain upright, her arms flailing as she struggled to regain her footing. She was sure Bo, running beside her, would be amused. And why not – if she were watching herself right now she'd probably be hooting with laughter.

Now her joggers were soaked through, it was icy cold, the sun nowhere to be seen behind the thick blanket of grey clouds, and she was fed up with everything. This morning jog was not lifting her mood as it should. If she was five years old, she'd probably chuck a tantrum, but she was a big girl now with big girl problems and she needed to pull on her big girl boots to deal with it all. Being an adult could really suck sometimes.

Ignoring her burning desire to give up and crawl under a rock, Ivy continued to jog with the grace of a sack of wet cement. The mist gradually cleared enough for her to glance down at Bo legging it beside her – she'd named him after one of her favourite characters of all time, Bo Duke from *The Dukes of Hazard* – and smiled at the loyal pooch, grateful for his steadfast company. Much like herself, it did him good to come for a jog. Bo was renowned for digging crater-sized holes in her aunts' treasured backyard if she dared leave him alone for an entire day. He was always up for fun, and while his stamina and endless energy were challenging at times, his goofiness gave her endless smiles, and his unconditional devotion gave her a certain kind of comfort that only a dog could give – something she especially needed right now. He truly was her best friend, and was the only male in her life she'd ever been able to properly trust and rely on. Giving Bo a quick pat on the head, she turned her attention back to the road.

Pushing onwards even though all she wanted was to climb beneath her warm feather doona again and go back to sleep, Ivy headed for the creek that flowed down from the surrounding mountains and passed through Healing Hills. Crystal clear and icy cold, it was moving a little faster today due to the rain. The water rushed over boulders in its haste to reach the bottom of the valley. Slowing, and then stopping, she bent down and cupped her hands, relishing the water as she tipped it into her parched mouth. Bo followed suit and furiously lapped at the water before flopping himself into the creek as he chased floating twigs. Ivy smiled, amazed at his resistance to the cold. But there was no time to sit here and wallow – she had a healing session booked in with two troubled teenagers and she wasn't about to let them down by not doing the best she could for them.

Standing, she whistled to Bo and he bounded out of the creek, shaking the droplets from his spotty coat before happily joining her once again. Crossing the rickety little bridge that spanned the creek, Ivy began jogging up the steepest part of the hill. With her breath escaping her in little white clouds and her calf muscles burning from the exertion, she turned a bend to head up the home straight. She gave everything she had for the last few hundred metres, gratitude for the beautiful land she called home filling her. Beside her Bo matched her pace with fortitude, his tongue hanging out the side of his mouth. Ivy loved this part of the seven-hundred-acre property, the summit giving her a magnificent panoramic view of Healing Hills in all its glory. Beyond the grand two-storey homestead her family had lived in for four generations, rolling green fields gave way to a labyrinth of woodlands, plateaus, gorges and scribbly gum trees, all of it goosebump-worthy, the vast expanse of untainted countryside jaw dropping to say the least. And the air up here, it was just so pure. She was a blessed woman to be able to call this her home. And her home she was determined it would remain.

Reaching the business sign hanging from the timber railing that read: HEALING HILLS, ALICE, MAY AND IVY TUCKER, HEALING WITH HORSES, she slowed and bent over at the waist, breathing the mountain air in deeply before her usual routine of warm-down stretches.

***

Legs folded beneath her as she sat in the shade of a towering jacaranda tree, Ivy smiled at the two teenagers enjoying their afternoon tea of homemade carrot cake and herbal tea, revelling in how far they'd both come. Imposing yet gentle, perceptive yet non-judgemental, the healing horses had silently helped both Max Jacobs and Michelle Harrison gain essential insights into their inner demons and innate strengths, in turn giving them the drive needed to work through what was needed, and they'd come along in leaps and bounds because of it. Contrary to what many believed, people's problems didn't always need to be talked about, mulled over and dissected – and that was the beauty of healing horses. One of the other huge benefits of equine healing for teens was it encouraged them to focus on the well-being of another while realising their moods and anxieties affected all around them, including animals – they needed to stay calm and focused while riding or they'd risk falling off or spooking the horse and they needed gentle movements and temperaments when working on the ground with the horses too. Ivy made very certain to push these facts home before anyone who came for the healing sessions stepped foot into the healing arena. The safety of both the horses and the clients was imperative.

'So, Max. Pastor John tells me you've gotten yourself a job as an apprentice mechanic,' Ivy said before taking a sip of her peppermint tea.

Max nodded proudly as he swallowed his mouthful of cake. 'I sure have.' He held up his hands, the kind of grease that refuses to wash off embedded in his palms. 'And I got me some dirty hands to prove it.'

Ivy laughed. 'Good for you.' She gave him the thumbs up. 'I told you you'd get your dream job if you believed you were worthy of it, and look at you now.'

Max flipped his cap back from the front of his head and smiled shyly. 'Yup, and it's all thanks to you and the horses.'

'No, not really, Max. We've guided you, but you're the one who's chosen to find the courage to move forwards. So a big hurrah to you.'

Max's eyebrows scrunched together. After a few seconds he shrugged and revealed his teeth with a huge smile. 'I reckon it's thanks to all of us then.'

Ivy turned to Michelle. 'So how are things looking for the photography course?'

The girl jiggled on the spot. 'Really good – I start next week.' She reached out and touched Ivy's arm. 'Thank you so much for helping me organise it.'

'My pleasure.' She gave Michelle's hand a squeeze. 'And how was your AA meeting last week?'

Michelle popped the last of her cake into her mouth, talking between chewing. 'Great – I even got up and talked this time.'

Ivy clapped her hands. 'Wonderful. Good on you. I'm so very proud of you both.'

Max and Michelle looked at each other and grinned, their deep connection making Ivy wonder if there was a bit of a romance bubbling, but it wasn't her place to ask: she was here to give them hope, and a sense of security in life, and to help them find the strength within to get past their addictions and anxieties. So, with cake and herbal teas consumed, it was time to move on.

'Now, I'd like you both to close your eyes and sit in quiet contemplation for a few minutes. Have a think about how far you've come in the past eight weeks, how much better you feel about your lives and what you've achieved, before we move on to the next part of the session.'

'With the horses?' Michelle said, grinning.

Ivy nodded. 'Yup.'

'Yes,' Max said as he fist pumped the air.

'But only after a few minutes of meditation.'

Max and Michelle both squeezed their eyes shut. Ivy couldn't help but smile at their enthusiasm. After first being afraid of the horses, Ivy loved how both teenagers were now eager to spend time with their equine mates. The two had evolved from hating the world and everyone in it, to beginning to believe in themselves and others – and they'd both been off the drink and drugs for almost two months now. They still had a bit to go, but along with her and Pastor John's help back in Sydney, they were getting there, together. The very thought warmed her heart. It was gratifying to know she was making a difference to people's lives, and somehow giving back to the universe. Her work was what gave her the strength to get through her own inner turmoils, and to have faith everything was eventually going to be all right. Seeing how other people fought their battles to reach their full potential inspired her, and always had. She'd been watching May and Alice do healing sessions ever since she could walk, and her dream had always been to do the same. She'd been living that dream for the past five years – firstly as an offsider for Alice and May, and now as a group leader herself, thanks to her degree.

After ten minutes, Ivy softly and calmly asked Max and Michelle to open their eyes.

'So today,' she said, once they were back in the present moment, 'we're going to have our very first reiki session with the horses. Sound good?'

Michelle's green eyes glittered. 'Wow, really. Horses can do that?'

Max looked confused. 'What the heck is reiki? Sounds like some kind of karate.'

Michelle jumped in to answer. 'It's like a massage, but without all the touching. I haven't tried it, but I've always wanted to. I've watched documentaries on it, and it looks amazing.'

With Max still staring at her with a knitted brow, Ivy elaborated on Michelle's description. 'Yes, that's right. It's where the horses lend their hearts and souls to us, taking us on a deeper journey of self-discovery. They can remove emotional blockages just by being near you, or sometimes by touching you with their muzzles, chin, lips or forehead. It may sound a little strange now, but you just wait until you experience it.'

'Uh huh.' Max cocked his head to the side. 'Do I have to tell them anything?'

Ivy shook her head. 'Nope. All you have to do is lie on a massage table and the horses do all the work.'

Max's worried look finally gave way to a smile. 'Sounds pretty good to me.'

After Michelle and Max had removed their shoes and climbed onto the massage tables set up in the shade at the side of the roundyard, Ivy placed a hand on Max's and Michelle's legs. 'All I ask of you both is to close your eyes and allow the horses to do as they need. You might feel different sensations, like tingling, twitching, or a rumbling belly, and you might feel nothing but peace, but either way, it's all good and all part of your personal journey. Just trust in the horses, okay?'

Max and Michelle agreed and closed their eyes. Ivy walked over to the edge of the roundyard and opened the gate wide, allowing the horses to choose if they wanted to join them or not. Out of the eight horses in the paddock, five did. Ivy stood back to let them pass her, breathing in their beautiful horsey scent. Three went to Michelle and two to Max. The horses by Michelle's side began to gently rub their muzzles up and down her back. The two with Max decided to lay their heads on his shoulders, one on each side. They did this for fifteen minutes, only shifting to the opposite cheek, until Ivy asked both Max and Michelle to roll over onto their backs.

'I feel really warm,' Michelle mumbled dreamily.

Ivy placed her hand on Michelle's arm. 'That's normal. It's your energy shifting and dispersing. Just go with it.'

'Okay,' Michelle replied distractedly as the horses mingled by her side once more.

Max rubbed his eyes, yawning. 'Is it normal to feel so heavy and tired?'

'Yes, that's your body's way of healing itself from emotional blockages.'

'I'm really liking this,' Max said faintly as his eyes slipped shut and the two horses that had chosen him got back to work.

One horse stood at Max's feet and the other gently pushed its muzzle into Max's chest. From experience, Ivy knew this was the horses' way of channelling energy through whoever they were doing the healing work on – kind of like they were flushing Max of any toxins. It was always mind-blowing to watch. Horses were such magnificent creatures, with a unique way of helping people open their hearts. She knew all too well from her own experience with them – after her mother's death and when she was attacked – that when you really looked and listened through the lens of your heart, you could open the doorway to a world of feeling, allowing you the insight to work through your inner dilemmas. And the horses, in such a gentle yet powerful way, helped people do this by bonding with them in a way no human could, making her job as a counsellor so much more fulfilling.

The second part of the session lasted for almost half an hour, until the horses stepped back from the table. Three of them rolled in the dirt as a way to rid themselves of the energy they'd taken on, while the other two did the same by shaking themselves. Ivy marvelled at their intelligence, and also at their giving and loving natures. Dogs may have been said to be a man's best friend, but in her mind horses were humankind's graceful saviours. If only more people knew of, and put faith in, horses' healing powers, she believed there would be a lot less suffering in the world.

Giving Max and Michelle some time to come back to reality, Ivy then asked them to slowly sit up as she handed them each a bottle of water.

'How are you both feeling?'

As always, Michelle spoke first. 'I feel weird, in a good way. A bit light-headed, like I'm free of gravity or something.'

Max stretched his arms in the air and yawned widely. 'I second that.' He shook his head, his eyes full of wonder. 'I don't know how else to put it except – that was fucking amazeballs.'

Michelle giggled. 'I completely agree.'

Ivy laughed with them as she stretched her arms wide and pulled them into a group hug. Within seconds Michelle began to sob in her arms, and Ivy felt Max's arms tighten protectively around them all. This was a moment Ivy had been expecting.

'I'm sorry,' Michelle mumbled, sniffling. 'That just kind of came out of nowhere.'

'It's okay,' Ivy whispered, as she stroked Michelle's hair. 'This is a good thing. You're releasing emotional blockages that the horses have moved.'

Michelle nodded softly.

'You'll be okay, Michelle,' Max said quietly. 'I'll make sure of it.'

Ivy's heart swelled. Max and Michelle had been at their very lowest when they'd first come here and yet they were giving it all they had to make life better – and that took so much courage. This, right here, was why she had to save Healing Hills.

CHAPTER 2

Long Bay Correctional Facility,
New South Wales

Byron Sinclair sat at an empty table off to the side of the exercise oval, his determined gaze following the length of the razor-topped walls that had cast a shadow over his life since he had arrived here at nineteen, his whole life ahead of him when he'd been sentenced to ten years. He hated the goddamn walls. Hated feeling controlled, constricted, and worst of all, trapped. Now he was twenty-seven – so many years of his life were gone, in a way stolen from him, but it hadn't all been in vain. At the very least, this place had made him own his crime.

Her beautiful face flashed through his mind and his jaw clenched, along with his heart. He'd kept the letter all these years, had read it a thousand times, her words touching a place in his heart that no other woman had been able to reach, but he'd never responded to it. In times of weakness he sometimes wondered if he'd done the right thing, but he was no hero and he didn't want her thinking he was. She was better off forgetting he even existed because a good-hearted woman like her deserved only the best of people around her. It had been the briefest of meetings anyway and in the worst of circumstances. In the terrible state she'd been in he was sure she wouldn't recognise him if she saw him again – which was very much on the cards now. Lottie was right, he needed to steer clear of Ivy if he wanted to keep his old identity hidden because there was always the risk of her remembering him. He certainly wasn't proud of what had happened, and was happy to keep his past where it belonged, especially for his great aunt Lottie's sake – he owed Lottie that much after everything she'd done for him over the years. Changing his last name to hers six months ago had been an easy decision and only the first step in his new life. With his sister's help, a few forms and $157, the man who was sentenced to prison was gone. Not that he cared. He'd never fit the arrogant persona of a McWilliams man anyway.

Glancing down at the creased letter in his hands, Ronny closed his eyes for the briefest of moments, willing himself not to break down. After receiving mail from Lottie each and every week he'd spent in here, this was the last one he'd gotten from her and the last he ever would. He inhaled deeply, as though drawing on the earth for strength. He'd never shed a tear in this hellhole – his life depended on remaining hard as nails – and he wasn't about to lose his resolve now. There would be plenty of time on the outside for him to be able to grieve openly, especially once in the welcoming arms of Sundown Farm – the only place he ever felt truly at home. His emotions in check, he began to read Lottie's curled handwriting for the umpteenth time, hearing her motherly tone, her addictive laughter, her weighty sighs and her sniffles, just like she was sitting beside him. If only he'd gotten out two months earlier, he would have at least been able to hold her hands and say goodbye. He could have been there to take care of her in her final few months. Life could be so damn cruel.

My Dearest Ronny,

If you're reading this then I've finally decided to go knocking on heaven's door – let's just hope God lets me in, hey. It would be a right bugger if he doesn't when I'll be dressed in my Sunday finest! But all jokes aside, this letter is of great importance as it contains my final requests, which my solicitor will also be following through on. I wish with all my heart I could still be alive to see you walking from that godawful place, but this brain tumour has gotten the better of me and I know it won't be long before the Lord calls me home … a week or two at the most, my doctor says. At first I was afraid to die, but now I've come to accept my fate. I'm at peace now. Please know I will always be with you in spirit and will be watching you from above. I know you've had a tough run in your young life, Ronny, and I hope by doing this I can give you the future you deserve. You're a good man, with a big heart, and I love you like a son with all of mine, and I believe you deserve a break in life. So, I am leaving Sundown Farm to you, along with half of my life savings, which isn't a great deal in the scheme of things, but it should at least help you make a start back out in the real world – the other half of the money I am leaving to Larry, along with the right for him to live out the rest of his days at the workers' quarters on the farm. He has been by my side for the past forty years, and I believe his loyalty deserves reward. All I ask in return is that you care for the animals that have made Sundown Farm their home, and do your best to leave your past where it belongs. Don't give the people of this town a reason to gossip about something they really know nothing about.

Now, being the organised woman I am, I have thought ahead and asked my friends at the Country Women's Association to take care of packing up my personal belongings so you don't need to and to give it to charity, making sure to leave the furniture, household items, photos, and also my jewellery box – one day you will have a special woman in your life who will treasure the items inside as much as I have, I just know it. Even though all the women are very dear friends of mine after being involved in the CWA for over half my life, I have felt the need to not divulge your private matters to them, Lord forgive me. Instead, I have told my friends that you are working on a cattle station in the Northern Territory, which is why you haven't been able to visit me, and will be here as soon as you can. Not being one to make up stories, this is the best I could do. As I've said a hundred times before, I'm so sorry I forced you to go to the police and confess what you did, Ronny, but at least now you can get on with your life without forever looking over your shoulder. Fingers crossed it doesn't take you too long to get here now that you've been granted good behaviour.

Finally, my very last request is that on my wedding anniversary, February 28th, you spread my ashes in the place where I spread my darling Frank's all those years ago – up on the highest hill of Sundown. I want to remain with him in my happy place forever. Larry will be taking care of the urn until you arrive.

Rightio, I think that's everything. This dying business takes a lot of planning! Anything I've forgotten I'm sure you will figure out along the way. Larry will be here to guide you through the paces, if need be, and the girls from the CWA will be popping in every now and again to make sure you're both doing okay, and are eating decent meals.

Ronny, I truly don't know of anyone else in my life who is more deserving of all that means everything to me. I know you will love Sundown Farm as much as I have.

I love you,

Lottie xoxo

P.S. I've also left you the old Kingswood ... I know how much you loved it!

Ronny felt his heart squeeze tight as it had every other of the hundreds of times he'd read the letter. It was so hard to imagine life without Lottie in it, especially now he'd be calling Sundown Farm home. It was going to feel strange arriving there without her greeting him. Although he would be moving to where his past still lingered, he was fairly confident he'd be able to keep his true identity private – he and Lottie had succeeded until now. Once again, the heartbreaking memory of that night filled him with anger but he exhaled the fury away. He couldn't let it own him, like it had in the past. Ivy Tucker still lived in Bluegrass Bend, but he'd been just another face in the massive crowd who'd all stood mesmerised by her that fateful night. But like almost every other bloke in the pub *he* had noticed *her*, big time. He'd found it impossible to take his eyes off her as she'd performed; there was just something unique about her, something he'd never seen in any other girl before. And her voice, it was as sweet as an angel's, and filled with depth and potency. How anyone could want to hurt such an exquisite creature was beyond him.

But Lottie was right. That was all in the past, and he needed to focus on his future if he wanted to make a decent life for himself. So, to stop dwelling on the things he could never change he focused on what lay ahead of him. He longed for the vast Blue Mountain countryside of his youth, and to feel the peace that came with the absence of man-made monstrosities like this godforsaken prison so he could truly allow his heart and soul to breathe. Although, he wouldn't be going back to his childhood home, which had passed into the hands of the last surviving McWilliams man other than himself, his uncle, Douglas McWilliams. With his grandad dying of prostate cancer when he was just nine years old, his father's dramatic exit from this earth fifteen years ago, and his grandmother's death last year, his uncle was the next in line. He'd never been able to bring himself to like his uncle – a man who reminded Ronny too much of his own arrogant father. Douglas was the epitome of a narcissist and only ever did anything to benefit himself, even at the detriment of another. Ronny silently thanked Lottie again for giving him the chance to return to the land he loved so much, suddenly craving the sensation of climbing into the saddle and galloping full throttle through the eucalypt-dominated countryside at the back of Sundown Farm. On a horse was where he felt truly alive. He'd always preferred the company of a good stockhorse or a dog to a human because, unlike most humans, you could trust horses and dogs. And both animals could feel deep into your heart, and could know so much about who you were without you having to utter a single word. They never judged you, either, for anything. Ever.

Taking a sip from his bitter, lukewarm coffee, Ronny relished the fact he would never have to drink a drop of the foul-tasting gutter water again. And he would never have to eat another mouthful of something that made him think starving to death might be a better option. There was so much in this hellhole that he wasn't going to miss. This godforsaken place had given him no physical freedom, and yet, he'd tried to turn it to his advantage as best he could over the years, believing in the notion that true freedom came from within. Taking his big sister's advice, he'd used his time in here wisely, reading every book about personal growth and inner healing she'd brought him – Jon Kabat-Zinn and Deepak Chopra were his favourites. Through the solitude of prison life he'd finally been forced to discover who he truly was, had no other choice but to face up to his inner demons and choose what he wanted out of his time on this earth – and he wanted to somehow make a difference by helping those in need. It had taken nine months of intense study, but he now had his accreditation, and was excited with the prospect of teaching people how to calm their minds, and lives, through meditation once he got himself settled into life at Sundown. He didn't want to waste another precious second of his life hanging around the wrong kind of people – the ones who sapped you until you were dry and then dumped you when they'd gotten what they'd wanted. By being able to tap into his spiritual side – which until prison he'd never have believed for a minute he'd had – he felt as though he had somehow beaten the system, because he was walking out more alive than he had been when he'd walked in, both physically and mentally, and with a belief in himself he'd never had before. That wasn't to say he still didn't carry some skeletons, and there were still a few lingering inner issues he had to deal with, but he was going to do his very best to overcome it all – and anything else that came his way.

Looking to the cobalt blue sky, the endless expanse of freedom that had always given him hope, Ronny smiled. He was amazed this day had finally come – no more counts, no more lockdowns, no more being told what to do, no more being constrained to solitary confinement because he'd defended his life yet again, no more having his every move watched and being told when he could eat, shower, sleep. This moment had always seemed so far away he just hadn't been able to truly grasp it. But today, he was walking out of the prison gates and onto the next phase in his life.

It had been seven years, eleven months and two weeks, 2905 days to be exact, since he'd lived life on the other side of these walls, since he'd felt what it was like to go to the toilet in private, brush his teeth when he wanted to, hug a loved one for longer than five seconds, and eat his favourite thing in the world – a juicy steak dripping with creamy mushroom sauce, served with tender steamed veggies and crunchy beer-battered chips. There was so much living for him to look forward to, and so much life to catch up on.

Ronny regarded the letter lying open on the table, and contemplated what lay ahead for him. He knew it word for word, but still, reading it made him feel close to her. He found it hard to believe Lottie had left her property to him – nobody had ever handed him something on a silver platter – and with very fair requests on her behalf. He just hoped he could do her memory proud and make a good go of the place – Sundown Farm was Lottie's everything. Even though she had left him her life savings it didn't mean he'd have a tonne of money behind him, although much like Lottie, he shouldn't need much: he wasn't a material person and was quite capable of surviving mostly off the land, along with earnings from a job, just as Lottie had used her pension and the money she made from dressmaking. His new life was going to come with its challenges, of course, but the kind he welcomed with open arms. He had faith that he could do it.

He drew in a deep breath then exhaled slowly, readying himself for his walk to freedom. He'd survived life on the inside, now he had to see if he was going to survive on the outside. His heart galloped like a captive horse finally breaking free of its restraints. He'd always been able to cover his inner turmoils and fears well, though, so to any onlooker he'd be the picture of complete calm and composure – a skill he'd mastered from a very young age to avoid another lesson being taught to him by his alcoholic and extremely hot-tempered father. Boys weren't meant to cry, weren't meant to show any kind of emotion other than strength, not ever. Looking back on what he and his mother had gone through at the hands of his father, Ronny thought it was no wonder he'd been a rebellious teenager with a massive chip on his shoulder (how his poor grandma, bless her soul, had coped with him, he'd never know). He could also see where his pure hatred of any man who laid a finger on a woman, or took advantage of her, came from. After his years in prison, the chip on his shoulder was long gone, but his instinct to protect a woman? Never.

He stretched out his aching neck and noticed the clock up on the guard tower read 11.15 am. It was time. As if on cue, the loudspeaker crackled to life.

'Prisoner number 1456 to the rear gates of the prison.'

The yard became still, no man saying a word as all eyes fell upon him. Grabbing his bag of belongings, Ronny stood, the world seeming like it was moving in slow motion as he approached the place he was usually forbidden to set foot in – any other day, the guard on watch would have aimed his rifle at him and shot him if he'd dared taken a step further. But it was his official day of release. Some inmates congratulated him along the way while others eyed him with barely disguised envy. He felt bad leaving some of them behind, but many he couldn't wait to see the back of.

A guard stepped out to meet him near the gates, and escorted him inside one of the penitentiary buildings to finalise paperwork. This was it. He was going to be a free man. Life would be limitless outside of these walls – he would make damn sure of it.

***

Thirty minutes later, dressed in the jeans and T-shirt his sister had brought last week, Ronny walked through the gates, the sunshine somehow warmer, more embracing, on this side of the prison walls. No more handcuffs, no gun tower, no more numbers on his chest, just the hum of everyday life, and a certain kind of beautiful noise – the pulse of a normal, free, human existence.

The navy blue Commodore that caught his attention was much older than he recalled but the familiarity of it made him smile. He'd had many expeditions in it, including the one to Parramatta that had landed him here in the first place. The driver's door flew open and the only person still alive who truly cared for him unconditionally ran towards him, her long golden hair flowing out behind her as she threw her arms wide to envelop him. She reminded him so much of their mother. Ronny dropped his bag and embraced her, enjoying the scent of the musk oil perfume she'd worn for as long as he could remember.

'Hey, sis, it's so bloody good to see you.' He pointed to the car. 'And I see you still have Old Grunter.'

'Old Grunter has been damn good to me … you're going to have to fight me to get him back.' Faith chuckled as she squeezed him tighter, giving him a few hearty slaps on the back, and then let him go, her hands flying to his cheeks as she blinked back tears. 'It's bloody good to see you, too, bro.' She glanced at the prison walls with her intense amber-coloured eyes, eyes that mirrored Ronny's. 'And on the other side of them ghastly things. It's about fricken time. You should've never ended up in that shithole in the first place.' She shook her head. 'You and your damn hero complex … you don't need to go saving every damsel in distress, you know.'

Ronny grinned. 'I know, but I just can't help myself. Anyway, them's the breaks. You do the crime you gotta do the time, as they say.' He grabbed his bag from the ground and tossed it over his shoulder. 'So what have I missed the past eight or so years … you haven't secretly married and had seven kids or something, have you?'

Faith gave him a loving slap. 'Always the joker, aren't you? I've really missed you.' She entwined her arm in his, giving his bicep a bit of a squeeze as she did so. 'Far out, did you do anything other than lift weights in there? Your arm feels like a brick.'

Ronny shook his head, grinning. 'You can just call me Arnie.' He deepened his already deep voice. 'I'll be back.' He tried to keep a straight face, failing miserably as he buckled over with laughter. It felt so damn good to laugh.

Faith laughed with him, rolling her eyes. 'You're a far cry from Arnold Schwarzenegger, Ronny, but in a good way – that man is way too bloated looking, kinda like a puffer fish when you poke it, whereas you, on the other hand, are just right. Boy oh boy, the girls of Bluegrass Bend are gonna love you, and maybe even some of the boys!' She wriggled her eyebrows cheekily, avoiding his playful slap before tugging him towards his old car. 'Come on, let's get you home, Thor – we've got so much catching up to do. I've just gotta call into the butcher's on the way so I can grab you that T-bone steak you've been craving, and I'm going to wow you with a whiskey cream sauce I've perfected too.'

Ronny's mouth watered. Real food made in a real, love-filled kitchen. Dinner was going to be heaven. Actually, anything not out of a packet or a can – or resembling something that had been scraped off the floor – would be heaven.

'Whatever you cook wows me, sis, you're the best cook I've ever met.'

Faith smiled and reached up on her tippy toes to give him a kiss on the cheek. 'I'm honoured you remember my cooking after all these years. You'd hope I was good at it, seeing as that's what I do for a living now.'

***

Walking through the door of his sister's Randwick apartment, Ronny breathed a sigh of relief. The world had changed a fair bit in the years he'd been behind bars and as much as he felt blessed to be free, it was a bit overwhelming. He wasn't used to the whirr and buzz of city life at the best of times, but after years in jail, it was magnified, the distractions coming at him from every direction making his head spin: the smell of takeaway foods wafting from shops; the cars whizzing in every direction; horns and sirens and music blaring; people scurrying down the footpaths and across the roads like they were on fast forward; even Faith's mobile phone ringing from the dashboard had made him almost hit the roof of her car (which wasn't hard when he was so close to it). He'd tried to prepare for this moment through meditation and mindfulness, knowing full well it wasn't something he was going to conquer in a day, but actually doing it in real life was a whole other ball game. It was going to take him a little while to ease back into society, but he wasn't in a rush to achieve anything, so all in good time.

Standing in the cosy lounge room, he turned around slowly, admiring the bohemian feel of the place. It smelt of incense sticks and scented candles, which suited his laid-back hippy sister down to the ground, and had an awesome view of the park across the road. He was very impressed by the apartment – all the hard work and endless hours Faith put into her trendy tapas-style restaurant at Coogee Beach had clearly paid off. And to top it all, she'd achieved everything on her own, without the help of a man. A lover of her own company and fiercely independent, he doubted she'd ever get married and have children – Faith had always made it quite clear she didn't have a maternal bone in her body. He, on the other hand, couldn't wait to have kids.

'Nice pad, sis.'

'Thanks, I like it. I'm proud to be able to call it my own – even though the bank owns most of it.' Faith dropped the grocery bag she was carrying on the kitchen bench along with her handbag and car keys and then pointed down the hall. 'The spare room is just on your right, you can go and chuck your bag in there if you like while I make us a cuppa.' She busied herself unpacking the groceries. 'And I'll make you something for lunch … you have a choice of a ham and cheese toasted sandwich or some leftover lasagne from last night.'

'I'll take a massive portion of your famous lasagne, thanks,' Ronny said, already heading down the short hall, his six-foot-four frame meaning he had to duck to get through the doorway of the spare bedroom. His heart squeezed tight. Sitting in a stand beside the bed was the Maton acoustic guitar his mother had worked three jobs to save for, the guitar she had given him for his tenth birthday, the one material thing in the world that meant everything to him, and more. He'd known his sister had it, but he wasn't prepared for the emotion the sight of it evoked.

He picked the guitar up and ran his fingers along the mahogany timber, memories flooding his mind of him and his mum sitting on the lounge together, singing the tunes of Slim Dusty and John Williamson as he strummed away. His mum had always been so loving and so caring. If only he knew then that he wouldn't have her around for long, he would have hugged her tightly and never let go, and he would have made sure to tell her every single day how much he loved and adored her.

Gently putting the guitar back in its place – he would spend time later tuning it – he placed his bag on the queen-sized, plushly made bed and grinned. He was going to get himself lost in a bed this big, not that he was complaining. To be able to wake up when he felt like it to a day full of endless possibilities equalled pure bliss. Sitting on the bed, he bounced up and down, relishing the fact the bed had give in it, and didn't creak like it needed an entire can of WD-40. A ceiling fan circled above him, the cool breeze something he was unaccustomed to, and something he welcomed after years of sweating through summers in his jail cell. Through the bedroom window he could see children frolicking in the lush green park, their sweet laughter uplifting. It had been a very long time since he'd seen children playing and it made him think, once again, about how much he wanted his own. It was amazing how many things you took for granted in life until they were taken away from you. He certainly would never take anything for granted ever again.

Lacing his hands behind his head, he lay back and looked around the room, appreciation filling him when he spotted the men's toiletries neatly arranged on the timber dresser. Faith was always so thoughtful, just like their mum had been. Emotions threatened to overcome him but he allowed the memories of his beautiful mother to float away before the heartache took hold of him, because all he wanted to feel right now was the joy of finally being a free man.

CHAPTER 3

Ronny felt a weight in his chest as he waved goodbye to Faith. She smiled sadly back at him, blowing kisses as the bus pulled away from the kerb. He took one last look at her on the footpath, her resemblance to their mother stirring deep emotions within him. Faith was now the same age as his mum when they lost her. He wished he could reach out and wipe the tears from Faith's cheeks, and take the ache from her heart. He hated being the cause of her sorrow, but there was no other way. Faith couldn't live in the country and he couldn't live in the city. They were only going to be a couple of hours away from each other, but her busy work schedule was going to make it hard for her to visit him, and with him wanting to get a job as soon as possible, it was going to be equally hard for him to make the trip here. Faith had wanted him to take Old Grunter, but he'd told her to keep the Commodore – it was hers now and she needed a car. What kind of brother would he be, taking her only mode of transport when he had a reliable enough car at Sundown? And he had to renew his licence anyway – his previous one had expired while he was in prison. He would give driving a shot once he was home at Sundown Farm, where he didn't need to worry about running into another car – there was no traffic in the paddocks. He was so grateful Lottie had left him her 1970 model HT Holden Kingswood, a faithful banger. He gathered it would need some work, but at least it would get him from A to B for now, as it had done for Lottie for over forty years. He loved classic cars, and the Kingswood was unquestionably an Australian classic – more like an icon. One day he'd bring it back to all its glory by restoring it. Being a passenger to his destination was a safer choice, and a much more relaxing one too. This way he got to gaze out the window.

Making sure his guitar case was still positioned safely on the empty seat beside him along with the wide-brimmed black hat his sister had given him yesterday – he'd have to rough it up a bit, brand new hats were the worst – Ronny fidgeted in his seat, thankful he had no-one sitting beside him so he could stretch out a little. He'd been like a kid in a lolly shop at Roundyard Western Wear, wishing he could take everything home with him, but having to be careful with money, he'd just gotten the necessities: a pair of boots, a belt with a pouch for his trusty old pocket knife, a few pairs of jeans, and a couple of going-to-town shirts and some blue King Gee ones for work. He looked down at his new RM Williams boots, making a mental note to roughen them up a bit too. Real cowboys weren't meant to look all shiny and new. He and Faith had also popped into Kmart where he'd grabbed some essentials and a pre-paid sim for the second-hand iPhone she had given him, which, other than understanding how to play music on the damn thing, he had no idea how to use properly but would eventually figure out. In his bag beneath the bus were some of his old clothes from before he'd gone to jail, the ones that still fit him, seeing he wasn't a scrawny teenager anymore. Faith had kept his stuff in boxes for this very day, all of it now freshly washed and folded. Life was looking up and, man, it felt good to be back in the threads that made him the real country-born-and-bred man he was.

Plugging his earphones into the iPhone, Ronny selected the playlist Faith had made up for him with Slim Dusty, Adam Brand, Troy Cassar-Daley, Johnny Cash, Waylon Jennings, Clancy, Merle Haggard, Hank Williams, George Jones, Alan Jackson, Garth Brooks and Brad Paisley, and hit shuffle. What a line-up of legends! 'A Walk in the Rain' was the first song up – the poignancy of the love song giving him goose bumps as he softly hummed away to it. If only he had a woman to sing such beautiful lyrics to. Listening to his country music heroes always inspired him to pick up his guitar – he was looking forward to getting back into his music. He breathed in deeply as he smiled to himself and settled in for the trip. He couldn't wait to start the next chapter of his life – a chapter of freedom and limitless possibilities in the heart of the iconic Blue Mountains. It was what his dreams were made of, and in less than two hours, it was going to be his reality.

With Sundown Farm needing daily looking after it was a blessing Larry had decided to take Lottie up on her offer and remain there because Ronny was going to need all the help he could get. And thank God for Larry being there for Lottie throughout her battle with brain cancer – it eased Ronny's guilt at not being able to help her in her greatest time of need knowing she had someone she was close to by her side. When it came to the farm, Larry was the only one, other than Ronny of course, that Lottie would allow assistance from. Lottie had always been fiercely independent and had hated asking for help, only begrudgingly accepting Ronny's when he'd turned up on her doorstep with his grandma one Saturday afternoon when he was thirteen years old. That had become a routine every month thereafter until Ronny had gone to jail. The bond he'd formed with Lottie was similar to that he'd had with his mum – the woman who'd never been able to have children of her own gave him unconditional love. It was going to feel strange being at Sundown Farm without her around to keep him on his toes, but he was sure Lottie would still be there in spirit, just as she had promised in her letter. If there was an afterlife, which Ronny believed there was, Lottie wouldn't be able to keep herself away from the place.

As well as tending to the few farm creatures – two horses, Merle and Hank; three cows that Lottie had bought for killers but then had never been able to bring herself to eat, which she'd named Daisy, Dolly and Daffodil; a half-blind, half-deaf rooster called Nugget; chooks, he'd discover their names later; two ducks, Plucka and Donald; a grumpy old goat called Ned; a Shetland pony inherited from the next-door neighbours; and a retired farm dog, Jessie – and making sure the place was maintained and essentially kept safe until his arrival, Larry had also filled Ronny in on the day-to-day running of the farm and had kept him up to date with photos of the place during his time in prison. Being semi-retired, Ronny didn't expect much more from Larry, but Larry being Larry, he'd gone above and beyond what was expected of him and had done a lot of work to the gardens. With the help of a few of the CWA women, he'd also tidied up Lottie's place in readiness for Ronny's arrival. Ronny felt lucky to have made a mate in Larry many years ago – knowing full well it was a hard thing in life to come across people you could trust. He was looking forward to having a good old yarn and enjoying a few beers with his mate.

He also couldn't wait to get out on the land and get his hands dirty, see the fruits of his labour as the land gave back to him tenfold. He knew that would have to be done in his spare time, around the job he'd need to find soon so he didn't eat into the money Lottie had left him, which was already dwindling after paying for feed for the animals and the day-to-day running costs of the farm over the past few months. Hopefully the carpentry apprenticeship he'd completed six months before being sent to the slammer would land him a job pretty quickly.

An hour into the journey the concrete jungle was far behind him, and it felt great. It had been wonderful spending time with Faith, but there was no way he'd ever be able to live in a buzzing metropolitan hub like she did. Faith had always been the opposite of him, preferring the city to the country any day. Although an intriguing place, a few days in the thick of the constant noise and Ronny had been itching to get into the serenity of the bush. Their trip to the beach had been enjoyable, though. He'd imagined the ocean washing away the shit of the past eight years every time he'd dived beneath the crashing waves. Feeling the fine white sand between his toes had been absolute ecstasy – meditation with his eyes open. He found so much pleasure in the smallest of things now. It was as though prison life had made all his senses more aware.

Gazing out the window of the Greyhound bus, Ronny drank in the glorious countryside, admiring the scribbly gums and sunshine wattle stealing the limelight among thick bushland backdropped by walls of sandstone. The sheer drops made him feel as though he was on the edge of the world and gave him a sense of freedom he hadn't felt in what felt like forever. The blue haze lingering above the mountaintops that soared as if determined to kiss the heavens was the reason the Blue Mountains had got their name, the eucalypt trees emitting an oil that appeared blue in the sunlight. Every which way he looked, the panoramic views dominated the horizon and took his breath away. This part of New South Wales was a place of undeniable beauty. The deeply incised sandstone plateaus, the spectacular cliffs, gorges and valleys, ignited a fire in his heart that had long ago been extinguished by the confines of jail, and it was damn good to feel his passion for the land he'd once called home rekindle.

The turn-off to Wentworth Falls alerted Ronny he wasn't too far from Bluegrass Bend. A bolt of exhilaration shot through him. Next would be Leura, Kooloy and then twenty minutes after that his new hometown, Bluegrass Bend. His stomach back-flipped with what lay ahead – how was he going to feel, knowing his grandma was no longer here? Before he had time to contemplate it too deeply, the Leura turn-off flashed past and they were heading through Kooloy. Ronny pressed his face against the window as his heart picked up pace, wanting, needing, to take every single detail in. To his surprise, not much had changed. Even the pub he used to frequent with his mates looked the same. A few of the shops had gone, replaced by bigger stores, and there were a few more touristy-looking cafes, but other than that it was the Kooloy he remembered. And, unexpectedly, he felt nothing, no sentiments or ties to the place at all. He thought about this for a few moments, wanting to understand his reaction, or lack of. He gathered it was because all his loved ones had gone into the next life, leaving just a town in their wake. That's all he could put it down to. And he was more than happy to leave his past here, where it belonged.

Twenty minutes later a sign stated they were entering the village of Bluegrass Bend, 1080 metres above sea level and with a population of 8300. From the second Ronny laid eyes on the township he was captivated, the place as picturesque as he remembered it. Charming cottages adorned the streets, most of the gardens meticulously manicured. Cherry tree–lined nature strips gave way to stone footpaths adorned with pot plants, the shrubs and flowers within them colourful and flourishing. Each shopfront showcased the rich tapestry of the slightly eccentric town: clothing boutiques, a bookshop, antique shops and cosy cafes were scattered among the necessities, all with the magnificent Secret Valley as their vast backyard. It was such a welcome respite from the shopping malls Faith had made him traipse through all day yesterday in search of his wares. The people on the footpaths in town were unhurried, relaxed looking, the feel of the place very unlike the rushed city streets; this was definitely Ronny's kind of town – laid-back, countrified, and unpretentious. For the umpteenth time that day he smiled again to himself, forever grateful to his great aunt for giving him such an amazing opportunity. What a beautiful place to be calling home.

The bus pulled into a cul-de-sac at the back of the local train station. As it came to a stop, Ronny almost leapt from his seat, pulling on his jacket and hat, every inch of him longing to get off and breathe in the pure mountain air. Patiently, he waited for the people in front of him to gather their things and step from the bus, his guitar case at the ready. Finally, it was his turn. He breathed in the crisp, untainted air as his boots hit the ground and his soul exhaled. He felt as though this was his first decent breath in years. Although it was the middle of summer it was just eighteen degrees today, typical of the mountains, and the icy breeze made it feel even colder. Tugging the collar of his jacket up and around his neck, Ronny approached the bus driver, who was unloading the luggage, the sharp, fresh scent of impending rain lingering in the air, making him look forward to many cosy nights by the fireplace at Sundown Farm while snowflakes covered everything outside.

'Oi, Ronny, over here, mate.'

Turning as he slung his bag over his shoulder, Ronny beamed, spotting Larry leaning up against a bush-beaten tray-back LandCruiser, with what was clearly Sundown's farm dog, Jessie, tied up in the back. The bloke was hunched a little more from his years spent in the saddle, a lot more weathered looking and a lot greyer than Ronny remembered, although his hair was just as thick and wild as ten years ago, but it was unmistakably Larry Smith, his trademark up-to-no-good grin so wide it made his eyes crinkle deeply at the corners.

Ronny took a few steps towards him, smiling. 'Hey mate, how's tricks?' He held out his hand and Larry shook it so hard it made Ronny feel as though he was holding onto a jackhammer. Larry's sixty-eight or so years certainly didn't stop him from being on the ball.

'I'm alive and breathing so I'm great, no damn use complaining 'cause no bastard wants to hear it anyway.' Larry released his vice-like grip and gave Ronny a friendly slap on the arm. 'It's so bloody good to see ya.' His unkempt eyebrows met in the middle. 'Ya haven't been taking that steroid junk in jail though, have ya? You've almost doubled in size since I seen ya last.'

Ronny grinned. Larry had never been one to shy away from saying what was really on his mind. And that's exactly why they'd gotten on like a house on fire from the second they'd met. Larry was the salt of the earth, a man Ronny could trust with his life – the only man Ronny had ever been able to truly rely on for anything.

'No way, mate, wouldn't touch that shit if you paid me, I just didn't have much else to do in there, other than read or go to the gym.' He tossed his bag in the back of the ute as he eyed Larry's crocheted multicoloured jumper – not something the Larry from days gone by would have been caught dead in. 'And by the way, nice jumper, mate.'

Larry struck a pose, resembling not so much a model as someone who'd just been hit by lightning. He grinned as he rubbed the slight podge around his middle – another new thing for the stick insect Larry had always been. 'I've made me some special friends in the CWA. They've been taking real good care of me since Lottie left us, bringing me food and just popping in for a cuppa and a chat.

It's been nice companionship for an old codger like me – I've really missed your great aunt's company.' Larry rubbed his eyes and sniffed as if warding off tears. 'So, to cut a long story short, I volunteered to do a bit of gardening around the hall they use and in return the lovely ladies made me this – and the yummiest lemon meringue pie I've ever sunk my false teeth into.'

'Good on you for helping them out,' Ronny said with a smile, recalling how much of a ladies' man Larry had always been. He mightn't be the best-looking bloke around, and his age probably didn't help, but his charm always won the women over. 'Any *extra special* ladies in these newly made friends?'

Larry's mouth twitched as though he was fighting a smile. He wriggled his eyebrows. 'Let's just say there might be …' His lips broke into a stupid grin.

Larry certainly looked like a man in love, something Ronny thought he'd never see when it came to the usually hard-as-nails commitment-phobic Larry Smith. He gave him a friendly slap on the back, mischief written all over his face. 'Good on ya, Smithy, it's about time you settled down and got married, maybe had yourself some mini Smithies.'

Larry coughed as though choking on Ronny's words, then burst into snorts of laughter. 'Whoa, slow down there, cupid. I reckon we'd all agree I'm *way* past having me any ankle-biters.'

'True with the ankle-biters, but you're never too old to tie the knot.'

'Let's not jump ahead of ourselves here – it's all just for fun,' Larry muttered, the dreamy expression on his round face betraying him.

Jessie gave a short sharp bark, as though saying hello, her tail going round and round like a helicopter blade and her jowls stretched into a wide canine grin. Ronny leant in and gave her a ruffle behind the ears. She was tethered to the back of the ute by a rope thick enough to moor a yacht, which made him laugh – Larry always having been a stickler when it came to the safety of his animals. 'Hey there, girl, nice to finally meet you. Lottie used to mention you all the time in her letters to me.'

Jessie snuck in a lick to his cheek and Ronny laughed again as he rubbed the slobber off with the back of his hand. The dog sat and stared at him as if waiting for a command, like she somehow knew he was her new owner.

Ronny smiled at her. 'You can lie back down, girl.'

Jessie did as she was told, her tail thumping against the tray of the ute as she watched Ronny jump into the passenger seat of the LandCruiser.

Larry headed around to his side, nodding in Jessie's direction. 'Bloody good dog, she is, too damn clever for her own good most of the time.'

Ronny popped his guitar case between his legs before tugging on his seatbelt. 'I'm so glad you're staying at Sundown, Larry. It's gonna be nice to have a familiar face around, and priceless to have someone who knows the place like the back of his hand.'

Larry flashed Ronny a smile. 'Really? I was a bit worried you'd be wanting the place to yourself. I kinda felt if I stayed, I'd just be getting in the way.'

Ronny shot him a look of absolute astonishment. 'As if, Larry. You're like an uncle to me. I'm gonna love having you about the place. I'd be insulted if you left, especially seeing as Lottie wanted you to stay.'

'Well, that's just made me real happy to hear.' Larry grinned.

Ronny grinned back at him, feeling on top of the world.

***

Ten minutes later, driving through the wrought iron gates of Sundown Farm, Ronny experienced a warm rush of homecoming from the tips of his boot-covered toes to the top of his head. This beautiful place was now his home. Forever. He'd never had a forever home. It was the best feeling in the world. He still half expected Lottie to run out and greet them on the front verandah, her flour-dusted apron tied around her plump hips, her genuine smile bright enough to lighten his darkest of days. It saddened him beyond words that she wouldn't be there to take him into her arms and hug him until he felt like he couldn't breathe. At the very least, by being here, by making this place his home, he would have a piece of Lottie with him always – although he would give it all back in a heartbeat to have her alive again.

With proud eyes he surveyed the land before him, rising and falling like a gentle ocean. Lush, green and fertile, Sundown Farm was a country-lover's dream. Radiant afternoon sunlight bathed the land in its warm glow, the golden rays creeping to every nook and cranny of the place. Apple trees lined the gravelled driveway that led to the three-bedroom cottage, the fruit dangling from the branches a work of art. And no, they weren't all shiny, they were misshapen and different in size, and some probably had brown spots and the occasional worm, but they were real apples. No dangerous chemicals – Lottie never used harsh chemicals around her farm. This was fruit straight off the tree, and Ronny would be savouring each and every one.

Built on a gentle rise that sloped away gradually on every side, the timber cottage finally came into view. Many years ago the paint would have been smooth and unbroken, and the window frames would have been brilliant white upon the new wood. Now weathered over the years by the elements, the old relic of a farmhouse spoke volumes about hardships and hope, strength and vulnerability. With its rusting roof and slightly sagging porch surrounded by colourful manicured gardens, it resembled a house well lived in but also very well loved. Although it couldn't be described as magnificent, it had an early settlers kind of charm that was extremely appealing to Ronny.

Pulling up out the front, Larry left the LandCruiser running. 'I'm just gonna head back to my place for a bit. I've got a load of washing to hang out and I wanna catch up on the footy scores. And I reckon it'd be good for ya to have a look around the place without me tagging along like a bad smell too.'

Ronny slipped his seatbelt off. 'Yup, okay, mate. No worries at all.'

'Wanna catch up over a barbecue dinner tonight? I've taken some snags out of the freezer, and grabbed a tub of Mrs Crocket's finest potato salad and coleslaw from town, and I've even got some leftover chocolate mud cake that Shirl dropped off yesterday too.'

'Who's – oh, your new extra special friend. Yup, sounds good to me.' Ronny grinned wickedly at Larry before he jumped out, grabbing his guitar case before he shut the door. He retrieved his bag from the tray.

Larry leant out his window. 'Ya might as well take Jessie with you. She basically lives here at the cottage anyway … refuses to sleep down at my place. I reckon it's because she feels close to Lottie here.' He pointed to the backyard. 'She's got a dog bed on the back verandah, and her food and water bowls are out there too.'

'Righto.' Ronny undid the clasp attached to Jessie's collar, his heart aching for her. Jessie clearly missed Lottie as much as he did. The dependable pooch waited for her cue to jump off. He whistled and threw his thumb to the side, and Jessie hightailed it over the back of the tray. Landing on the ground with a thump, she scuttled to his side. Ronny beamed down at her. It felt damn good to have a dog by his side again.

'I'll catch ya back here around six, mate, and in true dinky-di style I'll bring beer too.' Larry spun the LandCruiser around and headed down the dirt track that led to the workers' quarters. He braked suddenly and a cloud of grit and gravel flew out from his tyres. Hanging his head out the window, Larry grinned and pointed towards the cottage. 'Oh, and I forgot to mention, watch out for Miss Cindy Clawford in there … she tends to catch ya out when ya least expect it! She's pretty harmless, but my God, she can be a loose cannon at times.'

Ronny adjusted his sunnies, the glare bouncing off Larry's back window making it almost impossible to see. 'Who in the hell is Cindy Clawford?'

'Lottie's cat. Someone brought her around about six months ago, saying the moggy was too much of a handful and if Lottie didn't want her then they'd have to get her put down.' He smiled warmly. 'And of course, Lottie took her in, being the beautiful woman she was.'

Ronny returned the smile. 'That's our Lottie.' Oh shit. He'd never been a cat person, but by the sounds of it he was going to have to quickly learn to be one.

'Yup, Lottie was certainly one in a million. Cindy's bowls are in the laundry and there are some cans of cat food in the cupboard. I've been giving her a feed every morning and night. The little bugger eats like a horse. And she doesn't need a kitty litter tray, she makes her own way out the cat door for her dirty business.' Larry slapped the outside of his door. 'Right, this time I'm really going …' And he was gone before Ronny could say 'see ya'.

Ronny stood in front of the homestead, bag in one hand and guitar case in the other. What was in his hands used to be all that he owned and now before him was more than he'd ever imagined possible. He was overawed that this was now his home. Jessie danced at his heels, her brindle coat merging with the dappled shadows cast by the towering blue gum trees alongside the cottage. The distinctive squawking of galahs grabbed Ronny's attention and for a brief moment he looked skywards, recalling Lottie telling him the early settlers used to make them into parrot pies. He didn't know if she was pulling his leg – Lottie was always up for telling a good yarn – but a bit of investigating on Google had confirmed her story.

Stepping through the little gate that led down the pebbled garden path, Ronny took in the quaint garden with its mix of roses, lavender and natives, including waratahs – it was so very Lottie to give anything that could have life the best life possible, and that included her beloved gardens. He noticed a pile of wood resting against the side of the house, and opposite that a vegetable and herb garden. Larry had cleared the beds of weeds, and Ronny was keen to get it up and running again. He'd make sure to grow enough to supply Larry with all he needed too. On the other side of the cottage the little lean-to carport drooped, as though the fight had left it and it could no longer stand up for itself against the elements. Ronny made a mental note to repair it before it collapsed on the Kingswood parked beneath it.

Climbing the front steps, Ronny placed his guitar case and bag on the couch near the front door and Jessie jumped up beside them, lying down for an afternoon snooze in a spot that was moulded to her form. He was certain he'd be doing the same thing himself on the odd lazy afternoon. Shoving his hands in his jeans pockets, he turned slowly while he surveyed the land spread out before him. The view from here seemed to stretch out forever, the tranquillity making him feel as though he was standing on top of the world. Lottie and he had spent many a night out here, gazing at the stars and just talking over a glass of rum, or three. Those were the days.

Turning back to the cottage he opened the flyscreen and it squeaked wearily. WD-40 was in order – another mental note. The keys were where Larry said he'd left them, dangling from the lock of the hardwood door – Ronny gathered there were no worries about burglars here. Unlocking the door, he finally stepped inside. The familiar smell was the first thing that hit him – rose oil. It was Lottie all over. She wore rose oil as her perfume and used to sprinkle it throughout the house too. He hoped the scent lingered for as long as possible.

He took off his boots then stood still, arms folded. It was hard to make out the details of the room after the bright sunlight outside, but after a few moments his eyes adjusted as the filtered light from between the curtains lit up the room sufficiently. The lounge room was exactly as he remembered it – unpretentious and welcoming. The walls were a soft hue of blue, and the furniture uncluttered and simple, but definitely cosy looking with plenty of cushions on the couches and plush carpet that made him want to roll around on it. One entire wall was a bookcase with books crammed into every possible inch of space, Lottie having been a very avid reader of anything she could get her hands on. A fireplace held pride of place, and an antique coffee table separated the lounge chairs from a television that looked almost brand new. Ronny guessed Lottie's old one must have blown up, Lottie not one to replace things unless they'd had their day. Over in the corner was an old-fashioned hutch-style timber desk and on top of it sat an out-of-date phone with the large dialing disk and curled cable hanging from the receiver with the Bluegrass Bend phone book beside it. Ronny smiled sadly. Lottie was certainly a woman from yesteryear.

Ronny turned and headed down the hallway from which the three bedrooms led off, stopping to admire the black and white photographs hanging on the walls and to peek into each room. He'd move into the room he'd always used, with its queen-sized bed and built-in cupboards. The third room was Lottie's. Going to the old oak dressing table, Ronny picked up one of the framed sepia photographs, the look in Lottie's and her husband's eyes one of undeniable love for each other. They wouldn't have been any older than thirty in the photo, their arms entwined as they'd beamed at the photographer – poor Lottie, losing her one true love at fifty-two to an aneurism. Lottie had loved Frank so much she'd remained on her own after his death, saying she could never love another when her heart was with Frank. At least now she would be with her beloved husband eternally. Ronny hoped to one day be lucky enough to feel a love as deep and everlasting as theirs.

He headed into the heart of the home – the kitchen. If Lottie wasn't busy sewing, or caring for the farm and all the animals she adopted, she'd very often be found in the kitchen, whipping up some culinary delight, not only for herself and the many visitors who dropped in, or to help out a sick neighbour or friend, but also for the local meals on wheels. Nobody ever went hungry when in the company of Lottie Sinclair. And it was never a chore for her – she loved to cook, and she was good at it. Leaning on the kitchen bench, he sucked in a deep breath, wishing at the same time he could get a whiff of Lottie's cooking once more when, out of the corner of his eye, he saw something lurch at him from behind the bin. He wasn't fast enough to get out of the way so he now had a tiny cat wrapped tightly around his leg, her shiny black coat enhancing her big green eyes. He tried to pry her from his leg but Cindy Clawford meowed warningly. Larry was right – the little terror had caught him off guard and scared the shit out of him.

Although still a little shaken, he had to laugh at her audacity as his adrenaline levels returned to normal. Her tail was twitching playfully, giving him the impression she wasn't taking things too seriously, even though she wanted him to believe otherwise. Warily, he leant down to pat her, and also to disengage her claws from his jeans. She meowed at him once more, but this time sounded a little friendlier, and pushed her head into his hand, her purring growing louder as he gave her a scratch behind the ears. Cindy allowed him to pick her up, and once in his arms she snuggled into his chest and almost disappeared inside his button-up shirt. That simple gesture gave Ronny hope that he could get past the fact he'd never been a fan of felines. He had a feeling they were going to become firm friends.

Glancing around the room with Cindy still nestled in his arms, the nostalgia that had subsided with the cat's attack rose again to claw at Ronny's heart. True to her word, and thanks to the ladies who had cleared the cottage with her passing, an odd assortment of cups still hung from hooks below the overhead cupboards that were full of Lottie's kitchenware. The imitation-marble laminate benches were well worn but in an adding-character sort of way and the basics sat atop – a toaster, kettle and matching coffee, tea and sugar canisters, and then there was Lottie's favourite biscuit tin from the nineteen-twenties – a hand-me-down from her mother. Ronny ran his fingers over it, appreciating the fact the CWA ladies had left it here. He'd had many a homemade biscuit from within it. Pots and pans hung from a wrought iron hanger above a concaved butcher's block which took centre stage, and rightly so. At over a hundred years old and retrieved from a butcher's shop that had shut its doors in the seventies, it added personality to the place. Ronny loved it as much as Lottie had. A six-seater dining table sat off to the side, with views out the windows of the horse paddocks. Last year's calendar hung askew on a nail above the stove and Ronny reached out to straighten it. It felt a little grimy. It struck him then that this was the first time the cottage looked a little dusty, and he wasn't walking in to the sound of ABC radio playing in the background. The thought squeezed his aching heart even tighter. Glancing at the windowsill above the sink, he spotted a photo of him and Lottie standing on the front verandah, smiling like they hadn't a care in the world. He remembered the day like it was only yesterday – his sixteenth birthday. Lottie had cooked him and Grandma a feast fit for a king in celebration. It had been such a beautiful day, filled with the love of family.

A wave of grief washed over him, engulfing him and taking him by surprise. He was never again going to be surrounded by Lottie's addictive laughter, or her warm spirit, or her unconditional love. Swallowing his emotions, he strode through a side door and into the laundry, where Cindy decided to leap from his arms and into her little basket sitting on top of the washing machine. He needed air. Now. He pushed through the screen door and out onto the back verandah. Breathing in deeply, he tried to keep himself under control. But it was here that reality finally hit him and his tears began to fall. Hard. Lottie was never coming back. She had given him all that mattered to her and he would never get the chance to thank her for all that she had done for him.

Leaning against the timber railings, he covered his face with his hands and allowed the sorrow he'd been suppressing to surface, his sobs coming from deep within as grief finally overcame him.

CHAPTER 4

The screen door squeaked in protest as Ivy walked outside with banana and crunchy peanut butter on toast along with her morning cuppa. Breathing in the scenery sprawling before her, she sat on the steps of the wrap-around verandah, the steam rising from her cup matching the fog hanging like a blanket over the distant mountains – the similarity somehow soothing her nerves about what lay ahead this morning. Their appointment with Gerald was first off the rank and she was relieved she didn't have to sit and wait half the day to see him. Yawning, she tried to blink the tiredness from her eyes, her body weary and her heart heavy. She'd had a horrible night's sleep again, her doona feeling the brunt of it as she pulled it up and tossed it off a million times. A midnight cup of chamomile tea with her equally sleepless aunts had done the trick for a few hours, but then she'd spent the wee hours of the morning cursing sleep and all it stood for.

The beauty of Healing Hills made her heart swell as she gazed out over the horses bathed by the morning sunlight now beginning to peek through the dispersing grey clouds – even after all these years the landscape never ceased to amaze her. Her gaze then travelled to the place way up on the hillside where she'd once lived with her mum and dad. They'd always intended to renovate the cottage to its former glory, but had never gotten the chance. The colonial-style house that had once been her home now lay as desolate as her heart could sometimes be – it was going to be a bittersweet moment when she sold it. With poignant memories of her early childhood stirring emotions deep within she moved her gaze hesitantly towards the high cliff face that dropped dangerously to a gorge one hundred metres below. The very place her mother had jumped to her death sixteen years ago – a place a piece of her heart would forever remain. Damn Ivy's cheating father for breaking her mother's heart. Bloody men! She sucked in a sharp breath and slowly blew it away, silently telling her mum how much she still loved her.

Off in the distance, just beyond the borderline of Healing Hills, a rainbow hovered, its arc of prismatic colours – red, orange, yellow, green, blue and purple – vivid, the vision hopeful and comforting, like a warm hug after tears. With the heavy downpour they'd had throughout all of last night she'd thought today was going to be as overcast as yesterday, but maybe it was going to be a nice summer's day after all. Her mood lifted a little with the thought. Mother Nature always had a way of cheering her up.

Bo did a yoga-like stretch on the corner of the verandah, then came and lay down beside her, his head resting on his paws. He eyed her thoughtfully as he whined a little. She leant over and gave him a cuddle. Her mate always recognised when she was stressed or upset. She knew how she felt wasn't helping but how could she feel anything else right now? Her aunts' entire future – and her own – hinged on this meeting today, and she prayed with all her might that she wouldn't somehow stuff it up, not now that May and Alice had finally agreed to selling her property and using part of the money to pay out Healing Hills' debts. It had taken hours of pleading with them, but in the end they'd caved, with the proviso that, if they were ever in the position to, they would pay her back. She'd firmly reminded May and Alice they wouldn't owe a penny after selflessly raising her as their own all these years. Yes, like her, they had wanted her to one day make the cottage her home again, but as she'd brought to their attention, there was no way she'd ever be able to live on the adjoining property if Healing Hills was no longer in the family – it would just be a constant, painful reminder of all they had lost.

She'd done all the research on renovating the cottage, including investigating an estimated sale price of the five-acre property with the local real estate agency and was impressed with the figure; the effort of renovating was certainly going to be worth it. Although, after obtaining three separate quotes from the only reputable builders in the area, Ivy had quickly realised she would have to do the majority of the work herself, along with the help of a carpenter, if she were lucky enough to find one willing to do the job at short notice. But she was getting ahead of herself – their bank manager first had to lend her the fifty thousand she'd need to achieve it. Her plan was risky, but they had to do something to save Healing Hills.

She couldn't bear the thought of leaving – it was as if she'd grown roots into the land here and tearing herself away would be like an ancient tree being ripped from the ground. And where would all the beautiful healing horses go if the unthinkable happened? This was her home, her aunts' home, their sanctuary, a place people came to save themselves, a safe haven for both young and old. Yes, she'd had dreams for the cottage, but she didn't need to hold onto bricks and mortar to keep her mother's memory alive – Jasmine Tucker would forever live in her heart.

***

The raucous sound of laughter dragged Ronny from his slumber. His instinct to shield himself from an inmate with a gripe wielding a handmade weapon sent him bounding from the comfort of his bed in seconds, fists at the ready. Who in the hell was laughing so damn loud and what was so damn funny and come to think of it, where in the hell was he? His head pounded like a freight train and he pressed his hands against his temples, groaning. Still half asleep as he tried to gain his bearings, he tripped over his boots then trod on a fork left on the floor from his midnight snack of two minute noodles which then sent him hopping on one leg as he nursed his stabbed foot. He was only saved from hitting the deck by clutching the open door of his empty cupboard. Thank God for small mercies.

Rubbing his knuckles against his eyes and then blinking himself to full awareness, Ronny adjusted his askew boxers and began to relax. He chuckled at himself as he heard the laughter outside once again, the lyrics from an old nursery rhyme coming to mind. Warmth filled him with the song.

Pulling back the blackout curtains, he peered into the backyard, straining to see through the golden sunlight now pouring in like a flowing river. It reflected off a few objects in the room, making him squint even more. He blinked a few times as his eyes took time to adjust, his pounding head becoming more of a steady thump now his heart rate had returned to normal. Damn his stupidity at drinking six beers with Larry last night. He should have known that he would have ended up with a massive hangover, having been sober for so long, but he'd been having too much fun catching up on the good old days to worry about it at the time. Copious amounts of water would be needed today, after a very strong cup of coffee, a greasy breakfast of bacon and eggs and a few painkillers. And of course no self-pity would be allowed, the headache was completely self-inflicted.

Resting up against the window frame Ronny inhaled the country scene sprawled out before him as he ran his hands over his recently shaved head, his dark hair barely a few millimetres in length now thanks to Faith's trusty old pair of Wahl clippers. Dew glittered on the grass, making it appear as if it was adorned with diamonds and just over the back fence two kangaroos bounded past. He smiled in their direction, loving the fact he could witness this first thing rather than a concrete cell and steel bars. Beyond the large backyard were some horse paddocks and the stables, and then the bountiful countryside seemed to stretch on forever. The National Parklands at the back of Sundown Farm made the place feel like it was charmingly isolated, although Ronny knew his neighbours, the Mayberrys, were hidden just behind the long line of mountain blue gums that created the border between their place and Lottie's, or should he now say, his place – the thought, as much as it was something he would be eternally grateful for, was still hard to swallow.

Bringing his attention back to the raucous laughter that had awoken him Ronny focused on the three kookaburras sitting on the clothesline, one of them staring fixedly at the ground below. It swooped down, seized its prey in its bill, and then flew back to its wire perch to eat it. Ronny wondered if it was the young bird he'd fed years ago, now an adult and still living here with its own little family. It was a comforting thought – and not a far-fetched one either. He knew for a fact that kookaburras mated for life, and the family unit usually consisted of a few generations with most of the young birds staying around to help raise their younger brothers or sisters. And it was all thanks to Lottie he knew all of this, including the Aboriginal legend that the kookaburra's famous chorus of laughter every morning was a signal for the sky people to light the great fire that illuminates and warms the earth by day – the sun. He liked the legend, as had Lottie who'd always loved legends and folk tales, but Ronny also knew the bird's laugh was actually used more as a territorial marker. Lottie had religiously fed the kookaburras every morning, which is why they would still be coming here, and he made a mental note to continue on with the ritual. He smiled to himself, the call of the kookaburra one of those unmistakable sounds of the Australian bush that will definitely give your ears a workout morning and afternoon, and it had awoken him on his very first morning at Sundown Farm. What a beautiful way to start his day.

A long, drawn-out meow drew his attention back to his bed. Cindy was stretched out on the pillow beside his – the little blighter must have snuck in through the night. Being susceptible to hay fever, the thought of cat hair all over his pillows made him cringe. He picked her up and placed her down on the floor, firmly reprimanding the cunning feline while trying to hide his smile. 'There'll be no sleeping in my bed, missy, so you better get outta that habit real quick.'

Cindy meowed back at him while clawing the rug beside his bed. Turning to the door, she strutted away as if to say, 'We'll see about that.' Her tail flicked as she disappeared around the doorframe and down the hallway.

Grabbing his T-shirt from the floor, he tugged it over his head and, spotting the letter that outlined Lottie's final wishes on his bedside table, he popped it in his second drawer so it wouldn't get lost. He glanced at his watch, shaking his head as he tapped the glass face a few times, thinking it must have stopped. But it hadn't. Holy snapping duck shit, it was almost eight o'clock. He had to head off in less than an hour. Talk about wasting the better part of the morning.

He hadn't slept past six am in as long as he could remember – even while he was at Faith's he still woke up at the crack of dawn.

Going out to the kitchen, he went in search of a stand-your-spoon-up-'cause-it's-so-strong cup of coffee, making sure to let Jessie in before he started his breakfast. The dog leapt from her verandah bed like a rocket and tap-danced at his feet. He gave her head a loving ruffle. He needed sustenance, then he had a small load of washing to do thanks to the fact he'd spilt half his midnight snack of noodles into his suitcase last night while searching for his boxers. He'd do that whilst running through the dip (the shower) to save time.

His belly flipped with excitement. Considering it was his very first day back at Sundown Farm – and his very first as a landowner – he was sure there'd be plenty to see and do. But before anything else, he needed to head into town with Larry to open a bank account and to also apply for his new driver's licence. Once they got back he'd have a stroll around the place to see what needed doing as well as checking out the shed where all his tools of his trade had been stored while he was in jail. Along the way he would make sure to introduce himself to all the farm animals Lottie had collected over the years. He couldn't wait to see her two horses, Merle and Hank, both geldings having shared many a ride with him over the years. And after all that he was going to try his hand at driving again now he was in a place without traffic. So much to do and he couldn't wait to do it all. Staring out the window while the kettle boiled and with Jessie now sitting on his feet Ronny beamed from ear to ear. Today was without a doubt going to be a magical kind of day.

***

Ivy pulled up in the last free parking space out the front of the National Bank and snatched her ringing mobile from the dash of her treasured 1964 EH Holden ute, which had previously been her aunt Alice's. 'Hey Aunt May.'

'Hi love, how far away are you?'

'I've just pulled up out front. I'll be in in a sec. Sorry to make you all wait like this.'

'That's all right. We were just getting worried. Is everything okay?'

'It is now. I'll explain what held me up later.'

'Okay, love, we'll meet you in Gerald's office.'

'Yup, righto.'

Ivy gathered her things from the passenger seat and floor of her ute while cursing under her breath. Her aunts had left an hour before her to run some errands while they were in town and must have accidentally locked Bo inside the homestead, which meant he'd had to relieve himself on the kitchen floor – the poor bugger had looked mortified when she'd discovered the mess. Now she was running late. Pausing to steal a glance at her reflection in the rear-view mirror, she grimaced at her wayward hair – having the window down on the way into town hadn't done her any favours. Huffing, she tossed everything in her hands onto her lap and quickly pulled her long black hair into a ponytail, then, grabbing her strawberry lip gloss from the centre console, she applied some, smacking her lips together. She sucked in a deep breath to calm her nerves and dived from the ute. Rushing for the front door of the bank, she spritzed on her favourite perfume, Roses de Chloé, tossed the bottle back in her bag, and pushed the door open with her boot while tossing her handbag over her shoulder. And ran smack-bang into a bloke on his way out. Every last bit of her composure unravelled as her paperwork went flying – it was going to take her ages to get it all back in some kind of order.

'For fuck's sake,' she mumbled as she eyed the mess then sank to her knees to pick it all up.

In her frazzled state she didn't take much notice of the man she'd collided with. His hand lightly touched her arm, making her jump as though she'd just been electrocuted. Heat seared throughout her. She glanced up at him, getting a look at his face, and her breath caught in her throat. Mr whoever-he-was was drop-dead gorgeous. Their eyes locked for a few seconds and for a fleeting moment she felt as if she knew him from somewhere.

A strong hand rubbed the dark stubble on his chin, his amber eyes full of concern. 'I'm so sorry. Here, let me help you.' He knelt down and began gathering the pieces of paper with her. His hand brushed hers, sending another shockwave throughout her, the sensation making her feel strangely drawn to him. Ivy shook her head as if in a daze. She'd never experienced such an immediate reaction to anyone before.

'Oh, don't apologise. It was my fault rushing in here like a maniac.' She smiled as she admired his chiselled features. Where in the hell did she know him from? 'And I'm so sorry for the colourful language, I'm just having one hell of a crappy morning.'

He laughed. It was the sexiest laugh she'd ever heard, husky and deep and a little suggestive. Of what, she had no clue. As much as she tried, she couldn't tear her eyes from him, or the glimpse of his burly chest inside the collar of his shirt. This man was the most delicious blend of tall, dark, handsome … and mysterious. It was all she could do not to reach out and pull him into a kiss right then and there.

'No worries, I can completely understand what a hell of a morning can do to a person – I've had them myself from time to time.' The hint of a smile at the corners of his lips made them even more kissable – if that was possible.

Desperately trying to curb her desire to tear every shred of his clothing off, right here, right now, Ivy gathered the paperwork in her hands to her beating chest. 'Please don't think I'm hitting on you by saying this, but do I know you from somewhere?'

The man looked a little surprised, and then shrugged as he rubbed his stubble once more with a calm assured confidence. 'Oh, I doubt it. I'm only new to town. Moved here yesterday.' Handing her a messy stack of paperwork, he stood quickly, as though he'd sat on a thorn. He shoved his hands in his jeans pockets. 'Anyhow, I better be off – let you get to wherever you were going in such a rush.'

Ivy stood too, feeling like a complete idiot – he clearly did think she was hitting on him. 'Oh, yup.' She gestured towards Gerald's closed office door with her thumb. 'Important meeting with the manager.'

He grabbed the front door and yanked it open, flashing her a dazzling smile. 'Might catch you around sometime,' he said, and he was gone.

Ivy watched through the glass as he tugged on the brim of his hat to greet a passer-by before sauntering away. A new man in town. And a very sexy one at that – she'd never been able to resist a hot country bloke dressed in his western best. Hmm. Her interest was piqued.

Shaking her head again, she brought herself back to reality. She didn't have time to swoon over some bloke she may never encounter again – he'd probably just turn out to be another arsehole like Malcolm who would break her heart anyway. And her heart was already broken enough. Nope, she wasn't going to even fantasise about going there with Mr Sex-on-a-stick. Spinning on her heel, she made a beeline for Gerald's door, sucking in a calming breath and squaring her shoulders before she opened it and stepped inside.

***

Might catch you around sometime?

As he hightailed it away from the bank, Ronny shook his head at his bad choice of words. The last thing he wanted to do was catch her around, even though her sweet perfume lingered in the headiest of ways. He strode down the street as though he was on a mission but his head was in a crazy spin, so he had no idea where he was going. But as long as it was far away from Ivy Tucker, he was heading in the right direction. He knew he'd run into her one day, though maybe not as soon as this, and he'd thought he'd be able to be happy to know she was out living her life, before moving on with his. Yeah, right! Who was he trying to kid? After seeing her in the flesh, it was crystal clear to him that was going to be much easier said than done.

With her long dark hair pulled up in a high ponytail, intense chocolate brown eyes and sensual womanly curves, Ivy Tucker was even more beautiful, even more captivating, than he remembered. Seeing her was exactly as it had been all those years ago – like a bolt of lightning hitting his heart. No other woman had ever been able to evoke such feelings, especially when they weren't even aware they were doing it. It was weird, considering he and Ivy were basically strangers, but then again, he felt as though he'd known her for a lifetime. The night he'd first laid eyes on her there'd been something magical, though he hadn't been able to put his finger on it, and he'd thought maybe when he saw her again those unexplainable feelings would have gone. But they had only intensified at the sight of her: seeing Ivy had brought back everything he'd felt for her that night. And if he was going to be perfectly honest with himself, what did he expect? Ivy Tucker had changed his life without even knowing – it was all because of her he was the person he was today, the person he was destined to be. If it wasn't for their paths crossing on that fateful night, Ronny doubted he'd even be alive with the dark path he'd been on at the time – the wrongdoings of his father leaving him with a massive chip on his shoulder. The friends he had chosen for himself before ending up in jail were the kind of people he was now glad to see the back of.

Now a fair distance down the road from the bank, he stopped and drew in a deep breath as a familiar voice grabbed his attention.

'Hey, mate.' Larry was approaching, pointing down a side street. 'The RTA is down that way.'

'Oh, right.' Ronny tried to smile but failed.

Larry picked up pace so he was soon standing beside Ronny. 'Shit, mate, is everything okay? Ya look like you've seen a ghost.'

'Well, I kinda have. I just ran into Ivy Tucker.' Ronny shook his head. 'And I mean literally ran smack-bang into her as she was heading into the bank.'

'Oh, fuck.' Larry took his hat off and scratched his head. 'Did she recognise ya?'

'Nah, I don't think so. She asked if she knew me from somewhere but I just said that wasn't possible because I was new to town.'

Larry tugged his hat back on and gave Ronny a firm nod. 'Good answer.'

Ronny's brows knitted together as he began to pace the footpath. 'I really hope it doesn't come to her later on, Larry. She's much better off thinking I'm still in jail, for all our sakes.'

'I reckon you're pretty safe. Ya don't look much like you did before ya went to jail.' Larry gave him a friendly pat on the back. 'Word of advice – don't stress about something ya have no control over.'

Ronny nodded; his training in meditation had taught him the very same thing. 'Yeah, you're right. Stressing isn't going to achieve anything.'

Larry winked as he flashed Ronny a tooth-filled smile. 'I'm always right.'

CHAPTER 5

Gerald Fromstein was as frazzled looking as ever, his office as muddled as he looked, even at nine forty-five in the morning. His desk was strewn with paperwork and more was piled up beside him on the floor, so high it resembled the Leaning Tower of Pisa. He was clearly under the pump, and Ivy felt sorry for him. Gerald had lived in Bluegrass Bend for all his life, and tried his very best to look after the interests of the locals he also classed as friends – Ivy had witnessed his kindness firsthand amongst some of their family friends. He understood rural life, and how demanding and challenging it could be, trying to survive off the land, so he usually bent over backwards to try to stop a property from being snatched from its owners. Ivy prayed he graced her with the same leniency.

Gerald said nothing as he perused the wad of paperwork she'd brought in – which she'd been able to get back into some kind of order – his glasses perched on the end of his long nose, the metal rims making his face look wider as the arms splayed outward to his protruding ears. He was clearly taking her proposal seriously, his thin lips pursed so tightly it seemed like he had none. Other than him clicking the end of his pen in and out – which was driving Ivy nuts – it was so quiet that the ticking of the clock on the wall sounded like bombs dropping. It was as though the clock was deliberately counting her life away and she wished she could stop it, reverse it or at least slow it down. She glanced at his hair, or lack of, trying to avert her attention from the anxiety she was feeling inside. Then for some reason she tried to imagine him naked – May had once suggested it as a way to calm nerves. Ivy subtly screwed her face up, the image of a naked sixty-eight-year-old man didn't do the trick at all. All she wanted to do now was burst into laughter. Not the ideal time to do so.

Looking from her aunt May seated on one side of her to her aunt Alice seated on the other, Ivy had to fight her urge to escape. Even though her aunts each graced her with a small smile, they looked as nervous as she felt. And Gerald's office was so small and poky, lacking any windows, that she was beginning to feel claustrophobic, as though the walls and ceiling were slowly closing in on her. An iridescent light blazed, the light so fake it grated on her eyeballs. No wonder Gerald always looked as pale as a ghost. How anyone could work under these conditions amazed her. She needed endless space and fresh air to be able to think straight – what she'd give to be able to breathe a lungful of it right now.

Gerald finally made a noise like he was trying to clear his throat but instead only sounded like he was choking, then he brought his small dark eyes to hers, the rings around them almost darker than the pupils. 'So, Ivy, are you the one behind this idea? Because I'm guessing, from my experience with your aunts over the years, they wouldn't have easily agreed to you selling your property to save Healing Hills.' His eyebrows met in the middle as his face became clouded with concern. 'Have you honestly thought long and hard about letting go of your mother's house?'

Ivy swallowed with difficulty, feeling as though she had a golf ball lodged in her throat. She pushed back her shoulders and sat up a little straighter. She needed to look super confident. 'Yes, Gerald, it was all my idea, and I'm very comfortable with selling the house.'

Alice grabbed her hand beneath the table and gave it a loving squeeze. The simple gesture made Ivy want to burst into tears. It was going to hurt to say goodbye to the cottage, but she wasn't going to say that out loud. Her poor aunts felt terrible about what she wanted to do, and she didn't want them carrying that unwarranted heartache; May and Alice had done so much for her throughout their lives and it was time she paid them back now she was in a position to do so.

'Hmm, well, I'll suppose I'll have to take your word for that.' Gerald pushed his glasses back up the bridge of his nose, and then sat back in his leather chair as he folded his arms. 'So tell me, Ivy, what other programs are you going to offer, other than the equine healing sessions, that is? You haven't mentioned exactly what they are in your notes.'

Ivy folded her hands on the desk and made an effort to talk slowly, convincingly. The new healing sessions were crucial to the success of her plan. 'Well, things like team-building workshop weekends for corporate offices to regain spirit in the workplace, emotional awareness workshops for schools, and couples' programs to rekindle relationships – all done with the help of the horses, of course. And I'd eventually like to offer meditation classes and have a room for massages and acupuncture – if I can find trained therapists to do so. It'll take a bit of advertising to get the word out there, but once it is, I'm sure people will be rolling through the gates.'

Alice smiled at Ivy and then at Gerald. 'She's certainly done all her homework, Gerald, and both May and I are very supportive of her ideas for the new programs. We feel, in the long run, if it's done properly, which of course Ivy, May and myself will make sure of, it will make Healing Hills quite a profitable family business.'

'Yes, I'm gathering you're both in agreement with it all, Alice, seeing as you're here with Ivy. And I'm over the moon you and May have finally seen sense in needing to make Healing Hills into more of a business than a safe house. Otherwise you're never going to survive in this day and age.' Gerald rested his elbows on the desk and folded his hands, eyeing Ivy for a little longer than was comfortable, before his lips curled ever so slightly at the sides, upwards.

Although feeling a little like she was standing in the spotlight of a hunter, Ivy sensed a glimmer of hope. She held her breath, wanting to squeeze her eyes shut as if someone was about to burst a balloon in her face, terrified of what Gerald was about to say next.

'Good God, girl!' Gerald leapt up as he smacked his hands onto the desk, making them jump in their seats. His smile broadened and filled his face. 'I love your ideas, and I think there's huge potential in what you're proposing for Healing Hills. I wish more young people had your vision and drive.' He began pacing as he rubbed his chin. 'Because we don't want to just look at a quick fix, which the sale of your property would be, we also need to look at the long-term effectiveness of Healing Hills as a lucrative business.' He stopped pacing as he threw his hands up in the air, and then shrugged. 'Otherwise you're all going to find yourselves back in this exact position in a year's time because you've fallen behind again.'

Ivy sat on her hands, which were itching to reach out and pull Gerald into a hug. Instead, she smiled, trying to contain her bubbling excitement. Just because Gerald liked her plans didn't mean he was going to give her the fifty-thousand-dollar loan she needed. 'It's fabulous you agree, Gerald.'

'Thank you, Gerald,' May and Alice said in unison, looking just as chuffed and surprised as Ivy was as they gave her a pat on the back.

Gerald rested against the desk as his broad smile faded, his fingers resembling spiders about to pounce. 'Don't thank me just yet, ladies. We need to talk the nitty gritty of terms first.' He took a sip from a coffee cup that read *You don't have to be crazy to work here, we'll train you,* his thick grey brows furrowing as he sat down again, tried to straighten his crooked tie, and then leant forwards to address May and Alice. 'Healing with horses is a fabulous service to the people who come to use it, but I agree with Ivy in that you need to broaden your market if you're going to survive in these tough times. Government grants and the small amounts you charge for your programs are not covering the costs any more, and as much as I know you pride yourselves on not being greedy with program costs, you simply just can't be charity cases any more, you have to price your services accordingly – and I'm relieved you've seen the sense in this.'

He sucked in a breath and shook his head as he removed his glasses. 'But, as much as I'd love to, I can't loan you the entire amount you've asked for, Ivy, when your income isn't proving you can make the repayments at the moment.'

'But can't I use the property as security, Gerald? Wouldn't that make all the difference?' Ivy noticed she sounded desperate now, but she didn't care.

'I know the train of thought you're on, Ivy, and it's the right one in some aspects. Although you can use the house as collateral for the loan, I still need to show that you've got sufficient funds coming in to support a loan of that amount … and at the moment you don't, with the sorry state of affairs Healing Hills is in. But just give me a minute ...' He popped his glasses back on and grabbed his calculator, his fingers going like the clappers as he punched in numbers while mumbling to himself. After less than a minute he looked up at Ivy again. 'I *can* offer you a loan of twenty-five thousand.'

Although there was an offer of sorts on the table, and it wasn't a big fat no, Ivy's heart still sank like a destroyed battleship – she'd been counting on the fifty thousand dollars to cover the costs of renovation materials and the expense of an experienced builder. At the going rate of ninety dollars an hour, how was she going to be able to afford a qualified carpenter now? And the job was way too big to achieve on her own – pulling kitchens and bathrooms apart was certainly not her forte. Besides, the council had told her they'd only approve the renovations if done by a qualified tradesperson. She looked at the floor, unable to meet Gerald's eyes for fear of crying.

'We'll gladly accept your offer, Gerald,' she heard May say. 'Thank you for your time and understanding.'

Ivy dragged her eyes from the floor and towards her aunt, blinking furiously. 'But, Aunt May, I can't see how we're going to achieve all this without the fifty thousand.'

May gathered Ivy's hands in hers. 'Where there's a will there's a way, love.' Her voice was soft and soothing, but it did nothing to alleviate Ivy's soaring tension.

Ivy shook her head sadly. 'There isn't always a way.'

Gerald stood. 'How about I give you ladies some time to chat? I need to go and make myself another cuppa anyway.' He moved towards the closed door then stepped back to grab his cigarettes out of the top drawer. 'Would any of you like a coffee or tea while I'm at it?'

There was a collective, 'No, thank you.'

With Gerald gone, Ivy jumped up from her chair and began pacing the room, managing to walk into the Leaning Tower of Pisa paperwork beside Gerald's desk in the process. She cursed her clumsiness as she knelt down to tidy it up. 'I don't see how you pair think we can do this with only twenty-five thousand dollars.' Her voice was a few notches higher than usual, and laced with irritation – she never spoke to her aunts like this and hated herself for doing so. She tried with everything she had to calm down. 'I mean, with building costs and wages and –'

'Sweetheart,' Alice said, voice gentle as always, 'we haven't got a choice. We either accept his offer, or say goodbye to Healing Hills for good – and I know I speak for all of us when I say that is out of the question. As you well know, I'm a firm believer in everything panning out just how it should, and I'm certain that if this is the path we are meant to be following, the universe will provide us with a way around this little roadblock.'

Ivy's eyebrows shot up. 'You consider this a little roadblock?'

May nodded her head like a bobble-headed doll on the dash of a four-wheel drive out bush bashing. 'I totally agree with Alice. Don't throw the towel in yet, Ivy. We will make it through this. Remember, we Tucker women never give up. Rah.' She punched the air.

The paperwork somewhat restacked beside Gerald's desk, Ivy rolled her eyes and huffed weightily as she stood. She was usually more than happy to be on her aunts' positive bandwagon, but today she just felt like ramming it off the tracks. Damn stress – it was exasperating. 'I hope you're both right, because we're going to need some kind of miracle to be able to achieve what we want with way less money.'

Alice reached out and touched her arm. 'Like I always say, Ivy, believe it will happen and miracles will follow.'

***

'I told ya, it's a bit like riding a bike … ya never forget how to do it,' Larry said as he lightly pushed Jessie off his lap and then slid out of the passenger seat of the Kingswood. He grinned as he leant on the window frame, his face covered in dry speckles of mud, as was his T-shirt, and his wild hair was completely flattened on one side from the wind that had been blowing through the open window. 'I might have to check me undies though, that massive roo jumping out of nowhere scared the friggin' life outta me. Thank God ya swerved when ya did or the bastard would have ended up on the front seat with us.'

'My oath, it coulda been messy if I hadn't spotted him in time,' Ronny said. 'Sorry I got us bogged in the Mayberrys' field, but I had nowhere else to go when I swerved. We're bloody lucky old Burt Mayberry didn't see it.'

'Yeah, he can be a cranky old bugger at times.' Larry chuckled, his eyes squinting at the corners. 'But no worries, I like me a bit of an adventure, keeps the old ticker ticking.' His bushy eyebrows shot up as he slapped the windowsill and then turned to walk away. 'I'll catch ya later on,' he called over his shoulder.

Ronny wound his window right down, grinning at the fact it wasn't powered and he had to do it the old-fashioned way – with a window winder. Once again, it was Lottie all over. 'Are you sure you don't want to come for a ride this arvo, Larry? It won't take me long to saddle old Merle up too.'

Larry shook his head. 'Nah, I got me a hot date with Shirl tonight and I wanna give meself enough time to shower and shave and dress dapper for her. We're stepping it up and going to the new Chinese restaurant in town, seeing as it's our three-month anniversary. Honey king prawns are her favourite.'

'You old romantic, you.'

'Yeah, who woulda thunk it, huh? I might even shout her some deep-fried ice cream with strawberry topping,' Larry added cheekily as he gave Ronny a wave and headed down the path to his front door. 'Catch ya tomorrow, mate, enjoy your ride on Hank. Just watch the bugger though, I don't know if ya remember, but he tends to toss ya from the saddle sometimes, just to make sure you're awake.' He instinctively rubbed his lower back as he shook his head.

Ronny returned his wave before he gave Jessie a rub on the head, then turned the Kingswood around and headed back to the cottage. It was great to see Larry so happily in love – the bloke deserved it. It had certainly been a long time coming. Hopefully one day Ronny could say the same for himself, and hopefully a lot sooner than Larry because he didn't want to run out of time to have a family. He longed for children, and that special woman to share his life with, now he had a life to share, because he had a lot of love to give. Which got him to thinking about Ivy again – although she hadn't really left his mind. Seeing her in town this morning had sparked the fire she'd lit within him all those years ago, and he wished things could have been different and that he'd met her under different circumstances. She'd make a man one hell of a wife one day.

Pulling up under the shade of the big old gum tree beside the cottage, Ronny's eye was caught by something in the backyard. What the heck were all the clothes he'd hung on the clothesline this morning doing strewn about the back lawn? He jumped out with Jessie in tow and wandered towards the back fence. His favourite blue Wrangler shirt now lay in shredded pieces. What the hell? Another few steps confirmed exactly how it had happened when he met Ned, Lottie's grumpy old goat that he'd tried to become acquainted with this morning. Ned had made sure to give him anything but a warm welcome as he attempted to butt Ronny each and every time he'd tried to give him a friendly pat. It hadn't been overly aggressive, but enough to let Ronny know Ned didn't warm to anyone easily. Ronny wasn't too concerned – he knew he'd get the belligerent goat to come around eventually. Eyeing the wayward animal, Ronny had to hold back a chuckle. A pair of his jocks hung from the goat's right horn and what appeared to be a sock hung halfway out of Ned's mouth. This should be no laughing matter but it was impossible not to see the funny side of it. Ned tipped his head, as if perplexed by the exasperated look on Ronny's face, his beady eyes watching Ronny's every move.

Telling Jessie to go sit on the back verandah, Ronny glared at Ned as angrily as he could while still trying to hold back a burst of laughter. 'You're a little shithead,' he said as he jumped the fence, arms outstretched. 'Come here, you bloody bugger, and give me back my sock – and my jocks while you're at it!'

Ned bleated loudly as if to say, 'Stuff you,' and then took off in a gallop, heading straight for the small gap in the fence he must have squeezed through in the first place, and towards his mate, a Shetland pony called Grace, not that she had any of that – Ronny had learnt she was as tetchy as Ned thanks to a few nips to his butt earlier. They certainly made for a good couple: grumpy and grumpier. What the heck Lottie saw in the two wayward creatures was beyond him, but then again she'd always been one to take in the downtrodden and love them. He knew that all too well. And out of respect for Lottie he would learn to do the same – he would love these two rascals if it damn near killed him.

Skidding to a stop at the fence he noted the hole he was now going to have to fix as the two ducks, Plucka and Donald, went waddling past with Nugget the Rooster following closely behind – the three feathered friends stopping to watch the commotion from a safe distance. Ronny glared at Ned as he stood on the other side of the fence, chewing his sock into obliteration. He could swear the goat was almost smiling. Behind him, Grace neighed as though cheering Ned on, while up on the verandah, Jessie watched, her head tipped to the side. Cindy Clawford sat next to the dog, her attention, too, focused on the event unfolding.

Ronny shook his head, chuckling to himself – he certainly had a captive audience. He shook his finger at Ned like he was a naughty child. 'If we're going to get along, there's gotta be some ground rules.' He swung his arm around behind him, gesturing to his mangled clothes on the lawn. 'There'll be no more of this, mister, or I'll be making myself a Jamaican goat curry.' Ronny knew he didn't mean it, but Ned didn't, and goddamn it, how else was he meant to threaten a goat?

Ned opened his mouth and dropped what was left of the sock, leaving his mouth wide, as though he understood every word Ronny had said and was in complete and utter shock that a human would ever consider eating him.

Ronny couldn't help but break into laughter at the sight before him – his blue pair of jocks still dangling from Ned's horn. Huffing, he then shook his head and groaned lightheartedly before beginning to collect his clothes from the ground while sorting out which ones would be binned and which ones were still wearable. With all these crazy animals there certainly was never going to be a dull day at Sundown Farm – and he loved the fact. And once he cleaned up here, he was going to go and spend time with some more Sundown animal friends, Merle and Hank.

***

As Ronny gave Hank a light scratch on the muzzle, the horse regarded him with big eyes that had the capacity to see right through a person and into their heart and soul. In response, the twelve-year-old buckskin gelding lifted his head slightly and gave Ronny a sniff. Ronny returned the gesture by placing his nose up close to Hank's and breathing in and out, mimicking a friendly horsey greeting – such a simple but effective way of bonding with a horse. Over in the corner, lying on some straw, Jessie watched from sleepy eyes. Outside, Merle whinnied his displeasure at not being the one chosen for a ride. Hank replied to his mate with a short nicker.

Ronny stuck his head out of the stable door, smiling at the slightly older horse. 'Next time, buddy. I promise.'

Merle gazed at him for a few seconds as though assessing if Ronny was telling the truth before turning his attention back to the feed at his feet.

Stepping back inside, Ronny couldn't help but feel pride in where he was standing. He'd built the stables from weathered oak planks for Lottie over a weekend visit not long before he'd been sent to prison, and he was proud to see the structure still standing, the many years not taking much of a toll. He hoped he was going to be lucky enough to get a job doing what he loved once more – there was just something so satisfying about working with his hands, and he treasured the feeling he got when he stood back and appreciated a job well done. But he didn't hold out much hope of snapping up his dream job in a town as small as Bluegrass Bend, and he wasn't keen to travel to neighbouring towns for work if he could help it – that would mean too much time away from Sundown, and he had to keep up with what needed doing around here too – he couldn't leave it all to Larry. If push came to shove, he would just take whatever he could get, for now, and just put his feelers out for a more permanent carpenter's job in the meantime.

He breathed in his surrounds as he knelt down to buckle his spurs around his boots. The place smelt of straw, leather and horse – three smells he absolutely adored. Half empty hay nets hung limply in the corner and the stable door sat with the top half pinned back by a rusted nail. Along the side wall hung a multitude of bridles, breastplates, reins and ropes. On the timber table beneath all this were brushes, combs, hoof picks, feed buckets and the like, and over a railing made especially for them sat four much-loved saddles alongside a few saddle pads – he was in absolute heaven in here. He stood and finished saddling up a slightly eager Hank, his spurs chinking with each step, excited himself at the thought of going for a late afternoon ride. Ronny put his boot in the stirrup and effortlessly threw his leg over before settling into the well-worn saddle. He gave Hank a gentle cue to get going and the horse made his way out of the stables and into the open, the gelding stopping momentarily to drop his head and snatch a mouthful of grass. Ronny gave the reins a firm tug, letting Hank know in no uncertain terms that he was the boss. Like a rebellious child, Hank whinnied then took a few steps forwards and once again lowered his head. Ronny could sense the buck coming seconds before Hank even moved. Sitting his butt firmly in the saddle while keeping his stomach and back relaxed, Ronny flowed with the horse's movements, making sure to leave the reins slack – Ronny knew if he tightened up, he'd just become a spring for the horse's exaggerated motion and bounce right out of the saddle. Like a rocking chair, a horse didn't keep rocking unless you rocked it. One buck, two bucks, and then Hank gave up, for now – Ronny wasn't going to slip into a false sense of security on this strong-willed horse's back.

Squeezing both his legs to cue the horse forwards, Ronny eased Hank into a trot and then a canter, knowing from experience that the best way to keep Hank from misbehaving was to work him, and work with him. Muscles rippling underneath his glossy coat and with his tail and mane flowing in the breeze, Hank's fluid movement gave Ronny goose bumps. He closed his eyes and revelled in the wind whipping past him and the sound of Hank's hooves pounding the ground, feeling absolute bliss. God, he'd waited for what felt like a lifetime for this very moment. With the sun on his back, and his wide-brimmed hat shading his eyes from the glare, he enjoyed the sensation of finally being at one with a horse and his surroundings – the sense of freedom that came with this was overwhelming after so long behind bars. Ronny's spirit soared. As Hank broke into a gallop, man and horse headed towards the National Park that Sundown Farm backed onto as time began to dissolve.

CHAPTER 6

Pulling the rope to call the ladder down, Ivy began to climb up into the attic, clutching her aunts' old bookwork in doubled-up lemon-scented garbage bags. She was being extra careful not to slip in her socked feet like she had the last time she'd climbed this very ladder a few years back. She really didn't need a twisted ankle at the moment, or a busted chin, there was too much to do and not enough time to do it in to go causing herself an injury. It had taken her all day yesterday and a few hours this morning to get the homestead's office into some kind of acceptable working order, her old-fashioned aunts finally agreeing it was time to let her bring the world of modern-day technology into their pen-and-paper office. Ivy couldn't wait to set up the Apple iMac she'd bought at the computer shop in Kooloy – it was going to make keeping the finances in order a whole lot easier and it was also going to make their accountant the happiest woman alive: May and Alice arriving at her office with a shoebox of receipts and a few books scribbled with half-remembered outgoings and incomings would now be a thing of the past.

It was no wonder they were in such financial strife. And it wasn't like Ivy could really be annoyed at them for that, her aunts had always just been more focused on working with the horses than crunching numbers. Ivy, on the other hand, was passionate about both, and she was more than prepared to divide herself between working at the desk and working out in the paddock – as well as giving all she had to the renovations and marketing side of things over the next few months. The thought of how thin she was going to have to spread herself made her temples instantly throb. Lord help her – she really needed to clone herself.

The memory of Gerald saying no to the extra money made her blood pressure rise – as if they were going to be lucky enough to find a fully qualified carpenter who'd work for a weekly wage when accustomed to charging a ridiculous amount of money per hour. The problem was doing her head in, to say the least, but she wasn't going to give up on wishing and hoping that the miracle Alice and May kept referring to would happen. In the meantime, she needed to make a start on the renovations ASAP. A trip to Bunnings in Kooloy while she was collecting the computer had provided her with some tools and loads of advice on DIY projects from the helpful staff. The work sounded fairly simple when explained to her, but putting it into action was going to be completely different.

Silence reigned in the dimly lit attic. As the scent of staleness and dust hit her, she looked over the boxes and garbage bags full of pre-loved things that had been stored here over the years. There were so many precious memories tucked away in here, some of which belonged to her ancestors. It was kind of like a graveyard for treasured items that were no longer used, but still had enough sentimental value to not be thrown away – the pain of parting with each item postponed until the sentimental value had faded. One day she would have to find the time to explore the hidden treasures. Placing the weighty bag down on the floor, Ivy went to the window on the far side of the room, being careful not to walk into the many cobwebs along the way, and wiped the grimy dust from the colourful stained-glass window.

The sunlight now streaming through made the hundreds of dust particles floating in the air appear diamond like, her memory of trying to catch the floating jewels with her mum making her smile wistfully. They'd spent many afternoons up here with her aunts, playing dress ups from the old boxes of clothes. If she closed her eyes she could still hear the laughter as she swirled around in garments five times too big for her. With her arms wrapped tightly around herself now she slowly twirled, mimicking those movements as her memory swept her away to a time and place when her mother was still alive. Her heart soared with the recollections as a lone tear ran down her cheek. She let it fall. How she wished her mother were still here to share her life with. Ivy took a deep breath, and gently blew away the heartache, imagining it dispersing into the filtered sunlight.

Not wanting to dwell too much on the things she couldn't change, Ivy tried to be grateful for all she had, and the beautiful women who were still on this earth to share her life with. The gratitude brought a smile to her lips. She was making her way back to the ladder when she spotted her guitar case sitting in a corner. Her heart sank and she stopped in her tracks, her smile now stolen. In days gone by, music was her life, and her life was full of music. She used to feel a melody in everything: the pitter patter of rain, the croak of a frog, the clip-clop of horses' hooves, even the sound of her footsteps on the timber floorboards of the homestead. As a child she used to make musical instruments out of everything, from old tin cans, milk bottles filled with rice, pots and pans, to blowing on blades of grass like it was a harmonica. Music used to be the one thing in life that could change her mood in an instant, the one thing that had the power to lift her spirits on the darkest of days. Along with the healing horses, her music had been her saving grace when her mother had killed herself. But then that bastard had taken all that away from her when he'd tried to rape her and then, when she wouldn't succumb to him, tried to take her life. She trembled with the awful memory. The mind was a powerful thing – she knew that all too well after her years of training to be a counsellor, but as much as she understood how she was unconsciously connecting what had happened with the fact she'd been in that place at that time for her music, it didn't make it any easier to remedy. She wished she could just click her fingers and make everything better, but it wasn't that simple. She'd tried for a few years, time and time again, to at least take her guitar out of its case, but she hadn't even been able to do that. So, before she'd begun her online study, she'd put her guitar up here – out of sight, out of mind. Apparently. Not that it had worked; her passion for music, although buried all these years beneath distractions and keeping herself busy, was still deep within her. There was no denying it – just like her mother, music ran through Ivy's veins and made her who she was. She just prayed that with her aunts' gentle encouragement and loving support, and through her own will and sheer determination, she'd eventually get past her anxieties.

Hesitantly, and with her feet feeling a little like lead weights, she went over and ran her fingers down the guitar case, collecting a thick layer of dust on her fingertips. A muscle twitched involuntarily at the corner of her eye and her heart picked up pace as her mind flicked back to that night. A muffled sound escaped her lips as the scar that ran from her chest to her belly button ached. Flinching, she jerked her hand away from the case and brushed the dust onto her jeans as fresh tears filled her eyes. She tried to blink them away, wiping the few salty droplets that had escaped down her cheeks with the back of her hand. She'd cried enough because of what that monster had done to her, probably enough to fill all the oceans in the world. She just wanted to move on and forget it had ever happened. If only she could bring herself to strum her guitar once again, to sing again, maybe the memories of that terrifying night would finally stop taunting her, and the occasional nightmares would stop too. It angered her that not only had her attacker assaulted her body, he had also stolen her passion, her sacred love of music. The sound of an acoustic guitar was a balm to her soul, the hypnotic sensation of picking the strings a soothing quality she still craved. To be able to lose herself to the melody of her guitar once again would be magical. It would be a dream come true.

In a daze, she took a few steps backwards then sat down, trying to regain her composure with some deep breathing and silent affirmations. There was a young woman arriving very soon for a healing session and May and Alice had asked her to work one on one with her – which Ivy was eager to do, as she could draw on her own experiences to help her on an even deeper level. The woman was a victim of domestic violence, and Ivy needed to be a pillar of strength for her, for she was meant to be the healer, not the one who needed healing. And being a fully qualified counsellor, she wanted people to think the best of her, to believe that she was capable and strong and didn't need help, that instead she could help them. There was no way Ivy wanted others to know that at times she felt weak or scared – it was always a lot harder to dig deep within yourself and heal, than it was to help others to heal. However, she was learning the hard way that the problem with keeping up a front and pretending everything was okay was eventually you started lying to yourself, and that wasn't constructive. Seeing her guitar shoved away up here like a bad memory was a kick in the guts, and a reminder that everything was not okay. She needed to get that part of herself back, but finding the strength to do that when she had so much other stuff on her plate was almost impossible. She drew in a deep breath and exhaled slowly, feeling her body relax somewhat. All in good time – she had to believe that there was rhyme and reason to everything that had happened and eventually she would be at one with her music again.

'Ivy, are you still up there, love?' Alice's voice carried up the ladder, snapping Ivy from her thoughts. 'May will be back from the train station in a minute, love, and I need you down here to welcome Leah.'

Ivy leapt to her feet and tiptoed over to the ladder. She smiled down at Alice, who was looking very smart in her jeans and the aqua-blue shirt Ivy had had made for them all with the Healing Hills logo on it. 'Yup, sorry Aunt Alice, you know me … got a bit sidetracked. I'm coming now.'

Alice waited for Ivy to join her and then helped her close the ladder back up. 'What have you been doing up there? I thought you might have gotten lost among all the boxes.' She wrapped a protective arm around her niece and gave her a loving squeeze. 'I was about to send out a search party.'

Ivy knew from the compassionate look in her eyes that Aunt Alice had cottoned on to the fact she was a little distressed, so she glanced away, not wanting to get into the whole scenario right now. They'd been there many times before. And although she usually went to her aunts when she needed some parental advice, she didn't feel like doing so right now. She needed to stay focused on the afternoon ahead and not go getting herself more upset.

'Oh, you know, just got a little preoccupied wandering about – there's so much interesting stuff up there.'

'Tell me about it. We really need to clean it out one of these days. Who knows what hidden treasures we might discover, hey?' Alice uncoiled her arms from around Ivy's shoulders and headed for the spiral staircase that led down to the entrance hall. Turning, she gave Ivy a knowing smile. 'And Ivy, don't go beating yourself up, you'll play it again one day, my love. I just know you will. And I know your heart is hurting at the moment, but it will heal, and you will go in search of love once more. You won't be able to help yourself, sweetheart, you're a romantic if ever I've seen one.'

Ivy smiled warmly at her aunt as she fought to keep her emotions in check. She should have learnt by now that there was no keeping anything from Alice, or May for that matter – the two women were so in touch with those around them. 'Thanks for the vote of confidence, Lord knows I need it.'

'Oh, no you don't, Miss Ivy Tucker – I know you struggle at times but you're much stronger than you give yourself credit for.'

Ivy blinked back tears as the knot in her throat tightened. 'Thank you, Aunt Alice, I try to be strong but sometimes all I want to do is crumble into tiny little pieces and cry for all of Australia.' She sniffled.

Alice reached out and pulled her in tight. 'I know, love. You just need some more time, and to be gentle with yourself. That's all. There's no need to rush into healing … it will happen when it's meant to.' She pulled back and shrugged. 'And who knows? A miracle might be just around the next corner … magical things always seem to happen when you least expect them to.'

Ivy wiped her tears away. 'I'd like to believe you're right.'

'I always try to be.' Alice gave her one last squeeze. 'Are you sure you'll be okay for today's healing session?'

Determination filled Ivy. 'Yup, one hundred and ten per cent sure.' She tucked her hair behind her ears. 'Helping people gives me the strength to heal myself just that little bit more, and being able to relate to their pain makes the session all the more healing for them, I'm sure – not that I'm going to tell Leah of my own experiences, of course.'

Alice nodded. 'You're a clever girl, Ivy.'

Ivy smiled. 'I love you, Aunt Alice.'

Alice reached out and gently tapped Ivy's cheek. 'And I love you.'

***

Wisps of clouds that looked as though a painter had swiped their paintbrush across the cobalt sky and a breeze so gentle it was more like a caress met Ivy outside the homestead. The sun was just warm enough to whisk away any lingering coolness from the dawn, giving rise to goose bumps as Ivy stepped down off the verandah. It was a perfectly beautiful summer's day for a healing workshop.

Introductions done and a morning tea of date scones with jam and cream and homemade strawberry and chamomile tea savoured, Ivy smiled warmly at Leah Harwood. It was time to begin the session. First, Leah would acquaint herself with her chosen horse, Harmony, in the middle of the sheltered roundyard – which Ivy confidentially considered her official counselling arena. With her calm, kind and gentle nature, Harmony was a brilliant choice for Leah. The gorgeous palomino mare had always been one of Ivy's favourites among the twelve beautifully intuitive horses they had at Healing Hills, with her glossy-as-silk golden honey coat and champagne-coloured mane and tail, and her ability to help people through whatever it was they were struggling with. Almost fifteen now, Harmony had been with them since birth – a foal from Zena, one of the greatest horses she and her aunts had ever come across in the art of horse healing. She'd been the horse that had helped Ivy get through the excruciating heartache of losing her mother. The charismatic Zena was now buried in a field specially reserved for their beloved horses.

After standing back a little and allowing Leah some time to bond with Harmony by grooming her with a rubber curry comb, Ivy began the nitty gritty of the session, doing her best to allow Leah to feel comfortable at the same time. It didn't appear like that was going to be too hard to do as Leah delicately wrapped her arms around Harmony's neck and gave her a quick hug and a kiss on the cheek. Harmony responded by dropping her head and gently pressing her muzzle up against Leah's heart, and remaining there, her eyes closed. Ivy knew this was Harmony's unique way of deeply connecting with a human in need, a form of horse-to-human reiki. It was a powerful practice to observe, and even more so for the person receiving healing energy from the horse. It gave Ivy goose bumps just watching it.

'What's she doing, Ivy?' Leah asked in almost a whisper as she softly placed her hands on Harmony's neck, her facial expression that of someone gazing at the miracle of a new baby.

'She must be sensing an energy blockage in your heart, so she's performing some reiki on you. Just try to breathe slowly as she works her magic.'

Leah nodded, clearly at a loss for words. After a few moments she glanced back at Ivy – her eyes glistening with unshed tears. 'I can't put it exactly into words, but it feels like she's drawing some of my sadness away.' She shook her head slowly. 'I've never experienced anything like this before – how does she know?'

'Our four-legged staff members are very gentle and remarkably intuitive. They can sense any surface uncertainty as well as deep-seated emotional distress without you having to say a word. In effect, they hold up a mirror for you to view yourself so you can really reach within and begin the process of healing.' Ivy strolled a little closer to Leah, lowering her voice, being careful not to interrupt Harmony. 'When our energy system is out of balance, healing takes place through exposure to the electromagnetic field of the horse's heart, which is scientifically proven to be five times stronger than that of the human heart. So when we are in this space, it's an innate human trait for our heart to rise in frequency too, especially when we are invited into their space with such grace, as Harmony just invited you. In turn, we are gifted with a feeling of belonging.'

Leah glanced at Ivy as the tears she'd been holding back began trickling down her cheeks. She opened her mouth to speak but nothing came out. Harmony lifted her head at this point and rested it on Leah's shoulder as she began nibbling Leah's shoulder-length hair. Leah giggled and sniffled at the same time.

'What they say is true, Ivy, horses really are beautiful creatures. I thought I was going to be terrified, seeing as I've never been this close to one before, but I feel so at peace with her. Kind of like I'm part of her herd.' She smiled through her tears as she rested her hand on Harmony's cheek. 'This might sound weird, but I feel like I can truly let go and be myself near her, and I seriously haven't felt like that in years, around anyone.'

Ivy smiled, her heart welling as she watched horse and human connect, just as she had hundreds of times before; each and every time as potent as the last. 'It's not weird at all. Horses aren't predators and they don't judge, instead they give you a place to feel safe, and a sense of feeling wild and free. They open their hearts and souls to us so that we can do the same for them.' She reached out and softly touched Leah's arm. 'It's wonderful you're feeling so comfortable and connecting with Harmony so quickly, it means you're very open to healing.'

Leah nodded enthusiastically as she dried her tears on a tissue Ivy handed her. 'I sure am. I just want to be the happy woman I was before everything turned to absolute shit.'

'And you will be,' Ivy said, as she wished the same thing for herself. She placed her hand on Harmony, silently thanking the horse for a job well done. 'So tell me, Leah, what do you struggle the most with when you're around other people?'

Leah stopped stroking Harmony's mane as she thought about this, her eyes displaying a depth far beyond her twenty-three years and her slumped shoulders displaying the massive emotional weight she'd been carrying. 'Definitely trust, and a sense of belonging anywhere – I always feel like the odd one out, like I'm the black sheep, not only of my family, but the world around me.'

'Okay, very good, let's work with the trust issue first, because I think Harmony has already made you see you can belong by making you feel like a part of her herd, yes?'

Leah broke into a heartfelt grin, her eyes sparkling with elation. 'Oh my goodness, yes, she has. Wow. I didn't really see it that way until you pointed it out.' She gave Harmony a scratch on her withers. 'So what would you like me to do now?'

'What I'd like you to do is walk around to the back of Harmony, and stand as close as you can to her, without making any sudden movements.'

Leah's face drained of colour and her eyes widened in fear. All traces of her smile were now gone. 'I don't know if I can do that. What if she kicks me?'

Harmony had been trained for this very thing, and there was no threat of her kicking out at Leah, but Ivy kept her voice soft and gentle as she observed Leah's body becoming tense. 'You'll need to trust me when I say she is not going to kick you. And you're not going to know if you can do it unless you try, are you? You've just told me how safe you feel around Harmony, and you know I've only got your best interests at heart, so just bear this in mind as you make your decision.'

Leah nodded before easing herself, step by tiny step, around behind Harmony, to stand about a metre from her back end. Folding her arms in front of her, she lightly swayed back and forth.

'Can you go a little closer please, Leah? In your own time, of course.'

Leah hesitated but then took a step closer and halted once again. She ran her hands over her face and through her hair. She took a deep breath and then took another step, and another step, until she was almost touching Harmony. She grinned as she looked at Ivy, the traces of the happy young woman she had once been lingering in her smile. 'I did it, and she hasn't kicked me,' she whispered.

Ivy beamed too. 'Great work! You just showed an immense amount of trust in both myself and Harmony.'

Leah nodded, visibly chuffed with her massive effort. 'I did, didn't I?'

'And nothing bad happened, did it?'

'No. It didn't.'

'Good work, Leah. Okay, you can come back around to her front now.'

Leah ran her hand along Harmony's coat as she walked back. 'I know I don't need to talk about what's happened to me, and in the past when I have been to my psychologist I haven't wanted to, but is it okay if I do? In a strange way, I feel like talking about it to you, so I suppose I should.'

Ivy nodded gently – this was exactly what she wanted to happen. 'Of course, how about we all sit down, though, so you and Harmony can be at the same level.'

Leah nodded. 'Sure.'

Ivy motioned to Harmony to lie on the ground with a simple sweep of her arm, and Harmony followed her request, going one step further as she lay on her side, completely relaxed.

Leah shook her head in awe as she sat down near Harmony. She began to stroke Harmony's coat as tears fell once more. This time, she didn't wipe them away. 'It's so horrible, being beaten by the person who's supposed to love you. It's like you're caught in this dark room with no windows or doors, like you have no other option but to stay in there with this person who's hurting you.' She began to sob, the cries coming from deep within. 'I'm sorry.'

'There's no reason for you to apologise.' Ivy placed her hand on Leah's, her heart wanting to reach out and take her pain away. She knew all too well what it felt like to be trapped by a dangerous man. 'Take your time. There's no rush, and if you want to stop, that's okay too.'

Leah shook her head. 'No, I really feel like I need to do this.' She took a deep breath and wiped her puffy red eyes. 'After years of leaving bruises in places people could never see them, my ex-boyfriend almost killed me.' Her voice broke and she took another deep breath, exhaling it slowly, her lips and hands trembling. 'I woke up one night to find him pouring petrol over me and the bed. I don't know how, but after a struggle I managed to get past him and out of the bedroom, but he ran after me, holding a smouldering cigarette, laughing hysterically. And then everything went blurry and by some miracle I escaped out the front door, unharmed.' She looked down at her hands folding and unfolding in her lap. 'I honestly thought I was going to die and I kept thinking, *I can't die yet, I have so much life to live*. So, when I found myself at my next-door neighbour's house, I swore I was finally going to leave him – and I did. And as hard as it's been this past year to put one foot in front of the other, I have, and my journey has brought me to Healing Hills, to Harmony and to you, Ivy.' She looked up and held Ivy's gaze. 'And I'm so very grateful for that.'

She flopped forwards and rested her face on Harmony's shoulder as she twirled the horse's mane around her fingers. 'My God, I feel like a huge weight has just been lifted from me, and all within a matter of hours.'

Ivy felt a flood of gratitude for this moment – she knew all too well that acknowledgement of inner struggles was the very first step to healing. Like a bulb that had been buried beneath the ground, Leah had just sprung forth and blossomed victoriously, her fears and buried emotions exposed and all because she'd trusted Harmony and Ivy. Ivy wanted to jump with joy at the enormous progress Leah had just made but instead she remained calm and composed, although she was beaming from ear to ear.

'I'm so happy Harmony and I have been able to help you open up and feel what it's like to trust again, Leah. It'll only be onwards and upwards from here for you. Trust me on that one.'

Leah grinned at Ivy, a sparkle in her eyes that had not been there before the session. 'Oh, believe me when I say this: I trust you fully on that one.'

***

Pulling up in the drop-off zone out the front of the train station, Ivy left her ute running as she leapt out to help Leah gather her backpack from the tray, and to give her a huge congratulatory hug. 'You did brilliantly today, Leah. I just know you're going to move forwards in leaps and bounds now.'

'I hope so.' Leah returned Ivy's tight hug and then pulled back. 'I can't wait until I come back in two weeks. I loved spending time with you and Harmony today.'

Ivy lightly touched Leah's arm. 'Thanks, Leah. We've loved spending time with you too. And please know you can call me any time you need to, okay?'

'Thank you, that means a lot.' Leah smiled. 'I can't thank you enough, Ivy. What you and your aunts do with the horses at Healing Hills is amazing. I'll be making sure I tell all my friends and family and everyone at work about you.'

Leah held out her arms and they hugged once more before Leah padded off to her train bound for Sydney. Ivy watched her walking away, giving one final wave before she disappeared down the steps. She felt an immense sense of fulfilment – to be able to give people a hand up from the hole they'd fallen into was not only gratifying, it was an absolute honour. Leah wasn't miraculously healed, and had a fair bit of work in front of her before she could totally move past what had happened with her ex-boyfriend, but with the help of Harmony, Ivy had eased Leah's heartache enormously and taught her she could safely begin to trust again and feel like she belonged.

CHAPTER 7

Tapping his boots in time to the catchy Darius Rucker tune 'Wagon Wheel', Ronny almost choked on his last mouthful of steak at what Larry had just said. Grabbing a napkin, he wiped his lips and took a swig from his Coke while trying to ignore the sultry, lash-framed stares he was getting from a table of three young women opposite them. Talk about being blatantly obvious. Every time one of them went to the bar they'd stare at him the entire way. He would smile respectfully, and nod his head in greeting, but that's as far as it was going to go. Women who flirted excessively did nothing for him, never had and never would, no matter how long it had been since he'd been with one. He required a little mystery, needed to dig beneath layers to discover a woman's truth, and he prized authenticity and thoughtful conversation above lipstick and high heels. These women prowled like lionesses and he felt like fresh meat – definitely not a sensation he was keen on.

He dropped his voice to a whisper so the women couldn't eavesdrop on the conversation, as they had been for the past ten minutes. 'You've got to be kidding, Larry! There's no way in hell I'm gonna stand up on some stage in front of half the bloody town and be auctioned off, because believe it or not, I don't like parading around like some big-headed boofhead with all eyes on me.'

'Well, we'll have to see about that,' Larry said with a wide grin, his eyes flashing mischievously. He took a sip from his beer and then pointed the neck of it towards Ronny. 'Oh, and I forgot to tell ya, ya have to do it in your boxers too. Hope ya own some 'cause it'd suck having to do it in your jocks.' He chuckled heartily, clearly enjoying the fact he was making the usually hard-as-nails Ronny Sinclair blush.

Ronny's jaw dropped as he frantically shook his head, resembling one of those clowns that you fed balls into in a sideshow alley. 'There's no bloody way, Smithy.'

Larry pretended to be intensely serious, although the cheeky glint in his eyes said otherwise. 'Oh come on, it's all for a good cause, mate. And also all in good fun. There's two other local boys doing it, so you won't be alone.'

Ronny huffed and rolled his eyes. 'I know it's for a good cause, and I want to be involved somehow for Lottie's sake, but isn't there something a little more subtle I can do, like man the barbecue?'

Larry shrugged as he took another swig from his stubby. 'Nope. That's my job.'

'But –'

'No buts about it, 'cause it's too late to back out – I've already dobbed ya in for the job, and the girls at the CWA are really excited now that they've met ya in the flesh. And how can ya say no to them after that awesome lamb stew they dropped off a few days ago?' Larry rolled his eyes with pleasure.

Ronny had to agree, his mouth watering even though he was full to the brim after lunch. 'It was the best damn stew I've ever eaten … and those suet dumplings, oh my God, I thought I'd died and gone to heaven.'

'So that's the clinch then. You'll never get their dumplings again if ya pull out now.' Larry wriggled his eyebrows. 'And Shirl reckons you'll make a fortune for the cause with all the women around this town bidding for the hot new bloke. Ya don't want to go letting them down now, do ya? Especially after everything they did for Lottie.'

Ronny pushed his practically licked-clean plate away and threw his hands up in the air. 'Okay, okay, I surrender. I'll bloody well do it.' He shook his head, chuckling. 'I wonder what I'm going to have to do for whoever buys me.'

Larry dropped his voice and leant across the table, encouraging Ronny to do the same. 'Who knows – they might want ya as their sex slave?'

'Oh stuff that, I'm not gonna be nobody's sex slave.' Ronny frowned as he shook his head defiantly, muttering to himself. 'No way, Jose. I don't just jump in the sack with anyone.'

Ignoring Ronny's protests, Larry motioned towards the table of cackling women. 'Oh come on, if it's someone like one of them three sheilas over there ya might find it a bit of fun … but if it's someone like Gertrude Browningstone, ya might find yourself in strife. She's a bit of a cougar.' He tipped his head towards the other side of the pub indicating a woman who looked like she already had one foot in the grave but was dressed like she was in her twenties. A smouldering cigarette hung from her lips.

Catching them looking at her, Gertrude graced them with the sassiest smile she could muster then blew a smoke ring into the air.

Ronny shuddered then swallowed down hard. 'Oh fuck, Lord help me.'

Larry looked back at the women who couldn't take their eyes from Ronny. Nodding at them in greeting, he smiled and raised his beer. The three women responded by raising their wine glasses and giggling like a group of horny schoolgirls. Larry met Ronny's gaze, clearly amused as he laughed heartily. 'Yes siree, it's quite clear that the girls are gonna be fighting over ya.' He took the last swig from his beer. 'And by the way, I was only kidding about the boxers, we don't want women passing out on the night … probably best ya wear clothes.'

Ronny threw his napkin at Larry. 'You bloody bastard! And to think I was going to do it in my boxers.'

Larry gave him a wink. 'You're a good sport, Ronny, always have been. I knew you'd come to the party for us, mate.'

***

Pressing the last of the thumbtacks into the corkboard, Ivy smoothed the poster out, praying that someone qualified, decent, able-bodied and dependable would be interested in the job – someone who had a builder's licence and could basically start yesterday. Wasn't too much to ask, was it? She'd put an ad in the *Bluegrass Bend Advertiser* a week ago, the day after Gerald had agreed to the loan, but so far all she'd gotten was an eighty-something-year-old who looked like he might have a heart attack if he lifted a hammer, and a giggly twenty-two-year-old with bloodshot eyes who she'd been sure was spaced out on God knows what. After a week of waiting the twenty-five thousand dollars had gone into her bank account this morning, and with limited time until the big wigs from the city branch started hounding them to catch up on the repayments of the Healing Hills mortgage, she was super keen to get the project started – she needed the cottage to be on the market in less than eight weeks' time.

The manager of the post office, Beryl Matheson, looked over the counter, her bright pink lips curled into her usual chirpy smile and her hazel eyes magnified by the thickness of her glasses. 'I really hope you find someone soon, love. It's damn tough finding good workers these days, with most of the young ones running off to Sydney to make a decent start at life. And the bloody government makes it too damn easy for the ones who stay here to sit at home on the dole.' She rolled her eyes, sighing. 'My poor Rodger is finding it harder and harder to find a decent set of hands to help him out on the farm. I just pray the day doesn't come when he'll need me to quit my job here. I'm not cut out for hard labour, and how else would I catch up on all the goss around town?'

Beryl had always been old-fashioned in her ways, believing it wasn't any kind of a place for a woman out in the paddocks and fields – which is why she worked in the post office and had always left the farming side of things to her husband. Ivy liked to believe a woman could work the land just as well if not better than a man, but had learnt not to argue the fact with Beryl after a few slightly heated discussions down the pub.

'This sure is the bush telegraph in here.' Ivy laughed as she approached the counter. 'I hope we find someone soon, too, Beryl. I really want to get the renovations underway. There's a bit of work I can do on my own, but there are some things I really need a carpenter for, seeing as none of us have any clue where to start when it comes to the nitty gritty of renovations. We don't want the place falling down on whoever buys it.'

Busying herself sorting the mail, Beryl completely missed Ivy's joke. 'Yes, love, just like a woman's job of ironing, cleaning and cooking, and doing more than two things at once I might add, there are jobs that are only done well when done by a man.' The bell over the shop door jingled and Ivy turned to see Shirley Jones trying to come in while balancing several packages in her hands, one heeled foot resting against the door while the other remained on the footpath. She looked completely frazzled, her legendary curly red hair windswept and more unruly than usual. Ivy ran over to help her.

Shirley blew a lungful of air through pursed red lips and then smiled. 'Oh thanks, love, there should be more of you helpful youngsters around here for us oldies.' She motioned outside with a tip of her head while trying to straighten her blouse. 'Some kid on a skateboard almost wiped me out as he went scooting past. He didn't even bat an eyelid. I had a good mind to chase after him and give him a piece of my mind, but I don't reckon I'd get very far in these heels.'

'The wicked little bugger,' Ivy said as she headed for the counter and plunked the packages down.

'Too bloody right.'

Beryl threw her three-bobs' worth in by mumbling about the state of the world as she began weighing the parcels then placing them in one of the massive postal bags behind her.

Throwing her keys in her oversized handbag, Shirley unrolled a poster and placed it on the counter. 'Is it okay if I pop this up on the community board, Beryl? It's a bit last minute, seeing as it's on in three days, but better late than never. I've been snowed under at work and haven't been able to find much time to do my voluntary secretarial duties for the CWA. Shame on me.'

Beryl scrunched her eyes up as she peered at the poster, as though her glasses weren't thick enough for her to read it. A smile shot across her face. 'Ooh, a cancer fundraiser, great stuff. And only twenty-five bucks a ticket.' She gestured at the corkboard on the sidewall. 'Of course you can, Shirl, you know you shouldn't need to ask.' She wriggled her perfectly manicured eyebrows, smirking.

'Especially one that factors in bidding for three hunky, spunky slaves for a weekend.'

Shirley grinned wickedly. 'And especially ones as fetching as the slaves we've got.' She fanned her face. 'Although Frank and Jed are good-looking sorts, I have to quietly admit the third one's an absolute hottie. The girls are going to go crazy trying to win him.'

With all this talk of hunky spunky men, Ivy's interest was piqued – she couldn't help herself. Being local boys and having gone to high school with them, she knew Frank and Jed well, and agreed both young men were easy on the eye, but who was the third hottie pattotti? She leant on the counter so she could read the poster.

'Really? So who's the one all the women will be fighting over? A local guy?'

Shirley nodded. 'His name's Ronny Sinclair, he's a newcomer to town, a stockman from up north who's inherited old Lottie Sinclair's place, Sundown Farm.'

Ivy gasped. 'Ooh, I think I know who you're talking about.' The image of the hunk of a man who had almost bowled her over at the bank last week came to her – his handsome face had been lingering in her mind but she'd refused to give him much attention, until now. She nudged Shirley. 'And oh my God, you're right, he's absolute eye candy. Although I reckon he might be a bit of a Casanova by the looks of him – he's too good looking not to be.'

Shirley shook her head. 'Oh, I don't know about that, Ivy. I met him the other day when I called in to see Larry …' Shirley smiled at the mention of Larry's name, her cheeks appearing rosier, '… and he seems like a really nice bloke, you know – trustworthy and dependable and most certainly very down to earth – a far cry from a show pony. I reckon, seeing as he's Lottie's great nephew and Larry speaks so very highly of him, he'd be one of the good ones – you know, a bit of a keeper.' Shirley wriggled her eyebrows for emphasis.

Ivy's eyes widened. 'You really got that impression?'

'I sure did, and I'm usually spot on with my first impressions of people.' Shirley gave Ivy a little nudge back. 'But I will completely agree with you on the fact he is very, *very*, handsome.'

'Hmm,' Beryl said, catching both Shirley's and Ivy's attention as her brows furrowed in thought. She sucked in an excited breath and then glanced at Ivy while tapping at the poster. 'There you go, love, if you haven't found yourself a handyman by this weekend you should go along and bid for him. Seeing as he's new to town, I'd be guessing he'll need a job, and then after he's fulfilled his slave duties, maybe you can keep him on to finish off the renovations – if he's any good, that is.' She clapped her hands together. 'Tah dah, problem solved.'

'Sounds good, Beryl, but the only thing is I really need a qualified carpenter for most of the jobs I need doing – council requirements.'

Beryl scrunched her face up. 'Oh bugger.'

Shirley's eyebrows shot up. 'Hang on a minute,' she said slowly. 'Ronny did ask me if he knew of any local building work going on, so maybe that means he's qualified in something to do with the building trade. And I'd say unless he's miraculously found something in the past couple of days, you might be in luck.' Shirley drummed the counter with her long fingernails, every finger adorned with a chunky gold ring. 'And believe you me, with the solid build of him, I'm guessing he'd be damn good at anything involving hard labour … especially if he has to have his shirt off.' She grinned then covered her mouth as though shocked at her brazenness.

Beryl half chuckled and half snorted as she once again rolled her eyes. 'God, listen to us would you? We're like a pair of old tarts.'

'Yeah, but we're sweet tarts,' Shirley spluttered, chortling. If Shirley's eyebrows went any higher they were going to join her fiery hairline.

Ivy grinned at the two women acting like hormonal teenagers and folded her arms, pondering the idea for a few moments. Maybe she'd been too quick to jump to conclusions, because she was on a man-hatey trip at the moment, and maybe Ronny was one of the nice guys. He was looking for work in the building industry, and from what she'd seen of him the other day, she knew he'd be capable of hard work. Being Lottie's great nephew there was a good chance he had her dependability and trustworthiness … he could very well be the very man she'd been looking for – for the renovations job, that was. She was not going to let herself fantasise about him being her knight in shining armour – she'd done that with blokes too many times before and only ended up getting her heart broken one way or another. Nodding her head slowly, she smiled broadly. 'Beryl and Shirley, you two are absolute gems. This is the best damn idea I've ever heard. If I win him as a slave I'll get to see how he works for a few days before I offer him the renovation job – if he's a qualified tradesman, of course. A win-win situation.'

Shirley did a happy jiggle. 'Wonderful, that's all sorted. I'll see you on Saturday night then?'

'You surely will.' Ivy beamed. 'I'll be there with bells on.'

'Great. Make sure you bring your lovely aunts along too … I haven't seen them in ages.'

'I'm fairly certain we'll all be there.' Ivy started towards the front door, an extra spring in her step. The sexy new bloke in town was in need of work, and there was a possibility he was a builder – this might be the little miracle she and her aunts had been wishing for. Fingers crossed their prayers were about to be answered by the powers that be, and Ronny Sinclair would be just the man they needed for the job.

CHAPTER 8

Driving around the block for the third time in a row, Ivy, May and Alice chattered excitedly about the lack of parking spots. Not being able to find a park was such a rarity in this part of the Blue Mountains. Hell, there weren't even parking meters in Bluegrass Bend, and only one set of traffic lights – country living at its finest. Resigned to the fact they were going to have to walk a little to get to the pub, Ivy headed to the Coles car park. She didn't mind at all, she needed to chill out and the walk would give her the opportunity to do so. She was feeling a little nervous – she'd never bid for a slave in an auction before and was apprehensive about bidding for the man she'd bumped into at the bank, because as much as she didn't want to admit it to herself, his handsome face had been lingering in her thoughts way too much. Had he felt the spark between them as she had? Could that be the reason he'd shot off like a bull from a gate? And she was worried the bidding would get too high and she would have to pull out of it – a hundred and fifty bucks was her limit, as she and her aunts had agreed. They really needed a worker and fast, even if it was only for a few days. And on top of that, she didn't know how she was going to feel if she ran into her ex, which was a given, seeing as the pub was Malcolm's second home and he was never one to miss a social outing. She sighed. There was so much to worry about and, true to form, she was overdoing it. Sucking in a deep breath, she parked and switched off the engine. She needed to stop stressing and just let the evening unfold. Leave it in Fate's dependable hands.

'It looks like every man and his dog has turned out for the fundraiser.' Alice clapped her hands with delight. 'How wonderful to see the town pull together for such a great cause, it makes me all warm and fuzzy inside.'

'It certainly is, Alice,' May said as she climbed out of the ute. 'Cancer is an absolute bitch. I can't wait until the day they discover a cure. We've lost too many friends and family over the years to the horrid disease.'

Ivy gathered her handbag from the floor and then clambered out, giggling at herself when she tried to do so with the seatbelt still on. Shutting the door, she tried to catch her reflection in the window, feeling a little uncomfortable in the fitted dress her aunts had insisted she looked amazing in. She had to admit she liked the feel of the soft fabric against her skin, and the earthy hues matched nicely with her brown knee-high Dan Post boots, she was just concerned that the neckline was too revealing, the hint of her ample cleavage something she was unaccustomed to.

'Come on then, Ivy, we're already an hour late. I hope they haven't started the bidding for our slave yet.' May tugged her silky shawl over her bare shoulders. 'And stop worrying, you look beautiful, as always.'

Ivy graced her with a smile as she pulled the dress up a little at the front, only for it to fall back down. She rolled her eyes. She really needed to find her inner goddess one of these days – believing she *was* sexy would be a damn good start.

'Thanks, Aunty May, but I reckon you're both just a little biased.'

Alice tutted and shook her head. 'Oh, hosh tosh. You're an absolute stunner, Miss Tucker – just like your mum was. And I can't for the life of me understand why a man hasn't counted his blessings and swept you off to get married.'

Ivy shrugged and said quietly, 'It's because the right one hasn't come along yet, that's all.' She looked down at the footpath, emotions welling. She angrily swallowed them down. Men weren't worth her tears. 'And after what Malcolm did to me, I kinda want a break from blokes for a while – they're nothing but trouble.'

Alice drew her niece to her. 'I don't blame you, dear, just don't turn all bitter and give up on love, okay?' She pulled back gently and tipped her head towards May, smiling compassionately. 'Because you really don't want to end up like May and me, a pair of old spinsters who can't have cats because they're allergic to them. You, my beautiful girl, deserve all the happiness that true love can give you.'

Ivy offered a resigned sigh. 'Thanks, Aunty Alice, I haven't given up on love just yet.' She tried to sound convincing, but to be perfectly honest, she was pretty certain she'd end up exactly like her two aunts. Although, on the plus side, she'd be able to have the cats because she wasn't allergic to them. She groaned inwardly with the thought.

'That's what I like to hear, love.' Alice grinned. 'Now let's go and have ourselves some fun.'

They headed off in the direction of the pub, chattering about this and that along the way and before they knew it, they were walking through the front door of the Bluegrass Bend Inn, the chatter of the patrons along with the music blaring from the jukebox like a slap to the face.

A woman standing at the door handed them each a small glass of pink champagne from a drinks tray along with a pink heart with a pin on the back of it. As though reading Ivy's mind, she smiled and pointed to the heart. 'We thought it would be a nice little gimmick for the night to unite us all in some way. You can pop it on wherever you like.'

Ivy smiled and attached it to her dress, right where her heart was beating beneath it. Alice and May did the same.

Humming to the tune of 'I Walk the Line' by Johnny Cash she smiled at the huge turnout, the many familiar faces around the room giving her the same warm and fuzzy feeling Alice was speaking of earlier. The way a country town pulled together always made her proud. She could feel quite a few sets of eyes upon her, the attention making her cheeks flush. She didn't like being in the spotlight, although it was nice to know her effort of getting dressed up was being appreciated.

Alice placed her hand on Ivy's back. 'We're off to get ourselves a shandy, love, do you want anything?'

'Um, I'm not really sure what I feel like yet … how about I just come with you.'

'Might be a good idea. I'm not sure we'd find our way back to you through this lot anyway.'

The trio worked their way through the throng as they sipped on their champagne. Being a beer drinker, Ivy was having trouble swallowing it, but she did so out of good manners, although the contorting of her face was out of her control. Stopping along the way to say hi to friends, the three finally made it to the horseshoe-shaped bar just as they'd finished their glasses. In seconds, May and Alice had been separated from Ivy, the growing mob forcing their way between them in their haste to get served. Leaning on the bar, her shiny black hair lying over one shoulder of her dress,

Ivy scanned the beers on tap and decided on a schooner of XXXX Gold. She was the designated driver tonight so she needed to pace her drinks and stick to lighter beer, and not being a huge drinker, she didn't mind at all.

After giving Ivy a forced smile, the head barmaid, Amy Mayberry, begrudgingly went to work pulling her beer. As Ivy watched her ex-friend, she recalled the event that had ended their close bond in their final year at high school. It was almost seven years ago now, but Ivy remembered the night like it was only yesterday – the images were hard to forget. Finding Amy in the bushes on the night of their debutante ball, as naked as the day she was born, with her legs wrapped around what was Ivy's first love, Brett Jones, and her tongue shoved down his throat, had been like a knife through Ivy's chest. After telling the entire ball over the microphone that Amy was the high school tart (as a scorned woman she had the excuse of not thinking straight at the time), she'd run all the way home from the deb and hidden in her room for a week, crying her heart out, her tissue usage enough to warrant a sponsorship with Kleenex. May and Alice had eventually dragged her from her bedroom, kicking and screaming, in a bid to get her to go back to school, with a firm command to brush her unkempt hair and teeth, and then to hold her head high as she walked through the school gates, because although she'd ratted on Amy in the heat of the moment, in the big scheme of things she wasn't the one who had done wrong.

Upon returning to Bluegrass High, the gossip around the school hallways had been that Amy had liked Brett long before Ivy had gotten with him, and that Ivy had basically stolen him from Amy, and so Ivy deserved to be cheated on. Amy had made sure everyone knew that Ivy was still a virgin and wouldn't sleep with Brett. The 'fact' that Amy had had a crush on Brett for ages was news to Ivy, and she was guessing it was a big fat lie just so Amy could make herself look like the victim. It was as though Ivy was the one who had done wrong. Ivy knew she shouldn't have been surprised, because guys always came first in Amy Mayberry's world, no matter what. Ivy had certainly learnt who her real mates were during the aftermath.

Amy and Ivy had never spoken again, though they were civil enough to each other – as you had to be in a tiny town – and Amy had never once offered an apology for what she had done. Looking back, Amy had done Ivy a huge favour – Brett Jones wasn't the kind of guy she would ever have wanted to end up with and was now in jail for selling drugs to teenagers. And Amy wasn't the kind of friend a girl wanted – she was so self-involved she didn't give a hoot about anyone else's feelings, her reputation as the town tart a perfect example of her selfishness. Any guy who would go near the likes of Amy Mayberry did not appeal to Ivy.

While waiting for her beer, Ivy scanned the faces at the bar. Her heart leapt out of her chest when she spotted Malcolm and, standing beside him, the guy who had been buck-naked the day she'd walked in on them. She almost ran to the toilets to avoid him seeing her, but found some inner strength and stood her ground – as her aunts had said after the deb ball all those years ago, she'd done nothing wrong and should hold her head high. To any onlookers the two men resembled the average pair of country blokes out for a good night. As she stood tall watching them, she felt a little weird about knowing their secret but at the same time somehow privileged. As her heart rate returned to normal, she thought about how many things people hid from those close to them, and the outside world, for fear of being judged or ridiculed. And she'd be the first to admit she was guilty of judging too quickly at times too – it was human nature. Even so, it was sad. And it made her wonder how many more people here had things they never wanted anyone to ever know – surely some had secrets that had the power to ruin lives? If only everyone could feel safe to open up and be their true selves instead of pretending to be someone they weren't just to please everyone else – at the same time making themselves miserable – the world would be a beautifully loving place.

Malcolm caught her gazing at him and in turn acknowledged her with a meek smile as he raised his beer. She returned his smile with a broad one – surprising Malcolm and even herself. She realised now that she hadn't had the intense feelings of love for Malcolm she'd thought she'd had; it had been more the desire to be *in* love. Of course she'd liked him, a lot – he was a genuinely likeable bloke – but now she could see him without rose-coloured glasses and she could honestly admit to herself he wasn't The One. The very idea jolted her and got her thinking about her ex-boyfriends. Had she ever truly been in love with any of them? Deep in thought, she jumped when Amy thumped her beer down on the bar, the amber liquid sloshing and spilling over the glass. Ivy almost asked her to top it up, but refrained. It wasn't worth the argument it would most certainly cause.

Amy flicked her head so her long blonde ponytail swished like a horse's tail, her glittery earrings swinging as she did so. She stopped chewing her gum. 'That'll be four bucks.'

How about a please? Ivy dug in her wallet and then handed the money over, trying to smile as she did so. It didn't hurt to try to be friendly although her tongue was going to bleed if she bit it any harder.

Unsmiling, Amy snatched the money out of her hand then turned to serve the next patron. She graced the young bloke with the biggest smile she could muster as she leant in just enough for him to peer into her cleavage. Ivy watched as the guy licked his lips. Yuck! Sighing heavily, she turned and leant against the bar, tired of feeling as though she was back at high school each and every time she was anywhere near Amy.

She took a sip from her beer, enjoying the malty flavour, and scanned the sea of faces once more to see if any of the blokes took her fancy. Not that she was going to be following through if there was, she just wanted to see if there was any hope of her finding a happily ever after in Bluegrass Bend. But nope, there was no lightning moment, no sparks, not even a flicker. Hopefully her real knight in shining armour was still out there somewhere, trying to find his damn horse to ride in on when the time was right. Knowing her luck, he'd find himself a donkey and ride off into the sunset without her. She groaned inwardly. Yup, that'd be her bloody luck. Maybe she *was* destined to wind up a lonely old woman, with cats.

Alice and May appeared in front of her, halting her train of depressing thoughts, both grinning like billyo. Clearly they'd already enjoyed a shandy after their glasses of champagne and were now onto their next drink. Her aunts were lightweights when it came to alcohol, much like herself, and it didn't take long for them to be merrily tipsy.

May patted her on the arm. 'Come on, love, let's get up near that stage and find ourselves a good spot. I just ran into Shirley at the bar and apparently she's going to start the bidding for the slaves in five minutes. I wonder who's going to be up first – I can't wait to see what this new bloke in town is like.'

'Neither can I. I just hope my heart holds out if he's as sexy as Shirley says,' Alice added with a titter. Ivy had decided not to tell May and Alice about her run-in with the sexy newcomer because they'd just start on the whole universe-throwing-him-in-her-path thing and she hadn't been in the mood for that.

Not wanting to fall into a hole filled with self-pity, she mentally shook her fears away and strode forwards. It wasn't in her nature to be so, well, so downright negative and miserable, and she needed to snap the hell out of it. And she secretly couldn't wait to see Ronny Sinclair again so she could perve on his manly scrumptiousness, as did most of the females in town by the looks of women to men ratio tonight. Yes, Frank and Jed were popular amongst the locals, for being such likeable blokes and being easy on the eye for the women, but both were taken – Frank was married and with a fiancée Jed was halfway to the altar himself. So it seemed as if news had spread like wildfire about the new stud in town. Very unusual for a night at the pub, the Bluegrass Bend men usually were the ones to outnumber the women, but not tonight ... by a long shot.

The microphone roared to life as the charismatic Shirley Jones took centre stage. Beneath the spotlight, her bright red smile was as dazzling as her copper hair. Ivy smiled up at her from where she stood with Alice, May and Beryl. Like Ivy's aunts, Beryl had clearly enjoyed her share of white wine tonight too – her face glowed a warm red hue and she wore her goofy grin. Beryl always liked a bit of a tipple, and she was a cracker when she'd had a few; Ivy knew she'd be dragged onto the dance floor at some stage of the evening. On the other side of Beryl stood a stocky, middle-aged man Ivy had occasionally seen around town but wasn't overly familiar with. From the proud-as-punch smile on his face as he gazed at Shirley, she gathered he was the Larry Shirley had mooned over at the post office the other day. She caught his attention and gave him a wave, and he returned the gesture.

The crowd hushed as Shirley began. 'Good evening, ladies and gentlemen, it's wonderful to see so many of you here for tonight's fundraiser. It makes me extremely proud to be part of such a loving and supportive community. We've already made three thousand dollars tonight with the entry tickets and meat raffles, so hurrah for Bluegrass Bend!'

The crowd cheered and whistled and raised their glasses in the air and after giving them a few moments to celebrate Shirley continued on, her smiling face now turning serious. 'Sadly, cancer has affected all of us in different ways. Some of us have had it and travelled the long, hard road through chemotherapy, others are still fighting the battle with grit and determination, and there are those of us who have lost loved ones to the terrible disease.' She sniffed and cleared her throat. 'Only a few months ago, we lost one of our oldest and dearest Bluegrass Bend residents, Lottie Sinclair, to brain cancer. Lottie fought hard, always remaining positive and never giving up, but sadly, in the end, the cancer won. Tonight is in her memory, and in memory of all of those souls who have lost their battles. We're raising much needed funds to help find a cure for this life-stealing disease and to aid in funding some of our local residents who need regular trips to the city for their treatment.' She motioned to the side of the stage with a dramatic sweep of her arm. 'And who better to start tonight's slave for a weekend auction off than our dapper local lad, Frank Albano.'

The crowd gave Frank a rowdy warm welcome to the stage and, swept away with the excitement, Ivy, her aunts and Beryl cheered along with them – the atmosphere of the room addictively electric. Being the larrikin Frank was renowned to be, he strutted out, turning this way and that as he flexed his arms and puffed out his chest, mimicking a bodybuilder – which he was a far cry from – the entire time grinning cheekily. He was revelling in the limelight. Ivy recalled him being exactly the same at high school – forever the show pony and always happy to be the centre of attention. And unlike most of the other girls, she'd never found it attractive – but did find it hilarious to watch.

And then the auction began with Frank's wife, Rosa, who was at the front of the sea of people, bidding forty dollars.

'And we're off and racing,' Shirley sung into the microphone. She laughed as she pointed in Rosa's direction. 'But you already have him as your slave, Rosa, being married to him.'

'Yeah, but at least if I pay for him he has to do what I ask him to do, like vacuuming and ironing, doesn't he?' Rosa called out. Her girlfriends squealed beside her.

Frank pulled a face of mock horror, sending the crowd into hysterics once more.

'Yup, he sure does Rosa.' Shirley was still laughing as she eyed the crowd. 'So do we have fifty?'

'Yup, I'll give ya fifty,' a bloke called out.

The spotlight fell over the bidder and Ivy recognised him as one of Frank's fellow footy team members. 'My lawns need mowing and my car needs detailing – you up for it Frankie boy?' The lanky redhead held up his beer, grinning stupidly.

'Oh fair go, Chopstick,' Frank called back, his smile widening.

And then the bidding ramped up, with the spotlight flying this way and that. The final price ended up at one hundred and thirty dollars. Frank jumped off the stage and ran to his winner – a lady from the local Bendigo Bank – and gave her a hug. She hugged him back, grinning like the cat that had gotten the cream.

Shirley captured the crowd's attention. 'So one slave down and two to go people – next up we have the very suave and forever charming, Jed Freeman.' She waved to someone offstage, as though the person was hesitating about stepping out.

And out came Jed, his face glowing a bright shade of red as he tried fruitlessly to dodge the spotlight. Reaching Shirley he gave the applauding crowd a shy wave, shoved his hands in his jeans pockets and then stared down at his shoes like they were an object of complete fascination.

Shirley wrapped her free arm around his shoulders, and gave him a squeeze. 'He's a quiet one, our Jed, but they say those are the ones to watch out for.'

Wolf-whistles followed, along with clapping and squealing. Jed chuckled and shook his head.

Shirley stepped forwards. 'So who's going to start the bidding for this fine specimen of a man?'

'Me!' A young woman jumped up and down, waving her hands in the air.

Shirley grinned. 'Great, but how much?'

'Oh, yeah, oops – thirty dollars.'

'So we have thirty folks, but I reckon we can do much better.' Shirley wriggled her brows. 'So come on now, give us your best shot.'

And they were off and racing again, with bids coming from every direction of the packed pub. Ivy couldn't help but feel sorry for Jed – he looked like a fish out of water up on stage. She wanted to run up and hug him. Within minutes, he was saved from standing there any longer when the bidding war came to a standstill at one hundred and forty-five dollars.

'Sold to Missus Peterson,' Shirley cried out.

The well-known CWA lady cheered with delight at her win, her champagne glass raised high in the air.

Shirley clapped along with the crowd as Jed hightailed it off the stage and then claimed the spotlight once more. 'And last but not the very least, we have Lottie's great-nephew and the new owner of Sundown Farm as our final slave tonight. So please give a round of applause for Ronny Sinclair!'

The audience exploded into whoops, hollers, cheers, clapping, and with the entrance of Ronny Sinclair, ear-piercing squealing and wolf-whistles. The reaction was ten times that of what Frank and Jed received. It was as though Chris Hemsworth had just entered stage left, albeit way younger, and way sexier – in Ivy's opinion. It suddenly felt very hot inside the pub and she fanned her face with her hands. In a pair of jeans, a button-up navy shirt, cowboy boots and a black, wide-brimmed hat, Ronny Sinclair demanded every single woman's attention without even trying. And the om tattoo on the side of his neck let her know he was a spiritual man too – hubba hubba. Yum! She hadn't noticed it the other day as she'd been too focused on his eyes and amazingly muscular chest. And *bam*, there was the lightning she'd been looking for less than an hour ago – the exact same feeling she'd had when she ran into Ronny at the bank, although this time it was even more intense. The fact that he looked so familiar irked her, but he would have told her if they'd already met when she'd asked him the other day. Maybe they'd known each other in a past lifetime – something she strongly believed in.

Ivy let her eyes wander over every single glorious inch of him as she tried to shake the feeling of knowing him. Ronny Sinclair certainly looked like he'd been around the block, and she'd always had a preference for the bad boys – from the aura he gave off, she sensed he might harbour a bit of an edge – but on the other hand, everything she'd heard about him told her he was a good man. He smiled charmingly at the screaming masses of women, his slightly quivering lips and the sweep of his hands over his short, dark hair giving away the fact he was a little uncomfortable on stage. Ivy liked that, never keen on a man who liked to flaunt his sex appeal – and Ronny Sinclair had bucketloads of it. As much as she hated to succumb to his charms, she grabbed hold of the bar stool beside her as she felt herself go a little weak at the knees. He. Was. Divine. Damn it, how was she going to work alongside this magnificent man if she won him as her slave for the weekend? Thoughts of spending the time naked beneath the sheets with him made her blush and she felt tingles all over. So much for being anti-men – although she'd been doing quite well until Ronny hunky-spunky Sinclair crashed into her life. She mentally slapped herself. She needed to snap out of whatever this was – a man was not the complication her life needed right now.

As much as she fought it, her heart fluttered as though it was filled with butterflies. Taking a swig from her beer, she tried to calm her lustfulness, biting down on her lower lip. His rugged looks and rough-around-the-edges image that would stop most women in their tracks made Ronny undeniably manly; Ivy bet he could sweep a woman into his big strong arms and protect her for a lifetime. She weirdly felt like she'd already been within the comfort and shelter of them there burly arms. The feeling confused her, as did the feeling of being drawn to him. What was it that Ronny had that no other bloke in here did, other than his good looks? Because for her to have such intense feelings of attraction, there had to be something underlying. Maybe it was because there was something of a warrior in him combined with an appearance of gentleness that made her heart reach out. She laughed quietly at her train of thought. As usual, she was going way too deep when maybe it was simply because Malcolm had really messed her up. Thinking Ronny could be the man she'd always longed for was more wishful thinking thanks to the champagne and beer. And for God's sake, she didn't even know him from a bar of soap.

Get a grip, Ivy Tucker.

But she couldn't help herself. Her gaze once again settled on his handsome face. With his sharp cheekbones and angular jaw darkened with a little stubble, the strong brows and eyelashes so thick they should be illegal, Ronny looked like he'd been chiselled from granite. She wished she could see his eyes better. Eyes always revealed so much to her, but the spotlight beating down on him made it impossible.

Now the gathering had calmed down, although a few women were still squealing and whistling their approval at the manly masterpiece on stage, Shirley pointed to Ronny's shirt, where his pink heart badge was pinned to the top part of his sleeve.

'And looky here, all you ladies, not only is he damn good looking, but he also wears his heart on his sleeve.' She chuckled, as did Ivy and the rest of the crowd. 'Now, who's going to begin the bidding tonight?'

Ivy wanted to shout out, but there was no way in hell she was going to be the first one to bid – it would make her look desperate. May and Alice playfully poked her in the sides, telling her to do otherwise. But she bit her tongue as a woman from the middle of the crowd shouted, 'I bid fifty smackaroos for the sexy cowboy!' saving Ivy the embarrassment.

Shirley pointed at the middle-aged lady as she jiggled on the spot, the spotlight now on her. Ivy knew her from the doctor's surgery: she was the receptionist, and usually so quiet and reserved. Funny what a sexy man could do to a woman.

'So we have fifty dollars, thanks to Barbara starting the bidding. Do I hear sixty dollars?' Shirley called as she skimmed her eyes over the throng before her.

'I'll give ya sixty,' shouted Gertrude from her usual place at the bar, her extremely tight clothes doing nothing other than making her look like mutton dressed up as lamb.

'We have sixty smackaroos, do I hear seventy?' Shirley called with a wide grin.

Ivy was just about to call out when someone beat her to it.

'Eighty! I bid eighty dollars.'

The spotlight moved to the bar where Amy stood upon it, *Coyote Ugly* style, making it obvious just how sexy she thought she was. The display made Ivy want to gag.

May waved her hands in the air. 'We bid one hundred dollars!'

The spotlight shifted to them and Ivy shaded her eyes from the brilliance.

Shirley's excitement raised a few notches as she called out to the crowd, 'One hundred dollars! Does anyone want to bid higher? Come on, ladies, you know you want him as your slave for the weekend. How could you not?' She waved her arm at Ronny. 'Look at him!'

Ronny visibly blushed, his smile shy. Ivy could see him scanning the crowd, the glare of the spotlight making him squint a little. She could swear his gaze lingered on her a little longer than anyone else, or maybe she was just being delusional.

'One hundred and twenty bucks,' Amy yelled from her perch on the bar. She winked at Ronny, and then licked her lips suggestively. The men in the crowd cheered her on. She gushed with their attention.

'One hundred and thirty dollars,' Ivy retorted, her arms upstretched. There was no way she was going to let Amy Mayberry sink her teeth into Ronny Sinclair. Her sudden desire to protect him startled her. But with everything going on around her, she had no time to ponder it – another woman joined the bidding war from the back corner of the pub.

'One hundred and forty dollars!' A collective cheer followed.

Ivy had no idea who the new bidder was, she couldn't see that far, and goddamn it – they were almost at their limit already. There was no way they were going to win this hunk of a man if the auction kept going the way it was. Her heart sank, not only because they needed a worker, but because she felt a need to get to know Ronny better. She had no idea why, but something was telling her there was more to this man than met the eye, and that intrigued her.

'One hundred and fifty dollars!' she called as she held her breath, wishing at the same time that all the other women in this place would just disappear. She wanted to throw her hands over her ears so that she didn't hear a higher bid.

'One hundred and sixty bucks!' Amy squealed as she snapped to attention on top of the bar.

Ivy wanted to scream and her temples began to throb. Damn Amy Mayberry – couldn't she keep her sticky fingers off the new bloke? May and Alice looked at her and shook their heads dejectedly, an indication that their bidding was now over. Ivy dropped her gaze and stared at the floor. *Damn it.* Her fantasy of being able to get to know him better crumbled at her feet – there was no way she'd be asking him out.

'One hundred and seventy!' a voice called from the left, followed by a collective squeal of the girl's friends.

'One hundred and eighty!'

'One hundred and eighty-five!'

'One hundred and ninety!'

The bidding was on fire, with offers coming left, right and centre, the spotlight moving so much it now resembled something at a rave rather than a country pub. Shirley's gaze was flying around the room like a ball in a pinball machine.

'Two hundred,' Amy retorted, her voice now desperate.

'Two hundred and fifty dollars!'

The spotlight shone in Ivy's direction and she looked over to see Beryl shaking her arms in the air while jumping up and down. 'I bid two hundred and fifty dollars for the fetching Ronny Sinclair!'

Amy cursed loudly from her place atop the bar and then jumped down to her usual position behind the beer taps, the scowl on her face priceless. Ivy said a silent hurrah as she fought not to punch the air. Even though they wouldn't be inviting Mr Ronny Sinclair in as their slave at Healing Hills, she didn't want Amy to have him either.

Shirley gave Beryl the thumbs up, before saying, 'That's a huge and muchly appreciated bid from the lovely Beryl Matheson. Do I hear two hundred and sixty?'

The crowd went silent. Ivy grinned at Beryl and softly clapped her hands, once again holding her breath. Beryl reached out and pulled Ivy to her, squeezing her tightly. May and Alice followed suit and threw their arms around the pair. They stood, entangled, waiting. The pub had gone so quiet Ivy was sure she'd hear a pin drop.

'So that's two hundred and fifty going once, going twice …' Shirley dragged it out, making sure to give the crowd plenty of time to change their minds and resume the bidding war.

The silence now extended, Shirley clapped her hands together loudly. 'Going three times, and sold, to Beryl Matheson!' She pointed at Beryl. 'Good on you love.'

The crowd exploded once again into raucous applause. Alice and May squealed and danced as Beryl whispered into Ivy's ear, 'I did that for you three, love, you just give me the hundred and fifty dollars you were going to spend and I'll chuck in the hundred.'

Ivy began to protest but Beryl shushed her. 'You do a wonderful job out there at Healing Hills and I want to do this for you and your aunts. So please, don't say no.' She tipped her head towards the bar and grimaced. 'And there was no way in hell I was going to let Amy Mayberry win him. God knows what that woman would expect from the poor bloke.'

Blinking back thankful tears, Ivy embraced Beryl, as did May and Alice. The four of them did a happy jig as Shirley wound down as compere. Ivy stole a moment from the celebration to look up at Ronny. His eyes rested fleetingly on her as he smiled, sending another jolt of lightning through her. She already couldn't wait for the moment she got to work alongside him.

CHAPTER 9

With Shirley's spirited encouragement, the crowd gave Ronny one more enthusiastic hurrah before the band began their first set. A classic Garth Brooks honky-tonk tune drowned out the thrashing of Ronny's heart against his chest. As the saying went, hearts were wild creatures and that's why God chose to cage them, and Ronny sincerely believed this. He wished he could control what was going on inside him, control his emotions, but just like the other day at the bank, it was impossible when all he wanted was to take the gorgeous woman standing only metres from him into his arms and kiss her full, glossy lips. Uninvited feelings washed over him – longing, shame, remorse, protectiveness, apprehension, and something he couldn't quite put his finger on – and he suddenly needed to be somewhere private. He gave one last charming smile to the dissipating crowd, fighting to keep his eyes from Ivy's face, as he had the entire time he'd been standing up here, the burn of her gaze on him doing things that normally only a seductive touch would do.

The spotlight now on the long-haired lead singer, and the disco ball and flashing party lights now in full dazzling swing, the crowd's attention finally turned from the stage to having a boogie on the dance floor. Ronny fought his urge to run and instead took measured steps until he reached the back of the stage, where it was quiet and he could be alone. Relief flooded him. Leaning against the wall, he slid down it, squatting and breathing deeply while trying to steady his racing pulse. Seeing Ivy two times in a week was too much. He still hadn't gotten over the last time he'd run into her – especially with her beautiful face visiting him in his dreams every night since. He'd known there was a big possibility she'd be here tonight, and he'd thought himself ready for such an encounter, but having her only metres from him, bidding for him, was a whole other story. And it wasn't only the effect of the perfect curves of her luscious body in that breathtaking dress or the sexy cowgirl boots that made him want to trace his fingers all over her long, slender legs, it was also her shyness, her hesitation, the way her lips moved when she spoke to the women beside her, that made her downright irresistible. And how close he had come to being her slave for the weekend. How would that have panned out? Thank God the elderly woman beside her had been the winning bidder, because he had no idea how he would have coped having to be in the company of the beautiful Ivy Tucker for two entire days. He wasn't a man who condoned lies, and just being in her company would make him feel like a liar if he didn't reveal who he was. He'd already hightailed it out of the bank to avoid answering truthfully after she'd asked if she knew him from somewhere. Out of respect for Lottie, he could never tell Ivy the truth. Besides, the past was better left where it was; Lottie had been correct in saying he needed to forget Byron McWilliams ever existed if he was to have a clean slate to build his life upon, and to do that with a clear conscience, he had to try to stay away from the captivating allure of Miss Tucker, as hard as that was proving to be.

Closing his eyes, Ronny took a few more moments to regroup before he went out and faced the crowd. Usually always up for a bit of socialising, all he felt like doing right now was escaping to sit by a campfire with his guitar.

'Ah, there you are, Ronny. Beryl and the girls are dying to meet you.'

Shirley's voice made him leap from the ground and then try to cover his turmoil by mustering the biggest smile he could. But Shirley must have seen through him, because her smile was replaced by a look of concern as she put her hand on his shoulder and gave it a gentle squeeze.

'You okay, Ronny? You look a bit shaken.'

Ronny blew air through his lips as though it wasn't a big deal while he shooed off imaginary flies. 'Nah, I'm fine thanks, Shirley, just felt like a deer in the headlights out there, that's all. I'm not used to being in the limelight.' *Especially after spending the last eight years in prison.*

'Oh, sweetie, that's completely understandable. I've had the job of compere in this town for as long as I can remember, so I tend to forget how nervous people can get when all the attention is on them. You did a damn fine job of it, though, I must say. The crowd loved you, especially all the ladies.' Shirley took Ronny by the hands, then tugged him gently forwards as she headed out the door that led to the dance floor. 'Come on then and I'll introduce you to the ladies you'll be slaving for.'

Ronny stopped in the doorway as his heart skidded to a halt. *Ivy was with the lady who won. Oh shit. Surely fate wouldn't be so cruel …*

'Um, what do you mean by ladies?' He emphasised the *s*.

Shirley winked and grinned at him, her white teeth glowing under the ultraviolet lights. 'Yes, ladies, in the plural sense, meaning you'll be slaving for more than one lady – and I reckon you're a lucky lad, because these three ladies you're about to meet are some of the nicest in Bluegrass Bend. I couldn't really think of anyone else I'd rather slave for, to be honest.' She turned and dragged him towards the thumping music, and before Ronny knew it, he was being introduced to Ivy and her two aunts, May and Alice Tucker. Nearby, an effervescent Beryl Matheson was shaking her tail feather on the dance floor. Spotting him, Beryl rushed over and hooked her arm through his, all the while grinning like a kid in a candy shop. Ronny liked her instantly.

'Ladies, this is the ever-so-charming Ronny Sinclair,' Shirley shouted above the music.

The four hollered their hellos, and then stood unspeaking, until Ivy broke the slightly unnerving silence by reaching out and giving him a friendly hug, her lips brushing his cheek along the way to his ear. His skin heated with her feathery touch.

'So, we meet again,' she whispered.

Stunned by her unexpected gesture, Ronny swallowed his shock before someone noticed it and hugged her back, the sensation of her warm body pressed against his and her eyelashes fluttering against the side of his neck sending a blazing fire through him. God, how he wanted her right now, wanted to be the man who helped chase the demons away that still shadowed her beautiful brown eyes. Time stopped for the briefest of moments, making him wish it would stay like that forever. But a forever, he and Ivy would never have. If only things had been different and they had crossed paths under much better circumstances, but they hadn't. End of story. He needed to get a grip. She clearly didn't remember him, as a hug like this would have been out of the question if she'd had an inkling who he was. The very thought gave him a jolt of much needed courage.

'So we do,' he whispered back.

They untwined but, before pulling away completely, Ivy went up on her tippy toes. Her hand still rested on his shoulder and her warm breath on his ear was like an aphrodisiac as she spoke loud enough to be heard above the music.

'We're so happy to have you for a few days, because Lord knows we need you.' She turned to Beryl and smiled warmly. 'And it's all thanks to this little bundle of loveliness, I might add.'

A tuft of Ivy's hair tumbled across her face as she smiled at her friend and Ronny had to resist the impulse to reach out and tuck it behind her ears.

Beryl nodded enthusiastically. 'Yes, I thought these ladies could use your help more than me. As much as I'd love to have you swanning about my house doing handyman duties, I think it might cause an argument with my hubby – he'll want you helping him down the paddock.' Beryl patted him a few times on the arm.

'That was generous of you, Beryl,' Ronny replied, the whole time feeling Ivy's gaze burning into him.

A tap on his shoulder made him spin around. He turned to see one of the women who'd been bidding for him, the one brazen enough to jump up on the bar, smiling suggestively at him. She was a stunner, but didn't come close to the captivating beauty of Ivy.

'G'day, I'm Amy,' she shouted over the music, then reached out and touched Ronny's arm, leaving her hand there as she continued, 'I just wanted to introduce myself, you know, welcome you to Bluegrass Bend and all – especially seeing as you're my new neighbour.'

'G'day, Amy.' Ronny held out his hand. His brows furrowed. 'And just how am I your neighbour?'

'My parents are Burt and Trisha Mayberry. I live with them on the farm.' Amy looked at his outstretched hand and laughed. 'That's a little formal.' She pulled him into a quick hug before planting a kiss fair on his lips. She stepped back, hands on hips. 'Now that's more like it.'

Shocked by Amy's audacity, Ronny didn't return the gesture. He just stood staring at her, trying to work her out, while at the same time noticing Ivy was throwing daggers in Amy's direction. He shoved his hands in his pockets and rocked back and forth on his heels. 'Well, um, it's nice to meet you, Miss Mayberry.'

'Miss Mayberry, huh? I don't think I've ever been called that. Such a gentleman – how sweet.' Amy smiled provocatively as she reached out and rubbed his arm. 'I'm on my break now – so how about me and you share a drink at the bar, you know, get a little more acquainted now we're going to be living next door to each other? That way I'll know you're not a serial killer and I'll feel safe to come borrow a cup of sugar …' she wriggled her eyebrows suggestively, '… if the need arises.'

Before Ronny could politely knock back her invitation – he wanted more time with Ivy and her aunts and Beryl – Amy peered over his shoulder, looking at Ivy as she grabbed him tightly by the hand. He sensed the tension between the two women increase.

'Do you lot mind if I steal this handsome man for a little while? I'll have him back before you know it, if you're lucky – or maybe after I get lucky.' She laughed raucously.

Ronny spotted May mumble something under her breath to Alice, and at the same time Beryl rolled her eyes. Ivy looked as if she wanted to throttle Amy – if looks could kill, Amy would be dead. Clearly, none of these women held a high regard for the vivacious Miss Mayberry. Feeling completely out of his comfort zone, and wanting to ease the growing tension, Ronny took hold of the situation. He couldn't be rude to Amy; she'd never done anything to him, and he had to live next door to her and her parents.

He leant towards Ivy. 'I have a feeling she won't take no for an answer. Won't be long.'

Ivy's friendly persona had waned a little as she reached into her handbag, her lips now tight. 'No worries, Ronny, you aren't my slave just yet, so no need to hang around us lot all night.' She pulled out a card and handed it to him. 'This is our business card. My mobile number is the one at the bottom. Just give me a call over the next couple of days and we'll sort out when you'd like to come out for a few days' work.'

'Sure, how soon do you want me?'

'The sooner the better really … we're in desperate need of some help around the place.'

Ronny was disappointed the mood between them had turned from friendly to businesslike, although he knew he shouldn't be – this was way safer. Two days near Ivy was going to be tough enough without them being too chummy. He stared at the card, not wanting to look Ivy in the eyes for fear of giving something away. From behind him, Amy gave his arm a tug. 'Oh, righto … I'll give you a call tomorrow then.' He finally looked up, giving her a smile.

Ivy graced him with a smile in return, but this time it wasn't as genuine as before. 'Sounds like a plan, hear from you then.' And then she turned her back on him.

May, Alice and Beryl gave him a wave as they said their goodbyes. The three women were adorable. Ivy Tucker, on the other hand, was to die for – if it ever came to it again, Ronny knew he would lay his life on the line for her as he'd done once before.

***

For fear of passing out from overheating, Ivy refused to be dragged onto the dance floor again by her aunts and Beryl – she'd already boogied her butt off for the past three songs. Instead she paid for her drink at the crowded bar and found a spot where she could covertly watch Ronny and Amy. Every now and then, Ronny would gaze around the room, as if looking for someone, and Ivy would shrink against the wall, the fact she was standing in the darkest corner of the pub giving her a little respite. She prayed they didn't bust her – Amy would get a big kick out of that, and it would make her business relationship with Ronny a little uncomfortable if he thought she was perving on him, even if she had to admit she was. He was the rugged kind of handsome she'd always found attractive, and he had a mysteriousness that drew her to him like a bee to honey. But although he was good eye candy, she had no idea who the man beneath the sexy exterior was, and if he was going to be doing work at Healing Hills, even if it was only for two days, she needed to know. Observing how he acted around Amy would certainly give her a fair idea; most men became putty in Amy's hands with her drop-dead looks and exuberant personality, not to mention her obvious eagerness to get them in the sack. Ivy found those types of blokes shallow, and she didn't want a shallow man hanging around Healing Hills for too long – if that was the case with Ronny, he could do his two days of free work and then bugger off, with no offer of a permanent job. It was imperative they kept Healing Hills a safe haven for the people who came there for healing and having a bloke around who might take advantage of their vulnerability would be unacceptable.

Taking a sip from her lemon, lime and bitters – she'd had her share of beers now to still be legal to drive – Ivy saw that Amy was doing a lot of touching whereas Ronny was keeping his distance, every bit the gentleman. Even when Amy leant into him, he would lean back a little. He did, however, seem to be enjoying her company as he smiled and laughed at everything she said. Images of the two ravishing each other plagued Ivy's mind, making her skin crawl. It irked her that there was a possibility they might sleep together, which would most certainly be on the cards if Amy had anything to do with it. Was Ronny the type of bloke that would fall for Amy's cheap charm? Anger flushed through her. God. Was she jealous? Maybe. She had no idea why other than the fact Amy got all the handsome ones. But then again, hadn't she been thinking only a few days ago that she didn't want to get involved with another man for a while? So why was she letting this bother her so much? *Snap out of it, Ivy*. Maybe the few drinks she'd had were making her not think straight. Or maybe she was just rebounding after being hurt by Malcolm, because as much as she'd tried to be strong, and now realised she didn't feel as strongly for him as she'd thought at the time, he'd still hurt her, deeply.

Gazing at Ronny's face, the way his jaw clenched every now and then, the way his strong hand curled around his beer, the way his movements and gestures emitted a sense of gentle kindness and a deep, inner strength, she felt again there was something familiar about him. Maybe he just had one of those familiar faces, or she'd seen him around town when he'd been here visiting Lottie. That could certainly be the case.

Deciding she'd seen enough, Ivy headed off in the direction of the toilets. Maybe Amy had, once again, unwittingly done her a favour by showing from the get go that Ronny was just like every other man. It would certainly help her to resist Ronny in all his blow-your-socks-off sexiness. Ivy clung to that idea. She'd had her little moment of feeling weak at the knees in his presence, now it was time to put her imaginary business hat on and focus on the huge job ahead of her – saving the one and only true love in her life, Healing Hills.

CHAPTER 10

With her shiny new toolbox in her hands, a wad of DIY brochures beneath her arm and sheer determination in her heart, Ivy followed the winding pebble path she'd been down countless times with her mum through the native gardens that could do with a little sprucing up but overall were pretty good thanks to her aunts' love of gardening – the perfume of the many roses taking her back in time to a fleeting evocation of summers past – before stepping onto the front porch of what used to be her family home. She instantly noted the weather-beaten timber decking needed oiling and pulled out her mobile phone and added *decking oil* to her growing list of things to get. Bo was beside her, a monstrous fresh bone in his mouth and a spring in his step. She pointed to the shade beneath a towering mountain blue gum beside the cottage, instructing the dog to eat his bone there and to stay put. Bo quickly did as he was told. Ivy thought the treat would keep him busy for a good hour. The past week he'd discovered how much fun chasing Aunt Alice's new ducks was, and although she was fairly certain Bo wouldn't harm a fly, his game still made her nervous.

Resting her hands on the sandstone walls, Ivy closed her eyes as memories of her early childhood flooded her. Apart from the recollection of her mother and father arguing whenever he'd decided to grace them with his presence, there were many joyful times when it had just been her and her mum. She could almost hear their raucous laughter as they raced around the house, her mother threatening to tickle her. It had been a game they'd played before bath time. Hide and seek had been one of their favourites too, and she smiled as she recalled how her mum hid in places blatantly easy to find her – always thinking of her little girl. And then there were the quiet times, when she and her mum would do craft together, play board games, watch movies or read books. So many memories – and they were so very precious now that's all she had left.

The house was a hundred years old and she'd quite often imagined it had ghosts. She remembered sitting with her friends beneath her bed sheets, each with a torch tucked under their chin to make them look scary as they told stories to frighten the wits out of each other. She smiled. There'd been many a happy day within these walls.

Drawing in a deep breath, she opened her eyes. She didn't want to reminisce to the point of heartache – she'd done that many times before. She needed to stay focused on the job at hand, and not get sidetracked.

The cosy, three-bedroom cottage had so much character, she was sure it'd find a new owner quickly. It just needed some tender loving care to bring it back to its former glory. Ivy approached the weary-looking front door, smiling as she recalled the time she'd run into it and broken her front tooth. A lick of varnish, she thought, and it would look like new. Out of habit, she took off her boots and left them on the verandah; her mother had always insisted on bare feet to preserve her clean floors. Dragging the door open, she winced as the bottom scraped across the floorboards and made a mental note that it needed trimming. She stepped inside. Silence greeted her, and a smell that she could only explain as home. The windows were curtainless and golden sunlight bathed the inside of the home in a warm glow. She couldn't help scrunching her face up at the décor, though. The tangerine and fuchsia walls had to go – she'd chosen soft creamy pastels for the interior. After trawling through hundreds of home and garden magazines, she'd finally chosen the design she thought would suit the place: country-style charm with a modern twist. She could just imagine it now, with throw rugs tossed over cosy couches to curl up on on wintery nights. It was going to look beautiful and feel so welcoming that people would be in a bidding war to buy the place.

Walking through the lounge room with its big open fireplace, Ivy headed down the hallway to the kitchen. Although empty now, she and her aunts had kept the home clean and tidy over the years, out of love for the old place. As she peeked into the bedrooms and peered into cupboards, making notes along the way of what needed doing, memories of her childhood and teenage years poured out from every inch. After her mum had passed, Ivy had spent many a night in here with her friends in swags and sleeping bags. It had been the perfect adolescent's hideaway, far enough away from her aunts to have the music loud but close enough if an emergency arose. Looking up at the ceiling in her old bedroom, Ivy shuddered as she noticed the only occupants of the house had woven their webs between the exposed timber beams. Although she hated killing anything, these spiders would have to go, they made her skin crawl and it wasn't a good look for buyers. If only she wasn't so terrified of them she would carry each one out, but a can of fly spray would have to do the trick.

Stepping into the kitchen at the back of the house, Ivy recalled all the times she'd sat on the countertop while licking cake batter from the mixing bowl – most of it smeared over her hands and face by the time she was finished. Her mum had always giggled as she'd wiped her clean. She missed days like those and was saddened by the fact she'd never get to make memories with her mum again. She wasn't going to be hard on herself by thinking she had to be stronger – the loss of a parent was something a child, no matter what their age, never completely healed from.

The décor in here was as bad as everywhere else in the cottage. Before her mum and dad had moved in here it had been used as a workers quarters by the neighbouring farm, and her grandmother had bought the place for them as a wedding present. What were people thinking back then? The lime-coloured laminate benches combined with orange cupboard doors and the orange and yellow floral wallpaper that covered the kitchen walls were a little overbearing to say the least. And the open overhead cupboards made the room feel minuscule, when in fact it was a very decent-sized kitchen, big enough to add a small laundry off the side of it. A tiny window sat above the kitchen sink with a teasing view of the sprawling green countryside behind the cottage. Opening the room up with a set of French windows would be magical, if she could afford it. A flutter of excitement filled her belly with the thought of how beautiful it could all be. She decided to get to work.

Seriously, how hard could it be? Loads of people turned to DIY to save on costs, although admittedly, usually there was a man involved to help with the bigger jobs. She wasn't giving up on the hope they would find a qualified, affordable tradesman, if they hadn't already in Ronny Sinclair, to help with revamping the kitchen and bathroom and adding a new laundry to replace the one that was part of the back verandah. She couldn't give up – or she might as well chuck the whole plan in right now. Hopefully Ronny was going to turn out to be capable, though there was no guarantee he'd take the position if she offered it to him. But then again, other than the wage issue, why wouldn't he leap at the chance if he was looking for building work?

She still hadn't heard from Ronny about when he might be able to start work, so she was on her own for the moment. After lengthy conversations about what they'd do with the limited funds, May and Alice had offered to handle all the healing sessions so Ivy could concentrate on the renovation. Ivy had thought it a great plan, since her aunts were a little past back-breaking labour. She'd made sure to let her clients know about the change and, thankfully, all had been happy to do their sessions with May and Alice for the next couple of months.

Today she would start hammering down the floorboards that had warped over time and then put her hand to anything else she could do on her own. She had to at least make some sort of start, because time was ticking and she was beginning to wonder whether the charismatic Ronny Sinclair was going to stand up to his half of the bargain and be their slave for a weekend. He'd said he would be calling her yesterday, and he hadn't – typical bloody man. Maybe Amy Mayberry *had* successfully wooed him into her dungeon and he was still lying handcuffed to her bed while she performed sexual rituals on him. As crazy as it sounded, Ivy wouldn't put anything past the woman – Amy always got what she wanted, especially when it came to men.

Keen to not think about Ronny and Amy getting naked together and wanting to make a start, she went back to the lounge room. She wanted to hang the banner she had rolled up under her arm that read HOME IS WHERE THE HEART IS; her little bit of inspiration to get the place in tip-top shape. She turned slowly around, trying to decide on the wall she would hang it on. Placing her toolbox down, she opened the lid and gathered what she needed – a hammer and a nail – feeling somewhat accomplished already just by acting like she knew what she was doing, even though half the tools in the box still perplexed her. Going up on her tippy toes, she tried to position the nail so she could hammer it in. Just as she was about to strike, her phone chimed in her pocket. Huffing, she grabbed it. Not recognising the caller ID, she answered in a businesslike tone of voice.

'Hello, Healing Hills, Ivy Tucker speaking.'

'Hi Ivy, it's Ronny Sinclair.'

'Oh, hi.' Distracted from the job at hand by the surprise she felt at Ronny finally calling, Ivy dropped the hammer. It bounced onto her socked toes and the pain sent her into a tirade of expletives as she jumped around on one leg, holding her throbbing foot. Her phone dropped to the floor. She could hear Ronny calling out to her but she needed a second to catch her breath.

'Bloody hell, hang on,' she yelled as she jumped around a few more times before bending to retrieve the phone. 'Sorry, I dropped the damn hammer on my foot.'

'Are you all right? You didn't break anything, did you?'

'Nope, I'm all good now thanks.' She actually wasn't, her toe was throbbing like hell, and she felt like a complete idiot, but Ronny didn't need to know that. She wanted to be a pillar of poise and fortitude in his eyes – the attributes of a proper boss.

'Good, glad that's all it was, because for a second there I thought you were cursing at me for ringing you.'

Ronny's laugh made her tingle all over and she hated how he had that effect on her. She didn't want to fall underneath his charismatic spell each and every time she had anything to do with him. A wall needed to go up, to protect her heart, but goddamn it she was having trouble finding the bricks to do so. She sat down on the floor to assess her toe, grimacing as she removed her sock. It wasn't broken but she was going to have a doozy of a bruise.

'Oh, really? Why would I curse at you for ringing me?' *Oh, that's right. Because you were an arse and didn't do as you said, like every bloke I've ever known, and because you're also friends with the town tart.*

'I thought you might have been annoyed at me for not ringing you yesterday, like I said I would. Things just got away from me and –'

'Oh, I didn't even remember you saying that, so no problem at all,' Ivy said, not interested in listening to his excuses. She hated telling white lies, but she wasn't going to let this gorgeous man know he'd gotten to her, no way, Jose. Poise and – what was the other thing? Fortitude.

'Oh, that's good. I didn't want to start off on the wrong foot. I was meaning to call, but got stuck out in one of my paddocks fixing a leaking water pipe well into the night, so I didn't get a chance. Sorry.'

Was Ronny telling her the truth, or was it *his* water pipe he was having fixed by the one and only Amy Mayberry? Ivy felt like slapping herself. How was it her business if that were the case? She silently willed herself to get the hell over whatever it was she was doing, because it was the height of ridiculousness. This was business, and Ronny was basically a stranger to her, simple as that.

'Like I said, no probs, Ronny, these things happen when you've got a property to run. I completely understand.'

'Great, thanks, anyway, the reason for my call, I'm free this weekend so I thought I could come out to your place and fulfil my slave duties.'

His voice was so dreamily husky – listening to him was like sliding her body into a bathtub filled with warm water on a cold winter's day. Her slave for the entire weekend – her heart fluttered with the thought but she slapped it back into line. *Get a grip, girl.* She cleared her throat.

'That sounds perfect, Ronny.'

'Excellent, what time do you want me out there?'

'Oh, say, sevenish? Or is that too early for you?' Was that a little bit of sarcasm she heard in her voice? For God's sake, what was wrong with her? She lay back and stared at the ceiling, noting it needed painting too – her to-do list was growing by the minute.

'I'm always up and about way before then, so not at all. Anything you need me to bring, like any particular tools?'

'Oh, Shirley mentioned something about you looking for work as a builder. Do you have any builder's tools?'

'Sure do, I'm a carpenter by trade so I have plenty here in the shed. Is there some work around the house you need me to do?'

'Something like that ...' Ivy punched the air as she jiggled her legs then flinched when she smacked her sore toe against the doorway. Allelujah! Their miracle may have arrived, just as May expected. Praise the powers that be! She fought to keep her voice calm. 'We're in the beginning stages of renovating a cottage, and we've been having a really hard time finding a qualified tradesman to do the job, which as you'd know is a council prerequisite, so you're going to come in very handy over the next few days – and hopefully even longer, if you think you can handle the workload.'

She almost slapped her hand over her mouth. She couldn't believe she'd offered him the job before he'd even proven his worth, but she was desperate and in desperate times a person was known not to think straight. She held her breath, waiting for his response, which was taking way longer than she expected. She could swear she also heard him curse under his breath. Her irritation with him returned, in full force. Who did this bloke think he was? Shirley had said he'd seemed pretty desperate for work. So what was the damn problem?

'Cat got your tongue, Ronny?' She definitely said that with sarcasm, and she hoped he picked up on it too. Raaa!

'Oh, sorry, yeah, um, hmm, well, thank you for the kind offer, Ivy, but how about we just wait and see how I go over the weekend first? I'm, um, pretty busy around here at the moment so I'm not sure if I can take anything else on right now.'

'But I thought you were asking around for work? Shirley said you were pretty keen to start something as soon as possible and she's not one to talk bullshit.'

'Oh, yeah, I was just feeling it out, that's all. Shirley must have got the wrong impression.' Ronny chuckled awkwardly. 'I wasn't too serious about getting anything straight away. I haven't really had a chance to settle in here yet.'

Ivy bit her tongue hard, keeping her usually slow-to-ignite temper in check before she said anything she couldn't take back. Her stomach shifted uneasily. What wasn't he telling her? Shirley was a trustworthy woman, so Ivy knew she was telling the truth when she'd said Ronny was keen to start work soon. Was Ivy's job offer not good enough for this bloke? She thought he would have jumped at the chance. Her mind went into overdrive and she started to worry that Amy had been in his ear and told him some bullshit story about her, like she had done when they were at high school. *Deep breaths. Calm thoughts.* She couldn't lose her cool – they needed Ronny Sinclair, as much as she hated to admit it. Hopefully, after a few days of working together, she could charm him into agreeing to take the job. Then a bolt of panic hit her. He was already sounding blasé and she hadn't even told him about the crappy wages situation yet. Could things seriously get any more challenging? She wanted to bang her head against the wall.

'Ivy, are you there?'

'Oh sorry, um, okay, we can do it that way if you like … but I really do hope you decide to take the job.' She pushed herself up from the floor and hobbled over to the window to check if Bo was where she'd told him to stay. He was. She couldn't help but smile at him.

'Yeah, I think it's for the best if we just see how things pan out.' Ronny sounded confident – almost too confident.

Her smile for her obedient pooch vanished. What in the hell did he mean by 'for the best' and 'we'll just see how things pan out'? She wanted to ask him but the words seemed to jumble in her mouth before she could get them out. And probably for good reason.

Sucking in a breath, she spoke carefully. 'Right then, that's all settled. I'll see you bright and early tomorrow. Thanks for the call.'

'No worries, Ivy, see you then.'

'Oh, Ronny …'

'Yup?'

'Do you know where we are?'

'I've got the address on the business card you gave me the other night so I'll find you.'

'Okay then, bye.'

'Catch ya, Ivy.'

And the line went dead, as did Ivy's hope for her plan to save Healing Hills. They were no closer to finding a qualified tradesman to do the job, and the only one in town she had any hope of affording had better things to do – apparently.

Exasperated and defeated, she sat on the floor of the empty house as the tears she'd been holding began trickling down her cheeks. A person could only remain strong for so long, so fuck fortitude and poise – a good cry had never hurt anyone, and at this moment, in the privacy of the cottage she had once called home, a good cry was exactly what she needed. Hugging her knees to her chest, Ivy cried for those she had lost, the love that she was sure she'd never find, the music she was afraid she'd never play again, the cottage she had to sell, and the place she had come to call her home that she was on the brink of losing. As she cried, she prayed with all she had that somehow, some way, everything was going to turn out even better than she'd expected. She had to hold onto that hope, because without it, she had nothing.

CHAPTER 11

Ronny pressed the end button and then shoved his mobile phone back into his pocket as he paced the gravel driveway with Jessie and Cindy Clawford on either side of him. He punched a fist into his palm as his jaw clenched. Damn it, and just when he thought his life was finally heading in the right direction. Talk about being put on the spot – so much so he hadn't been able to think straight. And his mind was still in a whirl from it. Ivy had sounded desperate for him to take the job on, and he'd basically told her in no uncertain terms that he wasn't interested. A big fat lie, and he'd regretted it as soon as he'd said it. He could tell she knew he was lying too – but it was too bloody late to back-pedal. Now what was she going to think of him? He felt like the biggest arsehole on earth and he wouldn't blame her for thinking the same thing. But what was he meant to do, go and work day in, day out with the one woman he should be doing his very best to steer clear of, a woman who made him feel things he'd never felt before?

Stopping before he carved a path into the drive with his boots, Ronny knelt down and gave Jessie a ruffle on the head and Cindy a scratch behind her ears. He was trying his best to make sense of the run of coincidences that had brought Ivy back into his life. First, he runs into her at the bank, then she wins him as her slave for a weekend and now she's offering him his dream job. He was well aware that his future hinged on how he handled the situation. On the one hand, he could just do his two days and never set foot back on Healing Hills – but Bluegrass Bend was such a small town that she would most certainly find out if he took a job somewhere else and then Ivy would most certainly hate him forever because he'd left her and her aunts stranded in their time of need. Or he could take the job on, do a good deed for people in need of his help, just like he had promised himself he'd do when he got out of prison, and get paid for something he loved doing. And when the job was done he could get on with life at Sundown Farm as Lottie had begged him to in her letter. It didn't sound too hard but he knew putting a plan like that into action would be a different kettle of fish. It didn't have to be hard, though; if he could promise himself he'd keep the past where it was and not say a word about that night, maybe he and Ivy could be friends. Not close friends, but acquaintances. He hated lying, but was keeping a secret lying? Maybe if he kept a bit of a wall between them, she wouldn't feel comfortable enough to ask him questions about his past and he wouldn't have to lie to her. He'd just go to work, do his job, and then go home – keep it all very businesslike.

He wished Lottie were here so he could talk to her about it, but then again, he had a fair idea of what she would say: *Keep away from her and concentrate on your own life, Ronny*. Maybe he could have a word with Larry, seeing as his old mate knew everything there was to know about the situation. Yes, that's what he would do. He needed someone to bounce his thoughts off, and Larry was the only person he could do that with.

***

The Bluegrass Bend bakery was humming with life, their award-winning pies drawing people in from far and wide, adding to the regular lunchtime rush to make the place a bit of a madhouse. Ronny and Larry sat outside at one of the tables, wanting to enjoy the beautiful summer's day away from the hustle and bustle. They leant across the table, making sure to keep their voices low, not wanting anyone nearby to be able to eavesdrop on their conversation. Ronny was well aware news could spread like wildfire on the bush telegraph and he didn't want his dirty laundry aired on it. He could just imagine it:

Have you heard that the new bloke in town is a murderer – you know, the one who's taken over Sundown Farm?

Oh my God, you're kidding me! Lottie Sinclair's nephew really murdered someone?

He sure did, with his bare hands, and he's just spent eight years in prison because of it. Lottie was lying when she said he'd been working away on stations up in the Territory – the hide of her to not let the Bluegrass Bend locals know that a convicted criminal would be living among us.

Lottie Sinclair a liar? I never would have thought it.

And that's not even the most shocking thing.

Oh, really?

It was all because of that Tucker girl.

Ronny shuddered at the thought. That conversation was *never* going to take place, if he had anything to do with it. Lottie deserved to retain her reputation as a woman of her word – which she most certainly was; she'd only said what she had to protect him, and in return he had to protect her honour.

After listening intently to Ronny's take on the events over the past week, Larry sat back, silent, a contemplative frown creasing his face. Ronny dropped his gaze to Larry's seafood mornay pie, swimming in tomato sauce. He shuddered at the sight – he hated tomato sauce – and took a bite from his lamb and fennel sausage roll, not knowing what to make of Larry's loss for words – it was very unlike him.

Larry sighed and folded his arms, his pie remaining untouched and his forehead creasing even more as he leant forwards. His eyes almost closed as he squinted into the sunshine, evidently forgetting his sunglasses were perched atop his head. 'I wish I had a clear-cut answer for ya, Ronny, but I honestly don't know what to tell ya to do, and I don't know what our Lottie would say in this instance either.' He held his hands up, mimicking a pair of scales, weighing the situation up. 'Ya could just say ya don't have enough time to take the job on but then it'd look really bad of ya to take a job somewhere else, and believe me, the Tucker women will find out if ya do that almost before ya know it yourself. Or ya could take the job on and keep your head down but then there's always the risk that the more time Ivy spends with ya, the more likely it will be that something will trigger a memory and she's going to recall who ya are, or ya gonna cave in and tell her the truth – and I know ya want to avoid that more than anything … and fair enough too.' He threw his hands up in the air, huffing. 'So, what to do? Fuck only knows. There's only one thing we know for sure and that's you're between a rock and a bloody hard place.' He sat forwards again, pulling his sunglasses on as he did, and finally took a bite from his pie.

Ronny groaned as he nodded. 'Tell me about it. I really need the work and Ivy and her aunts seem like they'd be nice people to work for. It would only be for a couple of months, until the renovations are completed, so it's not like I'm taking on something where I'll be around Ivy forever.' He shrugged. 'And I don't want to piss Shirley off either, seeing as I asked her about work in the first place. It's going to make me seem like I'm a bullshit artist, and I really don't want the girls from the CWA thinking that of me, especially when they were like family to Lottie, not to mention the fact Shirley's your girlfriend.'

Larry shook a finger towards him and exhaled heavily. 'It's bloody difficult being in a small town, where everyone knows everyone's business – well, they like to think they do – and because of that everyone has strong opinions of what a person is like based on mostly hearsay. So if ya make yourself out to be someone you're not right off the bat, no matter what your reasoning, it's gonna be a bloody hard uphill battle to prove otherwise.' Larry took another mouthful of his pie. 'I reckon you're just going to have to bite the bullet and take the job on, otherwise you're probably going to draw more attention to yourself and get a shitty reputation. And believe me when I say that ya don't want to get on the wrong side of Shirley – she's a top sheila and I love her to bits, but boy oh boy, she's not one to take kindly to people who bullshit her, and she won't be backwards in letting ya know that either.'

Grinning at Larry's strained expression, Ronny felt a surprising flood of relief. Having someone he trusted with his life telling him to do what he'd been feeling in his gut the past few hours was just the shove he needed. 'I'll give Ivy a call tonight and let her know I'll do the job. That's if she still wants me to, after the way I was with her on the phone.'

Larry shoved the last of his pie into his mouth then wiped around his lips with a paper serviette. 'Ya know what, I reckon that conversation is best kept for when ya see her tomorrow. Ya only told her this morning that ya weren't really ready to take work on, it's a bit of a fast turnaround to call her back now and say otherwise. Just tell her ya slept on the idea and decided you'd like to help them out, and you're looking forward to doing a job ya love.'

'You know what, Larry, I reckon you're right.'

Larry gave him a toothy grin. 'I'm always right, although Shirley likes to tell me otherwise.'

'You should've learnt by now that the woman is always right.' Ronny laughed as he opened his can of Coke. 'Speaking of Shirley, how was your date night?'

Larry beamed from ear to ear. 'Oh, mate, it was bloody tops. The best damn date I've ever been on. That woman is one in a million, I tell ya. I'm one lucky bloke to have her in my life.'

Although genuinely pleased for Larry, Ronny couldn't help but feel a little envious of his mate's happy relationship. He wanted to find someone to spend time with too, maybe even find a one-in-a-million kind of love – though he knew that was not an easy feat. He ignored his own despondency and instead beamed broadly.

'That's what I like to hear. Did you end up getting that deep-fried ice cream you were on about?'

'Oh, I went one step further and pulled out all the stops.'

Ronny winced playfully. 'Do I need to know what that one step further was?'

'Oh come on, it was nothing like that, ya dirty bugger. I do have a bit of class.' Larry blew on his fingernails and then pretended to shine them on the Hawaiian shirt Shirley had given him. 'After dinner I took her to the movies and we snuggled up in the back row and ate choc-top ice creams, and I stole a few kisses from her too.'

'Like I said, you're an old romantic at heart.'

'Yeah, I gotta admit Shirl's brought that side outta me – I felt like I was seventeen again, but don't let anyone know, otherwise my hard-as-nails reputation will be completely ruined.' He gave Ronny a wink.

'After keeping my big dirty secret safe all these years, your closet romanticism is definitely safe with me, Smithy. I owe you one, mate.'

'And what big secret might that be, Mr Sinclair?' A woman's voice interrupted their conversation and as he held his breath, Ronny turned to see Amy Mayberry's breasts trying to escape from her top, her chest at his eye level as she leant on his chair.

Shit, how much of their conversation had she heard? His heart took off at a gallop as he looked up into Amy's wide eyes. 'Hi, Amy … um, well.' He felt like he was speaking through cotton wool, his mouth had gone so dry from panic.

Larry saved him. 'Now if he told ya his big secret then it wouldn't be one, would it?' He grinned teasingly at Amy as he spooned four sugars into his cup. 'And on top of that is the important fact that he'd have to kill ya if he told ya.'

'Oh my God, that makes me need to know even more!' Amy smiled seductively as she put her butt on the armrest of Ronny's chair and then slid her arm around his shoulder, her denim skirt riding so far up her thighs barely anything was left to the imagination. Ronny had a strong urge to pull the fabric back down to give the woman some dignity. 'Oh, come on now, boys, I love secrets and they're certainly safe with me.' She ran her fingers across her chest in the shape of an X. 'Cross my heart and hope to die, and all that.'

Ronny doubted Amy could keep anything secret so he tried a diversionary tactic, desperate to get the focus off what she'd heard. 'So, Amy, you should pop in for a cuppa sometime, seeing we're neighbours now.'

It seemed to work as Amy gave him a smile that would turn most blokes to mush. 'Ooh, I'd love to, Ronny … thanks for the invite. I might take you up on it this weekend if you're going to be around.'

'Oh, shit, I'm over at Ivy's this weekend, fulfilling my duty as her slave, so maybe take a raincheck and you can call over the following weekend, or something.' He shrugged. 'Whenever suits you really. I'm pretty much always there.'

'Other than this weekend, that is.' A sour look fleetingly crossed Amy's petite features before she recovered and gave him a dazzling smile. 'But that will be lovely for you, I suppose, going to slave for Ivy … in a boring kinda way. She will certainly have plenty of handyman jobs for you seeing as she can't find a man who will love her enough to do it for her.' She laughed cruelly. 'I kinda feel sorry for you having to slave for her an entire weekend. I couldn't think of anything worse.' She sighed then shrugged. 'But a man's gotta do what a man's gotta do, hey.'

Ronny bit his tongue, annoyed with Amy for speaking about Ivy that way. Ivy Tucker was the most loveable woman he'd ever met. But he shrugged his shoulders nonchalantly. 'I signed up for the gig, so I suppose so.' He wiped the last of his sausage roll from his fingers. 'And to be honest, I'm actually looking forward to checking the place out. Healing Hills sounds like heaven on earth to a horse lover like me, and I really like Ivy and her aunts.'

'But you barely know them.'

'I like to think I'm a pretty good judge of character.'

'Fair enough, different strokes for different folks, I suppose.' Amy ruffled his short hair, completely oblivious to his change of mood. 'I'll take a raincheck, handsome, and call over when I get a night off.'

Ronny fought to stay friendly, Amy's blatant dislike of Ivy getting deep beneath his skin. He'd cottoned on to the fact there was bad blood between the two at the fundraiser, but he didn't go for bitchiness, and Amy was being a bitch. He was having a hard time stopping himself from telling her so.

'Okay, Amy, sounds good. Whenever suits you.' His voice was expressionless. He regretted asking her over but he couldn't go back on his invitation now. He mentally slapped himself as he tried to at least remain pleasant; she and her parents were his neighbours and he didn't want any bad blood with them from being nasty to Amy.

Thankfully, Amy seemed completely unaware of his true feelings. She gave him a wink. 'I'll hold you to that invitation, Mr Sinclair.'

A slightly uncomfortable silence fell and Amy graced Ronny with a come-get-me smile.

'So, come on then, are you going to tell me what this big secret is?'

Ronny groaned inwardly. His tactic hadn't worked at all. 'Oh all right then, you've twisted my arm, I'll let you in on the secret, but as long as you promise to keep those lips of yours sealed.'

Larry kicked Ronny's shin under the table and Ronny fought not to shout in pain. He threw Larry a sideways glance. Larry gave him a stern but discreet look and then avoided Amy's gaze by pretending to be completely captivated by the froth on his cappuccino.

Amy clapped her hands together as she wriggled off the armrest and planted her butt on Ronny's lap. 'Well, come on then, tell me, tell me – I'm dying here.'

Ronny whispered into Amy's ear so Larry couldn't hear him.

Amy's mouth dropped to the floor and her hand flew to her chest. 'Oh my God, really?'

Ronny nodded, his face serious. 'Yup, no word of a lie.'

Amy shook her head in absolute disbelief. 'Well, fuck me dead; I never would have guessed it. And trust me when I say this, it makes you a whole lot sexier in my eyes, because you're more of a challenge.'

'Really?' Ronny sat back in his chair. 'Well, there you bloody well go.'

Amy's phone chimed in her bag and she plunged her hand into it in her haste to answer. 'Hello. Yes, okay, no problems. Oh shit, really? What an absolute arsehole. Men, hey? Can't live with them, can't live without them.' She paused for a moment, shaking her head as if in total disbelief. 'Oh honey-bunny, that sucks, big time. I'll be there in five and we can go get ourselves some retail therapy.'

She tossed the phone back in her bag. 'Gotta run, girly problems.' She leapt off Ronny's lap and, just like the first time they'd met, landed a kiss fair on his lips. 'Catch you at your place sometime soon you handsome man.'

Ronny ached to wipe his lips. 'Okey dokey.'

Larry and Ronny watched her dash off down the footpath, the atmosphere between them heavy.

As soon as she was safely out of hearing range, Larry smacked his palm down on the table. 'What the fuck did ya just do, Ronny? I mean, I know it's your life and all, but really? Amy Mayberry, of all people? We've spent years keeping your past –'

Ronny held up his hands. 'Hold your horses, Larry. As if I'd tell her about that.' He had never seen Larry so burred up. He had to put him out of his misery to stop the bloke from busting an artery. 'I told her I'm a virgin.'

Larry's anxiety melted away as he burst into uncontrollable laughter. He kept trying to speak but found it impossible because he was hooting so hard.

Ronny laughed with him. Once half composed again, he said, 'Am I forgiven now, Lazza?'

Larry finally took a breath, his eyes wet with mirthful tears. 'My bloody oath ya are, but I'm warning ya – the whole town is now going to think you're a virgin.'

Ronny shrugged. 'Don't care really, it's better than them knowing the truth.'

'Fair point,' Larry said before sculling the last of his cappuccino. 'Anyhow, times a-ticking so we better get cracking if we want to get the horses shod and the weeds cleaned out of the dam before sundown.'

***

Stepping from the hardware store, her arms ladened with bags filled with decking oil and every nail and screw imaginable, Ivy froze as she caught sight of Amy and Ronny canoodling like lovers on a chair out the front of the bakery. A cry stuck in the back of her throat and envy engulfed her as she watched Ronny lean in and whisper something in Amy's ear, then Amy's face lit up like it was the most amazing thing she'd ever heard – the drama queen. Ivy felt her heart wrench. Larry sat at the table too, and seemed a little embarrassed by Ronny and Amy's open show of affection, and she couldn't blame him.

Not wanting to be spotted, she tiptoed to the side of the footpath and stood behind a manicured shrub just tall enough to conceal her, wincing as one of the twigs grazed her arm. She ignored the droplets of blood, unable to take her eyes from the pair. They looked so damn happy it infuriated her – life just wasn't playing fair. And obviously her initial thoughts had been correct – the two *were* together. The real reason Ronny hadn't called yesterday was right there in front of her – Amy I'll-get-whatever-bloke-I-want Mayberry. Ivy's heart sank as she imagined the two of them ravishing each other in every position possible, before the realisation that Ronny was the same as every other bloke she'd ever come across overwhelmed her. How could her instincts have been so wrong about him? He'd seemed so different. If she were to be completely honest, she'd held a glimmer of hope that the hot new bloke in town might be a true gentleman, a guy who wanted something more than a fling, *her* knight in shining armour, seeing as the rest of the blokes in Bluegrass Bend were either already taken, players, commitment phobic or – as she'd very recently learnt – gay.

After watching as Amy planted a kiss firmly on Ronny's lips and strutted away, Ivy returned to her ute. She'd planned on grabbing one of the bakery's pies for lunch, but there was no way in hell she was going over there now. Like wet fingers upon a candle flame, any fantasies she'd harboured about Ronny Sinclair – and there had been plenty of them since she'd first laid eyes upon him at the bank – had been extinguished by what she'd just witnessed. As much as she hated to admit it, she was attracted to the bloke, and she felt, somewhere deep inside, like she'd already known him for a lifetime, as though they were somehow already connected. It was a foreign feeling, but she liked it, a lot. As much as she wanted to deny it to herself, she was excited to see if things might eventually develop between them. And now he'd gone and ruined it for her. Forever.

She shook her head, disappointed in herself. She clearly wasn't thinking straight, lusting after a man she knew nothing about. This connection she'd been feeling with him was just her imagination playing tricks on her. *Desperation to be in love*, she thought. The same as it had been with Malcolm. Damn her emotions and her romantic fantasies – she should have learnt by now they never came to fruition. Part of her wanted to storm over there and tell Ronny he was being a dickhead, giving his heart to a woman like Amy, but another part of her, a very big part, knew it was none of her business what Ronny Sinclair did – or what Amy Mayberry did, for that matter. They were both adults, and if they wanted each other, then so be it. Maybe it was a blessing he wouldn't be taking the renovation job on.

Revving her ute to life, she pulled out into a gap in the traffic, keeping her eyes straight ahead as she drove past the bakery and towards Healing Hills.

CHAPTER 12

Brilliant hues of orange and red poured out over the horizon like a pot of spilled molten lava. The spectacular sunrise danced on Ronny's windscreen, making it difficult for him to see the road. He leant forwards in his seat, adjusting his hat and then his sunglasses. After the kangaroo episode the other day, he was being extra cautious to not run into one.

The azure sky overhead showed no sign of rain, and he was glad – it would make his day a whole lot easier. He'd made sure to pack all the essential tools to get a renovation job on the roll – his cordless drill, pry bars, circular saw, electric planer and mitre saw, as well as his well-stocked toolbox. Thank God for Lottie keeping all his tools of the trade safely stored wrapped in sheets; everything was still in perfect working condition albeit a little outdated. But he didn't care how old his stuff was, as long as something worked he didn't believe in replacing it to get the new you-beaut model. He was a firm believer in being thankful for what you had, especially after experiencing what it was like to have nothing but the basics in prison.

Thinking Healing Hills might be a nice place to sit and strum some tunes on his lunch break, he'd brought his guitar, which was now sitting beside him on the front seat, strapped in safely with the seatbelt. He hadn't really had much of a chance to play since arriving at Sundown Farm, other than a few times while watching the sunset on the back verandah, and he hoped Ivy wouldn't mind the fact he'd brought it along. Although why should she, being the amazing musician she was? He hoped she'd agree to play some tunes with him; perhaps it would ease the tension between them, not to mention his own nerves.

He drove without haste down Bluegrass Bend's main street, appreciating that they had all they needed for day-to-day living. With its narrow streets, cosy cottages, independently owned shops, and beautifully manicured gardens, the town really was the epitome of chocolate-box charm. He loved it here.

He waved to the few people already out and about on the footpaths – some getting their morning papers from the newsagency or grabbing brekkie from the bakery, but the majority were out for their daily walks with beloved pooches. Not that he knew any of them by name – and only a handful of them by face. The calm pace of the lifestyle here made him forever grateful he called this wonderful place home – he wouldn't want to live anywhere else.

Pulling into one of the many empty parking spaces, Ronny grabbed his wallet from the dash and made a beeline for the bakery. It might be nice to break the ice by turning up with a peace offering for brekkie. He didn't know if Ivy drank coffee, but he was going to get a vanilla latte for himself and take a punt by getting her one too, along with a couple of the bakery's cherry danishes.

Ten minutes later he was headed out of town and towards Healing Hills, the landscape a collage of apple, cherry, blueberry, peach and chestnut farms, open fields with horses, sheep and cattle, rolling hills that dropped into rocky mountainsides and blissful nothingness. His mouth watered as the scent of the danishes made him think of biting into them, but he wanted to wait and eat with Ivy, although he was going to make a start on his coffee. Humming Gary Allan's 'It Ain't the Whiskey', Ronny flicked down the sun visor and then turned the song up as he hit the hundred zone and accelerated. A buzz of excitement washed over him. Although he wasn't getting paid for the next couple of days, it felt good to be going to work as a carpenter for the very first time in almost nine years – even if it meant he was going to be near a woman who made his heart go like the clappers. He held high hopes he was going to be able to handle the effect Ivy had on him. Self-control was a quality he'd learnt to master in prison thanks to meditation, and he was hoping he'd also be able to master it in Ivy's company, too, because there was no way they'd ever have a future together, no matter how much he craved it. The only way they could ever be together would be if he told her who he actually was, and that was never going to happen. He doubted the feelings he had for her would be reciprocated anyway – Ivy didn't seem the least bit interested in him. And besides, he truly believed she deserved someone better than him, a man with a squeaky-clean past and a bright future, a man who didn't have to hide things from her.

Glancing at his mobile phone in the holder on the dash, he marvelled at the Google map showing him the exact course to take to get to Ivy's place. He had a fair idea of where it was, but he wanted to be there on time and didn't want to risk taking a wrong turn and pissing Ivy off any further by being late – he'd already done enough by knocking back the offer of work in the first place.

The map told him he'd be on her doorstep in less than ten minutes, and the knowledge made his stomach tighten in more ways than one. How was she going to be around him? How was he going to be around her? Was she going to let him take the job on, or would she tell him to bugger off? He wouldn't blame her if she did.

He started as the phone rang – Ivy. Talk about ESP. He smiled broadly at the sight of her name then answered.

'Good morning, Miss Tucker.'

'Hey, Ronny, just wanted to make sure you're still okay for today and to give you a heads up on how to get to the cottage.'

Ivy sounded very … businesslike, and there was a trace of sadness in her voice. He wished he could reach through the phone and hug it out of her, but then again he wouldn't be able to do that in person either.

'Yup, sure am, I'm actually not too far from your place now.'

'Far out, you're keen then – it's only six thirty.'

'Yeah, wanted to make a good first impression and all that.' Ronny chuckled but Ivy didn't join him.

'Righto, well, I'm heading over to the cottage now to make a start on oiling the back deck. You could usually come along the main drag to get to it but there's some council workers doing a drain out the front of the cottage today and the road's blocked off, so it would be easier for you to cut through Healing Hills.' She sucked in a breath as though in a rush. 'So when you pull into the driveway just head on past the homestead and shortly after there'll be a sharp right turn past the stables, take that one and after a kilometre or so it'll lead you up to the cottage. Oh, and I have a dog that's not overly keen on men, so don't get out of the car until I come out and introduce the pair of you.'

'Will do, Ivy, see you soon.'

'Yup.'

And she was gone, in more ways than one. Part of him wanted the Ivy who had embraced him the night of the fundraiser back. But then again, maybe treating their relationship as purely business was the best way – it meant there was way less chance of giving in to temptation. And boy oh boy, she was a huge temptation.

With the map announcing he'd reached his destination, he slowed the Kingswood to a stop and peered out his window. A metal business sign hung from rustic timber posts, stating he'd most certainly arrived at Healing Hills. Turning down the long gravel drive and crossing a cattle grid, the Kingwood rattled as he drove through a wrought iron gate that looked as if it had been forged a century ago, and probably had. He felt as though he'd just driven through the gates of heaven. He brought the old girl to a halt once more, wanting a few moments to absorb the beauty of Healing Hills. The sight before him stole every last bit of oxygen from his lungs, the lush green landscape disappearing into a horizon thick with fog. The mountains lay in a great line like the spine of the land, dominating the panorama in the most evocative of ways. Up on a rise the silhouettes of horses were just visible. Ronny's heart swelled at the sight of them. They were such exquisite creatures. Healing Hills was Mother Nature at her glorious best. Just like Sundown Farm. He drove slowly so he could soak up the surrounds properly. The green blanket of grass all around him made him consider ditching the car and running across it barefoot – maybe not a good look for his potential employers though – they'd think he'd lost his mind. Driving onto Ivy's property seemed so unreal – he would never have believed it if someone had predicted this day.

The glimmer of the homestead's roof came into view and shortly after the building itself. Yet again Ronny was impressed – the place was the epitome of what a country homestead should be: majestic yet rustic, grand yet inviting. He could just imagine sitting on the wrap-around verandahs and strumming his guitar while admiring the view that seemed to go on into infinity. Ivy was so very blessed to call this her home. Someone exited the homestead's front door and gave him a wave and he squinted into the sunshine to try to make out who it was.

He pulled up out the front and leant on his windowsill, tipping his hat in greeting. 'Morning, Alice, top day for it.'

'It sure is, Ronny. Mother Nature's being kind to us today.'

Alice walked towards him, her fluffy hot-pink robe and matching slippers making Ronny smile. She was certainly the kind of person who glowed from the inside and warmed all around her. She reminded him of Lottie and the likeness somehow made him feel closer to Alice. Ronny switched off the engine as Alice opened the gate that led down the garden path.

'Would you like a cuppa before you start, love?'

'Thanks for the offer, Alice, but I grabbed one from the bakery on the way and I don't want to go irritating the boss by turning up late. I might find myself fired before I've even started.' He chuckled, even though he believed every word he'd just said.

Alice stood by the car and waved a hand through the air. 'Oh, don't worry about Ivy, love, her bark is worse than her bite.' She sighed, her smile fading. 'And about that … I wanted to have a quick word with you before you head over to the cottage. Can you spare a minute?'

Ronny took his sunglasses off, wanting to meet Alice's apprehensive gaze properly. Anxiousness pummelled his stomach. Did Alice know something she shouldn't? 'Sure, I can spare five minutes, if you need them. I don't have to be there until seven.' He fought to keep his voice even.

'Goodo.' Alice eyed him thoughtfully. 'I wouldn't normally bombard someone I'd just met with our dramas, but I feel this situation calls for it and I like to be upfront with people. You see, we're in a really dire situation with the renovations on the cottage. If we don't get them done soon, so the cottage can be sold, there's a big chance we could lose all of this.' She gestured to the sweeping countryside while blinking back tears. 'And none of us could bear it. This place means everything to us. Nowhere else would ever feel like home.'

Ronny felt as though a red-hot coal had been placed against his chest and sorrow stole his smile. 'Oh, Alice, I'm so sorry. I didn't know.'

Alice patted his arm kindly. 'I know. And I understand Ivy's a bit annoyed because Shirley said you were looking for work and then you told Ivy you weren't.' She eyed him inquisitively. 'Is there a particular reason you wouldn't want to take the job here? And please don't be afraid to tell me what it is, because I won't judge you.'

Ronny felt like crawling under a rock. Fuck it – he didn't want to lie to Alice, of all people, but there was no way he could speak the truth. Thank God he'd already decided to take the job, because he wouldn't be able to live with the guilt of leaving May, Alice and Ivy in the lurch now. He could understand how much Healing Hills meant to them, and he wanted to do everything he could to help. He cleared his throat, willing himself to sound convincing.

'No, not at all, actually, I've reorganised a few things at Sundown Farm so I can take the job on now – that's if you still want me to.'

'Oh my goodness! Thank you, Ronny.' Alice almost leapt through the window as she reached in and gave him a kiss on the cheek.

Moved by her gesture, Ronny took a few seconds to respond. 'I'm glad I can help in some way. I'm so sorry to muck you about the way I have. I didn't mean to cause any unnecessary stress.'

Alice nodded as she sniffled. She wiped at the tears that had escaped down her cheek, smiling through them. 'No need for apologies, Ronny, you're here now and happy to take the job on and that's all that matters.'

Ronny wanted to get out of the Kingswood and give Alice a hug, but he didn't feel a hundred per cent comfortable doing so. 'I sure am, and I'll be here as much as you need me to be.'

'Thank you.' She pulled a tissue from the pocket of her robe and blew her nose. 'There is the subject of wages to discuss, and I'm a bit worried you won't like what we can afford, but I'll leave that conversation for you and Ivy to have.' She chuckled. 'I think I've said enough.'

Ronny already knew he'd take whatever they could afford. There was no way in hell he was going to abandon them in their time of need. 'It will be fine, Alice.'

She held his gaze. 'Geez, I hope so. You truly are one of the good ones; I knew it the minute I laid eyes on you.' She folded her hands and placed them against her chin. 'And you know what else? I've been praying for a miracle to help us through this hard time, and I'm thinking you might be it.'

Ronny laughed uneasily. *If only you knew the truth, maybe you might think otherwise.* 'I'm not sure about being a miracle, but I'll sure do my best to do everything I can to help you lovely ladies out.'

'And humble too.' Alice smiled fondly. 'Just a word of warning – Ivy's not in the best frame of mind at the moment, the poor darling has had a lot to deal with of late, so if she seems a bit tetchy, please just take it with a grain of salt, won't you?'

Ronny offered Alice an understanding smile. 'Don't worry, I will.'

Alice looked at her watch. 'Anyway, I better let you go. It's two minutes to seven.' She patted the car. 'And nice wheels by the way, Ivy's going to be very impressed.'

'Really?'

'Yes, Ivy's a classic car lover from way back. She's got a 1964 EH Holden, her pride and joy. It used to be mine.' Alice chuckled. 'She was absolutely mortified when I went to trade it in for my new car, so I decided to give it to her for her twenty-first instead.'

A woman after his own heart – how many exciting layers did Ivy Tucker have? 'Well, I look forward to seeing her pride and joy. I've always loved the old classics myself.'

'Excellent, something you'll both have in common then.'

Ronny tapped his guitar case beside him. 'I think we have a few things in common …'

Alice dropped her head and peered into the car, her eyes widening as she did. She took a step back, one hand fluttering to her chest. 'Oh, a guitar … you play, do you, Ronny?'

Ronny was confused by Alice's reaction – it was almost as if he'd brought along a loaded gun. 'I sure do, have since I was an ankle-biter. Is it okay I've brought it along?'

Alice coughed gently before smiling. 'Of course it is, with me, but it might be a different story with Ivy. You'll have to check in with her on that one, though.'

'I don't want to upset the apple cart any more than I already have. Can you tell me why?'

Alice shook her head. 'You haven't really got time for me to explain it all to you now, and it's not really my place to do so.' She tipped her head to the side, her eyebrows furrowing. 'Can I ask, though, how do you know Ivy plays the guitar, because she hasn't touched it for almost ten years?'

Fuck. Ten years? That coincided with that horrible night. Ronny's heart squeezed tight and his brain went into overdrive as he did his best to try to cover the huge mistake he'd just made – his first slip-up, but hopefully his only one. He rolled his eyes skywards, feigning thought, even though it was a ploy to get his gaze as far away from Alice's questioning one as he could. 'Oh, I'm not sure, but I think Lottie might have mentioned it to me.'

'Oh, I see. I didn't know Lottie very well so it's strange she mentioned such a thing … but there you go.' Alice did her best to smile, but Ronny could almost hear her mind whirring.

He shrugged his shoulders like it wasn't a big deal. 'Anyway, I'd better get going because now it's a minute past seven and I'm officially late – catch you later on maybe.' He gave his best charming grin, as he revved the car to life and drove off, not waiting for her goodbye. He looked in his rear-vision mirror just as Alice waved and he stuck his hand out the window to return the gesture, mentally slapping himself for being so damn stupid. He'd just proven how easily he could slip up, and he was going to have to do his very best not to do it again – that had been way too close. From the look on Alice's face, a seed of doubt had been planted and the last thing he wanted was for that seed to grow.

CHAPTER 13

The crunch of tyres out the front of the cottage, as well as Bo's energetic bolt around to the front and then his incessant barking, alerted Ivy to Ronny's arrival. Putting her paintbrush into the tray of decking oil, she glanced at her watch. He was pretty much on the dot too. After talking to him on the phone earlier she'd been expecting him about ten minutes ago, but clearly he'd been sidetracked somewhere along the way. Her do-good aunts instantly came to mind. She hoped to God neither of them had already been in Ronny's ear about him taking the job, because she didn't want him changing his mind out of pity. She was no charity case. Nevertheless, he'd certainly scored a brownie point by being on time. Not that she was going to tell him that after he'd let her down four times – okay, twice he'd done so unwittingly – in the past week.

Mumbling to herself, she went to make her way out to greet him but discovered she'd painted herself into a corner against the timber railing of the verandah – she'd failed to think ahead, the classic mistake of a deck-oiling amateur. Thinking quickly, before Ronny decided to get out of the car giving Bo the opportunity to possibly take a chunk out of him, she climbed over the railing and jumped the two metres into the garden without a second thought.

Bad move. Where she'd expected garden mulch to be was actually the concealed concrete septic system she'd forgotten all about. Her left foot twisted at an awkward angle and an excruciating pain shot through her ankle. Everything blurred as she screamed and crumpled to the ground. The pain merciless, her eyes filled with tears and her head spun, and for a moment she thought she was going to either heave her breakfast up or pass out.

After a few deep breaths she was calmer, although the pain was only getting worse. Accustomed to what a sprained ankle looked and felt like after falling down the steps of the attic a few years back, she knew what she'd done, and also knew roughly how long it was going to take her to heal. This was the last thing she needed. Feeling completely defeated, she stared down at the offending ankle, already swollen and beginning to bruise, as heavy tears rolled down her cheeks.

'Why do I have to be such a damn klutz all the time?' she wailed between sobs. She reached out and gently touched her ankle with a clammy hand, wincing as soon as her fingers met with the swelling. The bruising appeared to be getting worse before her eyes. She needed to get ice on it, and the sooner the better. Then she remembered Ronny was still out the front, and hang on – she strained her ears – Bo wasn't barking anymore. Oh hell, what had happened? Feeling a complete and utter fool, she tried to pull herself up to standing by yanking on the shrub beside her. She was halfway up when the branch snapped and she thumped back down to the ground again, only this time it was firmly on her butt. Part of her wanted to laugh. Could her situation get any worse?

After a few seconds of wishing she could start her day over again, she sat up slowly, cursing as she tried to remove leaves, twigs and bits of mulch from her hair.

'Shit, Ivy, are you okay?'

Ronny's hands were reaching out to her. For a split second she worried about how dreadful she must look, then the sensation of his skin against hers sent a shot of something through her, like she'd just downed a tequila slammer – and she liked it. A lot. And a lot was way too much.

Bo skidded in alongside her seconds later, sneaking a lick to her cheek. A smile tugged at her quivering lips as she wiped his slobber away with her hand, but it was quickly swept away by the pain of her ankle.

'Um …' At a complete loss for words, Ivy's eyes met with Ronny's concerned amber gaze, now only inches from her, and for a few blissful seconds she felt as though she were going to fall into that beautiful sea of gold. Blinking then focusing on the whole manly package, her stomach somersaulted and then back-flipped for good measure. The sight of Ronny in his jeans and singlet, wide-brimmed hat shading his face and the look of concern was almost too much to cope with right now. And if that wasn't enough to send a girl into la-la land, his burly arms flexed in all the right places making the tattoos upon them dance as he held her hands. Damn it all, why did she have to be so attracted to him? She noticed a small scar above his lip and had the urge to gently place her fingertips upon it before kissing him – so much for keeping her feelings businesslike.

'Earth to Ivy …' Ronny's voice was gentle as he lightly squeezed her fingers.

She looked into his eyes, still finding herself speechless. Curse the man for having this effect on her when she didn't want him to, and especially at a time like this. She felt her cheeks flame – Ronny's drool-worthy yumminess had taken her attention off her throbbing ankle for a few short moments, but now the initial shock of him being here in the flesh was over, the pain was returning in full force.

'Oh, Ronny, sorry, I'm a bit dazed from the fall.' She glanced down at the black-and-blue monstrosity that used to be part of her foot. 'I think I've sprained my ankle. No, actually, wipe that – I'm positive I've sprained my ankle.'

Ronny moved in closer to her, the sensation of his body pressing against hers as his arm went around her waist sending that damn jolt through her once again. 'Here, let me help you up.' He scanned her ankle before lifting her, grimacing at the same time. 'Jesus, you've done a damn good job of it. We're going to have to get some ice on that bugger soon as.'

Ivy put her arm around his shoulder, noticing how broad and strong it felt and also how scrumptious the hint of his spicy aftershave was – the scent of it making her feel as though she'd somehow arrived home. She tried to mentally shake the sensation away, at the same time feeling as though something was scratching at her soul. It was a ridiculously crazy feeling – the pain must be rendering her senseless. She allowed him to take her weight as she attempted to stand on her good foot, still trying to make sense of what she was experiencing. She knocked her swollen ankle against an over-excited Bo and a pain shot through her, making her cry out and collapse into Ronny's arms. She blinked back fresh tears. Bo whined beside them as he peered up at Ivy.

'It's okay, buddy, it's not your fault,' Ronny said kindly as he gave Bo a quick pat on the head.

The gesture melted Ivy's heart. She learnt so much about a person from the way they were with animals, and Ronny was being an absolute sweetheart to her beloved pooch, and with her for that matter. Just as the thought passed through her mind Ronny took her entire weight and effortlessly picked her up. She put her arms around his shoulders and melted into him. The comfort she felt doing so freaked her out a little. Why did she feel so at peace with him when she barely knew him? She'd never felt like this with anybody before. Ever. Especially a man.

Hugging her close to him, Ronny stepped out of the garden with Bo padding beside him. Ivy was taken aback by how relaxed the dog was with his newfound friend. She'd never seen him trust a male so quickly, especially when the man was placing his hands on her; Bo would usually be baring his teeth by now, ready to defend her with his life, so clearly her pooch felt as at ease with Ronny as she did. Ivy felt so good in his arms. It was a bizarre, familiar feeling of being safe and she didn't know what to make of it – like everything else about this moment. Maybe she was correct in thinking the pain was sending her a little loopy.

Walking around the side of the house, Ronny made for the front steps. 'I'll get you inside and organise some ice, and then I think we should take you to the hospital.'

'Oh, please, no doctors, there's no need,' she groaned, and shook her head. She'd had more than her fair share of visits to the Bluegrass Bend emergency ward, and she didn't feel like having to do it again today, especially not with Ronny as her chaperone. How embarrassing. She was meant to be keeping a professional distance from this guy, and acting like a boss should, and here she was, a typical damsel in distress.

'By the looks of that ankle, I reckon there's a huge need. And I'm not taking no for an answer. I wouldn't be able to forgive myself if you've broken something and I don't take you to get checked out.' Ronny gave her a don't-argue-with-me look and if she hadn't been in so much pain, Ivy would have burst out laughing at his poor attempt to be serious with her.

'Okay, then,' she said lightheartedly. 'If you insist.'

'I definitely insist,' Ronny said as he carried her through the front door, and then stopped, glancing around the empty room. 'I was hoping to have a couch or something to put you down on, but looks like you're stuck in my arms for the minute. And I'm gathering from the lack of furniture in here there's no fridge either?'

Ivy felt a little giddy, whether from being in so much pain, or being in the most hunky, best-smelling man's arms, she wasn't sure. She hoped it was the former, because otherwise she was heading into very dangerous waters. For one, Ronny was taken, and secondly, she didn't want to fall for the likes of a man who could fall for a woman like Amy Mayberry. And thirdly, while she was at it, men were supposed to suck, and couldn't be trusted, and Ronny Sinclair was as manly as you could get.

'You'd be right in guessing there's no fridge.'

'Okay, so where are we going to get ice from?'

'The homestead – I can ring my aunts and get them to bring some over.'

'No need, by the time they do that, I could have you back there. And you need something comfortable to lie on while you've got some ice on that ankle too.'

You look pretty comfortable to lie on … Ivy couldn't believe she'd just considered that. If she were on her own she would have slapped her forehead to try to rid herself of the unwelcome dirty thought. But far out, how could any woman control herself around this gorgeous hunk?

Ronny turned and walked back outside to the Kingswood. Balancing Ivy, he wrangled the passenger door open and skilfully manoeuvred his guitar onto the back seat, being extra careful not to bang it, or Ivy, in the process.

'You play the guitar?' Ivy's voice was waiflike.

'I sure do, and I sing too.' He chuckled to himself as he placed Ivy gently on the front seat, his laughter making her heart quiver. 'Well, it's probably more like I *try* to sing. Music is one of my biggest passions in life, aside from horses and meditation.'

'It used to be one of mine too,' she said softly. Her pulse quickened as tears stung her eyes but she fought them back, along with the painful memories of that night, wishing she could just dump them where they belonged – in a garbage bin. If only it were that easy. Regardless of what was going on inside her heart and soul, she wasn't going to allow the sight of a guitar to evoke that horrific night, especially around Ronny. He didn't need to know about her awful past.

Ronny shut the passenger door and then leant on the windowsill. 'Why isn't it anymore?'

'Why isn't what?' she replied distantly.

'Why isn't music your passion anymore?'

Ivy snapped to attention, dragging her thoughts back from that night. 'Oh, it's a long story, and one I'm tired of reliving. Let's just say my musical talents are a thing of the past, and leave it at that, okay?'

'Okay.' Ronny looked miserable as he motioned to the back seat. 'I'm really sorry I've upset you by bringing it along. I won't bring it again. Promise.'

Ivy instantly felt bad. Who was she to quell his burning desire for music? She waved her hands through the air as if warding off a swarm of mosquitos. 'No, don't you dare leave it at home. You play it whenever you like … it'll be nice to hear some acoustic tunes around here again.' She hoped she didn't live to regret what she'd just said, but she wasn't going to be a total bitch and tell him to leave his passion for music at the gate.

Ronny's face lit up. 'Are you sure?'

'Totally, and speaking of common interests –' Ivy gently tapped the side of the Kingswood, '– this is a very impressive ride, Mr Sinclair.' She pretended to be prim and proper as she said it, but her attempt was pathetic. If she weren't in so much pain she would have laughed out loud at herself.

Ronny ran around the other side of the car and jumped in, a lone dimple dancing on his left cheek as he smiled at her. 'Why thank you, Miss Tucker, I must say I do love it.' He mimicked her poshness, his mischievous grin making Ivy smile for the briefest of moments before she began to squirm in her seat. Her ankle was throbbing like a jackhammer was inside of it.

Ronny revved the car to life. He placed his hand on her thigh for the briefest of seconds, leaving the skin beneath her jeans scorched from his touch. 'Are you all right?' he said, worry stealing his smile. 'You look really pale.'

'Yeah, I think I just need some painkillers, that's all.' She smiled nervously, the desire she had to lean over and kiss his very devourable lips completely unacceptable for so many reasons. She tried to shift her focus, noticing her voice was a little shaky. 'I adore classic cars. I've got one myself.'

Ronny turned the car around and headed back to the homestead, being careful of Bo running along beside them. 'Yeah, your aunt Alice said you had an old EH Holden. Can't wait to check it out, I love the old classics.'

Ivy's eyebrows shot up. 'Oh, did she now?' She folded her arms. 'And when did she tell you this?'

Ronny remained casual. 'This morning, when she stopped me to offer me a cuppa.' He pointed to the styrofoam cup in the cardboard drink holder between them, as well as the brown paper bags. 'But I'd already brought brekkie along – for both of us.'

A warm rush set Ivy's heart ablaze. Who was this man and where had he come from? And why couldn't she have gotten to him before Amy had? This totally sucked. Damn the universe for playing with her like this. Just when she'd sworn off men for a while here comes Ronny Sinclair into her life – so perfect, yet so unattainable. She groaned inwardly, reminding herself that any man she allowed to see her vulnerable side eventually broke her heart. They just weren't worth it. Any of them. No matter how sexy or charming or kind they were. And that most certainly included Ronny.

Ronny's voice grabbed her from her thoughts. 'Your coffee will be a bit cold now, but hopefully the danish will still be tasty.'

Ivy grabbed one of the bags and peeked inside. 'Oh my God, cherry and custard danishes are my favourite.' She closed it back up. 'As much as I hate to say it, though, I reckon I'd throw up if I ate right now with the pain I'm in, but I'll deffo eat it later.' She reached over and gave his arm a squeeze. 'Thanks, Ronny, that was very thoughtful of you.'

'No worries at all, just trying to impress the boss, and I even got you a vanilla latte.' He glanced towards her and wriggled his eyebrows. 'Have my tactics to impress worked?'

'Seeing as vanilla lattes are also one of my favourites, yes, they have.' Ivy gave him a cheeky smile. 'But don't go getting too cocky now.'

The homestead came into view and Ivy breathed a sigh of relief. She needed some ice, and some codeine, desperately. 'What else did Aunt Alice talk to you about?' She tried to sound nonchalant even though she was dying to know the details of their conversation.

'She wanted to have a word with me about not taking the renovation job, but the thing is …' Ronny turned to face Ivy, keeping one eye on the earthen track ahead as he did so. 'I wanted to tell you in person this morning that I would love to take the job – that is, if you'll still have me of course.'

Ivy eyed him cautiously, one brow quirked. 'Why the sudden change of heart?' She hoped to God it wasn't because of Alice, because she didn't want Ronny taking the job out of pity. She held her breath as she waited for his reply.

'I just thought about it a little more and it seemed like a win for all of us.' He shrugged. 'I need some extra cash to help with the bills at Sundown Farm and I know you ladies really need a qualified carpenter to do the job.'

'Okay then, good answer.' Unable to look Ronny in the eye, she looked down at her ankle, frowning at the ghastly sight of it. 'There is the small matter of the wages we need to discuss, though.'

Arriving at the homestead Ronny switched the motor off and turned in his seat. 'Yup, shoot.'

'We can only afford a weekly wage, not the usual hundred bucks an hour you carpenters normally charge.'

Ronny rubbed his chin, eyeing Ivy thoughtfully. 'Okay, so what are we talking here?'

Ivy fought to raise her eyes to his, ready for him to knock the job back once again. 'Say, seven hundred bucks a week, for five days a week … and I'll even throw in morning smoko every day.'

'Wow, smoko every day.' Ronny smiled as he held out his hand. 'I'd be crazy to knock that back. It's a deal.'

Ivy's mouth dropped open as she stared at him in shock, her lashes heavy with unshed tears.

'I'm hoping that's a happy reaction?' Ronny said carefully.

Ivy nodded as she reached out and pulled him into a hug. 'Yes, yes, it is. Thank you, Ronny. I honestly didn't know what we were going to do if you didn't say yes.'

'Well, thank *you* for still giving me the job after I was a complete arse about it yesterday.' Ronny got out and made his way around to her side.

'Yeah, about that, why didn't you want it when I first spoke to you? Is there something I should know before you take the job on, like you're an axe murderer or something?' She giggled.

'Close, but not quite …' Ronny gave her a wink and shook his head as he opened the door and slid his hands around her waist and legs to lift her out. 'You just caught me off guard when you offered it to me, that's all. I hadn't really gotten my head around the fact I had an entire farm to take care of, but Larry helped me figure out that, with his help, I'd be able to handle doing this job too.'

'Well, hurrah for Larry,' Ivy said, as she once again enjoyed the feeling of being in Ronny's arms. Her twisted ankle was proving a positive in this way at least. She wondered what Amy I-think-I'm-shithot Mayberry would think of her boyfriend carting her around. She certainly wouldn't be happy about it. Ivy couldn't help but smile at the thought.

'Yup, a whopping hurrah is in order for Larry,' Ronny said as he tipped his head towards the homestead. 'Now, we better get you inside, get some ice on that massive lump growing out the side of your foot, and then get you to the hospital for some X-rays.'

'Yes, sir.' Ivy saluted like she was in the army. 'It appears I'll be following you, so lead the way.'

CHAPTER 14

Ronny stood back while the doctor assessed Ivy's X-rays, the silence of the room a little uncomfortable. He was trying to keep his eyes off Ivy, the natural beauty of the woman still capable of taking his breath away even as she looked a little worse for wear in a hospital bed. Holding her in his arms had felt so right that he hadn't wanted to put her down. He could still smell her musky perfume lingering on his singlet, and it smelt damn good. He subtly breathed it in as he paced the room, his concern for her making it impossible for him to stand still.

Ivy glanced over the doctor's shoulder and gave him a small smile, her face scrunching up as she mouthed, 'Sorry it's taking so long.'

Ronny smiled then shrugged, mouthing, 'That's okay.' As much as he should, he honestly didn't care where he was, as long as he was in Ivy's company. Although he was feeling a little strange being back in a hospital with her, the images of that night almost a decade ago making his heart squeeze tight. The guilt he'd felt after running away and leaving her at the emergency department had been inconceivable – but what else was he meant to do, given the situation? At least this time round he was doing what a man should do and sticking around.

Thinking back to Ivy's comment about not singing anymore, his heart ached. How devastating for a woman as talented as her to lose touch with something that was so much a part of her. He'd wanted to say, *No, don't say that, you're the most beautiful singer I've ever heard, and the way you play your guitar, like you're strumming everyone's heart in the room as they watch you, is mind blowing.* But he couldn't, otherwise Ivy would hold the same suspicions as Alice. He wasn't supposed to know she'd once been a brilliant musician. Wasn't supposed to have ever crossed paths with her before the day at the bank.

Was the reason she couldn't play the guitar or sing anymore something to do with that fateful night? The time frame would certainly fit. His instincts were telling him yes, but he couldn't be absolutely certain and he wasn't confident Ivy was going to fill him in either. Whatever the reason, hopefully, with some gentle encouragement, he might be able to get her to embrace her passion once again, and now that he was going to be at Healing Hills for a month or so, he had plenty of time. Because if his instincts were right, and they usually were, he couldn't stand by and let a woman as talented as Ivy Tucker waste her gift because some low-life bastard took advantage of her. Ivy had been through enough heartache in her life, so if he could take some of that away for her, he would do everything in his power to do so.

'Well, Ivy, unlike the last time you were in here with a broken finger, the good news is you haven't broken anything.' The doctor's gravelly voice broke Ronny's train of thought and pulled him towards the hospital bed.

Ivy wriggled herself up to sitting. 'Well, that's good I suppose. And the bad news?'

The doctor offered a resigned sigh. 'It's not like the last time you sprained your ankle where you only had to rest for a week – this time you have a grade two injury, which means you have ligaments that are partly torn.'

'Bugger.' Ivy sat up straighter, concern twisting her features. 'What's that mean in regards to recovery time?'

'It means you'll need to rest up for at least two to three weeks, elevating your foot as often as possible, and in that time you'll also need to keep your ankle wrapped in a compression bandage. After that, you'll have to be very careful not to put too much strain on it for a few more weeks.'

'Oh, bloody hell, well that kind of puts a dampener on the renovation project,' she groaned as she hung her head in her hands. 'How the heck am I going to save Healing Hills now?'

'Sorry to be the bearer of bad news, Ivy, but you won't be doing any kind of strenuous work, because if you try to push past the pain, you might very well cause permanent injury to your ankle. And we certainly don't want that.' He looked at Ronny. 'You may have to rely a little more on your boyfriend for now, I think.'

Ivy glanced up at the doctor as her cheeks flamed. 'Oh, no, Ronny's not my boyfriend.'

The doctor smiled for the first time. 'Oh, pardon me, but with the way you two are around each other, I just gathered that was the case.' He shrugged. 'My wife is always telling me I'm too quick to assume.'

Feeling uplifted by the doctor's incorrect but very agreeable observation, Ronny reached out and lightly squeezed Ivy's arm. 'I can handle the renovations on my own. You can be the supervisor

– just tell me what needs doing, and I'll do it. Simple. So don't stress, okay?'

Ivy's desolation was written all over her face as she shook her head. 'No way, Ronny, not for a measly seven hundred bucks a week, you're not. It'd be wrong of me to expect so much of you.'

Ronny gave her a playful don't-mess-with-me look. 'I'm not taking no for an answer, Miss Tucker, so you better get used to the idea.'

The doctor cut into their conversation as he tapped his watch. 'Sorry to interrupt, but I have to run – we're understaffed, as per usual.' He patted Ivy's leg. 'I would highly recommend using crutches to get around with, too, Ivy, otherwise you could risk putting unnecessary pressure on your ankle. The nurse will take care of organising some for you.' He left the room, still talking over his shoulder. 'Say hi to May and Alice for me, won't you?'

'Will do, thanks, Dr Miller – again.' Ivy turned to Ronny, who was now seated on the end of the bed. 'Why are you being so nice to me?'

Ronny gave her a brazen smile. 'Dunno, maybe I've lost my mind.'

Ivy slapped him playfully. 'Oi, thanks a lot.' She eyed him thoughtfully. 'But seriously, tell me, why are you going out of your way to help three women you hardly even know?'

Ronny wished he could pour his heart out to Ivy and tell her everything there was to know, but he couldn't. Instead, he grabbed her hand and gave it a squeeze. 'Just because I can, and just because you're one of the most likeable chicks I've ever met.'

'Oh, shucks, thanks.' Ivy tried to hide her shyness by laughing his comment off, endearing her to Ronny even more. This beautiful woman deserved every compliment under the sun, and he wished with every inch of him that they'd met under different circumstances so he could have the chance to compliment her properly, to love her how she should be loved, and to protect her every single day for the rest of his life.

Ivy placed her hand on his arm. 'I think you've certainly fulfilled your slave duties for the day. So how about we leave the cottage until tomorrow now, and instead I can give you a guided tour of Healing Hills.'

'Are you sure you're up for that?' Ronny pointed to her ankle. 'I think you might be forgetting you're a little incapacitated.'

'I'll be right, it's not like I haven't injured myself loads of times before. And the painkillers the doc gave me are kicking in nicely.' She smiled stupidly in an effort to make him laugh, and it worked. 'I'll ride shotgun and just point out all the good bits along the way, kind of like a tour guide. And then, if you like, you can join us for dinner. Aunt Alice has her famous lamb and barley stew in the slow cooker, and believe me when I say it's to die for.' She rolled her eyes in pleasure.

Say no! SAY NO! Ronny ignored the little voice in his head and nodded. 'I reckon that sounds like a brilliant plan.'

'Good, that's settled. First things first, though, we better organise some crutches.' Ivy began to ease her way off the bed, wincing and groaning as she did. The sheet beneath her butt slipped and she just barely stopped herself from hitting the deck for the second time that day.

Ronny shot to her side. 'Hang on a minute; let me get a wheelchair first. I think it might be a safer bet until we get those crutches.'

Ivy laughed. 'You already know me so very well.'

Ronny grinned cheekily. 'I'm working you out.' He motioned to the door. 'I'll be back as soon as I get us some wheels.'

'Cool, thanks.'

Ronny headed out the door. He knew it was crossing the line, accepting Ivy's offer, but he couldn't help himself. He loved being around her and it felt good to enjoy a woman's company after eight years in the slammer.

***

Ronny pulled the Kingswood up beside the fenced paddock and switched the ignition off, lips stretched in a broad smile. The last hour had been wonderful, casually driving about Healing Hills while Ivy proudly showed him around. The view from the cliffs was amazing, the glistening dam and flowing creek were inviting and he hoped to one day dunk himself in the crystal-clear water. Learning of the history behind the place had been fascinating, with her family being here for generations. But he thought he had noticed a shift in Ivy's mood whilst they'd been gazing out at the valley below, very fleeting, but it made him wonder what had consumed her for those few seconds. But this, right here, was what he'd really been yearning to see. The sun was just beginning to set, painting the landscape sparkling gold and the limitless sky pink and fiery crimson. 'They are just the most magnificent creatures,' he said dreamily, the sight of the healing horses tugging at something deep inside of him.

'They sure are,' Ivy replied, just as dreamily. 'They never cease to amaze me with how they can help heal people.'

Ronny turned to her. 'You have such a wonderful job, getting to work with them every day. I'm envious.'

'Uh huh. I certainly count my lucky stars, although, it does come with its challenges too. It can be really tough, watching people suffer the way they do, especially children.'

'Yeah, I reckon it would be. I'd have a hard time keeping it together seeing kids' hearts broken, but on the plus side, you get to guide them towards healing, and in turn a fulfilling life.' He smiled softly. 'And that is an amazing thing to be doing for people, Ivy.'

'Thank you. I like to think I'm making a difference in the world, even if it's small.'

'You are, as are May and Alice, and I admire you all for it.' He rubbed a hand over his five o'clock shadow as he rested his head back. 'I would love to be able to do something like this one day. I studied meditation …' He paused, realizing he was almost about to say *in prison.* 'And I'd love to put it to good use by teaching other people how to use it to better their lives.'

Ivy looked impressed. 'Really? Have you got accreditation?'

Ronny nodded. 'I sure do. It took nine months to get it, and loads of intense study, but it was well worth it. Meditation has got me through so much in the past few years.'

'Yeah, it's helped me through a lot of stuff too.' Ivy reached out and lightly touched the om tattoo at the side of his neck and he had to fight from shivering beneath her touch. 'This has intrigued me since the first time I saw it when you were up on stage at the auction. I never would have picked you for a man who had studied something like meditation – but hearing that now explains everything.' She smiled in a way that made him long to reach out and pull her into a slow, passionate kiss. 'You're a very deep man, Mister Sinclair. It's a nice change to meet a man with spiritual interests. I really like that about you.'

Not used to such openness from Ivy, or to such overt compliments, Ronny smiled shyly. 'Why thankya, ma'am.' He tipped his hat playfully.

'Don't mention it, cowboy.' She replied with equal light-heartedness. 'And I'll hold onto that info – we may be in need of a meditation teacher once we start our new programs here.'

Ronny sat up straighter. 'Seriously?'

'Seriously.' She arched a brow. 'Although that's not only up to me, of course – it would be May's and Alice's decision too. And to do that we'd also have to do a background check on you, seeing as we're an accredited healing centre.' She smiled. 'Not that that would cause a problem, being the wholesome country bloke I think you are.'

Ronny's heart felt as though he'd just jabbed it with adrenaline, and he fought to keep his voice calm. There was no way in hell he'd ever be teaching meditation here. He thought quickly, not wanting to knock back another of Ivy's kind offers of work. 'Let's just see how we go working together on the renovations first, hey? You might be happy to see the back of me by the time we're finished.' He grinned as playfully as he could and then gestured out the window. 'Do you mind if I go say hi to the horses?'

Ivy shook her head, smiling. 'Of course not.'

He eagerly leapt out his door, needing to get away from her questioning gaze. 'Be back in a few minutes.'

***

Savouring her last mouthful of Baileys-infused tiramisu, Ivy gazed across the dining table at Ronny, the flickering candlelight emphasising his chiselled ruggedness. She was in complete awe at how he'd kept her, Alice and May laughing until their sides ached over dinner and into dessert. It was so nice to be in the company of a man who could hold a decent conversation, and a witty one at that. He'd even insisted on helping May and Alice clear the dinner dishes so they could make room for the dessert plates, with a firm request that Ivy stay seated. The laughter that had floated into the dining room from the kitchen as they cleaned up had been uplifting, making her wish her damn ankle wasn't knackered so she could have joined in on the fun – it was one of the first times in her life she was super keen to help with the dishes. He was the perfect guest, in every way.

Ivy sighed quietly as she sat back, her belly now filled to the brim with yummy food. The more time she spent with Ronny, the more she liked him, and that scared the wits out of her. She couldn't like him – she wasn't ready for a man to be in her life again and on top of that, he was spoken for, even if it was by Amy Mayberry; Ivy wasn't one to condone cheating, in any way, shape or form. She really needed to get a grip on her emotions, and her desire to rip every shred of his clothing off, before she found herself in a predicament she didn't need – or want – to be in.

As if feeling her eyes upon him, Ronny captured her gaze with his for the briefest of moments, the pull of attraction shimmering between them, the energy passing between them unfathomable. Her cheeks flamed, as did every inch of her body – her longing for him escalating with the intensity in his eyes. She couldn't deny there was a spark any longer; actually, it was more like a blaze. It was disheartening to know it wasn't going to get them anywhere. Settling further back in her chair with her one and only glass of red wine (she shouldn't have had any with the painkillers but she couldn't resist having a wine with dinner) she recalled the way he'd approached the horses a few hours ago with such tenderness and with such insight into how a horse ticked. The sight of him caressing their coats as he'd spoken so softly to them, and the genuine pleasure on his face as the horses had responded to his gentleness, had set her heart aflame. In her eyes, there was nothing sexier than a man who could speak the language of horses, and Ronny spoke it extremely well.

His last mouthful of dessert finished, Ronny sat back and moaned. 'I'm so full I feel like I'm going to explode.'

'Me too,' Ivy said. 'I had to undo my belt and top button after the stew, otherwise I wouldn't have been able to fit dessert in – and there was no way I was going to let that happen when tiramisu is my favourite.'

Ronny laughed and pointed to where his belt also hung open. 'I hear you loud and clear.' He turned his attention to May and Alice. 'You're bloody good cooks. I reckon I might have to move in.'

'Okay, it's a deal. I'll provide the food and you provide the muscles. We could do with a man around the house, especially one as lovely as you,' Alice said, chuckling.

'No complaints here about that idea,' May added. Her cheeks were flushed after two glasses of wine.

Ivy laughed at the pair of them then joined in with the playful banter. 'Now, now, you two, Ronny has his own place to look after, so don't go getting too hooked on the idea.'

May and Alice feigned dejection.

Ronny chuckled at their exaggerated sad faces. Then, glancing at his watch, his eyebrows shot up. 'Wow, I didn't know it was that late.'

'Time flies when you're having fun,' Alice said perkily.

'It sure does. I reckon I might have to hit the road. I want to have heaps of energy for my second day of slave duties tomorrow – it sounds like there's a lot to do in a short amount of time.'

'Yeah, you better get some rest. Who knows, I might break a leg tomorrow,' Ivy said, laughing.

'With the way you're moving about on those crutches that could be a huge possibility,' Ronny said, smiling cheekily.

'I'll have you know they're bloody hard to drive.'

'I'll have to take your word on that,' Ronny said as he pushed his chair back and stood. He began gathering the dessert bowls from the table.

Alice stood and took the plates from his hands. 'You leave them, Ronny. We'll clean up the rest – you've been helpful enough already. You get yourself home to bed.'

'You sure? I don't mind helping.'

'Positive,' May said as she joined Alice in clearing the table.

Ronny did his belt up and then pulled his keys from his pocket. 'Okay, if you insist. Thanks for having me for dinner, I really enjoyed it.'

Alice reached out and touched his arm. 'We've really enjoyed having you. It's been a lovely night.'

'Yes, it has been. I haven't laughed so much in ages. You're welcome any time, Ronny,' May said. She leant in and gave him a quick peck on the cheek. 'Catch you tomorrow, I'm off to stick these plates in the dishwasher.' She smirked good-naturedly at Alice. 'In a very disorderly fashion, no doubt.'

Alice pulled Ronny into a hug and squeezed him tight before stepping back. 'And I better go help her, otherwise there'll be plates where there should be glasses, and cutlery where there should be plates – May is shocking at packing a dishwasher.' She smiled broadly. 'Night, Ronny.'

'Night, May, night, Alice.'

Ivy manoeuvred herself upright by holding onto the side of the table, and then began trying to place the crutches under her arms. 'I'll hobble you out, Ronny, once I get these buggers sorted.' One of the crutches fell sideways, bounced off the side of the table and then crashed to the floor. Ivy looked at Ronny and grinned sheepishly. 'I think I need to get a licence for these things, they're lethal.'

'Here, let me help you.' Ronny retrieved the crutch from the floor and then wrapped an arm tightly around her waist as he placed it under her arm.

The heat of his body permeated Ivy's skin, making her feel a little giddy as her pulse quickened. God, how she wanted to kiss him. This hunk of a man was like a damn drug, sending her skittish each and every time he was anywhere near her, and something told her, if she dared have a taste of him, just like a drug, she'd be addicted to him.

Once the crutch was positioned properly, and she was as balanced as she could be, he loosened his grip. 'Is it safe to let you go now?'

'Maybe,' was all Ivy could say as she gazed into his golden eyes. Their lips were so close she could feel his breath upon her skin, and the way his chest was peeking out at her from the collar of his shirt made her want to tear his clothes off him. She hungered to lean in and taste his lips and it took every bit of her resolve not to.

Ronny broke the intense moment as he stepped back and cleared his throat. 'Well, I better get going. I think it might be best if I walk myself out. It's a long hallway with plenty of obstacles for you to trip over – which you're a champ at, by the sounds of the stories your aunts were telling tonight.'

Ivy grinned at his teasing. 'I like to perfect everything I do, even tripping over. Practice makes perfect, as they say.'

Ronny flashed a charming smile before he leant in and kissed her cheek. 'Night, Ivy, thanks again for dinner.'

'Thanks for joining us. Night, catch you bright and early.'

'You certainly will,' Ronny said as he disappeared down the doorway.

Listening to his footsteps fade, Ivy's hand went to the place on her cheek that still burned pleasurably from his kiss. If only she could make him hers.

CHAPTER 15

Coffee in hand, Ronny spun around, the bemused look on his face making Ivy giggle. She was balancing on her crutches in the doorway of the bathroom, demolishing an iced vovo – her favourite biscuit of all time, as she had told him several times while devouring almost half of the packet at smoko. She'd certainly impressed him with her scoffing skills. Being a lover of food he adored a woman who could chow down without worrying about how many hundredths of a millimetre it was going to add to her waistline, and what a sexy waist she had along with all the other womanly curves that were in all the right places.

What I'd give to be that biscuit ...

Mentally clouting himself for having such carnal thoughts – he'd had enough of them last night on his drive home after dinner, and then in his dreams – Ronny diverted his attention to Bo and Jessie, sitting on either side of Ivy. The dogs were still panting after playing fetch in the backyard with him and drool hung from their lips as they eyed Ivy's biscuit. He was full to the brim himself, having savoured every crumb of May's banana cake, though he was regretting eating a third piece now.

'I told you it was pretty bad.' Ivy smiled and then licked the coconut from her fingertips before pointing to the head-spinning design of pink, green and purple tiles in the shower recess. 'God only knows what they were thinking when they chose the colours back then, but with the pain I'm in at the moment, I wouldn't mind a bit of whatever they were on. It might just take the edge off a little.'

'Uh huh,' Ronny said. He contemplated the pink bathtub with a shake of his head, and then turned back to her. The dogs had given up any hope of getting the biscuit and were making themselves comfy on the floor near the doorway. 'I think whatever they were on back then would do a lot more than take the edge off, Ivy. I reckon you'd quite possibly be wasted for days.'

Ivy cracked up and he relished the fact she'd been cheerful and relaxed around him all morning. After the moment between them just before he'd left last night, he wasn't sure how she'd be around him today, but it was as if nothing had happened. They'd spent the two hours before smoko evaluating what needed doing in the kitchen to make the house saleable, and their conversation had been flowing and easygoing. Even though he hated seeing her in pain, her fall had certainly been a blessing in disguise: it had broken the ice between them and now it felt as though they were actually on their way to being great mates.

He stepped into the shower. 'You weren't bloody wrong in saying it was pretty bad in here. With all the colours and patterns I don't know where to look first.' He imitated temporary blindness by blinking and covering his eyes.

'Yep, I'm hearing you.' Ivy nodded and pretended to shade her eyes. 'The weird thing is, I never noticed it when I was a kid. I used to think all the colours and patterns were pretty cool.' She tipped her head to the side, her long hair swishing around her shoulders. 'But now, it kinda makes me feel as though I've been sucked into a seventies vortex and I should be wearing bell-bottomed pants and a tie-dyed shirt.' She gave him the peace sign and grinned.

'Hmm, sounds pretty damn stylish to me, I reckon you would've made a good seventies hippy.'

'Why thank you.' Ivy tried to playfully curtsey on her crutches but failed miserably as she stumbled to the side.

Ronny dived towards her, saving her from hitting the deck as he grabbed hold of her arm. He placed his hands on her waist and left them there as she tried to regain her sense of balance. The sparks that flew between them made him swallow down hard. 'So I'm gathering you haven't got the hang of them yet.'

'I'm such a bloody oaf, it's like I've forever got two left feet. The amount of injuries I've sustained in my lifetime …' She rolled her eyes. '… You've got no idea.'

'I reckon I might have after the past couple of days with you, and also after the stories your aunts told last night,' Ronny replied gently, his lips softly smiling but his heart breaking for what this beautiful woman had been through. *And I've witnessed your worst injury too*, he wanted to say, as his eyes subtly passed over the place on her torso where a scar would most certainly be. God, how he wished he could be honest with her. This was a hell of a lot harder than he'd thought it would be. Ivy eyed him a little curiously, as though reading his thoughts. Ronny felt as though the bathroom was slowly closing in on him, the weight of keeping the truth from her almost too much to bear. Yes, he had his reasons for doing so, and he felt they were warranted – he owed so much to Lottie – but there was also a huge part of him that truly believed Ivy deserved to know who he was. Who was he to take that right away from her?

He tried to calm himself, employing the meditation techniques he'd used in prison to slow his racing pulse. He couldn't let Ivy see his angst, and he couldn't go blurting out everything just because he felt compelled to in the heat of the moment.

The questioning look faded from Ivy's eyes as she smiled. 'You've come to my rescue a few times, so I suppose you do have a fair idea I'm a professional klutz. I feel like a bit of an idiot, to be honest. First you find me in the garden and have to rush me to hospital and now you're constantly stopping me from falling off my crutches.' She sighed. 'And here I was trying to pretend I was your composed and self-assured boss.'

Ronny's heart sank even further. 'Please don't feel like that, Ivy. I reckon you come across very composed and confident – in all the right ways of course.' He wished there was some way he could take away her self-doubt. 'And just for the record, I actually find your clumsiness cute.'

'Really? You find it cute? Come on, you don't have to be nice just to make me feel better.' Ivy graced Ronny with a shy smile that had the power to send him crumbling to the floor.

He shrugged casually as he fought to keep his emotions in check. 'I'm not playing nice, I'm just being honest.'

'Well, I have to say I like you being honest, thank you.'

The look in Ivy's eyes made heat flame through him, and as she gazed at him, he felt something evanescent, profound, pass between them. Ivy's cheeks flushed as she bit her bottom lip. Ronny quickly looked away before he lost all sense and kissed her. He knelt down to give Jessie a pat, trying to lighten the atmosphere.

'And while I'm being honest, even though I find it cute, you and your two left feet are going to send me grey before my time.'

'My aunts would probably agree with you on that one.' Ivy laughed a little self-consciously as she took refuge from her crutches by leaning against the doorway. 'And back to the subject we were on before you heroically came to my rescue – I would've loved living in the seventies. They had the best music back then.'

She offered a dreamy smile that was laced with delight, the gesture making Ronny want to reach out and trace his fingers over her full, glossy, kissable lips. Instead, he gave one last pat to Jessie's head and stood. Grabbing his cup from the vanity he sculled the last of his coffee before placing the empty cup in the sink. 'Fleetwood Mac, the Eagles, Led Zeppelin, Pink Floyd – I'd have to agree with you there. I would've very easily lived back then, too, when life was simple, and music and peace and love was everything.' He shoved his hands in his pockets. 'And they had really cool cars back then too.'

Ivy raised her eyebrows. 'Even though you like to meditate, I would've never picked you for a peace-loving hippy kind of bloke, Ronny Sinclair.'

'Really? Why's that?'

'I dunno.' Ivy shrugged. 'You just look more … Viking-ish … like you should be bearing a sword or a battle axe and a shield, and you've kinda got a don't-fuck-with-me aura to go with it. Definitely not something a peace-loving hippy would exude.' She grinned.

'Well, I'm glad my grand plan is working …'

'What do you mean?'

'I want people to believe I'm hard as nails and can't be fucked with.'

Ivy's brows furrowed as she eyed him inquisitively. 'Really? Why would you want people to think like that? Wouldn't you rather they thought you were approachable?'

'Not really, because as much as we like to think everyone around us is virtuous, there's a lot of people out there who just want to take what they can get from you, no matter the cost. So, if they're wary of me from the start it means they'll tread carefully and not try to take advantage of me as easily as they would, say, a peace-loving hippy kind …' He smirked playfully as he wriggled his eyebrows.

Ivy nodded. 'Fair point, I guess.'

'If you haven't already noticed, underneath the hard exterior I'm a bit of a softy, though.' He dropped his voice to a whisper. 'But make sure you keep that to yourself, so I don't ruin the reputation.'

Ivy winked as she zipped her lips. 'Your secret's safe with me.'

Ronny laughed as he turned back to stare at the wallpaper above the sink, the swirling design making him feel a little woozy. Or was his light-headedness because he was in the presence of the most beautiful woman he'd ever seen? Whatever it was, the wall was a welcome distraction. He had to divert his eyes from Ivy before she noticed the hunger in them – if she hadn't already – her long, boho-style skirt and tight singlet doing more for him than a woman dressed to the nines in some flash clothing would. And the hint of her musky perfume made him want to brush his lips over the place her pulse was rhythmically throbbing in her neck. This desire was driving him insane.

Pushing it down, Ronny pretended to be focused on the job at hand, even though he already knew what needed doing and how he'd do it. 'It's no worse than the kitchen, really. But, yep, it is pretty out there. That wallpaper is so bloody bright you almost need to wear sunnies in here.' He gave the vanity a rap with his knuckles then kept chatting as he investigated every nook and cranny. 'It's all cosmetic stuff, really. I can deffo do a revamp on the cheap by painting the tiles rather than replacing them, and I can resurface the claw-foot bathtub and vanity to make them look like new. And we can just replace the fixtures and maybe even install a rain shower to snazzy the room up and make it feel modern – most of that can be bought off eBay for a steal. It'll look amazing in here and probably add about ten to fifteen grand to the sale price, at the very least.' He spun around and flashed her a smile. 'Sound good to you?'

Ivy's eyes darted to his face from where – he was certain – she'd been checking out his arse. *Busted.* She gave a slight flutter of her lashes as her cheeks faintly flushed. Ronny couldn't help but feel flattered.

'Um, yup, all sounds perfect to me.'

'Great, I'll make a start on it today. I'll just have to head into the hardware store first, grab a few things, and then I'll get cracking.' She turned away, the pulse in her neck now quickened. God, how he wanted her with every fibre of his being, but she was forbidden fruit and that was that. He crossed his arms over his chest as if to stop his heart reaching out to grab hers. When she turned back to him she was composed, the flush in her cheeks gone.

'I need to sit before I ask you the next question, and because my ankle is throbbing like hell.'

'Here, let me help you.' Ronny reached out and placed his hand on her arm, but her skin scorched him and he pulled away, tucking his hand into his jeans pocket. He had to stop touching her as he was treading very dangerous waters, his desire for her growing by the millisecond.

'As much as I'd love you to carry me around all day, I have to learn to get around on my own, but thank you,' Ivy said as she hobbled past him and then eased herself down on the side of the bath. 'How much do you reckon it's going to cost now you've had a good look around the cottage and seen what needs doing?'

'Well, let me work it out … but it will only be a rough estimate. Is that okay?'

'Of course, I just want a ball-park figure so I know what I'm looking at spending.' Ivy offered a resigned sigh. 'And so I know I have enough to cover the costs before you make a start. We don't want to go overboard and leave me with a massive bill I can't pay.'

Ronny sat down beside her and pulled out his notebook from his shirt pocket. He began jotting down figures. 'Seeing as we're going to keep the kitchen benches and cupboards and just refinish them with some timber-look laminate as well as replace the handles with some new ones, and I can get some really cool lighting off the internet so the biggest cost will be a new stove and cooktop, it'd be safe to say the kitchen will be around the six thousand dollar mark. And that includes putting new vinyl flooring down too.' He looked to Ivy. 'Is that all right?'

Ivy nodded, smiling broadly. 'That's much less than I'd thought I'd be looking at, so, so far, so good.' She gave him a friendly pat on the back. 'I envisioned I'd have to cut corners a lot more than you've suggested, so I'm pretty damn stoked.'

'Excellent.' Ronny went back to scribbling. 'I've been researching stuff on the internet the past couple of days so I can get up to speed with costs of building materials these days, and with everything we've talked about for the bathroom, I reckon three or four thousand should cover it.'

'Sounds great, but I'm confused – I thought you'd be well aware of the costs of building, seeing as you've been doing it for so long.'

Shit, he'd put his foot in his mouth again, just like he had yesterday with Alice. He seriously needed to be a hell of a lot more careful with what he said. He faltered before recalling what Lottie had mentioned in her last letter to him. 'Oh, yes and no, I've been mustering up north for a few years now so I've kinda fallen out of sync with the costs of building materials.'

'Oh, okay.'

'And then we've got to think about repainting the inside of the house, redoing the vinyl flooring throughout to match the vinyl you want for the kitchen, and then you'll be looking at about two grand to do the internal laundry because we'll have to call in a plumber for part of the job.' He ran his fingers over his razor-short hair as he mumbled a few more figures to himself. 'So, I'm guessing twenty grand should cover it, take or leave a few grand … plus my wages on top of that.' He whistled through his teeth, his features twisting with concern. 'Is that cutting the mustard for you?'

Ivy beamed from ear to ear. 'It sure is.' She reached over and squeezed Ronny's arm. 'Thank you.'

'What for? I'm just doing my job – a job I love, by the way.'

'For coming into my life exactly when I needed you.' She held his gaze and smiled appreciatively. 'Seriously, I believe in fate, and my aunts and I have been praying for a miracle to get us out of the deep shit we're in, and then you come along and make this renovation feasible.'

Ronny's heart skidded to a stop as he found himself at a complete loss for words. If only she knew he'd done what she was speaking of once before, in a massive, yet so different, way. He smiled, trying to hide the heaviness of the guilt he felt at keeping everything from her. After heaving in a deep breath, he said, 'Well, Ivy, you've come into my life at exactly the right time too. I needed some work to help with the running costs of Sundown, so I reckon we're square on that one.' He grabbed his tape measure and began working on the list of what he'd have to buy from the hardware store in town. He needed to do something, anything, other than sit and look into her beautiful chocolate brown eyes any longer. 'Why don't you go and rest a bit while I get started, you're looking a little weary.' She was actually looking gorgeous, as always, but he needed to get some time on his own, away from the hypnotic effect she had on him, to get his head straight before he had a change of heart and spilled the beans to her.

Ivy grinned. 'Oh shucks, thanks, so you're kicking me off the job already?'

'Sure am, I work much faster alone anyway, and you need to follow your doctor's orders by resting that ankle of yours.'

Ivy glanced at her watch and then stood, this time properly balanced on her crutches. 'It's time for me to take my painkillers anyway, and they tend to knock me out a bit, so I might do as I'm told and go and have a bit of a rest – maybe read for a while.' She looked back at him as he measured up the bath. 'Are you sure you don't mind me not going to the hardware store with you? I feel bad leaving everything to you.'

Ronny stopped what he was doing and placed his hand on her shoulder, giving it a gentle squeeze. 'Seriously, I'll be fine. It's not like you can drive at the moment anyway. And it'll be a lot faster for me to grab what I need and get back here without you hobbling along beside me.'

Ivy glanced down at her bandaged ankle. 'Hmm, very good point. We have an account there so just put anything you need on that and I'll fix it up when they send me the bill.'

'Righto, easy done. And, Ivy, I meant what I said at the hospital about being able to do it on my own and you being the supervisor.' He gestured at the doorway, where Bo was snoring and Jessie was flicking her paws like she was running in her dreams. 'So go and rest before I carry you into the bedroom myself and padlock the door so you can't get out.'

'Well, seeing you're putting it so sternly …' Ivy saluted him. 'Yes sir.'

Wish I could lock myself in there with you and pleasure you senseless, was the next thing that came to Ronny's mind as he watched her leave. He silently swore. Damn it. No matter how hard he tried, he couldn't control his thoughts. But for God's sake, he was going to have to learn to.

He waited until he'd heard the clunk of the bedroom door closing before he downed his tools. What the hell was the universe playing at? Leaning on the bathroom sink, he stared out the large bathroom window and looked to the endless blue sky. 'What do you want from me?' he whispered, shaking his head. Running his hands over his face, he pinched the bridge of his nose, groaning from the throbbing behind his temples. How the fuck was he going to get through an entire month of this? He'd come here thinking he was going to be able to handle it like a man should, but clearly, given Ivy could mesmerise him simply by being near him, it wasn't going to be as simple as that. With the amount of times he'd bitten his tongue to stop from telling her the truth so far, it was a wonder it wasn't bleeding. Being around her was dangerous, but there was no way he could back out of it now. He had to help her and her aunts. There was no way in hell he was going to walk away and risk being the reason they lost everything, because Ivy Tucker deserved to have all she dreamed of, and more.

CHAPTER 16

Ivy slowly blinked open her sleep-heavy eyes. She couldn't even remember closing them in the first place, so it was a nice surprise to be floating out of slumber, enjoying the fact she didn't need to jump up out of bed and hit the ground running. Not that she'd be able to but it was a welcome change for her mind to not be going a hundred miles an hour as soon as she woke up. The luscious, relaxed feeling floating through her was something she hadn't experienced for ages, and it felt damn good to not be wound up like a coil. Was it the painkillers she'd taken, or because she finally had a man in her life she could rely on? She wanted to believe it was the latter.

She glanced at her watch, surprised it had been four hours since she'd lain down. Ronny had been right in saying she'd needed a rest; she hadn't realised how exhausted she was. Ah, the hunky, spunky carpenter, Ronny Sinclair. What a blessing he was turning out to be. She'd grown very accustomed to having to do everything on her own, so it was a nice feeling to have a man about the house. She allowed herself the luxury of fantasising about having a man like him to call her own, to go to sleep beside every night and to wake up to every morning, to love with all she had, and to be loved equally in return. How beautiful that would be. If only Ronny wasn't with Amy, and as much as she hated the fact he found a woman like Amy someone he could care intimately for, Ivy considered allowing herself to fall head over heels for him. And the way she'd caught him gazing at her a few times, and the warmth in his touch, she had an inkling he felt the same way.

She still couldn't shake the feeling she knew him from somewhere, though. Each and every time she was around him, she felt as though she'd known him for years. Had they been involved somehow in a past life? Or had they already briefly crossed paths in this one? Maybe. But wouldn't Ronny have said something at the bank? Perhaps it was just as simple as she'd first thought – she'd seen him around town when he'd been here visiting his great aunt Lottie. But then why did she feel so connected to him, as though a piece of string was tying them to one another? It was a very strange sensation, and one she'd never felt before.

Rolling on her side, she stretched her arms above her head. She had to stop dissecting everything and trying to make sense of it, because sometimes in life you had to just let things unfold in their own time. Something would eventually explain why she felt she knew him and until then, she needed to focus on the wonderful new friend she'd made in him. That he was someone very reliable who could do the renovations – and be mighty fine perving material at the same time – was a bonus.

She eyed the book lying open beside her on the bed. Before drifting off she'd been reading the wise words of Deepak Chopra on how to overcome her fears so she could once again pick up her beloved guitar and sing. The book had been a gift from her aunts almost two years ago, but she'd only found the desire to read it after the incidents of the past couple of weeks: the heartache she'd felt at seeing her beautiful guitar abandoned in the attic; the godawful nightmares that had left her clutching her pillow too many nights recently; and then hearing Ronny speak about how much his music meant to him, and seeing how carefully he manoeuvred his guitar onto the back seat when he went to put her in his car – it had melted her heart and made her own passion scratch at her soul as though it were tired of being caged. Talking with Ronny, and hearing his deep passion for his music as he spoke about how much he loved playing his guitar and singing, did more than bring goose bumps to her skin, it had peeled back the bandage she'd wrapped around the gaping hole in her heart and left her aching to hold her guitar once again. It was the final kick up the butt she needed, making her realise it was high time she took action, instead of running from the pain of her past. She couldn't go on instilling the importance of combating your fears into everyone she worked with in her healing sessions when she wasn't doing it herself. But she also understood she couldn't beat herself up over this either – it wasn't going to help her situation. One step at a time … As May and Alice had kept gently reminding her, when the time was right, her focus would shift to the future rather than the past, and then she'd be ready to take the next step in her healing journey.

It felt amazing to have finally reached that point after nine years of running from it. And once again, Ronny Sinclair had been the catalyst. Fate had certainly provided her with an earth angel – if only said earth angel wasn't with one very infuriating Amy Mayberry, life could be close to perfect.

Sighing, she picked up her book and placed a bookmark between the pages, noting she only had another twenty or so pages to go. She was already familiar with most of the things the author spoke of, like the importance of meditation and distraction techniques to help you get over your fears, but reading it helped reinforce what she knew deep down she needed to do. She was actually excited at the prospect of putting everything Deepak Chopra had written about into action, even though facing her fears head on was going to be terrifying. Setting your mind to do something was the first step but actually doing it was a completely different matter. She knew she would have to take small steps, one foot in front of the other, but like all the previous times she'd tried and failed, this time, she wouldn't give up. Because she knew that if she didn't find the courage to finally conquer her fears and rid herself of the grip that awful night had on her, she would be destined to live the rest of her days without her music, and that possibility was even more terrifying than anything she'd already gone through.

She huffed as she rolled her eyes. Damn fear and all it stood for. She refused to be one of those unfortunate souls who let fear overtake them any longer.

Determination filling her, she gazed around her old bedroom, grateful for the fact her aunts had insisted on putting one of the spare beds from the homestead in here for her after returning from the hospital, with Ronny's help, as well as a couch in the lounge room and a fridge and some cutlery and crockery in the kitchen so she and Ronny had somewhere to make lunch and snacks. It saved them having to make the trip back to the homestead all the time, which was a difficult feat for her on crutches. May and Alice had also made a trip into the grocery store yesterday afternoon, returning with enough food stores to last them a month at the cottage so she could stick to her promise of providing Ronny with smoko every day – it was a hike back to the homestead to get anything. Ronny had tried to tell her several times that he didn't expect her to follow through on her offer now she'd hurt her ankle, but she was determined to look after him since he was going out of his way to help her. It was the very least she could do.

She gazed through the curtainless window at the beautiful country view, the undulating landscape drenched in a golden hue from the mid-afternoon sunlight. There was nothing of great significance to see, no buildings or roads, no cars or people. Just rolling green hills dotted with wildflowers, the horizon way off in the distance as though the landscape went on into eternity. It was this beautiful infinity that quite often helped Ivy find clarity. She smiled wistfully – it had been a long time since she'd awoken to the view from this bedroom window. And yet she could still recall so many happy times she'd shared with her mother in this very backyard like it was only yesterday. For it was out there her mum had spent many hours teaching Ivy how to play the guitar, and where they'd made mud pies and played hide and seek, and where they'd enjoyed many a day out in the sunshine while her mum had gardened or lain with Ivy cuddled into her arms as she'd read her stories. It was also where Ivy had fallen from the branch of the big old oak tree and encountered the first of several broken bones. Sadly, she barely had any memories of her father, the man never having bothered to get back in touch with her after leaving them all those years ago. And to cope with that she'd learnt to shut him out of her mind, and heart, completely.

With the memories of her mother floating in her mind a pang of nostalgia hit her and squeezed her heart tight. This house *did* mean more to her than bricks and mortar and a way to pay off debts, she just hadn't wanted to admit it for fear of disappointing her aunts. Pretending everything was all okay and she was hunky dory with selling the place was her way of trying to cope, but as per usual, all she was doing was ignoring her true feelings. But what was she meant to do? There was no other option. She had to sell it. Tears stung her eyes and as much as she tried to blink them away, they began rolling down her cheeks. It *was* going to hurt to sell this place. A hell of a lot. She'd always dreamt about the day she'd make it her own, imagined what it would be like hearing the pitter patter of her own children, envisioned living a life here just like she had with her own mother, as short as it was, but with a reliable loving husband by her side, but that day was never going to come now, and until this very moment she hadn't allowed herself to truly feel what it was going to be like to let it go. Yes, she was still determined it was the right thing to do, and she didn't want to be living next door to Healing Hills if her aunts were living somewhere else, but God, how she wished things could have been different, that life hadn't placed her in this position. But she was helping her aunts, and that was that. If May or Alice got even one whiff that she was upset about letting the cottage go, they would forbid her selling it, with no further discussion. And that would be the end of everything.

The flash of Ronny tearing past the window with a Frisbee in his hand broke her gloomy train of thought and she couldn't help but smile through her tears when she spotted Bo and Jessie racing after him, the look of pure pleasure on Ronny's face priceless as he laughed out loud. Bo and Jessie were clearly having a whale of a time too. It was an unusual sight – a Frisbee wasn't usually still attached to a human when a dog chased it.

Feeling as though she was missing out on all the fun, Ivy pulled herself together. She put on a happy face, and got ready to go outside and join in. She grabbed her crutches from where they were resting on the bedside table and then, after slipping her feet into her thongs, she slowly made her way out of the bedroom and down the hall, stopping off along the way to make a quick trip to the loo.

Passing through the kitchen on her way to the back verandah, Ivy stopped to wash her hands and face at the kitchen sink – the tools and cans of paint in the bathroom made it a little too difficult to manoeuvre about in. She'd also spotted bits and pieces of building materials in the lounge room, giving her a huge sense of relief that the renovations were underway. She was impressed with the progress Ronny had made in one day, and could only imagine what he was going to achieve in a few weeks. Turning to grab a tea towel from the oven door, she halted, grinning at what was sitting on the kitchen bench: a sandwich on a plate, covered in plastic wrap, a note attached to it.

A sanger for the sleeping beauty … hope you like egg, lettuce and mayonnaise.

Smiling like a lovesick teenager, Ivy folded the note up, kissed it, and then tucked it into the pocket of her skirt. She was suddenly ravenous, not only for the food, but also for her hired help. This was the sweetest gesture ever, and made her want him even more. Pulling the wrap off she picked up one half of the double-decker sandwich and took a bite, moaning with how good it was. This was the best damn egg sandwich she'd ever tasted; the man clearly knew his way around a kitchen. Carefully, she pulled open the pieces of bread and pinched a piece of the egg mixture from the middle, trying to figure out what he'd put in it to make it taste so delicious. First she eyed it suspiciously, then she rolled it around on her tongue. Curry powder, that's what she could taste, and something else. She couldn't for the life of her work out what that something else was and it frustrated her.

A captivating sound dragged her attention from her egg investigation and to the open window. Was she hearing what she thought she was – her favourite love song of all time? Her heart started thudding heavily in her chest as she held her breath. Something flickered inside her, like the wick of a candle being lit. Hesitantly, she peered out the window, not wanting Ronny to catch her, for she didn't want him to stop if he was shy of an audience. The sight she found stole every last bit of oxygen from her in an almighty sigh. Her lips curled into the biggest smile as emotions swelled inside of her. And everything shifted as her fear of men, and of falling in love, and of being heartbroken yet again, faded to the background. This man before her was the one she wanted to fall in love with, the one she wanted for her own, the one she'd been longing for her whole adult life. If only she could make it so.

Ronny sat beneath the big old oak tree she used to climb, his back resting against the trunk and his guitar in his lap, both dogs now relaxing beside him. In his jeans and a singlet, his wide-brimmed hat shading his handsome face, completely oblivious to the outside world as he sang his heart out, it was a scene worthy of a hot guys of the bush calendar. That, right there, the essence of Ronny Sinclair, was absolute heaven for her. What she'd give to have him love her, to *make* love to her, to be able to hear his wonderful voice every day. And she could just imagine what his touch would feel like, how his kiss would make her feel … she'd be putty in his strong, hardworking hands. Tingles ran through her at the thought of making love to him.

The rhythmic strum of the guitar floated into the room like an angel sent down from heaven and picked her up on its wings. She allowed herself to float within its trance. 'Once in a Lifetime Love' by Alan Jackson was the most beautiful song on earth to her. Every single word of it made her feel as though she was wrapped in a warm embrace, taking her to a place far away from all the heartache and pain and challenges of everyday life. The world around her faded as she listened to Ronny; time stood still. It was just her, and Ronny, and the lure of the music. And it was ethereal, exquisite, mind-blowing. Ronny's voice reminded her of the country music legend Waylon Jennings, deep and husky and strong, and filled with promises of tomorrow, the manliness of it inciting shivers all over her.

Lost in his voice, Ivy rested her face in her palms and began to quietly sing with him as she continued gazing out the window, taken back to when she was young and carefree and unashamedly innocent. And it was a wonderful place to be, if only for a few minutes. She felt free, and, for the first time in a very long time, she knew she was completely safe.

As if sensing her watching, Ronny lifted his head and turned towards her, his lips curling into the sexiest of smiles when he spotted her through the window. Unperturbed by his audience of one, he continued to sing as he gazed at her, making her feel as if every word passing his lips was from his heart to hers. Could it be true? Her hands fluttered to her chest as she smiled softly back at him, feeling as though Ronny was caressing every inch of her with his voice. Was he really singing *to* her, or was he just singing *at* her? She wondered if he'd ever serenaded Amy, and jealousy coursed through her as she remembered he was taken.

She shook her head as her hands dropped from her fluttering heart, the magic moment lost in an instant. How could a woman like Amy end up with a bloke as sensitive and as deep as Ronny Sinclair? And what was Ivy doing so bloody wrong to not be able to find a man like him to love her? Her emotions bubbled to the surface as tears filled her eyes, but she blinked them away as she took a few deep breaths. Life could be so freaking unfair, but she had to make the most of what she had right now, and not dwell on what she didn't – or never would – have.

The song finished, Ronny stood and gestured for the dogs to join him back inside the cottage. Ivy turned away from the window, taking a few moments to gather herself before he came in. She was shaky and a little light-headed, but also strangely focused. Some powerful things had just happened to her in those three minutes. Firstly, that was the only time in nine long years she'd felt uninhibited enough, compelled enough, and safe enough, to sing. Her first step to being able to pick her guitar up again, and it had happened so naturally. And secondly, she knew in her heart of hearts that she was falling hard for Ronny, and had been from the instant she'd laid eyes on him back at the bank. As much as she wanted to deny it, there was something about him that made her feel safe, and somehow loved. She wanted him, real bad. In any other situation she'd be doing her best to woo him. She sighed as a mixture of happiness and sadness washed over her. It felt so good to acknowledge her feelings for Ronny, even though she couldn't act upon them. Just in those few minutes of being lost in his musical world, something had shifted inside of her, and she liked it. A lot. As she picked up the other half of the sandwich and took a bite, her hunger gnawing at her empty stomach once again, she remembered what her mum had once told her in this very kitchen: *Unlike humankind, music doesn't ever discriminate, sweetheart. There's always going to be a song, a lyric, a melody, a beat, for each and all of us to connect to on some level. It has the power to relieve the tension of an awkward silence. It can speak to you in so many different ways and can release you from the sometimes unfair expectations of society so you feel free to be who you truly are, to emanate what makes you uniquely you. And it is so powerful it can also be the saviour from an addiction, and from life itself. So promise me, sweetheart, that you will always have music in your heart, and a song upon your lips, for it will get you through almost anything life challenges you with. I can promise you that.*

Her mother had always been a mystical person and so gifted with her musical talents. Not a day had gone by without her mum instilling some spiritual way of thinking in Ivy.

'Hey there you, did you have a good rest?' Ronny appeared at the back door as he made sure to wipe his boots on the mat before stepping inside. Unlike Bo and Jessie, who came tearing into the cottage at break-neck speed, sliding in beside her for a pat. As she gave her two canine mates some love, Ivy noted Ronny's thoughtfulness. Her mother would have been very impressed.

'Sure did, I passed out for a few hours.' Ivy shoved the last of the sandwich in her mouth before one of the dogs snatched it from her hand, and then pointed to the empty plate. 'And can I say, this is the yummiest sandwich I've ever tasted.'

Ronny placed his guitar on the kitchen bench, right beside where she was standing. His smile was enough to send her legs weak as he brushed past her. 'I'm glad you think so.'

She ached to reach out and rub her fingertips along the timber or pick the strings of the guitar only inches from her. Dragging her eyes away from it she looked at Ronny. 'What did you put in it to make it taste so good?'

'Oh, nothing in particular, just a whole lotta love.' Ronny winked at her, grinning.

'Oh come on, Mr Led Zeppelin, tell me your secret.'

Ronny went to the fridge and pulled out a can of Coke. 'If I do I'll have to kill you.' He held the can up. 'Want one?'

Ivy nodded. 'Aw, come on, pretty please … with strawberries and cream on top.'

He walked towards her, handed her the can, and then leant in to whisper, 'As well as the usual suspects of mayonnaise and curry powder, a sprinkle of mustard powder and a little bit of dill.'

Ivy had to stop herself from visibly shivering as his warm breath travelled over her ear and down the side of her neck. How did Ronny make egg sandwich ingredients sound so damn sexy?

She arched a brow. 'Really? Interesting. Where did you get mustard and dill from?'

Ronny shrugged casually. 'The pantry. May and Alice thought of everything but the kitchen sink when they went shopping.' He leant against the bench opposite Ivy and took a swig from his drink.

Ivy gazed at where his singlet pulled tight across his chest and swallowed hard. What she'd give to be able to trace her lips all over his tanned skin. There was a smudge of dirt on his left cheek and she yearned to reach out and wipe it away. 'Hmm, a man who can cook, fix things, build things *and* sing … very impressive.'

Ronny chuckled. 'Now, I wouldn't go that far, but thanks.'

Ivy snapped open her can and took a sip, needing to do something, anything, but stare at his delectable body. It was making her ache in places she didn't want to. 'Seriously, your voice is beyond amazing. It gets inside of you and warms you from the inside out. Do you ever perform at gigs?'

Ronny smiled shyly as he shook his head. 'Nah, I kinda like to sing when nobody's around. I get too nervous when people are watching and I tend to forget the words.'

'Well, if you don't like an audience, why did you keep singing when you knew I was watching you from the window?'

'Not sure really, other than that I feel comfortable around you, and you were at the window, not really right up in front of me, like people would be if I was on stage. I don't mind singing around a campfire with a few mates, I just don't reckon I'm good enough to make people sit and listen to me at a pub, that's all.'

'Are you serious? Your voice sounds a lot like Waylon Jennings. And he was a superstar. You're taking away people's God-given right to listen to your voice by not sharing it.' Ivy grinned playfully. 'And that's very selfish of you.'

'Now you're just being nice.'

'No, I'm not. Like a wise man once said to me, I'm just being honest.' She winked at him. 'But seriously, I know a good voice when I hear one, and you, my friend, have something very special.' She gazed at him, admiring how humble he was as he remained silent. 'I've had a lot to do with performing in the past, and I know a good thing when I see one.'

'Do you really think so?'

'I know so. You shouldn't waste your talent, Ronny, you need to get out there and show it off.' She threw her hands up in the air, her eyes wide. 'You might be the next big thing. You never know until you give it a go, as they say.'

Touché. Why was it so damn easy to give great advice to somebody else, when she knew this was exactly what she should be telling herself, too?

'I dunno, Ivy. I've sometimes daydreamed about performing in front of a crowd, but honestly, I wouldn't have a clue about where to start. I've never thought I was good enough to do it really, but you're almost giving me the courage to maybe give it a go sometime.' Ronny's thoughtful expression broke into a smile. 'Seeing as you're so clued up, I reckon you could teach me a few things, you know, about performing and maybe how to project my voice to a room full of people. And maybe, if I decided to do a gig, you might like to come and do it with me?'

Now it was Ivy's turn to doubt her abilities. Shit, she should have kept her mouth shut. She laughed nervously, all her irrational fears bubbling to the surface like a pot about to boil over. 'I don't think I'd be the best person to teach you anything about it, Ronny. I could maybe hook you up with someone who would be, though, if that would help.'

'Oh, thanks but no thanks, I'd only do it if you helped me, and sang with me.' He smiled at her, eyes beseeching. 'Like I said, I feel comfortable with you, and it's a rarity for me to feel comfortable with anyone.'

Ivy's hands were trembling, as were her lips and legs, the thought of being up in front of a crowd scaring the crap out of her. The last time she'd done that was the night everything had turned to shit. Instinctively she touched the place on her stomach where one of her scars now was.

'Come on, Ivy. It might be a bit of fun. And it'll give you something to do now that you have to rest up a fair bit with your ankle the way it is.' For the briefest of moments, she swore she could see pity in his eyes.

She dropped her hand and tucked it behind her. She had to open up to him, she didn't want him thinking she was fobbing him off after everything he was doing for her, and all he'd already done for her, consciously and unconsciously. 'I wish I could say yes, Ronny, but something happened to me a long while ago, something really bad, and it took away my ability to play my guitar and sing.' She gave a resigned sigh. 'I'm terrified of performing again, and am scared of having a panic attack up on stage in front of everyone, so I'd probably be more of a hindrance than a help, at the moment.' Tears were stinging her eyes and as much as she tried to fight them off, heavy drops rolled down her cheeks.

In three quick strides, Ronny stood before her. He took hold of her hands and gently squeezed them, his eyes gazing into hers with so much concern it touched her heart. How could this man care so much for her in such a short time? But then again, how could she feel so deeply for him? There had to be something otherworldly at work here, the connection between them was way too strong for it to be imagined.

'My God, you're shaking like a leaf.' He pulled her into his arms. 'Please don't feel pressured. I'm sorry, I didn't want to make you feel like this.'

Ivy allowed him to comfort her as she melted into his arms. 'It's not your fault. I've just got a lot of stuff to work through before I can play again. That's all.'

He pulled back a little so he could look into her eyes, his arms still wrapped protectively around her. 'If there is any way I can help you through it, I will. I know just how much it means to be able to follow your passion.'

Ivy wiped the tears from her cheeks. 'Thank you, Ronny; I think I'll take you up on that offer at some point. It'll be nice to have someone I trust to ease me back into playing and singing.' She sniffled. 'Amy Mayberry's one lucky woman to have a man like you to love her.'

Ronny's mouth dropped open in shock before giving way to a look of absolute amusement. He shook his head. 'What are you on about? I'm not with Amy. What in the heck made you think I was?'

Ivy's cheeks blushed a bright shade of red. 'Oh, um, I just gathered from the night at the pub that you might have been an item, and then when I saw you with her at the bakery last week, I just assumed you were together.'

Ronny's eyebrows scrunched together for a few seconds before his eyes widened and a smile spread across his face. 'Oh, I get it now. You saw Amy sitting on my lap and you thought –' he chuckled as he shook his head, '– there's no way in hell I'd fall for a woman like Amy Mayberry. Don't get me wrong, she seems like a nice enough person, but that's as far as it goes.' He dropped his hands from around Ivy's waist, and took a step back, his eyes never leaving hers. His smile faded. 'Do you really think I'd be the kind of man who would go out with a woman like her?'

Completely ashamed, Ivy looked at the floor. 'I was hoping you weren't. But I wasn't sure after seeing how cosy you looked at the bakery.'

'I think I'd be a little too deep for Amy's liking. And I'm well aware I'd just be another notch on her bedhead, and I've got a lot more self-respect than that.' Ronny placed his fingers underneath her chin and gently tipped her head towards him, capturing her eyes with his. 'You're the kind of woman I'd usually fall for, Ivy Tucker. Someone who is creative and kind and who knows what she wants out of this life. I need a lot more than what's on the outside of a woman to turn me on. I need layers, and you have plenty of those.'

'And therein lies the problem.' Her voice was a whisper.

'What's that, Ivy? What problem?'

'You said, *usually*, and the thing is …' Ivy stopped and turned her head to gaze out the window, her breathing shallow.

'What is it, Ivy?'

She turned back to face him. The look in his eyes was so touching she felt weak at the knees. 'You're exactly the kind of man I've been praying for, and here you are. But life is never that simple. There has to be a catch. I thought it was that you were with Amy, but now that's not the case, surely it has to be something else. I can feel you holding back from me, Ronny, and I can't understand why. Is there something you're not telling me?'

The shocked expression on Ronny's face told her everything she needed to know. Silence settled between them. He *was* hiding something from her and that realisation brought back all the unwanted emotions Malcolm's betrayal had caused her. Was Ronny going to be another man who somehow broke her into tiny little pieces? Well, if he wasn't going to be honest with her, she wasn't going to give him the chance.

Before she had time to escape from the room, Ronny's hands drifted back to her hips. They settled there and pulled her closer. She inhaled sharply as she once again touched his warm chest, chiselled to absolute perfection. The wild beating of his heart against her felt so damn good, and she hated it. She desperately wanted to pull away, but desperately wanted to stay in his arms too. His breathing quickened, as did hers. He leant in and, without a word, placed his lips against her neck then caressed it with delicate kisses so faint, they were like butterfly wings flickering against her skin. She moaned softly as she gave in to him. He slowly made his way towards her parted lips, their breath mingling. She could feel her mind and body in a tug of war. She knew she shouldn't be doing this, not when he was keeping something from her, but she couldn't help herself. Her heart fluttered inside her chest and every inch of her craved to be at one with him.

And then his lips were upon hers. At first, he was soft and slow, giving her delicate butterfly kisses, teasing her, making her push her hands harder into his back so there wasn't an inch of space left between them. Then his arms moved from her hips and encircled her as he picked her up and placed her on the kitchen bench. As his kiss intensified, she could feel his heat spread through her body. His tongue circled hers in the most suggestive of ways, driving her to the brink before he slowed back down again, slowly sucking on her bottom lip. She gasped, the longing inside her more powerful than she'd ever felt with any man before. She couldn't let this continue. Her heart couldn't take any more beating. Ronny needed to be open and honest with her, or whatever this was between them had to be put to rest. Forever.

'Please stop,' she whispered as she turned her face away from him. 'You need to tell me what you've been hiding or you need to leave me alone.'

And just as abruptly as he had grabbed her, Ronny pulled away, eyes glistening. He took a few steps backwards. 'I'm so sorry. I shouldn't have done that. I shouldn't have taken advantage of you opening up to me.' He began pacing in front of her, rubbing his face and running his hands over his head. 'I promised myself I wouldn't give in to my feelings for you, no matter how hard you were to resist. And here I am, caving in.' He stopped and stared at her, his eyes piercing hers. 'I can't do this either. It's so wrong in so many ways.'

So wrong in so many ways … Ivy blinked back tears as anger filled her. What the hell was he getting at? Was she not good enough for him? The familiarity she'd been feeling for him stormed to the front of her mind – maybe that had something to do with it? 'I know I know you from somewhere, Ronny. What aren't you telling me?' She almost spat the words, the heartbreak Malcolm had caused her through his deceitfulness now at the forefront of her mind. And here she'd been thinking Ronny was different. Fool!

'There's plenty I haven't told you …' Ronny's voice was laced with sadness as he looked up at the ceiling as though begging a higher being to come to his aid. 'And they are things that are best left unsaid.'

'What do you mean? Why can't you just be honest with me?'

'Because I can't be.'

'What do you mean you can't be? What are you talking about?'

Ronny met her worried gaze with equally anxious eyes. 'There are some things I just can't tell you. And for that reason, I need to leave you alone.' He gathered his keys from the kitchen bench. 'Come on, I'll drop you back to the homestead. I think I might call it a day, and start fresh tomorrow, if that's okay with you. My head's not focused on the job at the moment and I don't want to go fucking up anything more than I already just have.'

'Don't bother, I'll find my own way back,' was all Ivy could manage as she stared out the kitchen window.

Ronny didn't budge.

With wild eyes, Ivy turned to him. 'For fucks sake, just go.'

CHAPTER 17

The dawn sunlight streamed through the partially open curtains like a flamboyant guest, hitting the sun catcher in Ronny's window and splashing colours around the bedroom. Ronny rubbed his eyes, begrudgingly climbed from his rumpled sheets and sat on the side of his bed, shoulders slumped as though the weight of the world was upon them. His doona was in a pile at his feet – he must have kicked it off during the night. Again. He groaned as he roughly rubbed his face. What he would give to have a good night's sleep – it might at least help him get through the days of carrying around a heavy heart. Three weeks down, and hopefully, if things went to plan, there were less than two to go. He could do this; he simply had to because he didn't have any other choice. Being a man of his word he was determined to get the job done as promised, because Ivy and her aunts deserved a happily ever after. He, on the other hand, had ruined any chance of that happening for himself – because he knew without a doubt now, after kissing her beautiful lips three weeks ago, that Ivy was his happily ever after. And that was never, ever, going to be. Over in the corner of the room Cindy Clawford stretched languorously in her cat bed. Then she strutted like a supermodel to his side for a scratch while meowing a good morning. He chuckled as he stroked her, her purring sounding like a mini generator. He was thankful for her companionship – it calmed him. 'I don't know how you felines do it, Cindy, but you've certainly won my heart without even trying.' He glanced at the Hilton-worthy pet bed he'd bought her from the pet shop in town and shook his head. Never in his wildest dreams had he thought he would have gone shopping for a cat bed. 'And it only took you three days of clawing at my bedroom door to get your way.'

Cindy gave him one last meow before sauntering out of the bedroom in search of the great outdoors – she would sit in the sun for a while until Ronny got her breakfast, unless it was raining, then she'd sit on the bay windowsill in the kitchen, watching the goings on outside until she spotted food being dished into her bowl.

'In my next life I want to come back as a cat,' Ronny mumbled as he yawned and stretched his arms high above his head, at the same time willing his exhausted body to life. He'd have been lucky to catch an hour's sleep last night. And every night had been the same for the past few weeks, since he'd made the massive mistake of showing Ivy just how deeply he felt for her. Talk about a moment of weakness. The look in her eyes when he'd told her he couldn't be honest with her and that they could never be together … he might as well have stabbed himself in the heart, it would have hurt less. He felt like the biggest arsehole alive, and there was nothing he could do to take it all back. And Ivy had barely spoken a word to him since, only stopping by the cottage to check out how he was progressing and to see if there was anything he needed her to do. And every time, of course, there was nothing. Ivy was off her crutches now and managing to hobble about, but he wasn't going to ask her to do anything. She still needed rest, and plenty of it, if she was going to make a full recovery. Besides, he couldn't have her around him too much, because after tasting her honey-sweet kiss, and experiencing the way her touch caressed him in the most mind-blowing of ways, he was more addicted to her than ever, and he didn't want to make the same mistake twice.

It was all very businesslike between them now, exactly how he had wanted it from the start. If only he'd had the strength to curb his hunger for her, they wouldn't be in this godawful mess. He knew he needed to do something to try to mend the rift because he didn't want Ivy hating him, and at the moment he felt as if she loathed him. And that killed him beyond words. But what was he meant to do? It wasn't like they could ignore what had happened. And there was no way on earth he could reveal who he was now, even if he wanted to, because he'd gone way past the point of it being acceptable to keep the truth from her – and May and Alice for that matter. He groaned again as he threw himself backwards against the bed. What a fucking mess.

He needed to call his sister and get a woman's perspective. Faith was always full of great advice, and Lord knew he needed some right now. She'd been away the past couple of weeks on a much-needed holiday to Koh Samui, and he hadn't wanted to bother her while she was on vacation, other than the occasional email to say hi or to comment on her Facebook posts, but she flew back last night and he couldn't wait any longer. Rolling over he grabbed his phone from the bedside table and dialled her number. It rang out. He left a message. She was probably still asleep.

Succumbing to the fact he needed to get up and start the day he stood and went to his drawers, grabbing jocks, a T-shirt and a pair of jeans – the letters Lottie and Ivy had written him while he was in jail dropping to the floor as he did so. He'd had them tucked beneath his dwindling pile of T-shirts for safekeeping – he obviously needed to do some washing. He picked them up as though they were made of glass, Ivy's letter now terribly thin and tattered after the number of times he'd read it over the years. Pain shot through his heart as if speared. Both letters meant so very much to him. He really should put them away in the safe in the office with Lottie's jewellery box, out of harm's way and also out of sight of any prying eyes. There was a lot in each letter that would certainly let the cat out of the bag. Not that he had many visitors, but it was always better to be safe than sorry. He made a mental note then shoved them back underneath his shirts.

Grabbing his towel slung over the bedroom door he wandered down the hallway. A nice hot shower would help him feel a little more alive than he was feeling right now and it always helped clear his head. Having completed the kitchen revamp, he was going to make a start on the internal laundry today, and he needed a sharp mind to do the job right. He'd organised the plumber to come around after lunch and he had a fair bit to do before then.

A loud rap at the front door startled him as he made his way through the cottage, snapping him out of his thoughts. He deliberated briefly whether to ignore it then diverted through the lounge room, grumbling to himself.

Larry's broad smile met him through the fly screen door and Ronny was instantly happy he'd answered the door.

'Morning, mate, long time no see.'

Larry chuckled. 'G'day, Ronny, thought I'd pop down and have a cuppa with ya before ya take off. Feels like we're passing ships in the night at the moment.'

'Yeah, you dirty stopout. I see you've been staying a fair bit at Shirley's lately.' Ronny opened the screen door. 'Come on in, I'll just go get decent and then make us a cuppa.'

Larry gave his boots a good wipe before he stepped inside. 'Don't go getting dolled up for the likes of me, Ronny, boxers and a singlet will do for a cuppa. I gotta head off into town to grab some feed for the chooks and horses soon anyway.'

'All right then, suits me, I'll run through the dip after brekkie.' Ronny tossed his towel over the back of the lounge on the way past. Entering the kitchen with Larry in tow, he went to the kettle. 'Coffee or tea?'

Larry pulled a chair up at the dining table. 'Oh, whatever you're having, I'm easy.'

'Yeah, that's what Shirl tells me too,' Ronny said, laughing as he grabbed two mugs from the cupboard. It felt good to laugh – he hadn't in weeks.

'Oi, fair crack of the whip,' Larry said, laughing with him.

'Coffee it is then, and the stronger, the better this morning.'

Larry folded his arms on the table. 'Ya still not sleeping, mate?'

'Not really, too much on my mind, and I can't seem to switch the bastard of a thing off when I go to bed. Even meditating's not really doing the trick.'

'I see … Ivy talking to ya again yet?'

Ronny spooned a heaped teaspoon of coffee and two teaspoons of sugar in each mug. 'Only if she has to, can't blame her though. I'm a dick, doing what I did to her. I should have kept my distance.'

'Well, yes and no … you're only bloody human and ya like the girl, a lot. Ya can't help that you had a moment of weakness.'

The jug switched itself off and Ronny poured the hot water into the two mugs. 'There's no excuse for my moment of weakness. Whatsoever. I really hurt her, Larry, and I hate the fact I've been lying to her about who I am all this time. She knows me from somewhere, and I've dodged her questions about it twice now: once at the bank, and then when I kissed her.' Ronny shrugged as his forehead crumpled. 'It's eating me up more and more – it's just not right keeping something so big from her. And May and Alice have been so lovely, even after what happened – and that makes me feel even worse. I appreciate the fact neither of them have had a go at me for it, to be honest.'

'Yeah, I know, it's a hard one, but I suppose you've got your reasons to not tell Ivy who ya really are. And ya can't change what's happened, so don't go beating yourself up over it too much, or you'll send yourself around the bend. Okay?'

'That's me, mate, I beat myself up over everything – I'll never change. I just have to try to accept what's happened and move on, eventually.' He placed a mug in front of Larry and leant against the kitchen sink. 'Speaking of which, I'm sorry I haven't been here much to give you a hand around the place but I've got this weekend free, so I'll be making up for my lack of being here by telling you to rack off … in the nicest way possible of course.'

Larry held his hand up as if he was stopping traffic. 'Don't apologise, mate. I'm the one who pushed ya into taking the job on at Healing Hills. I said I'd take care of things here while ya do it and I'm more than happy to – keeps me outta trouble.' He took a sip from his coffee, and then shrugged. 'Where would I rack off to anyway?'

'I dunno. Maybe take Shirl away for a romantic weekend? I hear there's a really flash place less than an hour from here called the Hydro Majestic, and they've got specials on at the moment. It's supposed to be top nosh. So I reckon get in while it's discounted.'

Larry's bushy eyebrows shot up. 'Oh yeah, I heard about it re-opening a few months back. Apparently the views over the Megalong Valley are bloody awesome.' He smiled as he nodded at Ronny. 'I reckon ya might be onto something there. Shirl would be mighty impressed if I took her away for a weekend to a place with all the bells and whistles.' He cupped his hand around his mouth as though there were a room full of people eavesdropping on their conversation. 'And this old bushy wouldn't mind playing at the life of the rich and famous for a weekend too.'

'Well go for it, Larry, you two lovebirds deserve to have a weekend to yourselves.'

'I think I might just do that, Ronny. Thanks, mate.'

Ronny held up a loaf of bread. 'Want some Vegemite on toast?'

'If you're making some, I'll have a piece, thanks, but if you've got peanut butter I'd prefer that … Vegemite tends to give me real bad indigestion lately.'

'Shit, Larry, that'd suck. I'm addicted to Vegemite.'

'Me too, always have been, but weird things start happening to your body when you're a geriatric like me, and sadly, Vegemite just doesn't agree with me anymore.'

Ronny dug through the pantry and resurfaced brandishing a jar and a pleased grin. 'Kraft, and it's even crunchy.'

'Brilliant.' Larry's expression turned serious. 'Listen, I've been thinking about this situation you've gotten yourself into with Ivy.' He offered a resigned sigh. 'I should have said something earlier but I've been a bit hesitant because it's a pretty sensitive subject and I don't want ya thinking I'm sticking my nose into your business.'

'You're not the kind of bloke to stick your nose in anyone's business, Smithy, so I know whatever you have to say will be coming from a good place.' Ronny popped the bread down in the toaster and turned to face his mate. 'Go ahead, I'm all ears.'

'I know Lottie was pretty adamant on keeping your prison life quiet – she went to great lengths to keep it all under wraps when it happened. I can definitely see her way of thinking and I respect she was just worried about what was best for ya at the time, but situations change and, well –' Larry scrunched his face up as though he was about to get smacked in it, '– would it really be the end of the world if ya told Ivy who you were?'

Ronny's jaw almost hit the floor. 'Are you fucking serious, Smithy?'

Larry's eyes never left Ronny's, and they were filled with genuine concern. 'Never been more serious in me life.'

Ronny pulled a chair out, spun it around, and then rested his forearms against the back of it. 'Have you really considered what she's going to think of me after lying to her all this time? What about the fact I never wrote back to her when I was in prison? It felt right at the time but now I see it was pretty harsh of me not to.'

'I sure have, and I reckon it would somehow sort itself out, eventually. Better to lay it all on the line – than live with questions and regrets.' Larry offered a resigned smile. 'And I have a question for ya too: have *you* had a long hard think about never having the chance to be with the woman ya love with all your heart and soul because ya thought keeping all this stuff from her was the right thing to do?' Larry shook his head slowly. 'Because in my eyes, that's not living, Ronny, that's merely surviving each day until the next.'

Ronny's gaze shifted around the room before settling on the view out of the window. 'How do you know I love Ivy with all my heart and soul?'

'I can see it written all over your face every time ya mention her name.'

He turned back to Larry as the toast popped up behind him. 'You can?'

'Yep, it's plain as day. Ya see, as much as I joke about it, I'm a man deeply in love, and I couldn't imagine my life without Shirl in it. She's my soulmate, and I reckon, with the amount of times fate has brought you and Ivy together, Ivy might just be your soulmate too.' He shifted uneasily in his seat. 'I can't believe I'm saying all this lovey-dovey stuff, but I'm all you've got now Lottie has left us, and I need to step up to the plate and tell things how I see them.' He cleared his throat, his eyes sad. 'And I promised Lottie I would do the best for ya and support ya in everything that made ya happy, no matter what.'

Even though his head was spinning, a wisp of a smile tugged at Ronny's lips. It felt so damn good to be talking to someone about his feelings for Ivy, instead of rolling everything around in his mind – because that was getting him absolutely nowhere. 'I gotta say, this is a pretty heavy discussion for you.' He stood and grabbed the toast from the toaster and smeared a thick layer of butter on each piece. 'And because I know just how hard it would be for you to open up like this, I'm going to think long and hard about what you've just said. I can't promise anything will change, but you're right, I do need to take a serious look at what's going on around me.' He turned back to the table with Larry's toast and placed it in front of him. 'You've hit the nail square on the head, Smithy. I do love Ivy, with everything I've got. And I don't want to wake up one day when I'm eighty, all alone because I lost my one true love thanks to a wrong decision. But on the other hand I don't want to make the decision to tell her, only to have her end up hating me more than she already does. That would kill me.'

Larry offered a small smile. 'Good. All I wanted to hear was that you'd at least think about it. Because then, whichever way ya choose to go, it'll at least be your decision, and not based on what Lottie thought was best at the time, God rest her soul.' He lifted his toast to his mouth then hesitated. 'Like I said, I know Lottie was thinking of your best interests, as she always did, but little did she know ya were going to fall in love with Ivy Tucker. And that, my friend, changes everything in my eyes.'

Ronny finished smearing a thick layer of Vegemite on his toast and joined Larry at the table. 'I know what you're saying. I just feel bad even thinking about going against Lottie's wishes after everything she's done for me.' He shook his head sadly. 'It's a fucking hard one.'

'Look, mate, if Lottie knew how in love with Ivy ya are, I think she might have a change of heart … just like I have. All she ever wanted was for ya to live a happy life, and if that means you having to open up about what happened almost ten years ago, so be it. At least then, whatever the outcome, you'll feel like you've done the right thing by telling Ivy the truth. And I reckon Ivy's the type of girl who wouldn't go blabbing it from the rooftops either, and neither are her aunts, for that matter.'

Ronny took a gulp from his now lukewarm coffee. 'True.'

Larry swallowed his last mouthful of toast. 'And speaking of Lottie, it'll be her and Frank's wedding anniversary this Sunday, so the time's come for us to spread her ashes.'

Ronny's heart clenched. He'd been avoiding having this conversation. He was going to find it hard letting the last piece of Lottie go. 'Yeah, I know.' He swallowed the emotions that were making his throat tight. 'I really miss her, Larry.'

Larry reached out and gave Ronny a friendly pat on the back as he, too, sniffed back emotions. 'Me too, Ronny, me too.'

***

Halfway to Healing Hills, Ronny's mobile sang from the dash. Turning the radio down, he pressed answer and then tapped loudspeaker.

'Hi, sis.'

'Hey there, my beautiful brother! How's things?' Faith's sing-song voice radiated through the Kingswood.

Ronny smiled. By the sounds of it, the holiday had done her good. 'Things, are, well, a little complicated at the moment.'

'Oh shit, what's happened? What have you done?'

'I've only gone and fallen in love with the one woman on this earth I shouldn't have.'

'And who might this woman be?'

'Ivy Tucker.'

Faith's gasp reverberated around the car. 'Oh far out, Ronny, you never do things by halves, do you?'

Ronny grimaced. 'You know me well, sis.'

'So what the hell have I missed?'

Ronny slowed as he came to a T-junction, then turned left. 'Well, to cut a long story short, against my better judgement, I was entered into an auction to raise money for cancer, and Ivy won me as her slave for the weekend, and then she needed a carpenter, desperately, so me being the thoughtful kind of bloke I am, I couldn't say no to a damsel in distress, and then, well, things were getting a bit hot between us and I lost my wits and kissed her. And she kissed me back. And then I told her we could never be together because I couldn't tell her everything about myself. And now she hates me.'

'Fuck me swinging, you really do get yourself into the craziest of messes without even meaning to.' She sighed noisily then continued to curse under her breath. 'How much do you love her, Ronny?'

'With every breath I take.'

'Okay, well, that's the kind of love worth fighting for.' She sighed again. 'There's gotta be a way to fix this, just let me think for a minute.'

Ronny sat in silence as he watched the lush green landscape fly past his windscreen. He swore he could almost hear his sister's brain ticking over.

'I got it. You have to invite her to dinner.'

Ronny laughed. 'What? You're a spinner, Faith. Is that your way of fixing everything in your life, just feed people and they'll come round?'

Faith chuckled down the line. 'Basically, yes. It's always worked a treat for me, so it shouldn't be any different for you.'

'Right. So I invite her to dinner, and by some miracle she says yes, and then what?'

'And then you do exactly as I'm about to tell you to.'

***

A sliver of silvery moonlight spilled into the room and intertwined with the flickering candlelight – the two women preferring the softness to a blinding overhead light. The warm glow wasn't adequate to ignite every corner of the large, country-style kitchen, but was enough to light up Alice's gentle face and tender smile. Ivy sat across the dining table from her aunt, her cup of hot chocolate hugged tightly between her hands, and smiled back. Her belly ached after eating half a packet of marshmallows but she didn't care right now, the sugary, squishy pleasure had been well worth it; sweet food was her comfort when she was emotionally wounded. Alice knew that, which was why she'd come knocking on Ivy's bedroom door just before midnight with a packet of marshmallows to lure her out. Her beautiful aunt had heard her crying in bed, and had come to her rescue.

'If you're so worked up about going around there for dinner tomorrow night, sweetheart, why did you say yes in the first place?'

'Because even though I'm mad at him for kissing me and then telling me in the next breath that we could never be together because he's not been completely honest with me, I still like him, a lot. I know that makes no sense after cursing every lying, cheating man who's ever lived these past few weeks, but I just can't help myself when it comes to Ronny.'

Alice remained quiet as she listened, her hand gently squeezing Ivy's on the table. Ivy sniffled and pulled another tissue from the box Alice had placed in front of her. After wiping her tears and blowing her nose she added it to the growing pile in front of her.

'Why have relationships got to be so damn hard all the time? I just want to fall in love with the man of my dreams, have a family, and live happily ever after – is that too much to ask?'

Alice chuckled softly. 'You're asking the wrong person. Because, from my own experience, yes, it appears so.'

Groaning, Ivy rolled her eyes. 'Oh, Aunt Alice, I just wish he could tell me whatever it is he's hiding from me.' She shook her head. 'I mean, what could be *that* bad?'

Alice's eyes widened as she sat back in her chair. 'You never know what skeletons a person could be hiding in their closet, and yes, they can sometimes have a huge effect on another. But in the end it's their past, and their life, so you have to respect them enough to let them open up about things if and when they choose to, because you shouldn't force anyone into telling you something they don't want to.'

'But what about this magical feeling I get when I'm around him? And I know he gets it around me too because I felt it in his kiss. Isn't that worth opening your closet up for, instead of letting something that could be amazing slip through your fingers?'

'Yes, and no, Ivy.' Alice smiled sadly. 'I wish I could tell you what you want to hear, sweetheart, but Ronny's a big boy and he's got his own mind, so you have to allow him to do as he sees fit.'

Ivy huffed. 'I know you're right, and I also know that Ronny has the right to keep his past behind him. It just breaks my heart to think that we could have had something so beautiful together.'

'I know, love. Life can really suck sometimes.' Alice tilted her head to one side. 'But on a more positive note, though, at least by going around for dinner you can hopefully mend the bridge and become friends again. I truly think Ronny is good company for you.' She smiled. 'Don't ever forget the fact he was the catalyst behind you finding the courage to sing again – even if it was just for that moment, watching him through the window of the cottage. Small steps, as they say.'

Ivy bit her lip to stop it from quivering as the memory overcame her. 'Yes, he did more for me in those few minutes than I could have ever imagined, without even trying.'

Alice rested her chin on her palms as her eyes glistened with unshed tears. 'Ronny really has been a miracle for us – in a few ways – so maybe you need to give the guy some slack and allow him to tell you whatever it is in his own time, as much as it pains you to do so. I honestly feel he's a good man, and he'll open up to you when he's good and ready to.'

Ivy reached out and gave her aunt's arm a squeeze. 'As always, I think you're spot on, Aunt Alice. I need to focus on my own life, and my own heart. For now anyway.'

'That's the spirit love. But even so, I think you're best going to Ronny's with an open mind and heart, just in case he does decide to confess to you.'

'And if he does, what if I don't like what he has to say?' Ivy tipped her head to the side in contemplation.

'Only you can decide that, Ivy. It's how you react that's going to decide your fate, not the secret itself.'

'Yes, I suppose that's true to a point, but like you said, there are some secrets that can blow your world apart.'

'Yes, and like I also said, sweetheart, it's all about how we perceive something.' Alice yawned as she glanced at the clock on the far wall. 'Anyway, I think that's enough excitement for the two of us for tonight. It's almost two and you, my girl, need to get your beauty sleep so you can enjoy your date with Ronny.'

'It's not a date, Aunt Alice, he just wants to make it up to me after being such an arse. That's all.'

Alice grinned wickedly. 'As I said, it's all about how we perceive things.' She tapped Ivy lovingly on the arm. 'Now come on, let's hit the sack before we both turn into pumpkins.'

'I think it's a little too late for that – it's already past midnight.' Ivy smiled as she stood and wrapped her arms around Alice. 'I love you so much, thank you for the chat.'

Alice embraced her tightly. 'Love you, too, Ivy.' She gestured out the kitchen window to where the night sky shone spectacularly. 'More than all those beautiful glittering stars in the sky.'

CHAPTER 18

Climbing the ladder to the attic was one tiny step at a time for Ivy, but it felt as momentous as walking on the moon, the nerves in her belly like fireworks. She imagined what it was going to be like to pick up her guitar case, carry it back down the ladder and open it to reveal the beautiful J-45 Gibson Sunburst she'd inherited from her dear mum. It was as though she was going to be seeing an old friend after too many years apart – she was nervous and excited all at once. And an old friend her Gibson was to her, having shared many memorable moments with it by campfires, under trees, on the couch and in front of crowds. She'd been playing since she was six – it was the guitar her mother had taught her on. Her bond with the instrument was immeasurable. Ronny had asked her to bring it along tonight, so they could strum some tunes together, and she was determined to do so. The timing just felt right. She was ready for this.

Sucking in a deep breath she took one more look behind her before she stepped into the dimness of the attic, and was met with the comforting sight of May's and Alice's beaming faces. They gave her the thumbs up, expressions filled with the same exhilaration Ivy was feeling. She smiled back at them before drawing in another deep breath and blowing it away, imagining she was whooshing her fears away with it. She made a beeline for her guitar, not wanting to get sidetracked and chicken out of doing this – no more was she going to run from her past. Not only was this going to be a huge step for her, it would also be a way to break the ice with Ronny, and she wanted to believe she could help him out too. Ronny Sinclair had too much talent to let it go to waste – he had to get himself up on a stage so others could bear witness to his amazing voice. She just hoped she didn't fall in a heap when she tried, as she had done many times before she'd decided to tuck the guitar away, although she was safe in the knowledge that if she did, Ronny would be beside her to help.

Placing her hands on the case, Ivy felt a rush of adrenaline and her fight or flight instincts kicked in in full force. A cold clammy feeling engulfed her as an impending sense of something horrific happening threatened to overwhelm her. She knew from first-hand experience this was the beginning of a panic attack – although she hadn't had a full-blown one in two years. *Come and get me*, she said with conviction, referring to the fear. She was not going to let it overcome her anymore. Her mouth felt dry, her breathing became shallow and her body started to feel numb, especially her fingers and lips – it was always the way. With her heart hammering against her chest, images of that horrible night flooded her mind but she shooed them away as if reflecting light from a mirror – a tactic Deepak Chopra had spoken about in the book she had read. Every bit of her wanted to run away from these horrible bodily sensations, but today she was staying put and facing her fears. Her legs were shaking and her heart was racing a million miles a minute, as if her attacker was approaching her once more, but she reminded herself over and over there was nothing to be afraid of, and that he couldn't hurt her anymore. It wasn't because of her music that it had all happened – it was entirely Warren Young's fault. He was the one who had chosen to attack her. It was as simple as that. And he was no longer walking this earth to be able to do it to her again. With a flood of determination, she picked the guitar case up, turned, and retraced her steps to the opening and back down the ladder, as if she was on autopilot.

May and Alice met her at the bottom and, after helping her tuck the ladder back up into the ceiling, they stood beside her and gently placed their hands on her shoulders. No words were needed. Ivy knelt and unlatched the case with trembling hands. Opening the lid, she reached out and ran her fingers along the stained timber, tearing up as she did. The photo of her and her mum she'd always carried was exactly where she'd left it, tucked beneath the guitar's strings. It was her lucky charm. She plucked it out and brought it to her lips, kissing it. 'I miss you, Mum,' she whispered. May and Alice gave her shoulders a loving squeeze.

Images again started bombarding Ivy, but this time they were positive ones, reminding her of all the times she'd sung to her heart's content, either by herself or in front of a crowd of family and friends, or at an event where she'd basically known nobody. She'd always been so confident back then, so careless and free, with a faith that she could conquer anything. She ached to be that person once more. She smiled through her tears, as a sensation of finally coming back home to her roots washed over her. And for the first time in nine years, like a flower bulb that had lain dormant, she felt the piece of her she'd tucked away finally beginning to emerge.

***

A rustic timber sign hanging from an enormous tree branch caught Ivy's attention as it gently swayed in the afternoon breeze. Bringing her ute to a stop, she gazed out her windscreen. Something about the sign made her feel all warm and fuzzy inside as she silently read it: WELCOME TO SUNDOWN FARM. She wound down her window. The crisp freshness from the surrounding countryside crept into the ute and encompassed her, and as she breathed it in, a smile tugged at her glossy lips. She still found it hard to believe this was really happening. That she was here, at Ronny's place, and she was going to play some tunes with him – as long as her nerves didn't get the better of her. She glanced over at the passenger seat, to where her guitar case was strapped into the seatbelt, and determination flooded her. She could do this. She could finally win the battle against her fears. She just had to. She told herself the same as she told all her healing clients: her dreams deserved to be reached for. It was about time she started practising what she preached.

Adrenaline flooded her and her heart went into a wild gallop at the very thought of strumming her guitar strings, but instead of allowing it to override her as she usually did, she closed her eyes and breathed through the unwanted sensations, clenching and unclenching her sweaty hands. She'd been on autopilot most of the day, trying to kid herself into thinking that coming here for dinner was no big deal. Yeah, right. Her stomach filled with a flurry of butterflies. She lifted her fingers to her lips as she recalled Ronny's hungry kiss and the way his hands caressed her skin in the most erotic of ways – her body responding to the memory with longing. She'd never felt like that with a man before – so desperate to make love to him, to feel him inside her as they became one, to fall over the edge of ecstasy with him – and every inch of her craved to feel it again with him. If only Ronny didn't have a past he believed he couldn't share with her, things could be so beautiful between them. She wished he could trust her enough to tell her whatever it was. It couldn't be anything that would make her think any different of him, could it? Curiosity ran rampant in her mind.

Stopped at the front gates of the property with the engine still purring, Ivy took a few moments to gather herself while gazing towards where the mist hovered over the mountaintops like a loving embrace. Her body was tingling in all the wrong places and she needed to get a grip, worried her flushed face would give her wayward thoughts away. This dinner was for them to build their relationship as mates, not lovers, and she needed to remember that. After what had happened between them a few weeks ago, she would have never predicted she'd be coming here for dinner, let alone be able to act somewhat normal around him again, but there was just something about his company that put her at ease. She'd wanted to stay mad at him for giving her a glimmer of hope that they could be together and then stealing it from her in the blink of an eye, but after a few days of drowning in self-pity, and using up every box of tissues in the homestead – as well as her aunts' sensible words about being open-minded if she and Ronny were ever going to have a chance – she'd found it impossible to stay angry. And it was in her nature to forgive – the way she'd reacted upon seeing Malcolm the night of the fundraiser was perfect proof of that. Her mother's favourite saying, *Love people the most when they deserve it the least,* was one of her life mottos. She thought the fact that she'd found it almost impossible to put a whole sentence to Ronny over the past few weeks was proof of that, her avoidance of him more out of awkwardness than ill feelings. She would explain that to him tonight if the timing felt right.

She released the handbrake and drove through the wrought iron gates then stopped at the fork in the road, trying to remember Ronny's next instruction. *Turn to the left when you pull in, turning right will take you to the dam instead of the house and it's a bit boggy up that way at the moment.* Indicating, she turned left, and then laughed at herself. Why was she indicating when she was in the middle of a paddock? Talk about nerves making her not think straight. Wanting to appear calm and collected when she arrived at Ronny's front door, she turned her radio up and hummed along to a Cold Chisel tune as she drove along the gravel path.

Driving past a row of apple trees surrounded by impeccably manicured lawns and flourishing gardens, she smiled. It was a woman's touch; Lottie had clearly taken great pride in her visitors' first impression of Sundown Farm and it was heartwarming to see that Ronny and Larry were following suit. Beyond the trees were rolling green fields that seemed to disappear into the far-reaching horizon. Ivy sighed softly. Like Healing Hills, Sundown Farm was absolutely breathtaking.

Soon she was approaching a charming colonial-style timber cottage with wide wrap-around verandahs. A multitude of wind chimes and pretty sun catchers hung from overhead beams, two hammocks hanging in pride of place – she imagined the view from them at dusk and dawn would be amazing. The gardens surrounding the quaint home were mighty impressive, with colourful blooms bright between the green leaves.

Pulling up under the shade of a towering tree out the back of the cottage, where Ronny had suggested she park, she switched off the engine and began to gather her things, though she'd grab her guitar later on. She spotted Ronny leaning on the banister of the back verandah as she got out of the ute, the dimples on his cheeks prominent either side of his knee-buckling smile. He waved to her then descended the front steps in two bounds. He was dressed in jeans and a western shirt, sleeves rolled up to his elbows, his muscular chest peeking out just enough to make her crave more of it – God, how she loved his burly chest. He was clearly still in his work clothes and, damn, he looked mighty fine. She sucked in a sharp breath, his rugged sexiness not something she could ignore. Images of ripping his shirt from his broad shoulders filled her mind – she just couldn't help herself.

'Hi, Ronny.' He was beside her now, the hint of his aftershave making her a little giddy.

'Hey, Ivy, found the place okay?'

'Sure did, easy as.' She held out a six-pack and a bag of Lindt chocolates. 'And I come bearing gifts.'

'Oh, salted caramel chocolate, my favourite, thanks.' He examined the beer. 'Never heard of this one?' Ronny took them from her, his hands brushing hers as he did. Ivy felt a familiar warmth seep all the way to her toes.

'It's local beer, thought you might like to give it a go.'

'I'll give almost anything a go once.' He looked at her, his lighthearted smile contrasting with the depth in his eyes. He shook his head as he looked down at his bare feet, groaning. 'Shit, sorry, talk about foot in mouth – that came out all wrong … I wasn't referring to –'

Ivy reached out and brushed his arm. 'Relax, I know you didn't mean anything by it.' She smiled. 'Let's just say that from this moment on, we're starting afresh, hey?'

He held the beers up, his charming smile back in full force. 'I'll drink to that.'

Ivy breathed a sigh of relief, the last bit of tension between them seeming to melt away. 'Excellent.'

Ronny wrapped his arm around her shoulder as he led her towards the pebble pathway. 'But first, let me show you around the place before it gets dark.'

***

While Ivy waited for Ronny to return a phone call from his sister in Sydney and grab them both a beer while he was at it, she made herself comfortable on the back verandah. Jessie scuttled up the back steps and joined her. Flopping down at Ivy's feet, the dog rested her head on her paws. From her cosy seat on the couch, Ivy took in the final glimpses of the beauty of Sundown Farm as twilight began to steal away the bright colours of the day. She smiled at the goat and Shetland pony in a nearby paddock; both still gnawing on the clover hay she and Ronny had just fed them. Cindy Clawford meowed beside her and she gave her a gentle stroke. Like Jessie, the adorable bundle of fluff had curled up beside her the minute she'd sat down. The cat's name had sent her into a fit of laughter when Ronny had first told her, while Cindy was hanging off the leg of her jeans. The feisty feline's welcome had been less than warm as she'd leapt at Ivy like a lion pouncing on its prey the second Ivy had set foot in the cottage. But the cat had soon been putty in her hands when Ivy had shown her what a good head rub felt like. And contrary to what Ronny had said about Ned before Ivy had met him in the flesh, the goat had been nothing but gentlemanly. With a cheeky grin, Ronny had put it down to Ned being a flirt. And then there was the half-blind rooster, Nugget, who had gone tearing through the backyard and run smack-bang into the clothesline. He had lain there in a daze for a good half a minute, and she'd been terrified he was dead. But then up Nugget had jumped like he'd been lying on a bed of fire ants and off he'd raced once again on a mission none of them were privy to.

Ronny hadn't been kidding when he'd called it the funny farm; she hadn't laughed so much in ages. And God, it felt good. Ronny had a certain way of bringing out the best in her, and there was a lot to be said for a person who could do that. She was so relieved they'd gotten past their moment of weakness, even though it had been a kiss she would never forget – or regret. Ronny Sinclair was the type of bloke she needed in her life as a mate – dependable, trustworthy and so very kind-hearted. Maybe this was the universe's way of teaching her to trust in men again, so she could finally find her true love? At first she'd thought Ronny had come into her life to save her from her renovation dilemma, but now she was starting to think that Ronny was her angel sent from heaven in more ways than one. He'd certainly come to her rescue a few times, as he was going to tonight with her music.

The fiery sphere of light in the distance gradually sank beyond the misty horizon, the copper hues giving way to a dusty mauve scattered with the occasional glimmer of a faraway star. As the light faded, so did the warmth of the day, until all that was left was the chill of twilight and the promise of a cool night to come. Ivy pulled the blanket from the arm of the couch and tossed it over herself and Cindy, being sure to leave the snoozing cat's head uncovered. She motioned for Jessie to jump up beside her, and she did the same for her canine mate, the blanket just big enough to cover the three of them. Ivy leant back further, all snuggled up with her furry friends as she continued to enjoy Mother Nature's show. A distant windmill was silhouetted against the velvety sky, the golden dusk now enveloped by the approaching night. And just as effortlessly as day had given way to night, the spectacular performance of the evening sky began. Like the glowing embers of a fire, stars twinkled as the full moon stole the show, illuminating the sky with glorious silver light. Warmth filled her. What a beautiful way to end an equally beautiful afternoon, and they still had dinner to go.

The creak of the fly-screen door caught Ivy's attention, and as the sensor light flickered to life, Ronny appeared with two beers in one hand and her guitar case in the other. 'Thought I'd grab it for you, save you having to get out of your comfy spot. Hope you don't mind?'

'Talk about pushy,' she said with a playful grin. 'Of course I don't mind.'

Ronny returned her lighthearted smile, making Ivy feel as though she had firecrackers going off inside her. She was about to make some sweet music with the sexiest man she'd ever met, which was almost as good as making love.

Ronny placed the case on the floor. 'Just going to duck back inside and grab mine, be back in a sec.'

When he finally sat beside her, his guitar in his lap, he asked, 'What song do you want to try first?'

Ivy thought for a few moments, and then smiled, the tune in her head bringing back many happy memories from her childhood. 'How about "Wish You Were Here" by Pink Floyd?'

Ronny smiled. 'Good choice, I love that song.'

'It was my mum's favourite.' Ivy smiled sadly. 'She used to play it on this very guitar all the time – it was hers before it was mine.'

'That's beautiful, Ivy.' Ronny gently touched her arm, his eyes full of compassion. 'You must really miss her.'

'I do. A lot.' Ivy swallowed the lump of emotion lodged in her throat. 'But I've grown to accept the fact she's gone forever, and I just try to be thankful for the fact I got to spend the first nine years of my life with her.'

'I understand how you feel. I lost my mum when I was young too.' He motioned to his guitar. 'And like you, my mum gave me this guitar – it's my most precious possession. Other than Sundown, of course.'

Ivy's heart tumbled. Their lives were so similar in so many ways. She wanted to reach out and pull him to her, but refrained, not knowing if he'd welcome the gesture. 'Oh Ronny, I didn't know your mum had passed. I'm so sorry.'

Ronny gave her arm a squeeze. 'No need to be sorry.' His jaw clenched and a muscle twitched in his neck. 'It's my father who should be sorry – but the son of a bitch got out of it the easy way.'

'What do you mean?'

'There's no gentle way to put it, really.' Ronny looked away from her. 'When I was twelve, my father bashed my mother to death and then he shot himself.' When he turned back, his eyes were filled with tears. Two rolled down his cheeks and he brusquely wiped them away before clearing his throat. 'The bastard should have rotted in prison as far as I'm concerned.'

Ivy gasped, and then covered her mouth, Ronny's vulnerability making her soul ache to the very core. 'Oh my God, Ronny, that's terrible.' She shook her head, blinking back tears, her heart breaking for this beautiful man before her. 'I don't know what else to say.' She threw her arms around him, unable to stop herself from comforting him any longer. Ronny responded by embracing her tightly, and she breathed a sigh of relief.

After a few moments, Ivy said, 'I kinda know how you must feel. Although my father was not so directly responsible for my mother's death, he still played a huge part in it.'

Ronny pulled back so he could look into her eyes – the poignancy in them stealing Ivy's breath. 'How?'

Ivy looked down at her lap. 'She jumped off a cliff because he broke her heart beyond repair when he cheated on her with a barmaid in town.'

'So that's why you looked so heartbroken at the cliff face when you were giving me the guided tour of Healing Hills.'

Ivy nodded. 'I can't believe you noticed. I've become pretty good at hiding my heartache.'

'Now I'm at a loss for words.' Ronny took both her hands in his. 'You and I have both lost so much, been hurt so badly. We're like kindred spirits.'

Ivy graced him with a small smile. 'I think you might be right there, Ronny.'

Ronny gave her a tender smile and her heart fluttered. The warmth of his thigh resting against hers, the strength in his hands, and the tender look in his beautiful amber eyes sent quivers throughout her. In a way she couldn't make sense of, she felt as though she was somehow home when she was with Ronny, as though she'd been lost all her life and had finally found her place. She wanted to love him so much, and she could feel he wanted to love her in return. Damn his rotten, stinking, stupid, hidden skeletons. They were ruining what could have been a fairytale ending.

Ronny was the one to break the magical moment as he pulled his hands away and focused once again on his guitar. 'Let's get this show on the road, otherwise we'll be eating at midnight.' Even though he said it lightheartedly, his voice was a little strained.

Ivy smiled to cover her disappointment at losing the comfort of his arms. She watched his fingers stroking his guitar strings. She wished it were her he was playing with those manly hands – a girl could always dream. She knew nothing was going to come of her longing for him after their kiss had turned sour, but he was certainly a nice distraction from the nerves beginning to build inside her at the thought of singing. Unclipping her case, she pulled her guitar out carefully. She'd replaced all the strings earlier that afternoon, and had accustomed herself to the feel of having it in her arms once again.

Ronny graced her with a smile so tender it melted her already syrupy heart. 'You ready?'

She nodded as she chewed on her bottom lip before drawing in an extended breath.

Like riding a bike, a musician never forgot how to play their instrument and soon Ivy was strumming the hypnotic tune along with Ronny. It was a shared journey that held them spellbound in enthralled silence. No lyrics were needed at first, the melody enough to flood her skin with goose bumps. This was it, the moment she'd been dreaming of, pining for, fearing … and it was more entrancing than she could ever have imagined. The music soared through the air like a wedge-tailed eagle on an updraft, taking with it Ivy's heart and soul. She glanced sideways at Ronny as he hummed the tune, his eyes focused on where his fingers were strumming his guitar. He felt her eyes upon him, and looked at her, smiling and nodding, as if to say, *See, you can do it.*

And yes, she could, with him by her side …

It was at that very moment that Ivy felt the weight she'd been carrying in her heart and soul since that horrific night lift and disperse like ice melting on a summer's day. Then, she found her voice and began passionately belting the lyrics. Ronny followed suit, their voices entwining and floating upon the gentle evening breeze.

***

Three hours later, the mouthwatering aroma of the beef Wellington cooking in the oven wafted through the cottage. Ivy could have sat on the verandah and sung with Ronny all night long, his intense husky voice addictive, although their stomachs had other plans and hunger had lured them inside. She licked her lips, belly rumbling with the thought of tucking into something that smelt so divine. It was close to nine thirty, so it was no wonder she was starving and about to chew her own arm off. They'd been enjoying singing together so much they'd simply lost track of time. Once again, Ronny impressed her with his skills. The man clearly knew his way around a kitchen, on top of everything else he was good at. What a catch he was – if only she could catch him. Still on a high after playing some tunes with him, she tried not to let the thought get her down.

Sitting at the breakfast bench, she watched as Ronny fussed about the kitchen, chopping vegetables like he was a pro. Country music played softly in the background. She'd offered a number of times to help him prepare dinner, but he'd refused, telling her to sit back and relax, so she was. She took a sip from her beer, feeling at ease while she admired how sexy he was as he roamed the kitchen. His jeans showed off the curve of his arse perfectly and his singlet was taut in all the right places across his back and chest. Yum.

Ronny looked up at her as though reading her thoughts, a cheeky smile on his kissable lips. He put his knife down and wiped his hands on the tea towel over his shoulder.

'Have you never seen a man cook before?'

Ivy tipped her head to the side. 'Come to think of it – nope.'

Ronny laughed, and then stopped. 'Are you serious? You've never had a man cook dinner for you?'

'Nope.'

'Holy crap. What kind of blokes have you been dating, Ivy?'

Ivy smirked at his mention of a date, and then shrugged. It was nice to imagine Ronny was seeing this as more of a date than just a friendly catch up. Maybe there was a little hope for them. 'I've clearly been dating Neanderthals,' she said with a grin.

'I'd have to agree with you there.' His gaze lingered on her, intensity filling his eyes. 'I really enjoyed singing with you. Your voice gives me goose bumps.'

'Aw shucks, thanks, Ronny.' Ivy felt her cheeks flame. She turned away and pretended to be engrossed in the candle flickering on the coffee table in the lounge room. 'Your voice gives me goose bumps too.'

Ronny snorted. 'Yeah, right.'

She spun back to him. 'Seriously, as I told you before, your voice is a gift.'

Now it was Ronny's turn to look away. Ivy watched his Adam's apple bob. When he brought his eyes back to hers, a smile adorned his yummy lips. 'Thank you, Ivy, it honestly means the world, hearing that from you.'

She flashed him a smile as the music playing in the lounge room grabbed her attention. 'Oh my God, "Goondiwindi Moon". I love this song.' She clasped her hands together and closed her eyes, letting Lee Kernaghan's voice sweep her away. Seconds later she jumped when Ronny grabbed her.

'Dance with me,' he said before dragging her from the stool and into the dimly lit lounge room.

Caught off guard, Ivy let him do as he wanted and before she knew it, she was in his arms, her head against his burly chest as they slowly moved to the beautiful love song. With his body pressed against hers, Ivy's heartbeat accelerated, but it had nothing to do with fear of being hurt this time and everything to do with what her body wanted. She felt herself go into a trance, the tenderness of the moment making the outside world fade away, leaving just her and Ronny, here together, alone, as their souls mingled. Emotions stirred deep within her and a lump formed in her throat, as though the words she'd been dying to say had stuck there and needed to come out. A tear trickled down her cheek, not from sadness, but from the sheer emotion coursing throughout her. Ronny must have sensed her shift in energy as he gently placed his finger beneath her chin and tilted her face so she was gazing into his eyes. As his arm slid round her waist, he wiped the tear away with his thumb.

'You okay?' His voice was so tender.

She shook her head.

'Want to talk about it?'

She so wanted to talk about it, wanted to tell him exactly how she felt. She wanted him to know she could barely take a decent breath because she was falling so in love with him. But should she?

He tucked a tendril of hair behind her ear. 'Come on, what is it?'

And she caved at the compassionate look in his gorgeous eyes, her walls finally crumbling, leaving her exposed and vulnerable and in danger of being hurt. And the beautiful thing was, she didn't care. 'I've fallen for you, Ronny, hard. I can't explain how, or why, after only knowing you for a short time, but there's just something about you that makes me feel like I've already known you for a lifetime. You somehow make me feel so safe, and so loved for who I am, and …' She stumbled over her words. 'I suppose what I'm trying to say is I –'

Ronny leant in and placed a kiss so gentle and lingering upon her lips it made her entire body quiver. She wanted, needed, craved him, was desperate for him to kiss her harder, but he didn't.

'I love you too, Ivy Tucker.'

And she stood there, silent, their eyes locked on one another's, as his words sank deeply into her galloping heart. No more words were needed right now; what she needed was to feel at one with him. She clasped her hands at the back of his neck, pulling him into her once again. His lips met hers, hard this time, and they were oh, so deliciously hungry as their breaths quickened and their tongues twirled. Fingers fumbled as they began tearing at one another's clothes. Naked, they tumbled onto the couch.

Ivy wondered if he'd ask about the scar on her stomach, but he didn't, instead tracing his fingers along it before he stopped and looked into her eyes, his handsomeness enhanced by the flickering candlelight. 'Are you sure, Ivy?'

'Uh huh.' She pushed her hips into his long, hot hardness. 'I want to feel you inside of me.'

Needing no more of an invitation, a sexy smile curled his lips as he cupped her breasts and leant in to caress her nipples with his mouth. He licked and sucked and bit to the perfect point of pleasure. Ivy gasped in ecstasy as his lips trailed down her stomach, halting to kiss and lick inside her thighs, and then, thankfully, to her pulsating heaven. His tongue was warm and slow and lingering and so damn perfect against her that she almost reached ecstasy instantly.

And then he stopped.

She sucked in a breath, teetering on the edge of bliss, her body quivering.

Ronny stood and grabbed her hand, his yearning for her evident. 'Come on, let's take this to the bedroom, where it's more comfortable.'

***

Propped up on his elbow, Ronny smiled wickedly, his desire to ravish Ivy again perfectly clear, before a knock at the front door chased his smile away. 'I wonder who the hell that is?'

Ivy groaned as she felt his body move away from hers. 'Do you have to answer it?'

'As much as I would rather stay here with you, I have to. Just in case it's an emergency.' He brushed a kiss over her lips. 'I'll be back before you know it.'

She smiled sassily. 'I'll be waiting.'

The knock sounded again, this time louder and more insistent.

'Yeah, I'm coming,' he called as he rummaged through his drawers, pulling out a pair of boxers.

'You get many late-night callers?' Ivy said playfully. She tucked her hands behind her head so she could grab a better look at his naked lusciousness. A tingle travelled throughout her at the thought of ravishing him again when he returned to bed.

'Never. Christ knows who it is. It can't be Larry, he's gone away for a romantic weekend with Shirl.' Ronny tugged the boxers on.

Ivy smiled. 'Well I suppose you won't know who it is until you open it.'

'True that.' He sauntered out of the bedroom. 'Back in a sec.'

Moments later, Ivy's stomach turned at the sound of the woman's voice. Her jealousy fired up. What in the hell was Amy Mayberry doing here, and so late? Tugging the bed sheets over her naked body, she eavesdropped on the conversation.

'I thought I'd use my open invitation to drop in with some wine, Ronny. You up for a bit of fun tonight, cowboy?'

Ivy gritted her teeth. How blatant could Amy be?

'Oh, um, I –' Ronny sounded extremely uncomfortable. Ivy wondered whether it was because he'd been caught out – maybe he was having a bit of fun with Amy on the side, like she'd first thought. Had Ronny lied to her face? Was that what he hadn't wanted to tell her? Her heart squeezed as anger flooded her.

'Oh, come on now, you party pooper, let loose once in a while.'

'Not tonight, Amy.'

Not tonight? What kind of answer was that? Ivy's anger turned to rage at the thought she'd been taken for a ride by a bloke once again. Fuck this. She was going to go out there and give Ronny a piece of her mind – and Amy, while she was at it. She wrestled out of the sheet and climbed from the bed, cursing when she remembered her clothes were strewn all over the lounge-room floor. Bugger it, she'd just have to wear one of Ronny's T-shirts and hope it was long enough to cover her.

'Oh come on, Ronny, I could feel how much you wanted me at the bakery and I know you haven't done anything like this before, after what you told me, but I promise I can teach you everything you need to know.' Amy giggled suggestively.

'I'm sorry, but I already have company tonight, Amy.'

Hands shaking, Ivy yanked open the top drawer and fumbled through it.

Amy's voice went up a few notches. 'Oh, have you now? So much for me being able to call in any time. Who's the lucky girl?'

Ivy smirked as she pulled a shirt from the pile – it was a small win that Amy wouldn't be getting what she wanted tonight. As she unfolded the T-shirt, a piece of paper drifted to the floor. She bent and picked it up, still completely focused on the conversation going on at the front door.

'I've got Ivy here for dinner.'

'Oh, I see. Well, would you rather I go?' All the sugary niceness had left Amy's voice.

You better say yes, Ronny, Ivy thought as she straightened up and looked at the paper in her hands. A letter. Her jaw dropped. This was her handwriting. What in the hell was Ronny doing with this? And all of a sudden the conversation no longer held any interest for her, Ronny and Amy's voices fading away as the walls began to feel as though they were caving in on her. Her blood froze solid in her veins as her heart stalled and then started beating frantically. She fought to take a decent breath as she looked to the doorway Ronny had disappeared through, and then back to her trembling hands. She leant against the wall for support, feeling completely numb. She had to remind herself to keep it together as her temples began to throb. And then it dawned on her in full shocking force as Ronny's words hit home. *There are some things I just can't tell you. And for that reason, I need to leave you alone.* Oh, how right he was. She wanted to scream, thump something, climb under a rock, anything but face what was right in front of her. Her heart ached beyond belief. Ronny had been lying to her about who he was all along. They'd just made the sweetest love. Twice. The bastard, taking advantage of her like this. He was not the person he'd led her to believe, nowhere near it. She should have stuck to her guns, stayed away – as her father had taught her all those years ago, men just couldn't be trusted.

Needing to get some clothes on, she slammed the letter onto the dresser, part of her wanting to tear it to shreds, and glared at it as she tugged the T-shirt over her head. What to do now? Storm out there and confront Ronny, in front of Amy, or wait until the wretched woman left? Her fists clenched tightly at her sides until her nails dug into the palm of her hands. The only thing she was really aware of was the sound of her heart pounding against her chest, and her pulse drumming in her ears. Her mind spun out of control, to the point she couldn't think straight. She didn't know what hurt more right now, that Ronny felt he couldn't tell her who he was from the beginning, or that he'd deliberately hidden this from her. This whole time he'd been pretending to be someone he wasn't. She felt like a complete fool. She wanted to run – far away from him, forever, but that meant she had to run past Amy, and she wasn't about to do that. Her head spun faster, and she was finding it harder and harder to breathe. She clutched the side of the dresser, afraid she was going to pass out. Ronny appeared at the doorway, his smile disappearing when he spotted the outraged look on Ivy's face and then the open letter.

'You're a fucking liar, Ronny Sinclair – or should I say, *Byron McWilliams*?' She tore past him and began gathering her clothes from the lounge room floor. She rammed one foot and then the other into her knickers, and yanked them up.

Ronny followed and stood staring at her.

'Please, Ivy, let me explain,' he said, and she had to refrain from slapping him across the face.

With her clothes now bundled in her arm she grabbed her bag from the bench and her guitar case from the floor, and then stormed to the back door on wobbly legs. Ronny reached out for her but she dodged him. 'Don't you *dare* touch me. I don't even know who you are. And why in the hell does Amy feel she has an open invitation to arrive at your doorstep at this time of the night?' She didn't wait for an answer as she fled the house.

Ronny ran after her. 'Please, Ivy, wait. I can explain everything. Please don't leave it like this.'

She spun to face him, her eyes narrowed. 'If there's one thing I hate in this world, Ronny, or Byron, or whoever the fuck you are, it's a liar, and you are the biggest fucking liar I've ever met.'

She ran down the back steps and into the soothing darkness of night. In less than a minute she was in her ute and revving it to life. Gravel flew out from the tyres as she skidded out the driveway. Glancing in her rear-view mirror, she spotted Ronny standing on the verandah, his head in his hands, and her entire world shattered into a million tiny pieces.

CHAPTER 19

By sunrise the following morning, Ivy's bed sheets were in a knot and, aside from a few fitful bouts of dozing filled with horrible dreams, she hadn't slept a wink. On her bedside table her phone vibrated for the umpteenth time – the caller ID one she didn't want to answer. Ever. When was Ronny going to take the hint? Beneath the jumbled sheets, her sweaty hands were clasping each other as though she was trying to reassure herself, and her head felt like a cyclone had blown through it. She needed to talk to her aunts – rolling everything around in her mind wasn't doing her one bit of good – but they'd gone to visit some friends last night and wouldn't be back until later this morning. No way was she going to talk about this over the phone – this was a conversation that had to be face to face. She knew May and Alice were going to be as shaken as she was, and she didn't want them driving home in a fluster, it would be too dangerous.

Throwing her pillow over her head, she groaned, wishing she could knock herself out so she could at least stop thinking about Ronny

Sinclair or whoever he really was. Ivy's world had caved in on her last night and she hadn't stopped to think about the fact he was the man who'd saved her from death until she was speeding down the highway towards home. She hadn't been about to turn around and go thank him – she'd already done that with a letter, which he'd chosen to ignore. And even though she'd tried to understand Byron McWilliams' silence over the years, giving him the benefit of the doubt, knowing he had ignored her heartfelt letter of thanks hurt beyond words. How could Ronny have made love to her so passionately, making her feel like the luckiest woman on earth, even as he was deceiving her on such a deep level? He'd definitely crossed a line that he never should have until he'd told her who he was. Damn him – he should have respected her enough to give her the truth and let her decide what she wanted after that. But he'd stolen that from her.

At least now she understood why she'd felt as though she already knew him from somewhere, and why she felt so safe within his arms – she owed her life to him. She just wished he'd told her everything from the start, because although she would have been shocked and needed some time to come to terms with who he was, she would have also respected him for his honesty. In the long run, his honesty would have only strengthened their relationship.

Rolling on her side, Ivy hugged her pillow to her. The pain of her broken heart made it hard for her to take a breath as sobs began to wrack her body once more. She let the heavy, endless tears fall, unable to deny how deeply her feelings for Ronny ran. But he'd broken her cardinal rule. And in the process he had broken her trust, and her heart. And as far as she was concerned, he'd lie to her again – a leopard never changed its spots.

***

As daybreak peeked over the mountaintops, sending a scattering of beautiful hues across the cloud-strewn sky, Ronny boiled the kettle for the fourth time. Normally another day dawning at Sundown Farm would bring joy to his heart, but today he couldn't even muster a smile. He hadn't had one second of sleep, spending the entire night either tossing and turning in bed or pacing the darkened rooms of the house. Now standing at the sink in his boxers with his arms folded across his aching heart, he gazed distractedly towards where the glowing rays of the rising sun reached down and kissed the landscape to life. Those rays should have brought warmth to his new day but they only solidified the harsh reality of his loss – Ivy, the love of his life. It was all he could do not to break down right now.

It was now ten hours since she had stormed out and he still hadn't been able to speak to her, and not for lack of trying. As time slipped away, so did his hope that they would ever work this out. Exhaling forcefully, he glanced at his mobile phone for the hundredth time. There were no missed calls, no texts, nothing from her. He'd never wanted a phone to ring so much in his life. He'd rung her several times, and left countless messages, but cold hard silence was all he'd received … and it was killing him. Yes, he'd made love to her without first telling the truth about who he was, but he'd been ready to, especially after speaking with Faith. He'd been on the verge of confessing and leaving the ultimate decision to Ivy, when Amy had intruded. Now he might never know if Ivy could accept him for who he was and love him regardless. How sweet his life, and hers, could have been. He would have loved her like she'd never been loved, like she *deserved* to be loved, every single day, until he took his final breath. He would have lived to make Ivy's every waking day the happiest it could be. But then the night had taken a different turn, and he'd allowed things to get out of hand.

Smacking his palm down on the sink, Ronny shook his head. If only he'd been honest with Ivy right from the start, back at the bank, how would things have turned out? He understood Lottie had done all she could to keep his true identity hidden, and he was also keen on the idea of a clean slate to establish his life on, but crossing paths with Ivy had changed all of that – and she was well worth the risk of Bluegrass Bend finding out his dark secret. Now he would regret his mistake for the rest of his lonely life. And he would most certainly be lonely, because if he couldn't have Ivy, he didn't want anyone. If only Amy hadn't turned up on his doorstep, he would have gotten the chance to break the news to Ivy himself. He was going to tell her everything. Slamming his hands down on the sink once more, he choked back his emotions. What the fuck was he meant to do now?

Already wired with caffeine, he busied himself heaping a teaspoon of Nescafe and two teaspoons of sugar into his mug before stirring it and taking a sip. He hated black coffee, but he couldn't be bothered grabbing the milk. And he knew he should eat something to help soak up the coffee, but he wasn't hungry. A quick glance at the digital clock on the oven only confirmed how time was ticking away; just over an hour and Larry and Shirley would come to help him spread Lottie's ashes. The thought of doing that made his already heavy heart sink even lower. Having to say his final goodbye to one woman he loved with all his heart was bad enough, but two in the same day was beyond unbearable.

Grabbing his mobile from the bench he dialled Ivy's number again, and after five rings it went to message bank – again. In frustration he tossed the phone across the room, the shatterproof case saving it from smashing to bits as it rebounded off the wall and then hit the floor. Fuck it, he'd leave the bastard of a thing there.

She wasn't going to call him back anyway. And he couldn't blame her – he was officially an arsehole and deserved everything he was getting.

Taking another sip from his bitter coffee as he stared vacantly out the kitchen window, he went over the horrid details of the previous night once more. A muscle twitched involuntarily at the corner of his right eye as his mouth formed a rigid grimace. The vehemence in Ivy's eyes as she'd called him a liar had torn him to shreds. She might as well have grabbed a knife and plunged it deep into his chest. It was as though she couldn't even bear to look at him – and he couldn't blame her. He was having a hard time looking in the mirror himself, completely ashamed of what he'd done. What a dickhead he was, thinking that hiding the truth from her all this time had been the right way to go. As much as he wanted to believe he'd been protecting her from her past, looking back on it now, he saw he'd failed miserably; all he'd achieved was hurting her, deeply, and that was the last thing in the world he'd ever want to do. What a fucking mess.

With his arms folded tightly across his chest he finally made a decision. Wandering about aimlessly while worrying himself sick wasn't getting him anywhere – he needed to take action. Although nervous of what might happen next, doing something was going to be way easier than standing still. The day ahead would either see the dawn of his new life or snap his dreams in two – because, come hell or high water, he was going to find a way to talk to Ivy. He needed to at least explain to her that he'd invited her to dinner to reveal everything – but was she going to believe him now? Though the chances were slim, it was worth a try. He would fight for her until there was not an ounce of hope left. If she wasn't going to answer his calls, he'd just have to drive over there. But first, he'd pay his respects to Lottie – it was time she was finally laid to rest with her dearly loved Frank.

***

The sound of a car coming up the driveway sent Ivy clambering from the couch. Tissues tumbled from her and scattered over the floor as she pulled on her ugg boots. It wasn't an overly cool day, but the iciness inside of her made her want to rug up. Her aunts were going to know something drastic was wrong the minute they laid eyes on her, because it was close to lunchtime, and she was still in her PJs with crazy bed hair, as well as sporting puffy eyes and cheeks from all the crying. She was officially a mess. If she could, she'd crawl under the comfort of her doona and stay there for a week. Tugging open the front door, she raced down the front steps and to her aunts, with Bo beside her. Her boy hadn't left her side since she'd arrived home last night.

Without a word, Alice hugged Ivy to her, and Ivy broke down sobbing.

'Sweetheart, what's wrong?'

'It's a long story, but the short of it is ...' Ivy turned her face to her aunt, lips quivering. 'Ronny Sinclair is not Ronny Sinclair at all.'

May had joined them now, arms full of shopping bags. 'What do you mean Ronny isn't Ronny?'

Alice wiped the tears from Ivy's cheeks. 'I think I know exactly what you're saying.' She cupped her face. 'Ronny is actually Byron, the man who saved you that night, isn't he?'

May gasped, the shopping bags tumbling from her arms. She stood frozen to the spot, her mouth hanging open but no words passing her lips.

Ivy found herself holding her breath. 'How do you know?' She stepped back and wrapped her arms around herself. 'Did he tell you?'

'No, sweetheart, of course he didn't tell me, I just had a feeling. He said something very odd a little while back, the first day he came to work here, that made me start wondering.'

Ivy covered her mouth, her eyes wide. 'What did he say?' Her voice was almost a whisper.

'He said something about you having a few things in common, referring to his guitar. It made me wonder how a newcomer to town could know about your love of music, considering you hadn't played for almost ten years.' She offered Ivy a resigned smile as she reached out and took her hands. 'He tried to tell me Lottie had mentioned it to him but that raised an even bigger red flag, seeing as you barely knew Lottie Sinclair.'

'Oh, Aunt Alice, why didn't you say anything?'

May folded her arms crossly. 'Yes, Alice, why didn't you say anything?'

Alice took a few moments to respond as she squeezed Ivy's hands. 'You both know how strongly I believe in fate, and I was worried I could be jumping the gun and stirring up emotions that didn't need to be stirred. I mean, what if I was completely wrong?' She shrugged as her eyes filled with sadness, then looked down at the ground and slowly shook her head. 'And I didn't want to interfere in the natural course of things either, because if it was the case, I hoped Ronny would be a decent man and tell you himself – which I truly believed he might when he invited you for dinner last night.' She shook her head. 'I'm deeply disappointed in him. I honestly thought he was one of the good guys.'

'And he still well could be, Alice,' May said gently as she placed an arm around each of them. 'We never know why a person has chosen to do something. And we can't forget the fact he saved our beautiful Ivy from the unthinkable.'

Alice nodded. 'Yes, you're right, May. We shouldn't be judging the man before we know his reasons.' She held Ivy's gaze. 'Have you given him a chance to explain himself?'

Ivy shook her head. 'No, I basically ran from his house when I found out. I didn't know what else to do. I was in complete shock.'

'And who could blame you for feeling like that?' Alice said.

May tipped her head to the side. 'So how did you find out if he didn't tell you?'

'I found the letter I wrote to him in prison.'

May gasped. 'How did you come across that? You weren't snooping around his house, were you?'

'Of course not, Aunt May … I went to grab a shirt from his drawer and it fell out of it.'

'Why were you getting a shirt out of his –' Alice tapped her nose. 'Oh.'

Ivy blushed beneath her aunt's knowing gaze.

'Well, if that's not the universe at work, I don't know what is.' Alice offered a soft smile. 'It's very sweet that he's still got it, don't you think?'

Ivy looked into the distance. 'I suppose it is. It would have been nice if he'd responded to it, though.'

'Well, maybe you could give him a chance to respond to it now,' Alice said, her brow quirked. 'And face to face would be best. All this texting and Facebooking you young ones do these days to communicate just causes more problems.'

Ivy fiddled with the belt on her robe. 'I don't know. I'm not sure if I could ever trust him again. And trust means everything to me.'

'Do you love him, Ivy?' Alice's voice was soft, gentle, but laced with urgency.

Ivy looked at Alice. 'With all my heart and soul.'

'Well, isn't love worth fighting for?'

'Yes – and no. I just don't know if I'd ever be able to forgive him for lying to me the way he has.'

'People sometimes think that forgiveness is weakness, Ivy, but it's absolutely not,' May said. 'It takes a very strong person to forgive.' She pulled her niece to her so their faces were only inches away from each other. 'And you, my dear girl, are one of the strongest women I have ever had the pleasure of knowing.'

'Ditto,' Alice said with a loving smile.

Ivy fell into May's arms. 'I really don't see myself as a strong person, so thank you for believing in me the way you both do.'

Alice wrapped her arms around the two and gave them a hearty squeeze. 'We want nothing but happiness for you, Ivy. And I think you know deep down what would make you happy – yes?'

'Yup,' Ivy said as sobs stole her voice.

'Well, my darling girl, you better go get your man.' Alice laughed softly as she released them. 'But before you do, I think you better go brush those teeth of yours and put a brush through that crazy hair while your Aunt May and I make us some lunch.'

Ivy laughed through her tears as she imagined how awful she must look. 'I reckon you're right. I don't want to turn up at his place looking like a mad woman.'

'Probably best to give him a call first, too, Ivy, just to let him know you'd like to have a chat about everything.'

'Yep, will do before I jump in the shower.'

With trembling fingers Ivy dialled Ronny's mobile number from the privacy of her room. She held her breath, waiting to hear his husky voice on the line. Instead, it rang out and then she was greeted by a computer-generated voice telling her to leave a message that would be converted to text. She hung up. The stupid things never got the message right anyway. She tried again. No answer. Her heart began to beat erratically. Was he ignoring her calls? She tried to rationalise it. Maybe he didn't have his phone near him. Maybe he was in the shower, or out in the paddock, or on the loo, or … in bed with Amy. A pain shot through her heart. She shook her head, angry with herself for jumping to conclusions. But she couldn't help it. He'd eroded her trust in him. Could she ever get it back? She decided to go for a shower, and then she'd try him again.

Ten minutes later, with her wet hair wrapped up in a towel and the bathroom still cloaked in lingering steam, she pulled her robe around her and dialled his number again. This time, it went straight to the voice-to-text message. She sucked in a breath. He'd turned his phone off. He didn't want to talk to her. And how could she blame him? He'd saved her all those years ago, and gone to jail for murdering the man who was going to take her life away – he'd lost all those precious years of living his life as a free man because of her. Instead of running from the house last night, she should have wrapped her arms around him and thanked him over and over. Tears filled her eyes and ran down her cheeks. She felt like the biggest bitch on earth. Yes, she was entitled to feel shocked and angry – he'd deceived her, after all – but shouldn't the fact he'd protected her with his life, and spent eight years in prison because of it, have outweighed all of that? Because the black and white of it was, if it weren't for him, she wouldn't be standing here today. And if the shoe were on the other foot, wouldn't she want to start life with a clean slate too, which is what she gathered he wanted, seeing as he'd changed his name? Was he such a bad person for wanting that? Panic filled her. She needed to get to him, now. Running to her bedroom, she put on some jeans and grabbed the first T-shirt she could find. While pulling it over her head, she slipped on her thongs and then slapped some lip gloss on her chapped lips.

She quickly ran her brush through her hair as she dashed out the bedroom door and down the steps, ignoring the dull ache in her ankle as she did so. The mat at the bottom took off beneath her feet as she hit it and she did a bit of a crazy dance trying to stay upright, smiling at herself when she succeeded. A chuckle from behind grabbed her attention.

Alice stood at the doorway of the kitchen, a tea towel over her shoulder. 'In a hurry to get somewhere love?'

'He's not answering his phone.' Ivy grabbed her coat from the rack near the front door and started tugging it on. 'I'm going to skip lunch and make my way over there. I need to talk to him.'

'Okay then, hang on a sec.' Alice disappeared and then reappeared with an apple. 'You have to eat something, sweetheart – I'm gathering you haven't eaten since yesterday and you don't want to go fainting on the poor bloke.' She tossed the apple in Ivy's direction.

Ivy caught it. 'Thanks, Aunt Alice.' She dashed over and gave Alice a peck on the cheek. 'Love you.'

'Love you too.' She watched on as Ivy headed back to the front door. 'Oh, and Ivy …'

Ivy spun around. 'Yes?'

'I think you're on to a winner with this one.'

Ivy grinned. 'I hope so.' And she disappeared out the front door, leapt down the steps and ran to her ute.

***

Standing atop the hill, Ronny clutched the urn to him. He wasn't ready to say his final goodbye to the woman who'd given him everything, but would he ever be? Larry stood beside him. His face looked as downtrodden as Ronny felt.

Shirley offered them a sad smile. 'Are you both ready?' Her voice was soft.

The two men nodded, and Ronny removed the top of the urn. Then, making sure the wind was blowing in the right direction, he positioned himself to tip Lottie's ashes over the cliff face.

'Fly free, Lottie, we love you,' he said as the ashes joined with the breeze and floated away from them. His eyes filled with tears and instead of blinking them away, he let them fall. A quick glance told him Shirley and Larry were doing the same thing.

'Love you, Lottie,' Shirley said, smiling through her sadness.

'We miss you,' Larry added as he pulled a handkerchief from his top pocket and then blew his nose loudly.

They all stood in silence for a few moments, their heads bowed as they paid homage to the woman who had touched their lives with her big loving heart.

Shirley was the first to break the silence, pulling a bottle of champagne from her handbag, along with three plastic flutes. 'Lottie had been saving this for a special day. Shall we?' she said, passing a glass each to Ronny and Larry.

'We shall,' Ronny and Larry said in unison.

Shirley filled their glasses and they raised them to the heavens.

'To you, Lottie, thank you, for everything. I just hope you can forgive me for letting the cat out of the bag,' Ronny said.

Shirley reached out and wrapped her arm around his shoulder. 'Of course she'll understand, Ronny. Love changes everything.'

'It sure does. I'm perfect proof of that,' Larry said with a chuckle.

'Good point,' Ronny said, smiling. He looked out to where the earth seemed to drop off the edge of the horizon. 'I just hope Ivy can find it within herself to forgive me.'

Shirley gave him a squeeze. 'She will, love, Ivy's a beautiful soul, just give her some time. It would have been a huge shock for the poor girl, finding out the way she did, and with her archenemy rocking up at your door too – everything would have hit her at once. She'll come round, I know it.'

'I hope you're right, Shirley. I really do.' He wanted to drive over to Healing Hills right this second, but it was good to get a woman's point of view and Shirley was right in saying Ivy might need some time.

Half an hour later, Ronny was back at the cottage. He was going to try Ivy one more time, and if she didn't answer, he'd give her some space for a day and head over to Healing Hills first thing in the morning, if he could stand it that long. Picking his phone up from the floor, he swore under his breath when he realised it had gone flat. He went in search of the phone charger, sure he'd left it beside his bed. Focused on the task at hand, he gasped as he walked into his room and spotted her naked body sprawled out on his bed.

Grabbing his towel from where he'd tossed it over his bedroom door, Ronny threw it towards her. 'For God's sake, cover yourself up.' He turned away, shaking his head. 'What made you think you could just waltz into my house and make yourself at home?'

'Oh, come on, Ronny, come to bed with me. I promise it'll be fun, especially seeing as it's your first time. I know you want to.' She giggled. 'Every man wants to be with me.'

Her voice was syrupy sweet, sickly so, and it grated on his already frazzled nerves. 'No, I *don't* want to. I never have.' He turned back to face her, relieved to see she'd sat up and pulled the towel around her. 'Now please, Amy, get dressed. I can't deal with this right now.'

Amy jumped from the bed, anger contorting her features. 'You can't deal with what right now? No man has ever said no to me.' She smiled conceitedly, shaking her finger towards him. 'Oh, I get it now. The reason you're a virgin is because you're gay and you haven't had the courage to come out of the closet yet.'

Ronny half-laughed as he threw his hands up in the air in mock defeat. 'Yeah, you got me all worked out, Amy.'

Amy nodded, the pleased look on her face clearly stating she felt like the smartest person on earth.

Ronny felt like bursting out laughing. How big-headed and stuck-up could a person be? To think he was gay because he wouldn't sleep with her. Really?

The sound of a vehicle coming up the drive dragged Ronny's attention out the window. A ute pulled up, and his heart stopped dead in its tracks. How in the hell was he going to explain his way out of this one? 'You have to get some fucking clothes on, Amy. Now.' His voice was tense, desperate even.

Amy turned to the window, a smirk upon her bright red lips. 'Does she know you're gay?'

'Nope. But I guess you're going to tell her.'

'Maybe. Maybe not. I'll do you a favour and help scare her off.' Amy dropped the towel, walked over to the window, tugged the curtains so they were far apart and waved brazenly.

Dread filled Ronny as he dashed towards Amy, threw his arms around her waist and tossed her onto the bed. 'What the fuck do you think you're doing?'

'Helping you, you big idiot. Because if I can't turn you, she definitely won't be able to.'

Gobsmacked at Amy's attitude, Ronny bolted out of the bedroom. If Ivy had seen Amy, she'd never let him near her again.

He made it to the front door just as he heard the ute rev to life. Panic filled him. *No, please ...*

He dashed across the driveway and stood in front of the ute, blocking her path. Ivy revved the motor, warning him to get out of the way, the look in her eyes one of complete hatred.

He held up his hands. 'It's not what it looks like.'

Ivy remained silent, the tears sliding down her cheeks ripping at his heart.

He leant on the bonnet. 'Please, this time, you gotta let me explain.'

Ivy revved the motor again.

Amy appeared from the house, now fully clothed. She waltzed over to Ivy's window. 'Just for the record, nothing happened. He's gay, so you can have him.' Then, sauntering away like a slinky cat, she disappeared around the side of the house to where she must have hidden her car. Seconds later, Ronny heard her drive away.

Still, no words passed from Ivy's lips.

Ronny hadn't budged. He wasn't letting her go like this.

Ivy threw the ute into reverse, skidded to a stop and then swerved around him, the back end fishtailing as she sped off down the driveway.

Ronny saw his world falling apart as she disappeared in a cloud of dust.

Running for the house, he felt something running beside him and a smile fleetingly passed his lips as he looked down at Jessie. 'I gotta go after her,' he said.

Jessie barked a reply, and Ronny liked to think she was saying, *My oath you do.*

Slipping and sliding down the hallway in his socks, he grabbed his keys from the dresser and then raced for the back door. Tugging on his boots, he motioned for Jessie to jump up on the back lounge and then sprinted for the Kingswood.

Twenty-five minutes later he had driven through the front gates of Healing Hills and was pulling to a stop in front of the homestead. He switched off the ignition, took a deep breath and then leapt out. Striding to the front door, he was met by May. He readied himself for an ear bashing, and was shocked when May stepped out onto the verandah and wrapped her arms around him.

'Thank you for saving our girl.'

He hugged her back. 'There's no need to thank me.'

'Well, I think there is,' May said with a smile. She sniffled and wiped her tears. 'Ivy's upstairs in her room. We gathered things hadn't gone too well when she came racing into the house a few minutes ago and ran up the stairs without saying a word to us.'

'Hmm.' Ronny pointed upwards. 'Can I please go up there and try to talk to her?'

Alice was at the door now, a grateful smile on her face. 'Thank you, Ronny, for doing what you did all those years ago.'

Ronny held up his hands and shook his head. 'Please, after hurting Ivy the way I have, I really don't deserve your thanks.'

'You would have had your reasons for not telling her, I'm sure.' She gestured for him to come inside and he did so, following May.

Alice waved an arm at the spiral staircase. 'Please be gentle with her, she's endured so much heartache.'

'I promise I will be.' And up he went, the whole time trying to figure out what to say first.

Silence greeted his knock at the door.

'Ivy, please talk to me.'

'Go away.'

'Nope.'

'Leave me alone.'

'Never.'

Heavy footfalls approached the door. It swung open and Ivy glared at him, her eyes as wild as her hair. 'What do you want from me?'

'Nothing and everything.'

Her eyes flashed. 'What in the hell is that supposed to mean?'

'Well, if you let me, I'll be sure to explain it to you in great detail.'

Ivy contemplated this, and him, for a few moments. 'Oh, bloody hell, okay.' She squared her shoulders and jutted her chin out and all Ronny wanted to do was take her in his arms and kiss her anger away. 'And it better be a damn good explanation.'

'I'll try my best.'

Ivy peered over his shoulder, as though looking for someone. 'I don't want to talk here, though. I love my aunts and I know they're only looking out for me but they don't need to hear all our troubles.'

He glanced behind him, understanding the fact she didn't want to do this with her aunts about to hear them. 'We can do it back at my place, where we've got privacy to sit and talk? I don't want to rush everything and miss anything out. I want you to know everything there is to know.'

Ivy folded her arms and tapped her foot, and for a moment Ronny thought she was going to renege on the whole listening thing. 'I'll be there in an hour, or so,' she said sternly.

'Okay, thank you.' He lightly touched her arm, and was relieved she allowed his hand to stay there. 'I promise you, Ivy, once you hear everything, I think you might forgive me for being such a dickhead.'

'We'll see,' she said as she bit her lip and turned away.

CHAPTER 20

The heat from the campfire chased the evening's crispness away and made Ivy's skin tingle pleasurably, the warmth seeping beneath her skin and into her bones. The hypnotic orange flames licked at the kindling and projected long shadows all around them. Like a well-choreographed dance the glowing embers seemed to move in rhythm with the flames, matching every dip and sweep as gracefully as an entrancing ballerina. It was mesmerising to watch and helped to calm the nerves in her stomach. A Sunny Cowgirls tune drifted from the stereo on the back verandah and Ivy found herself softly humming the familiar song. She was grateful for the music that was helping ease the tension hanging between her and Ronny.

Even though she was still angry with him, Ivy couldn't help but admire Ronny's burly frame, the way his muscles tensed as he picked up the logs and added them to the fire, and his tight arse in those jeans – the entire package was drool worthy. Needing to drag her eyes away, she looked at the sky where millions of stars blazed brightly among the deep ebony expanse of night, the brightness of the moon not taking away from the sheer brilliance of the glittery show. She recognised the Milky Way and the Southern Cross, the constellations something she'd always found captivating.

Ronny sat down beside her, and followed her gaze, smiling. 'It's beautiful, isn't it?'

'It sure is,' she replied softly.

'You know, when I was in prison, I used to lie in bed at night and dream of the day I'd be able to admire the beauty of a night sky again. And now here I am, doing just that.' He turned to her. 'And do you know what makes it even more special?'

Ivy brought her eyes to his. 'What's that?'

'The fact I get to do it with you.'

'Please don't say things like that.' She smiled sadly as she looked down at her hands clasped in her lap. 'What's going on with you and Amy? And please be honest with me.'

'Nothing's going on – I swear it. I honestly can't stand the woman after what she's done and I wouldn't care if I never laid eyes on her again.'

'Really?'

'Yes, really. I came home from spreading Lottie's ashes to Amy lying naked in my bed, without a hint of an invitation to do so. I don't have time for a woman like that.'

'And why did she say you were gay?'

Ronny shrugged casually. 'Because I didn't want to sleep with her, she just assumed I was gay.' A wayward smile stole his lips. 'I told her I was a virgin at the cafe the day you saw us, hoping it would make her leave me alone, but it didn't work, it only made things worse.'

'Okay.' Ivy stifled a smile – this wasn't the time – and turned so she could see his eyes in the flickering firelight. 'Ronny, I need to know why you lied to me about who you really are.'

He nodded and leant forwards as he hung his head. 'There were a couple of reasons.' He shifted in his camp chair so he could face her properly. 'Firstly, and most importantly, one of Lottie's final wishes was for me to keep my true identity hidden, so I could get on with my life without unfair judgement. And because she left me all of this –' he swept his arm around them, '– I felt bound to do as she asked. She did everything for me when she was alive, and left me everything she'd ever loved when she passed away, so I felt I owed her.'

'I can understand that, Ronny, I truly can, but it doesn't make what you've done acceptable. It was okay for you to not let everyone else know, but –' Ivy placed her hands over her heart. 'How could you look me in the eyes and make love to me the way you did and not tell me who you are?'

'Trust me, Ivy. It's damn near broken me, not telling you. I came close to spilling my guts to you many times while renovating the cottage. I'd planned to tell you everything over dinner last night, but then things got carried away and before I knew it, we were making love. And then, well, you know the rest.' He sighed weightily. 'At first I thought I was protecting you by not telling you who I was. You seemed to have gotten on with your life and I didn't want to bring everything back up for you again. And I also thought if I told you it was me who saved you that night, you would somehow feel indebted to me.' He looked away from her, his jaw clenching and unclenching as he stood. He paced in front of her, blinking fast. Ivy wanted to reach out and touch him, but she refrained. They needed to do this, wade through the heartache, so they could come out on the other side, hopefully together.

Ronny stopped pacing and turned to face her, his eyes filled with unshed tears. He knelt down in front of her and took her hands in his. Ivy noticed they were trembling.

'And I didn't want you to see me as a murderer, I wanted you to see me for the man I truly am – a man with a kind heart, not some kind of thug.'

Ivy couldn't contain herself any longer. This beautiful man had risked his life for her and spent years in prison because of it. And now he was afraid of her judging him. She let go of his hands and cupped his cheeks, looking deeply into his eyes. 'You saved my life, Ronny. But that's not why I love you the way I do. I love you because of the beautiful man you are. You make me feel so loved, so protected, and so safe to be who I truly am, warts and all. And you've gotten me to pick up my guitar and sing again. Now that is magic in itself.'

Ronny smiled. 'You truly love me, even after everything that's happened?'

'With all my heart and soul.'

Ronny pulled her into his arms and held her tight. 'I love you, Ivy, and have since the very first time I laid eyes on you – I just didn't know it back then.'

He placed a lingering kiss on her lips. Within seconds, the kiss turned hungry. Ivy's heart soared, the sensation of his tongue caressing hers sending shivers through her. Breathless, they pulled back and held each other's eyes – words unnecessary.

Suddenly, all around them was the quick flicker and crackle of light as hundreds of fireflies sliced through the night air with their sugary light. The winged beetles flashed incredible patterns of light, creating an explosion of colour. It was like a silent symphony, a mind-blowing tribute to their love. Ivy's eyes widened as she took in the magnificence surrounding them – it was like Mother Nature's fireworks. She liked to imagine it was their mothers' ways of letting them know they approved of their love. Ronny stood, pulling her to standing with him as he wrapped his arms around her, before reaching out and catching a firefly in his hands. After a few seconds he opened them again ever so slowly, allowing Ivy to marvel at the light within his palms as the firefly flitted upwards and away. Turning back to him she curled her fingers into the waistband of his jeans and dragged him closer.

'Kiss me again, my gorgeous man.'

***

Looking into Ivy's beautiful eyes Ronny didn't need any more of an invitation. Leaning in, he placed his lips against hers, heat spreading throughout his body as she returned his passionate kiss. 'I want to make love to you,' he whispered.

'I want that too,' Ivy replied breathlessly.

Ivy wrapped her legs around his waist and her arms around his shoulders as he lifted her. They made their way inside, their kisses continuing as they half stumbled through the back door and down the hallway. In his bedroom, Ronny gently placed her on his bed, the sliver of moonlight spilling through the curtains enough to subtly light Ivy's exquisite features. 'Are you sure you want to do this?'

Ivy didn't reply. Instead she sat up, removed the tie from her hair so it fell freely around her shoulders and then slowly began removing her clothes, her eyes never leaving his. Ronny ached to touch and kiss every inch of her beautiful skin as he watched her, but he stood his ground, wanting to drink her in as she stripped for him. She was entrancing and he wanted to take this slow, so he could savour every look, kiss, touch, lick and moan.

He undid his shirt and dropped it from his arms and then took off his jeans and boxers, and remained standing there, naked. Ivy gazed at his hardness and then she smiled wickedly as she lay back and closed her eyes. Ronny's gaze travelled the length of her bare, silky-smooth body, halting when he reached the scar on her stomach. Needing to run his lips over it, to kiss away the pain that night had left in her heart, he climbed onto the bed and lay beside her.

'I want you to just lie there and let me pleasure you.' His voice was husky with lust, and gently demanding. 'I want to taste every inch of you before I slide inside you.'

Ivy nodded as though unable to speak, her breath quickening.

He ran his fingers gently over her eyelids, the moan escaping her parted lips turning him on even more as he ran his fingertips over her mouth and then downwards. He gently tilted her neck to the side so he could kiss the place where her pulse throbbed. Ivy responded by pressing his face to her skin harder and he followed her cue and bit the place he was kissing. She cried out in pleasure. Then, unhurriedly, he traced the line of her throat with his lips and stopped to run his fingers over her breasts, circling her erect nipples before leaning in to lick them, then suck and graze them with his teeth. Ivy arched her back, her breathing fast and shallow.

Aching to be inside her, but craving her sweetness before he did, Ronny continued on his downwards path, making sure to trace the inside of her belly button, and slowing when he reached her scar. He kissed it inch by inch until he reached her inner thigh. Easing himself on top of her, he gently pushed her legs open, bringing his mouth down upon her sweetness. At first, he did nothing but blow warm breath over it. Gently, teasingly, he ran his tongue all over her lips before slowly sliding his tongue into her, savouring every drop. She was so wet and warm and tasted truly addictive. Ivy pushed herself into him as her hands went to the back of his head, groaning in pleasure. Licking, sucking and kissing her, his hands pressing on her inner thighs as he slid her legs open wider, he made her moan and writhe beneath him in ecstasy. Pushing his tongue in as deep as he could, he gradually moved upwards before sucking on her pleasure spot and circling it with his tongue. He could feel she was so very close, but he didn't want her to fall into paradise just yet.

'I want you inside me, now!' Ivy cried out.

Ronny smiled as he slid his lips up her stomach, over her breasts and her neck back to her lips. Kissing her with unrivalled passion, he began to unhurriedly slide himself deep inside her. She wrapped her arms and legs around him, encouraging him as her hands gripped his back and her nails dug into him gratifyingly. She held her breath. Her muscles tightened around his manhood, sending shivers through him.

Once completely inside her, he stopped, enjoying the sensation of being at one with the love of his life.

Ivy flicked open her eyes, and he met her desire-filled gaze. 'I love you,' he whispered.

'I love you too,' Ivy replied, her voice soft yet filled with yearning.

He started to move, taking his time, sliding out of her achingly slowly before sinking into her once more. His body quivered with every stroke, every touch, and every kiss. Ivy moved in union with him, her trembling hips meeting his at exactly the right time. As their thrusts became harder, hungrier, faster, their moans became louder. They grabbed hold of each other as they reached the point of absolute bliss and tumbled over the edge of ecstasy together, crying out as they did.

Satisfyingly exhausted, they cuddled into one another as they caught their breath. They curled up gently, their bodies moulded, each feeling as if they'd found their place, their purpose, and true, soul-deep love.

EPILOGUE

Four weeks later

Smiling at the two guitars sitting side by side in matching stands – he and Ivy had made such beautiful music together, and they were going to be doing a gig next week at the local – Ronny opened Lottie's jewellery box and reached for the blue velvet box that held his aunt's antique diamond engagement ring. He opened it to admire the exquisiteness of the ring as a wave of nostalgia washed over him. This ring had signified a marriage filled with undeniable love, and now he hoped it was going to signify a lifetime of love and commitment between him and Ivy. He wished Lottie were alive to share his happiness – that was, if Ivy said yes.

Hearing hurried footsteps coming down the hallway he quickly wrapped the box in a tissue and tucked it into his pocket.

Bounding into their bedroom with Cindy Clawford in tow – the cat now followed her everywhere, even down to the paddock – Ivy eyed Ronny's smart attire of black trousers and a sky-blue shirt. She reached out and straightened his tie. 'You're looking pretty damn handsome, Mr Sinclair.'

'Why, thank you, Miss Tucker … I can scrub up when needed.' He eyed her up and down, grinning suggestively. 'And you, my gorgeous lady, are looking pretty damn sexy in that black dress.' He reached out and playfully pushed one of the straps off her shoulders. 'I think I might have to make love to you before we leave.'

Ivy slapped his hand away lightheartedly. 'We're already running late because you kept me in bed well after the alarm went off. Not that I'm complaining.' She leant in and kissed the place on his neck that drove him wild, grinning wickedly as she went over to her dresser. 'But hold that thought until we get back home, won't you?'

'Oh, trust me, I'm always holding that thought,' Ronny replied as he gave her backside a playful slap.

After applying a quick swipe of lipstick, she grabbed his hand and gave it a tug. 'Come on, my handsome man, the auctioneer will be there in less than an hour, and I want to be there when she arrives.'

Ronny allowed her to drag him down the hallway at a hundred miles a minute, laughing the entire way. 'I think I better drive, otherwise it might be a bit of a *Dukes of Hazard* moment when you hit the dirt roads – and I want us to arrive there in one piece.'

Ivy grabbed her coat from the stand beside the door, smiling dangerously. 'Are you picking on my driving?'

'Never,' Ronny said, as though mortified with the thought.

''Cause if you are, you might find yourself walking to the auction,' she replied with a wink.

Before she disappeared out the door, he grabbed her hand and pulled her to him, his smile fading as he eyed her seriously. 'We still have time to pull out of this, Ivy. I honestly don't mind mortgaging this place to be able to keep your cottage and help with what's owing at Healing Hills.'

Ivy shook her head determinedly. 'No, like I've told you a million times before, I won't hear of it. This is our home; the cottage is just an empty house that I would feel much better about if there were people in it, creating a life.' She placed her hand over her heart. 'It will hurt, letting it go, but Mum lives in here, so I don't need the place to remember her by.'

'Okay, only if you're absolutely sure.'

'I'm one hundred and ten per cent certain.' She smiled as she headed out the door, still talking over her shoulder. 'I can't wait to see who buys it – if it sells, of course.'

'I have no doubt it'll sell today. The place looks amazing, if I do say so myself.' Ronny pulled a proud face as he followed her out, making sure the door was shut firmly behind him. Last time they'd forgotten to shut it they'd come home to a muddied pair of dogs asleep on their brand new couch. Bo and Jessie had been banned from the house for a week, but within three days Ivy had caved and had let them back in.

Ned eyed them over the fence and bleated a goodbye. Ronny gave his mate a smile, as did Ivy. He never knew what mood Ned was going to be in from one day to the next, but he'd grown to love the belligerent goat, and the pony, Grace, too.

'You got the keys, beautiful?'

Ivy dug in her handbag. Finding them, she threw them towards him. 'Sure do. When will the makeover on the Kingswood be finished – I can't wait to see it restored to its former glory?'

They climbed into Ivy's ute, hauling on their seatbelts. 'Oh, Dave rang yesterday, said they're just waiting on a few final parts and then it'll all be done.' Ronny grinned like a child in a lolly shop. 'I can't wait to see the old girl all done up.'

'Me too,' Ivy said with an equally excited grin. 'She's gonna look beautiful.'

Ronny revved the engine to life as Nugget tore across the drive in front of them with the two ducks in tow. 'Right, ready to do this?'

'As ready as I'll ever be.'

***

Watching the auctioneer at work through the parted curtains made Ivy's head spin. 'How does someone talk so fast?' she whispered to Ronny, May and Alice, who were huddled in closely beside her – all of them wanting a glimpse of the goings-on outside.

'I have no idea what she's saying,' Alice said.

'Neither do I,' May added. 'She sounds a bit like a chicken clucking.'

Ronny chuckled. 'I can understand her, and it sounds like you're going to be making much more than you first thought, Ivy. Look at all those people out there.'

Ivy grinned. 'I know, I can't believe how many turned up.'

Alice wriggled on the spot. 'Shh, it looks like they're getting to the nitty gritty of the deal.'

They remained silent as the auctioneer pointed from one couple to another, her voice getting louder and shriller by the second.

'Did she just say six hundred thousand dollars?'

'Uh huh,' May, Alice and Ronny said in unison.

They held their breath, watching, waiting, and praying. Ivy wanted to scream, she was so excited.

'Sold to the couple on my right for six hundred and forty-eight thousand dollars.'

Ivy, Ronny, May and Alice faced each other, eyes and smiles wide.

'Oh my God,' Ivy squealed. 'That's over a hundred thousand more than we'd first thought.'

The four of them embraced as they did a happy dance.

***

The lighting in the restaurant was soft and romantic. Ivy smiled across the table at her sexy dinner date, grateful that he'd gone to so much trouble to bring her to her favourite Italian restaurant. It was over an hour's drive from Bluegrass Bend, and usually very hard to get in to. Ronny must have booked their table a few weeks ago to be able to get a seat and the thought warmed her already flaming heart.

The crab and prawn linguini was to die for and as per usual, it hadn't disappointed. And now she was tucking into her favourite dessert of tiramisu.

'Thank you for bringing me here, Ronny, it's so beautiful.'

As always, Ronny charmed her with his smile. 'You deserve beautiful, Ivy, because you're beautiful – inside and out.'

'Why thank you, sexiness.' Ivy blushed as she spooned the last mouthful of decadent dessert into her mouth, and then moaned. 'Oh my God, this is heavenly.'

'Please don't moan like that … you'll get me all hot under the collar,' Ronny said as he caught her gaze, and seized it.

The intensity in his eyes made Ivy's heart skip a beat. It always amazed her that he could make her feel as though he was caressing her soul without even touching her. She watched as he reached into his pocket and pulled out a blue velvet box. Everything around her faded away, leaving just her and him, here, loving each other in a way not many were lucky enough to ever experience. She held her breath.

Was he about to ask her the big question? Or was this a celebratory gift for the sale of the cottage? She squealed on the inside with the thought of it being the former.

Ronny placed the box on the table and took her hands in his. 'Ivy, you're my absolute everything. I want you to be the first thing I see every morning and the last thing I see at night. You're my best friend, and my soul lover. I want to have children with you, dream with you, and love you for the rest of my days.' He smiled softly, his eyes glistening. 'Will you marry me?'

Ivy gasped as happy tears filled her eyes. She jumped from her seat and threw out her left hand, wriggling her fingers. 'Yes, Ronny Sinclair. I'd love to marry you.'

The restaurant erupted in applause as Ivy fell into the arms of the man who had already protected her and loved her for years, and was now promising to do it for the rest of his days. She was one lucky woman to have found true love with a guy as deep and as sensual as Ronny. She knew without a doubt their love would last this lifetime and she liked to believe it would proceed into the next.

'I love you, Ronny, with every single inch of me,' she whispered in his ear.

'I love you, too, Ivy. Always have and forever will.'

❋ Ivy's Playlist ❋

Lady Antebellum 'Just a Kiss'
Tim McGraw and Faith Hill 'It's Your Love'
Troy Cassar-Daley 'Bar Room Roses'
The Sunny Cowgirls 'Green and Gold'
Lee Kernaghan 'Goondiwindi Moon'
Johnny Cash 'Orange Blossom Special'
Merle Haggard 'Workin' Man Blues'
Hank Williams 'Your Cheating Heart'
Waylon Jennings 'Good Hearted Woman'
George Jones 'He Stopped Loving Her Today'
Clancy 'A Walk in the Rain'
Alan Jackson 'Once in a Lifetime Love'
Garth Brooks 'Tomorrow Never Comes'
Brad Paisley 'I'm Still a Guy'
Slim Dusty 'Lights on the Hill'
George Strait 'When Did You Stop Loving Me'
Keith Urban 'Your Everything'
Randy Travis 'I Told You So'
Adam Brand 'Cigarettes and Whiskey'
Catherine Britt 'Sweet Emmylou'
Dolly Parton 'Jolene'
Gary Allan 'Nothing On but the Radio'
Cold Chisel 'Rising Sun'
Chris Stapleton 'Whiskey and You'
Adam Harvey 'That's What You Call a Friend'
Miranda Lambert 'The House'

ACKNOWLEDGEMENTS

A huge hurrah goes to the fantastic team at Harlequin headquarters – my publishers Sue Brockhoff and Rachael Donovan, my editors Annabel Blay and Kylie Mason, the design magicians that have yet again wowed me with cover gorgeousness, and the rest of the extremely talented, inspiring and addictively enthusiastic team who have helped me make *Bluegrass Bend* the very best it can be. I'm extremely grateful to be part of such a supportive, talented bunch.

To my beautiful hunky manly-man of a hubby, Clancy. You inspire me in so many ways – the depth in your heart and your creative mind among the many reasons I love you so very much. You make me strive to be the very best I can be and infuse a strength within me I never knew I had until I met you. Thank you for loving me the way you do, for proving the love I was searching for existed, and for being my rock, my best friend and an amazing stepdad to Chloe. The healing horses in *Bluegrass Bend* are all thanks to you – you're the best! Love you with all my heart and soul.

To my incredibly spirited, always smiling and beautiful big-hearted little girl, Chloe Rose. You're my absolute world, darling. You teach me to see things in such different ways, and help me to capture the magic in each and every day. You're wise beyond your years and are the kindest soul I've ever met. I'm always finding myself amazed by you. I love you a trillion bazillion, and then some.

To my beautiful stepdaughter, Taylor, thank you for being such a kind and caring soul. You have a bohemian spirit that warms and calms all around you. Chloe and I are both very blessed to have you in our lives. Love you.

To my life guru, my confidant, my dad, John. You guide me through everything with such gentleness, and with an amazing amount of love. I wouldn't be where I am today without you backing me the entire way. I feel extremely blessed to have a father like you. Love you.

To my amazing stepdad Trevor. You've influenced my life in so many ways, and I will be forever grateful for you teaching me how to always try to see the positive side of life, no matter how hard life gets – it has gotten me to where I am today. And you always know how to make me laugh – which is priceless. Love you lots!

Wayne and Pam, you're the kind of in-laws every gal wants, and the best grandparents too – kind, thoughtful, loving and supportive. Thank you Pam, for always being super keen to read through my drafts, and to give me brilliant constructive critique. I value your opinion greatly. Chloe and I love you both very much.

To my beautiful sisters, Mia, Karla, Rochelle, Talia and Hayley – what a lucky chicky I am to have you all there to share my life with. You're all so very different and I love how true to the core you all are, and also how you all strive to be the very best you can be. And thanks for being such cool aunties too! Love yas lots!

Tia and Kirsty, the two gals that are always there for me, in the good times and the bad, no matter what, and are also happy to do the random spontaneous stuff that makes me laugh until my sides ache. I love that you both aren't 'normal' – and I say that in the most loving of ways! We weirdos like to stick together, huh! I couldn't imagine my life without you both in it. Love you both heaps.

To Kristie Armstrong, I'm so happy our lives have crossed paths. You just get me, as I do you. Forever mates we will be!

To my SS, Fiona Stanford, you've been by my side throughout my writer's journey and I can't thank you enough for being so supportive, caring and giving. And you never expect anything in return. You truly are one in a million. Love ya!

To my wonderful Aunty Kulsoom, thank you for always loving me, warts and all. And huge thanks for always being super keen to edit my drafts. I value your input, and my books are better for it! You rock, and I love you heaps.

To Rachael Johns – what would I do without you there to message almost every single day! I can't wait until I get to meet you in person so I can give you a big squishy hug.

To Len Klumpp, thank you for everything you selflessly do to support myself, and other Aussie authors. You're an absolute legend!

And last but certainly not least, the biggest, loudest, most deserved thanks goes to YOU, the reader. Without each and every one of you I wouldn't be doing what I love each and every day – and being able to work in my PJs with crazy bed hair is a massive plus too! I really hope *Bluegrass Bend* lets you experience every emotion possible along the journey, as well as leaving you all warm and fuzzy in the end.

Until my next book, keep smiling and dreaming!

Mandy xoxo

Turn over for a sneak peek.

The Stockman's Secret

by

MANDY
MAGRO

Available June 2020

Some secrets are so extremely powerful that, when uncovered, they can unite, and they can divide

Dropping to her knees
She clasped her hands tight
While staring into the eyes of the devil
She did as she was told, and prayed for all her sins
Although, she did not understand
How he could be speaking of heaven
When all he brought to her life was hell

PROLOGUE

Little Heart township
Way back when

Twelve-year-old Joel Hunter listened as the wild wind lashed the branches of the towering Bowen mango tree he loved to climb against the side of the house. A distant curlew called out, the lone bird's song eerie, and Joel was grateful to be tucked up inside, safe and sound.

Making the sign of the cross, he tightly folded his hands, closed his eyes, and drew comfort from his hero – his father – kneeling close beside him. Soft lamplight cast shadows across the bottom bunk bed, and over Joel's cheeks, grazed in the attack. The Muller boys has started bullying him when he became an altar boy at Little Heart Church – a role he was extremely proud of. Trying to ignore the relentless sting in his knees, hands and arms from when they'd dragged him from his pushbike and across the gravel, along with the horrible ache in his heart caused by the humiliation, he joined his dad in their usual nightly bedtime prayer. He watched as his father drew in a steady breath, his big chest rising, before sighing it away as his eyelids closed. Only then did Joel squeeze his eyes shut.

'Lord, I pray for my son, and that you would comfort him in this hard time. Please grant him the strength to forgive the three boys who've bullied him for being a loyal child of yours and protect him from any further harm. I trust you'll help the culprits to see the injustices of their ways, and hope that, in time, they and their parents will come to believe in the teachings of the bible, so they can live a wholesome life devoted to you, as we do in this house that you have blessed us with. Amen.'

His father finished, Joel quickly added, 'Yes, please, Lord, to everything Dad just said. Thank you for everything you do for me. Amen.' Then, swallowing hard, he blinked back another onslaught of tears. He didn't want to cry again. He wanted to be big and strong, like his dad.

A reassuring pat on Joel's back brought his gaze to that of his father's. 'Proud of you, son.'

'Thanks Dad, and thanks for going and talking to Principal Edwards, and the Muller boys' parents too. I just hope it doesn't make things worse.' Joel frowned. 'You know how much of a grump their father can be when he gets mad.' The time he'd watched Mr Muller yell at the lady who worked in the grocery store because she'd given him the wrong change flashed before his eyes.

'It won't, my boy. I promise.' With a groan his father rose from his knees, as did Joel. 'Their father needs to take a long hard look at himself, teaching his boys that violence is okay. Champion boxer or not, Michael Muller should know better than that.'

Shaking his head, his father heaved another gentle, weary sigh as he sat on the edge of the bed. 'I think after being suspended from school for a week, as well as having to attend the anti-bullying classes your mum is running down at the church with Mrs Kern, the three of them will've learnt their lesson, hopefully.'

Nodding, Joel sniffled, gruffly wiping the tears from his sore cheeks. He hated being a big sook, hated the fact he was all lanky arms and legs without an aggressive bone in his body. Hated the fact it was a girl – *the* girl, the one he'd had a crush on for the past year – the very pretty and very nice Juliette Kern, who had saved him from the bullies. He wanted nothing more to impress her, to make her see he was big and tough, a match to her gutsy spirit and tomboy persona, but try as he might, he just couldn't fake it. 'I'm sorry I was too afraid to stand up to them and Juliette had to chase them off by throwing rocks at them. I feel silly, having a girl do that for me.'

'Don't you dare feel silly, my boy.' Patting Joel's arm William half-chuckled, shaking his head. 'She's certainly a little firecracker, that girl. I think she'd scare most boys with how fiercely she can yell.'

Remembering Juliette's stern face as she'd protected him so fearlessly, hands on her hips while telling the three Muller brothers to rack off, Joel chuckled. 'She sure is a little firecracker.' And right then and there, he decided that would be her nickname – if she didn't mind it. 'I wish I was more like her.' His smile faded with the declaration.

Reaching out and pulling his son to him, his father ruffled his hair. 'Don't beat yourself up. You're a good boy, Joel, and you did the right thing by not stooping to their level. God wouldn't take kindly to you throwing punches just because they are.' He unfolded his towering frame and stood. Then, with a warm smile, he peeled back the doona and patted the animal-printed flannel sheet. 'Now, come on, it's time for bed, so in you hop.' He glanced to the top bunk. 'Zoe's already fast asleep, the sweet child.'

'Yeah, I thought she was just trying to get out of eating her peas and carrots at dinner …' Joel peeped up at his baby sister. '… but she must have been telling the truth about being super-duper tired.' His cotton pyjamas askew, he straightened them before climbing beneath the sheets. A flood of reassurance filled him as his father tucked him in and kissed his forehead. 'I love you, son, and I want you to know how proud your mother and I are of you for always telling the truth, and not resorting to violence.'

'Thank you, Dad.' His tears and fears all but forgotten, Joel smiled. 'And I love you too, to the moon and back, and beyond.'

'Now that's a whole lot of love, my boy.' His father's smile widened as he chuckled. 'I'm one lucky father, having a wonderful, kind, and very clever son like you.'

Joel grinned proudly as his dad's tender chuckle warmed him from the inside out. 'Night, Dad.'

'Night, Joel. Sweet dreams, son.' Leaving the lamp on, his dad padded to the doorway, paused momentarily as he offered a final reassuring smile and, leaving the door half-open, disappeared down the hallway.

Joel rolled onto his side, squeezing his eyes shut. He was even more tired than the days he'd help his dad train the horses. Hovering in between realms, it wasn't going to take him long to drift into dreamland, the shelter of his home and the unconditional love of his family giving him all the comfort he needed to let the horror of the day go. As his mum had said while gently tending to his scrapes and bruises, her frown deep and blue-green her eyes filled with compassion, he would live to tell another tale. He just hoped it was going to be a good one.

CHAPTER 1

Six years later

Juliette Kern fought to keep her eyes from the door to the cupboard tucked in beneath the spiral staircase, her heart racing a million miles a minute. The little area terrified her, the enclosed space so velvety black she couldn't see anything once locked away in there – as she had been more times than she cared to remember. But the fear of that room wouldn't stop her now, although she had to be extremely careful. Being caught wasn't an option.

Stepping into the lounge room, she sucked in a shaky breath. 'I've finished my bible study assignment, so I'm off to bed,' she said as casually as she could, then forced a yawn.

Brows furrowed, her stepfather barely acknowledged her, his steel-grey eyes glued to his weekly dose of the ABC's Australian Story. Juliette was glad for his distraction. She glanced to where he'd hung his belt and tie over the back of a chair, and icy fingers travelled up her spine.

Leaning over the back of the lounge chair, she brushed a kiss over her mother's cheek. 'Night, Mum. I love you.'

'Night, love.' Cradling her cup of tea, her mum looked up, smiling. 'Don't forget to say your prayers before you go to sleep.'

'Of course I won't,' Juliette replied before turning and treading back down the hallway.

Shutting the door, she rearranged her pillows and doona to make it look like she was in the bed and, just in case, turned off her lamp. Satisfied she'd done all she could, she grabbed her torch and thongs and quietly slid her window open. Balmy air mingled with that of her air-conditioner, and the scent of her mother's frangipani and jasmine blossoms hung heavily. Cattle bellowed in the distance and from the paddock down the driveway, her horse whinnied. Holding her breath, one long leg after the other, she hitched up her dress and glided out, sliding her window shut and slipping on her favourite diamante-studded Havaianas. Sticking to the shadows while moving fast across the back lawn, she vanished into the night, waiting until she was safely surrounded by the scrublands of Crystal National Park before she flicked her torch on. She couldn't wait to see Joel, or for the day she didn't have to live beneath her parents' roof.

* * *

Summer had arrived in Little Heart with typical Far North Queensland vengeance, with the balmy temperature still hovering in the high twenties hours after the fiery orb of the sun had slunk behind the distant mountain ranges. Switching the outside light on, Joel Hunter watched hundreds of insects swarming towards the sudden brightness, like soldiers into battle. A loud ding from his back pocket almost made him jump. He grabbed his mobile phone, flipping it open.

I'm down by the river, hiding behind a clump of bushes. Phone at the ready. I'll make sure I stay quiet. See you soon buddy.

Smiling, Joel punched back, *Thanks Ben, I owe you one.*

He couldn't believe this day had finally come. It was the day after his eighteenth birthday, he was officially an adult, and this was first day of the rest of his life. Now his high-school years were done and dusted, he had moved from beneath his parents' roof into the renovated ex-tobacco barn and become his father's right-hand man on the farm. It was an absolute dream come true. Now, all he needed was for her to say yes, and his life would be perfect.

He heard her hurried footsteps just before she appeared from the trail that led to her place. Right on time, she had a torch in hand, and her long, dark hair loose and swaying around her back.

'Hey there, beautiful,' he said, his heart careening at the mere sight of her. 'I've missed you.'

'Hey there, handsome.' Juliette ran into his open arms and wrapped hers around him. 'We only saw each other seven hours ago. But I missed you too,' she said, a smile playing on her glossy lips as she pulled back a little, rose up on her toes, and kissed him.

'So, did you tell your parents you were meeting me tonight?' he asked cheekily.

'Yeah, right.' Her radiant smile faded as she shook her head. 'I wish I could tell them the truth, but Dad would kill me if he knew I was sneaking out, meeting some boy … doing god-only-knows what.' She mimicked her stepfather's booming voice while rolling her eyes. She tried to force a smile – he could tell she was faking it because her lips trembled.

'I'm not just "some boy", Jules.' Her words cut, but he shook it off. Malcolm Kern, Juliette's stepfather and the town's pastor, was very strict about Juliette doing anything outside of school or church. Joel had high regard for the man, who'd always proven himself to be a devout Christian, and he always felt a little guilty breaking Malcolm's rules, even if he didn't know about it. 'I'm your boyfriend. We've been together for almost a year now, even if it's on the quiet, and our families know each other so well. Surely your parents would be happy about our love when you find the right time to tell them?'

'All in good time, my gorgeous man.' She gently touched his cheek and studied him with her dark eyes. 'I know you think you know my dad. Heck, the whole town thinks they know him because they see him up on his pulpit every Sunday, giving his sermons. But trust me – I know him the most, and he won't like me being with *any* guy, especially before I've turned eighteen.'

'You're only five days off it, though.' Not that Joel needed to remind her of her birthday, a date easy for him to remember when they were only a week apart.

'Yeah, I know.' She sighed with a half-shrug. 'Stupid, but I live beneath his roof, and I have to abide to his rules. Or at least do my very best to make sure he doesn't find out I'm breaking them.' She grimaced. 'Because if he did, I'd be in big trouble.'

'He's only so strict because he loves you, and wants the best for you, I'm sure,' he said, gently tucking stray hair from her face and over her ear, donned with the dangly heart-shaped earrings he'd bought her for Valentine's Day.

Sadness splashed across her face as she cuddled into him, slicing at his heart – he hated seeing her upset. Ignoring his burning urge to do what he so longed and go around to ask Malcolm Kern his stepdaughter's hand in marriage – not something easily done when Malcolm thought he and Juliette were just friends – he did his best to focus on Juliette.

He turned his face into her ear, whispering, 'I love you.'

'I love you too, Joel. So much.' She pulled back a little and smiled now. 'So, tell me, what was so important that I needed to sneak out to meet you?'

Feeling on top of the world, though a little nervous, he unravelled his arms from around her and grabbed her hand, savouring the sensation of his fingers interlaced with hers. 'Come on and I'll show you.' She allowed him to lead her, their footfalls softened by the blanket of leaves along the path leading from Hunter Farmstead to the burbles of Little Heart River.

'Where are we going?' she asked, her sweet voice hushed.

'To our special place.' He fleetingly reminisced their very first kiss by the river, and his heart quickened.

'I only have an hour or so before I have to be back, Joel.' She hesitated a little. 'The longer I'm gone, the more chance of Mum or Dad sticking their head in to check on me.'

'All good, Firecracker.' He flashed her a grin. 'This won't take too long, I promise.'

Juliette regarded him, and then nodded. 'Then let's get there, quick smart.'

The weight of the ring in his back pocket only added to Joel's nervousness. He couldn't get to the bank of the river quick enough. He'd been waiting for this day to arrive ever since he'd locked eyes with her across the packed Sunday church seven years ago. Tonight was the night he'd make an honest woman of her – if she said yes.

Juliette's voice broke his satisfying train of thought. 'Joel, there's something I have to tell you.' Softly said, she seemed apprehensive to speak what was on her mind, so much so his heart skidded to an almighty stop.

Trying to act nonchalant, he looked at her. 'Sure, Jules. Shoot.'

She bit her lip, and then released a sigh. 'Remember I told you I'd applied to James Cook University to do my Bachelor of Education?'

'Yeah …' He held his breath.

'Well, I got a letter back from them this afternoon, she said in a rush. 'I've been accepted.' She gave his hand a squeeze.

'Holy heck.' His thoughts took off like spooked wild horses, and his heart sank to his boots like lead. She'd have to move. The university was in Cairns, only two hours away but still too far. With the course going for four years, they wouldn't be living together anytime soon. He couldn't move with her. It meant too much to his father that Joel had taken the job by his side, and Joel was proud and keen to follow in his footsteps.

Her pained expression pulled him to a stop. 'Joel, please say something.'

He swallowed down his bitter disappointment – this meant a lot to her. 'Sorry. Wow, that's wonderful news! I'm so happy for you.' And he genuinely was – just not so much for himself. Not wanting her to glimpse his deep sorrow, he picked her up and spun her around until she laughed, just long enough to pull himself together.

She pulled back a little, her smile wide, warm and relieved. 'So, you're okay with it?'

'Of course, Firecracker,' he lied. 'You've always wanted to be a teacher, so who am I to stop you from reaching your dream?' He placed a lingering kiss on her lips as he eased her back to the ground. 'We'll be right. Long distance won't matter a bit.'

Her hands slipped from his shoulders. 'It's not really long distance,' she offered with a little shrug. 'I can drive here, and you can come visit me. Any time, day or night.'

'When we're not studying, or working, or ...' With hurt flashing in her eyes, he stopped himself from going further into the negative, a habit that frustrated her at times. 'But yeah, of course we can, all the time. What's four years anyway? We've got this.'

'You're the best boyfriend ever, Joel Hunter. Thank you for being so awesome.'

'I do my best.' He puffed his chest out and forced a gallant grin. 'And you are the most awesome girlfriend ever.' He wrapped his arms around her tiny waist, imagining her as his wife, and himself as her husband.

'Naw. I love you, so much.'

'I love you, too, Jules, always and forever.' It hit him that he didn't need to curb his plans, just tweak them a little. Their love would get them through the next few years. God was just testing them. The new awareness buoyed him.

Juliette pushed up on her tippy toes and pressed another strawberry-glossed kiss upon his lips. When she sank back down to the earth, she flashed him a familiar challenging grin. 'How about the first one to our secret spot, scores a foot rub?'

'Even though I'm always giving you foot rubs.' His swooning heart skipping beats, Joel matched her grin. 'You're on like Donkey Kong, Jules.'

'On like Donkey Kong?' She chuckled. 'My goodness, Joel Hunter, you're so darn *groovy*, I can't handle it.' With a wide smile, she lingered for a moment before clapping her hands. 'Right then, race ya to the finishing line!' Competitiveness flashed in her eyes as she spun in her thongs and took off, long black hair swishing around her waist, her turquoise boho-style dress floating at her ankles.

'Oi, no fair! You got a head start,' Joel called after her playfully.

'Come on and catch up, you slow coach,' she teased, her laughter hanging heavily on the air.

Joel chuckled at her exuberance. She always made him feel that he was acutely alive, and so very loved. She was beautiful, ethereal – his very own gift from the heavens. With beads of sweat trickling down his back, he trailed her swiftly, weaving through the thicket of trees and scrub towards the gurgles of Little Heart River. The river bordered and divided three properties – Hunter Farmstead, all of two hundred acres, the opulent Davis Horse Stud, close to nine hundred acres with a sprawling homestead and classy stables to boot, and Juliette's parents' house on a humble five acres. Juliette and her parents had moved there six years ago, when she was almost twelve, from a cramped flat behind the church. Word was the property had been a bribe from Ron and Margery Davis, but for what, Joel had never bothered to ask. He didn't believe the tale. Gossip was the devil's tongue, his mother always said. He just thanked his lucky stars that they were virtually neighbours, and they got to see each other a lot more than when she lived in town.

A full moon shimmered against the velvet black of night, spilling silvery light over the worn path they'd taken many times before. Clearing a fallen tree trunk just in the nick of time, he patted his back pockets, making sure the ring and the key were still safe and secure. He was still going to offer both to her – it was her choice what happened after that. His heart flip-flopped at the thought of her walking down the aisle to him, and then afterwards, to the very first time he and Juliette would make love, both waiting until fully committed.

Juliette's squeals of laughter carried from up ahead, bringing him back to the present. In the thick of the shadows, the path turned sharply, and he cornered it perfectly, the thicket of native trees finally giving way to a small clearing that was home to their small part of Little Heart River – their special spot. It always would be. One day, they'd bring their children here, to share it as a family. Just up ahead, Juliette was kneeling at the edge of the river, scooping up handfuls of the water lazily travelling over the rocky riverbed. She and the stream were lit up, dreamlike, by the silverly moonlight.

Hearing him approach, she looked over her shoulder, grinning. 'About time you showed up. I thought you'd gone and got yourself lost.'

'Oh, hardy-ha-ha, Little Miss Comedian.' Beaming from ear to ear, Joel fought to catch his breath as he looked to where Ben would most probably be hiding, ready to film the special moment with his video camera. A quick thumbs up from the shadows let him know they were good to go. 'You're lucky to have a boyfriend like me, who gives you a head start and then lets you win,' he said a little less breathlessly.

'Pull the other one, Hunter. I beat you, fair and square.' She gave him the forks and he grinned wickedly. 'Now you owe me an even longer foot rub than I usually get.'

'Talk about a bloody slave driver.' Joel playfully groaned. 'But if I have to …' He loved being able to touch her soft skin, so it was no chore to rub her feet.

Somewhere in the line-up of the huge paperbark trees that hugged the river's banks, a barn owl screeched. Seconds later, its mate replied.

Joel glanced upwards. 'Man, oh man, they sound eerie.'

'They do, huh.' Standing, Juliette joined him in trying to spot the birds. 'But I love how they mate for life.' She looked back at him. 'So romantic, don't you think?'

'Damn straight it's romantic.' His passion stirred by the privacy granted by the bushlands surrounding them, he grabbed the perfect moment to do what he came here for.

Offering him a delicate smile filled with love, Juliette regarded the trees once more.

Lightheaded with anticipation, Joel dropped to his knees.

Turning her attention back to him, Juliette tilted her head, bewildered. 'What are you doing?' She looked to the ground. 'Did you drop something?' She fell to her knees, ready to help him.

Unable to get a word out for the lump of emotion stuck in his throat, Joel just shook his head. He'd practised a huge speech at length, one filled with sentiment, but now, in the heat of the moment, he was finding it hard to string a sentence together. *Come on, pull it together, Hunter.*

Juliette took his hand, her gaze deeply concerned. 'Joel, is everything okay?'

'Uh-huh.' He fleetingly glanced to the blanket of stars, glittering like millions of crystals, before bringing his teary gaze back to the love of his life. Then, with a deep inhalation, he went to his back pocket, plucked out his grandmother's ring, and flicked the box open. 'Juliette Kern, will you do me the absolute honour of marrying me?' He held his breath.

'Oh my goodness! Joel …' Juliette's lips quivered into a happy smile, but before she could answer, heavy footfalls sounded.

They appeared out of nowhere.